Du Rose Vendetta

THE HANA DU ROSE MYSTERIES

K T BOWES

Copyright © 2019 by K T Bowes

Would you like to be part of it?

I'm a believer in 'try before you buy.'
There's nothing worse than forking out your hard earned cash
on a doozy and regretting it.
I don't want stinky reviews. I want you to love my work and feel
like you got value for money.

If you'd like to be part of that, you can go to my website,
ktbowes.com and join my mailing list.
I'll send you 4 free eBooks in return.

I will take care of your email address and won't be sharing it or
spamming you.

You can unsubscribe at any time. I promise not to send Rohan
Andreyev after you...maybe.

1

Other People's Dirty Laundry

"She what?" Logan Du Rose squinted at his wife, an expression of surprise lighting his grey eyes from within. "Say that again."

Hana sighed, wishing she hadn't started the conversation. Her friend had shared a secret and already Hana felt nausea rising into her throat at betraying her so soon. Four hours, twenty minutes and about five seconds. "Forget it," she said, pushing her feet beneath the sheets and snuggling into the comfortable bed.

"No way!" Logan snapped his book closed in a motion which made Hana wince. She closed her eyes and feigned sleep. A click sounded as Logan whipped off his reading glasses and placed them on the nightstand. He slithered beneath the sheets and propped himself up on one elbow facing her. The corded muscle beneath his shoulder flexed and Hana reached out a finger to trace the tattoo snaking around it. "Start at the beginning," Logan said, his tone soothing.

"No!" Hana squirmed with discomfort. "She told me in confidence and I shouldn't have said anything. I promised not to." She sighed. "But we tell each other everything and I didn't want to spoil things by keeping a secret, especially one that wasn't mine." Her eyelashes fluttered against the pillow and she pouted. "You'd know, anyway. Then we'd get into a vicious cycle of you trying to find out and me struggling to stop you. Before we knew it, we'd argue and then who knows where we'd be."

Logan smiled, his lips curving upwards in a gentle arc. He reached out his hand and placed it on Hana's soft cheek. His thumb caressed her lower lip. "And then we'd get divorced and then you'd bury me under the patio and then and then and then. I'm always amazed at how far your surmising goes." His dark eyelashes fluttered and amusement created crow's feet at the corners of his eyes. "What comes after that?"

Hana wrinkled her nose. "We don't have a patio. And you're too tall to go under the deck."

Logan gasped. "Geez wahine! You've thought about it." He jerked backwards and the voile canopy lining the ostentatious four poster bed rustled.

The laugh bubbled up from Hana's chest and banished the guilt for a moment. The genuine horror in her husband's expression made her snigger. She only stopped when he shifted onto his back and stared at the twinkling lights overhead. The tiny bulbs emitted an ethereal glow which bathed his olive face and smoothed out the contours. "Sorry." She forced his arm up and snuggled beneath it, wrapping her legs around his like a koala. "I've no plans to bump you off, I promise."

Logan grunted and closed his eyes and Hana felt chastened. He shook his head and his hair swished against the pillow. "It's okay," he breathed. "I can build a patio."

Hana snorted and jabbed a finger into his ribs, feeling him curl inward and snatch at her hand. She sighed. "Husbands don't count, do they?" Her voice held an edge of pleading. "I know you won't tell anyone."

"No," Logan concluded. "I won't."

Hana sighed. "Libby told me something today and I still feel shocked." She paused and considered her words. "She's a mistress."

Logan's hair swished against the pillow as he turned his head. "I thought that's what you said, but assumed I heard wrong. A mistress of what?"

"Of a man. Her boyfriend is married." Hana shifted onto her stomach so she could gauge his reaction, suspecting it would mirror hers earlier. But Logan's face remained impassive and he displayed his impressive ability to mask his emotions. "She says their arrangement suits her. They enjoy each other's company and he goes home to his wife. He doesn't expect her to take care of his dirty washing or look after him when he's old and infirm. I looked her in the eye and believe she's genuinely satisfied."

Logan twisted his lips and his brow furrowed. "So, it's just sex. There's no emotional attachment?"

"She says she loves him very much. They've been together five years. They have rules around their relationship. He texts and if it suits Libby, he visits her place. She only texts him in emergencies. They go out for dinner and to the movies like a normal couple. They just make sure they go to Auckland and not Hamilton."

Logan snorted. "Except they're not a normal couple. He has a wife."

"I know." Hana reached out and fingered the St Christopher around her husband's neck. The chain slid through her fingers and the fine hairs of his chest tickled her palm. "I was that wife once."

"You told her that?"

Hana nodded. "Yep. That's why she came clean. She said she values our friendship and didn't want to base our relationship on a lie."

"How did you leave things?" Logan stilled the soft fingers as the chain slithered across his skin. He clasped her hand. "Are you still friends?"

"Yes. Much as I dislike her revelation, I still like her. I feel as though we'd clicked on a deeper level. It's lonely up here sometimes and she filled a gap. I'd started to rely on her."

"It's lonely because you're married to me?"

"Yeah." A wistful smile parted Hana's lips and she placed a gentle kiss against Logan's muscular shoulder. "You're a Du Rose and if the local women don't already work for you, they spend their time lusting after you. It puts a distance between me and most of the women my age. I craved someone with shared life experiences who I could relate to and Libby seemed to fit. I still like her but I'm not sure how to move forward."

Logan snorted. "So, she doesn't work for me and doesn't lust after me." He scratched his chin and shot Hana a sideways look filled with mischief. "What's wrong with her?"

Hana released a sigh of exasperation. Logan's grey irises sparkled with understanding and his expression became serious. He pulled her close. She pressed her face against his downy chest and relaxed, a barrage of thoughts and emotions shifting around in her brain. "Do you want some advice?" His voice held a tenderness only Hana and his children ever heard. Gentle fingers stroked her hair as she nodded. "Base your opinion on her role as a friend. She's an adult making adult decisions about her life. That need not involve you. If her relationship status bothers you then have that conversation. You can explain you want no part of it but wish to stay friends. If she's the person you believe she is, she'll settle for that."

The tick of a clock filled the silence as Hana pondered Logan's words. She sighed. "It's difficult. We've been friends for six months without issue and I knew she had a boyfriend, just not the circumstances. It didn't bother me that she hadn't introduced us. I value her friendship and the children adore her, but what she's doing is wrong. There's another woman somewhere whose heart will break when she finds out." Hana's arms snaked around Logan's trim waist and she placed a kiss against his chest. "But you talk sense sometimes, Mr Du Rose."

"Do I?" He pulled away so he could gaze at her, his lips quirking upward into a knowing smile. "So, the toy-boy knows a thing or two then?"

Hana snorted. "Don't throw my age in my face, young man." She jabbed a crooked finger into his ribs and heard the satisfying sound of him groan as his muscles tightened. He was usually much quicker than her to react. "No night-time privileges for you now."

"Says who?" Logan threw the sheet over their heads and burrowed them both deeper into the bed. Hana squeaked as strong fingers slid beneath the waistband of her pyjama shorts and coasted across the delicate skin of her hip. His lips found hers in the darkness, tentative and searching. Hana blossomed beneath his attentions and allowed the burden of someone else's adultery to fade from her list of immediate concerns.

2

Raranga

Hana peered at her phone screen and winced. Logan had seemed preoccupied lately. She'd hatched a plan to distract him in the bedroom by taking more control. He checked the credit card every month and she hadn't wanted him to notice the book title she'd purchased. It meant going to elaborate lengths to send herself a gift card and then download the book. Hana stroked her finger over the screen and jumped as the view changed to a chaste black-and-white image of a couple kissing. "Who knew?" she whispered, fascinated by the graphic description. "Five different sorts of kissing and I have to do all this other stuff at the same time." She shrugged, thinking of Logan's lips over hers. The thought sent a coil of desire spinning through her gut. He kissed her with enough skill to turn her into a shivering wreck. She wanted to be able to do the same. Hana increased the font size and scratched her cheek. Her nose almost touched the screen. "Put his legs where?" she breathed, skimming the instructions. Her eyes widened. "Oh my!"

"What are you chuntering about?" The museum curator sounded brusque and Hana jumped and dropped her phone onto the table. A quick sleight of hand sent the screen dark. "Get on with that basket. We've got just over a week left until the mid-summer fair. We're meant to be showcasing Māori skills, not making ourselves look like imbeciles." He jerked a head towards the mess of wilting flax leaves sprawled on the table and Hana pouted. She picked up the weaving with reluctance and released the clothes peg to pick up where she'd stopped. Her clumsiness betrayed her as a length of flax burst free from her grasp. Unfurling like a green sea creature, its soft pointed end almost speared Will's eye. He let out a sigh of exasperation and glared at her poor workmanship. "I've no legs, Hana," he snapped, shifting his wheelchair backwards. "And you wanna take my eyeballs too?"

"Sorry!" Hana huffed. Her cheeks flushed at the memory of Logan's lithe legs and the position which the book said she should master to please him in the bedroom. She gathered the flax into her lap and began again, creasing its hardy skin along fresh lines and spreading green sap onto her knuckles. "This isn't easy," she grumbled.

"Finished." Phoenix slapped a perfectly formed rose onto the pile growing in the centre of the table. "Can I go now, please Mama? I don't want to do this all weekend. Sunday's almost over and I still want to play."

Hana stared at the neat green stem and the way the petals formed around a delicate central eye. She sighed and her leaf pinged free again. "Well, that's just unfair. How do you know how to do this? You're six."

"Papa showed me." Phoenix waggled a dark eyebrow and looked at Hana's pile with pity. "Just after my third birthday."

Will snorted and Hana shot him a look filled with barb. She jerked her head towards the other two children sitting at the table, their fingers flying as they created woven masterpieces. "Go," she sighed. "But stick together and don't speak to strangers."

Wiremu Du Rose tied off his last loose end and dropped the kete basket onto the pile. At eight-years-old, he already bore the characteristic Du Rose looks. Stunning grey eyes glittered from an olive face and high cheekbones. He nodded to the other two. "Come on," he said. "Nonie Leslie promised us a pie. They're leaving for their mini-break after dinner."

"Mini-break. Phoenix snorted and enjoyed the taste of the words on her tongue. Mini-break."

"Wash yer hands!" Will raised his voice. "Horoia ō Ringaringa! Wash your hands unless you want diarrhoea until Christmas."

Phoenix scrambled down from her chair with a giggle, nudging her brother's slender arm. His green-eyed gaze met Hana's across the table top, the harsh wooden edge bisecting an elfin face and shock of auburn hair. She gave him a smile. "Pie." She mouthed the action of eating to accompany the signed word and he blinked. Pointing at Wiri and Phoenix, she communicated he should stay with them and wash his hands first. Mac Du Rose lifted his chin and Hana watched his lips purse into a thin line. He cocked his head and a slender pink finger pointed to her. "Wiri," she repeated and the older boy touched his shoulder.

Mac placed his finished rose on the table with exaggerated care. Wiri helped him from the chair and waited while the child ran around to Hana's side and lifted his face for a kiss. "Stay with Wiri," she told him and he read her lips and nodded. The slam of the heavy museum doors and the sound of running feet heralded their escape from enforced drudgery and Hana sighed. She yearned to go with them and sample her mother-in-law's homemade pie. Thoughts of the New Zealand staple of steak and oozing cheese made her mouth water. Will nudged her elbow with his bony arm and jerked his head toward her sorry looking leaf.

"Get a fresh one," he ordered. "Start again."

Hana groaned and rested her forehead on the table. "I can't do it!" she protested. "You're a rubbish teacher."

Will's throaty laugh rumbled through the cavernous room. "White girls!" he breathed, intending it as a veiled insult. But his gnarled hand rubbed Hana's slumped shoulders in contradiction of his gruff exterior. "Make me a coffee and I'll let you off for today." He returned to the complicated weave on the table, removing pegs from the base of his basket. His wheelchair tyres squeaked against the floorboards.

Hana rose and escaped to the thin office behind the museum. The kettle heated while she sank into a swivel chair to wait. The issue with Libby wasn't settled in her heart but her options were limited. She could fling the usual Christianese at her and walk away, but that wasn't helpful. She liked Libby as a friend but disliked her life choices. Hana sighed, knowing she wanted to maintain the friendship, but hoping she could ignore Libby's love life. "Maybe it won't get raised again," she whispered. "Perhaps I can forget and just go back to how it was before."

Will's unexpected appearance in the doorway made her jump. "Yer man did a good job in here, didn't he?" he asked, navigating his chair through the widened doorway.

Hana nodded. "You'd never know this whole area used to be a bedroom, bathroom and sitting area." She tapped the workbench with her hand. "I think Logan's grandfather used this suite when he became ill."

Will shook his head. "You know he did, Hana. Stop fluffing. What's wrong?"

Hana poked her bottom lip out and sighed. "Nothing," she lied, though her body language said otherwise.

Will turned his chair to fit beneath the work bench and gave her a sideways glance. "As you wish, kōtiro," he whispered. "As you wish."

Hana hauled herself into a standing position and gathered mugs and spoons for their drinks. Her hand shook as she poured steaming water onto instant coffee granules. "It's Mac," she said, defying the tears which pricked behind her eyelids. "He still can't hear. The surgery didn't work."

Will's wizened face held sympathy and he took the strong black coffee without comment, setting it before him on the bench. A gentle finger nudged aside a pile of aged family documents extracted from the cavernous attic. "We need to stop eating and drinking in here," he said with a sigh. "Accidents happen."

Hana sank into her chair and took a sip of her coffee, wincing at the sudden burn to her lips. "Don't worry. It'll be me who ruins something."

"Oh dear." Will waggled bushy eyebrows flecked with grey and white. "We are miserable today."

"How can you say that, after what I just told you?" Hana's shoulders slumped further as her mind sought to shrink her until she grew small enough to hide from her problems. "My son can't hear or speak. The surgeon made me so many promises and I believed him. I let him take my child and cut his head open and for what?" The anger in her heart burned worse than the coffee on her tongue, rising and threatening to engulf her if she let it. "The surgeon is my brother's partner, so he's practically family. It's like I'm criticising his work, so it's personal. But it's my son's life we've messed around with. For nothing."

"What does Logan say?"

"Nothing!" Hana spat. "He just coasts along on his glorious Du Rose cloud of greatness and leaves me to worry about the children."

Will snorted. "Glorious Du Rose cloud of greatness. Can I add that to the list of family quotes?"

"Only if you want your wheelchair tyres popping," Hana growled. "Don't you dare!"

"I'm sorry, Hana." Will's hand trembled as he sipped his drink and she regretted heaping her burdens on his head.

"It's okay," she sighed. Jerking her head toward the pile of documents he'd moved aside, she forced herself to brighten. "What are you working on now?"

Will reached out tender fingers and patted the yellowed papers. "Letters belonging to Miriam Du Rose."

"Logan's mother? Are they from Reuben?" Hana couldn't help herself and leaned forwards as though desperate to catch each tentative word.

Will shook his head. "No. From her mother. Recipes and advice, but interesting. Her birth certificate needs digitising if you have time later. Then I can store the original in the safe."

Hana blew out a breath which ruffled her fringe. "Don't tell me. Her parents were itinerant sheep shearers called Mr and Mrs Smith from Invercargill and Miriam grew up thinking her name was Du Rose."

Will swallowed and considered his next words with exaggerated care. He took a sip of his coffee and wrinkled his nose. "You didn't put sugar in this," he complained.

Hana's lips parted in surprise. The protest budded in her chest but didn't make it free. Diabetes claimed Will's legs and the warning look in his eyes made her love him more than she already did. Her husband stood in the doorway behind her and every nerve ending tingled from her heels to the tip of her nose. She didn't need to turn around to know he stood watching her. Hana stilled and made her reply sound calm and collected. "I'll scan it this afternoon if you don't mind waiting. Is there anything else you need me to scan while I'm at it?"

"Not yet." Will blew on his coffee. "I'll make a pile in the tray, but this is more precious than the other stuff." He raised an eyebrow and Hana performed a graceful turn on the office chair.

Logan leaned against the door frame with his muscular arms folded across his chest. Hana read the amused twinkle in his grey eyes and felt her cheeks heat, knowing he'd heard the insult to his mother's parentage and decided not to challenge her. Guilt sent a nasty shiver through her chest and she almost wished he would rebuke her in front of Will as a punishment, but it wasn't Logan's style. "Would you like a coffee?" she asked, her voice wavering.

"No thanks." His strong fingers gripped his cowboy hat and lifted it off his head. His brows furrowed as he stared at the scuffs in the dark leather. "Walk with me?" It emerged as more of an order than a request and Hana's brow furrowed. She shot a look back at Will and rose, a naughty schoolgirl summoned to the headmaster's office. Will's throaty chuckle followed them across the museum and Hana fought the urge to run back and throw something semi-hard at his head.

They crossed the reception area under the scrutiny of the woman behind the desk. Guests milled in the foyer, picking up leaflets and putting them back in the wrong place. Logan stood out in his work clothes, tall, swarthy and worthy of a second glance. His boot heels clicked across the floorboards and Hana jogged to keep up with his long stride. Out in the sunshine he seated his hat back on his head.

"Where are we going?" she demanded. When he didn't reply she reached out and caught his elbow. "Slow down! I know you heard what I said. I'm sorry. It was rude and tasteless. Just tell me I'm wrong and get it over with."

Logan's expression relaxed as he glanced at her fingers clasping his arm and then at her face. "You're wrong," he said. "Mama knew who her parents were."

"Okay, then I apologise." Hana swallowed at the blankness in Logan's grey eyes. Impossible to read, he continued to punish her without raising his voice or showing his displeasure.

She blew out a breath and released him, turning on her heel and striding back toward the main house. Her mind ran through a list of quiet places she could hide to lick her wounds and smooth her ruffled feathers. "Oh, no you don't!" Logan's head butted her waist as Hana squeaked and rose into the air. Strong hands fixed around her thighs and she found herself facing the back of Logan's shirt with a frightening image of the gravel driveway moving in and out of view.

"Stop!" A girlish giggle forced itself free and a woman dragging a suitcase towards the stairs stopped to watch. "Everyone's looking!" Hana hissed.

Logan jerked his head upward in greeting to the woman and gave her a stunning smile. "Hi," he said, amusement in his voice.

"Is that extra?" the woman joked, pausing a moment more before continuing her journey. Her case bumped up the steps with an unhealthy thud.

"Let me down," Hana pleaded. "Everyone can see my butt."

Logan let out a snort of laughter and slapped her upturned bottom encased in jeans. "And a great butt it is, babe." The sound echoed off nearby buildings and Hana groaned. She wound her fingers into Logan's shirt and tried to push herself backwards off his shoulder, wasting her efforts as he increased his grip.

"Please let me down," she begged. "I said I'm sorry."

"No, you'll run away," Logan bit back. "I've ridden twenty-five kilometres since the sun rose. Much as I love a good chase, I don't have the energy."

"I won't," Hana whined. "I promise."

The second her feet touched the ground she bolted, dodging Logan's outstretched arms and hearing his grunt of irritation behind her. She held her breath until his footsteps sounded against the gravel before acknowledging she wanted him to chase her. Skirting the stable yard, she dashed into the hay barn and sped away from the wide doors. Shadows engulfed her near the back as she tried to hide behind stacked bales. Panicked mice scuttled from underneath and Hana slid and tripped over spilled hay. Logan caught her half way across, snagging her around the waist and pulling her with him as he fell backwards onto the prickly mattress of stalks and dried grass. A morepork woke in the rafters and gave a worried hoot.

Hana giggled as Logan wrestled her beneath him and pinned her arms. His biceps bulged through his shirt and hay dust stuck to the day-old beard covering his chin. His mocking grey eyes held her gaze as she wriggled against the scratchy mattress. "When are you gonna admit you lost?" His voice sounded tender and he traced a line along her cheek with his index finger. He tilted his body to pin her in place.

A lazy smile crossed Hana's lips and she studied her husband with feigned coyness, tilting her head like a budding flower. "Who says I lost?" she whispered and saw the grin break out across Logan's face.

He sighed and his gaze strayed to her mouth. "Well played," he replied. His lips felt rough against hers and Hana smelled sun cream on his cheeks. He snagged her wrists as though afraid she might run again, but when she struggled, he released them. Hana wrapped her arms around his neck and held on tight.

"I love you," she breathed against his skin and felt him relax beneath her touch. Her eyes held a smile and Logan kissed her until his rough beard pinked the soft skin of her chin. Hana's fingers strayed to his waistband and she pulled on the hem of his shirt until she felt soft flesh.

Something clattered in the stable yard, the sound bouncing off the surrounding ridge and returning as a muted echo. Logan shivered and caught Hana's fingers. "We have thirty seconds before Rawhiti pushes that wheelbarrow in here," he whispered.

"You could do it." Hana giggled at the offended look he gave her and her chest shook with laughter. "Spoilsport," she complained.

"You're a bad girl." Logan pushed himself backwards and sat up. He brushed hay and dust from his clothes.

"Na, you like me bad." Hana glanced sideways and her lips turned down. "Where's all the hay and the bags of silage? There's usually more in here."

"Hana, I need to talk to you."

She wrinkled her nose and hauled herself up with less elegance than her husband. Strands of hay poked from her fringe and she retrieved the pieces, crumpling them in her fingers. "What's wrong?"

Logan heaved out a breath and leaned his elbows on his knees. He stared at the floor between his boots. "The developers still want Reuben's side of the mountain," he said. "They're happy to negotiate. My lawyer seems to think they'll take the block near town and they've doubled their offer."

Hana felt herself withdraw, her emotions thrown into turmoil. "I don't know," she stammered. "It's your decision."

"It's our decision, Hana." Logan's gaze followed her as she stood to brush strands from her jeans. "We're partners, remember?"

She jutted her hip out and angled her body in a silent expression of defiance. Her jaw worked in her cheek until it ached, the tender kisses forgotten against the backdrop of pain. "Don't we need the paddocks for baling?" she snapped. She flapped her arm to encompass the barn. "This looks like we're running short of hay and silage."

Logan ran a hand through his hair and avoided the fire in Hana's green eyes. "No. Everything is fine. We don't need that land. But do we want to keep it, anyway?"

"Get rid of it." Hana shook her head and her red hair cascaded around her shoulders. She put a hand up to it, her brow furrowing as she searched for her clip.

"Hana!" Logan sounded sharp. "We need to talk about this. It's important to me. We don't inherit the land from our ancestors, we borrow it from our descendants. I need to make a decision that Phoenix and Mac won't hate me for later."

"I want no part of this." Hana backed away until the stacked bales prevented her safe passage. "It's your land, not mine. JD was your grandfather and he left it to you." She swallowed and felt the knot of anger forming in her chest. "When Mac's older and he finds out that man tried to kill him and me, he won't want it either." Her voice caught in her throat. "Do what you want with it, but don't involve me. Sell to the developers or fill it with land mines. I don't care, Logan."

Tears blinded her as she fled the barn, the memory of Jack's calm indifference burned into her psyche. Her mind saw him lift the gun and point it at her new-born and she squeezed her eyes closed against the image. Guilt compounded her misery. Logan had sat on the discussion for days, afraid to broach it with her. She'd seen it in the sideways glances he gave her and the dark cloud hanging over their interactions. "I'm sorry," she whispered. "I just can't."

"Hana, come back." Logan managed to throw his voice without shouting, perhaps sensing it would upset her less. Hana turned the corner, glancing back and seeing him standing in the doorway to the barn with his hands shoved deep into his pockets. She turned her face away and let the embittered ghost stay between them, just like it had for the past three years.

3

An Adventurous Spirit

Hana forced herself into the tight bodice with great difficulty. It prevented her taking full breaths and her breasts spilled over the top like a bar wench from the middle ages. She'd had to fasten the hooks at the front and then spin the whole thing around, which left her breasts still pointing at her left armpit. The cheap thong from a recent trip to Auckland felt like dental floss stuck between her butt cheeks. Hana slumped onto the bed and regretted it, leaping upright at speed. A sheen of sweat dusted her brow and sent her to the bathroom mirror for a last-minute inspection of her make-up. "Two minutes to touchdown," she murmured after a glance at the bedroom clock. She sighed with frustration. "And I'm knackered already."

Logan's truck roared onto the driveway and Hana tensed. She'd planned to meet him at the front door but low self-esteem made her want to hide in the wardrobe instead. She'd put the children to bed and made sure they were sound asleep, but still worried about being caught in the hallway wearing kinky underwear. After their earlier spat over JD's paddock she needed to make up some ground with her husband, but parading around the house required the covering of a modesty saving dressing gown which ruined the image of lasciviousness. Logan Du Rose's love languages were extensive and complicated.

Hana gathered her wits and snatched a last minute cram session with her eBook. The written instructions jumbled in her panicked mind and became mixed up. "Should've got the one with diagrams!" she groaned, knowing she couldn't. The children played games on her phone and she'd deliberately picked a sedate looking cover with a couple holding hands and giving each other adoring smiles. Pictures within the text were tasteful close-up images in black and white. Lips. A foot. "I hope it's a foot," she breathed, turning the screen off and putting the phone on her bedside table.

The front door slammed and Logan's footsteps padded along the hallway. Hana assumed a number of sexy vertical poses, abandoning them all at the last minute and clasping her hands behind her back. She looked more like a soldier on parade than a wanton seductress.

"Hey." Logan pushed the door open and froze. His dark windswept hair gave him a superhero appearance and his handsome features settled into a look of curiosity. Hana gulped as his gaze stroked her body from head to toe and he cocked his head to one side. His lips pursed, but he said nothing, passing through the door and closing it with his heel. Hana tensed, seeing the familiar glint catch fire behind his eyes. She didn't want him to ambush her moment and take control, though the temptation hovered in front of her like a security blanket. She forced steel into her spine and straightened her shoulders. Her left breast spilled over the top of her bodice as though making a break for it.

Logan took a step towards her and his eyes narrowed. His left hand reached for the buttons of his shirt, scrabbling at the top one. Hana breathed in the overwhelming power of Logan Du Rose and realised exercising control over her incredible husband would be like holding the tide back with her hands. She swallowed and took a fortifying, but shuddering breath.

"Let me." She met him halfway across the bedroom. The lust in his granite irises sent darts of weakness into her thighs. She reached for his remaining buttons and batted his eager fingers away with her hip as they strayed towards the skimpy thong. "Behave," she warned, injecting authority into her tone. The buttons resisted her shaking fingers and joined the conspiracy against her. "Bugger!" she hissed. She tugged in frustration and two of them popped off the shirt and skittered across the floorboards. Logan blinked and his pupils dilated enough to obscure his grey irises. Time stopped and Hana felt the advantage crawling away from her. Temper flared in her breast and she gripped both sides of the fabric and wrenched the shirt open. The remaining buttons shot in several directions and Logan's lips parted. Still, he said nothing and Hana hauled tomorrow's darning over his shoulders. None of that was in the book.

He helped her with his white tee shirt, lifting it over his head and revealing defined pectorals and abdominal muscles worthy of a photographic opportunity. Only the myriad scars from his childhood marred the image. Hana squeaked as Logan dipped his body and lifted her. Still battling for control, she resisted his move to put her over his shoulder and wrapped her legs around his waist. His belt buckle dug into her thigh and she pushed her fingers through his wavy hair and clamped her lips over his neck. The need to embrace five different sorts of kissing spun through her head as she sucked on the tender flesh. Logan groaned and slipped a finger between the string of her thong and her skin and the cheap material made a ripping sound. The elastic whacked her across the butt as it twanged and she bit Logan's neck too hard.

"Sorry," she whispered, her eyes widening at the blossoming hickey under his jaw line. The haemophilia took hold and the mark seemed to grow before her eyes. Her hesitation tripped her up and in a split second, Logan seized the advantage, tipping them both backwards onto the bed.

Hana's foot hit the bedside table and she heard her phone thud onto the rug. Logan seemed happy with one sort of kissing and in his strong arms, everything else went out of Hana's head.

4

Sand Houses

After another day of floppy flax baskets and a table runner which Will scoffed at, Hana felt ready to quit raranga for life. Logan was pressing her for an answer about the developers' offer and she couldn't decide without thinking of Jack and the ease with which he'd wanted to destroy her. The school run gave her time to regroup and she lifted Mac from his car seat outside the school gates after picking him up from the nursery. He patted her cheek to get her attention and made his sign for Phoenix; a butterfly motion with his fingers which suited his sister's sunny nature and perpetual motion. Hana shook her head. "No, baby. She's going to play at a friend's house tonight. We'll get Wiri now and then fetch Phoe later." Mac cocked his head and jabbed a finger at the school building behind the imposing fence. Hana set him down on the ground and signed her sentence instead. Mac's eyes flickered with understanding and then his nose wrinkled as though he knew something Hana didn't.

"Hey, how are you?" A clatter of high heels preceded the question and Hana whipped around, rewarded by a waft of strong hair spray.

"Fine, thanks." She pursed her lips to avoid further intoxication. There seemed no point repeating the greeting as the woman's question appeared rhetorical. Hana sensed if she dived into a litany of her most pressing issues, the newcomer would find someone else to talk to.

"Is Phoebe still coming round to play?" Manicured fingernails pushed an imaginary strand of glossy blonde hair away from decorated lips full enough to float a lifeboat.

"Phoenix." Hana gripped Mac's fingers with one hand and pushed the other deep into her jeans pocket to stop the woman seeing her ratty nails. "Yes, please."

"Such a dear little name. Jordan's quite taken with her. It's difficult moving into a new town, isn't it?" The woman dragged her feet and the sharp heels ground against the concrete pavement. "The friendship groups are a mine field filled with drama."

"Yes." Hana forced herself to adopt a more sympathetic guise. She'd spent time in the company of loneliness and the black cloud of depression. With an effort of will, she pushed the knotty issue of JD's paddock into the locked box in her mind and plastered a smile onto her face. "How are you settling?" she asked. "It's a small town but growing. You'll find your spot." Her mouth worked as her brain tried to dredge up the woman's name. They'd exchanged pleasantries a few times since the start of term and phone numbers when they arranged the play date. Hana contemplated dragging her phone from her back pocket and scrolling through for a clue, but didn't want to appear rude. She'd asked around and found out a little about the family before agreeing. Phoenix seemed keen to go. "I'll pick her up at six. You live in the new subdivision behind the school playing field, don't you?" The woman nodded and her full lips parted in answer.

"Gina!" A sing-song voice echoed off the building and more heels clattered towards them. Hana cringed at the sight of another new mother, not liking her but grateful for her provision of Gina's name.

"Hi, Louise." Gina's face brightened and her lips parted in a smile wide enough to reveal a diamond glittering on her left front tooth. The women oozed money in the kind of superficial, glitzy way Logan despised. Hana enjoyed the fleeting thought that he could probably buy and sell both their assets before breakfast without making a dent in his sizable fortune. And he'd do it in dusty cowboy boots with hay in his hair and dirt under his fingernails. She sobered at the reminder of their earlier dispute. JD's influence stretched its destructive fingers over her heart and she resisted, forcing herself back into the moment.

"Hi." Hana stood her ground in the tsunami of perfume washing over her. The women's mingled scents seemed to create a cloud which engulfed them in an untouchable bubble. Standing taller in their stilettos, they dwarfed Hana and Mac, gathering in a circle which excluded the other adults arriving to retrieve their children. Louise observed Hana with an expression like a slapped backside. Gina appeared impervious as she babbled about the weather and Auckland traffic.

"I don't miss it." She wrinkled a neat nose almost too perfect in its proportions. "I wanted my roots touching up again and couldn't leave it much longer."

Louise snorted. "I wouldn't trust my roots to the local salon. Anyone getting work done there wants their head testing. Talk about a leap back in time, you'll walk out looking like an escapee from the nineties."

Hana pursed her lips and held her breath. Betty had cut her hair the previous week, thinning out the fluffier layers and neatening the ends. She resisted raising a hand in self-conscious appraisal. Logan had told her it looked sexy as he ran his fingers through it and nibbled her neck. He didn't lie when she asked him if things looked okay. But then he'd seemed more distant lately. Hana opened her mouth to defend Betty's hairdressing skills and Louise interjected again. "My husband expects me to travel into the city. It's part of the deal with moving out to this hick town. He promised me the perks of Auckland if I came with him."

Gina's face took on a peculiar, tight expression and Hana watched her cheeks flush. She glanced sideways at Hana and then widened her eyes at Louise, as though issuing a silent plea for the other woman to stop disrespecting the locals. Despite herself, Hana's hand strayed to her hair and she tucked a stray curl behind her ear. Mac studied her with interest as though he understood the scene on a much deeper level, his deafness enhancing his other senses and giving him a unique perspective.

Spotting someone else she wanted to speak to, Louise gave a regal wave and clacked across the pavement towards her next victim. Gina pursed her lips. "Sorry. She's not as bad as she seems. Just tactless." The jewel flashed on her front tooth again.

"You knew her before you moved here?" Hana relaxed, stroking her son's auburn hair as his keen eyes studied a flitting butterfly.

"Yes." Gina blew out a breath. "My husband and her ex work together."

"Hi girls." An arm slid around Hana's shoulders and she felt the tension ebb from her body. Libby's voice held a soothing quality which brought peace. She gave Hana a sideways hug before releasing her. Gina flashed her diamond smile in response and Libby showed no sign of being either impressed or disinterested. Her face remained schooled into its impassive guise, a serene smile fixed on her lips.

"Hey." Hana glanced down at the neat body encased in Yoga gear and nodded. "How was your class?"

"Great." Libby clasped her hands in front of her and arched her spine into a gentle curve. She released it with a sigh of satisfaction, not a spare gram of fat anywhere to be seen. Tossing her long blonde ponytail, she grinned at Hana. "You should come."

Hana looked down at her dusty boots and the flax stains on her jeans. "Will's keeping me a prisoner in the museum. The stock men have built a fake town based on original drawings from the first Du Rose settlers and they're creating a Māori pa next to it. Will's responsible for designing the buildings and he's gone overboard with the number of baskets he wants." Hana sighed at the memory of the growing pile of weaving stacked in the corner of the museum. "That's not forgetting woven place mats, woven rugs, woven wall hangings and woven bunches of flax roses. He's using old documents to find out what they used. He's in his element, but I'm currently his slave."

Libby laughed and Gina gave them both an odd look. Hana identified it as a frown in the seconds which followed, but Botox had rendered the woman's forehead immobile. "How's it going?" Libby asked. "I'd always liked the idea of flax weaving but never got the opportunity."

Hana snorted. "Please feel free to pitch in anytime. I think Will's sick of my wonky attempts. He says I'm reducing his cultural heritage to dust."

Gina's eyes narrowed. "Oh, do you own that hotel in the mountains?" She lowered her voice and confusion crept into her tone, though her wooden features remained blank like the mask of a doll.

"Yes." Dread snaked through Hana's heart though she couldn't identify the source. She tried so hard to fit into the local scene and feel included in the thriving community. The label of Mrs Du Rose possessed the ability to segregate her from their warmth like a bucket of cold water. She swallowed. "But we don't live at the hotel anymore. My husband built a house higher up the mountain." She glanced sideways at Libby but received only an encouraging smile. Wisdom told her to stay out of it and not muddy their friendship with Hana's latest round of self-defeatist thinking.

"Ohhh." Gina drew the sound out before taking a step closer to Hana. She invaded her personal space until the urge to take a step backwards became overwhelming. Hana glanced down to find her son staring at her, looking for her reaction so he'd know what to think. Gina lowered her voice. "I didn't realise you lived there. Louise insisted I get the girls together. We planned to have a play date at her place, but her ex-husband's knocking a wall out to build a conservatory."

"Girls?" Hana held her breath and dreaded the answer.

Gina's head bobbed like a nodding doll. "Yes. Phoebe, Jordan and Holly."

"Phoenix." Hana made the correction while her brain scrambled for answers. Her heart sank. Libby gave her a look of sympathy and squeezed her arm above the elbow, offering physical comfort without getting involved. Holly had split Phoenix's lip on the first day of term over ownership of a crayon. It had been smoothed over as an accident but subsequent verbal and physical digs left Hana concerned enough to visit the teacher. The investigation was allegedly still ongoing.

Libby released Hana's arm as a little boy cannoned into her stomach. She cupped his cheeks in her hands and leaned down to kiss his hair. "Good day, sweetie?" she asked. He nodded up at her, sparkling blue eyes showing his pleasure at finding her waiting in the usual spot.

"Hey, Darren." Hana gave him a wave before scanning the crowd for her own children. She spied Wiri's dark head bobbing through the throng towards her. He cut through like a silent juggernaut, a couple of smaller boys swimming free in his wake. "Phoe's coming," he announced as he reached her. He stood on tiptoes and pursed his lips for a kiss, unashamed of his need for emotional affirmation from his chosen mother figure, even in public. He'd learned from Logan not to care about what other people thought. Hana envied them their determined oblivion. Gina glanced sideways at Wiri's greeting with Mac. The older boy ruffled the ginger curls and slipped an arm around Mac's slender shoulders. They shared a brief second of connection that said more than words.

Chaos interrupted the sweetness in the shape of two girls from Phoenix's class. Sassy and filled with indignation, they barrelled towards Gina with library bags flowing and scowls already set on their faces. Gina dipped at the waist and pursed her lips ready for Jordan's arrival. The lanky, dark-haired girl ignored her maternal overtures. "She's not coming," she stated. She placed one hand on her hip as though preparing to perform a complicated ballet move, the other clasped the fingers of the blonde girl she'd towed behind her. "Holly's coming by herself."

"Oh." Gina swallowed and glanced towards Hana. "We thought Phoebe wanted to play at our house."

Hana's brow furrowed and she corrected the expression after looking at Gina's smooth forehead. Already older than most of the other mothers, she blinked away the momentary fear that she'd be mistaken as someone's granny. The thought offered no comfort. She was a granny. Jas and Hope's granny. A growl of frustration escaped her throat and she narrowed her eyes at Wiri. "Did you see Phoe today, Wiri? What's going on?"

Wiri gave her a sage look filled with unspoken wisdom. He cocked his head to one side and raised his left eyebrow in reprimand, as though wondering why Hana would ask such a question. He jerked his head towards the blonde girl behind Jordan and Hana's heart sank. She scanned the swirling mass of bodies and saw her daughter stalking towards her with a face like thunder. Her grey eyes had changed to the colour of slate and she channelled latent fury. When she spotted Jordan and Holly, she gripped her stomach with her free hand in a display of academy award acting.

"She's got a belly-ache." Wiri backed up the ruse which told Hana he knew of Holly's gate crashing of Phoenix and Jordan's play date. She suspected they'd got together during the day and discussed it, despite Wiri's love of soccer during his lunch break.

Hana disliked the lie but had grown to dislike Holly more. She decided to speak to the teacher again about the low key bullying. Her daughter folded into Mac and Wiri's tight embrace without breaking step. Hana sighed and dredged up a sincere smile for Gina. "I'm sorry. She can come another time. There's a bug going around and you wouldn't want to catch it."

Gina's eyes widened at the veiled suggestion of vomiting and diarrhoea and accepted Hana's apology with haste. "It's fine," she urged, patting the top of Phoenix's head as the child nestled into Wiri's chest. "Another time, Phoebe. Hope you get better soon." She turned on her heel and strode towards Louise and a static group of other women wearing designer clothing.

Libby raised an eyebrow at Hana and she shrugged in return and shook her head. Holly spun around to follow Gina, but Jordan made doe eyes at Wiri and fluttered her lashes. "Hi Wiremu," she said. Her cheeks flushed pink as his grey-eyed gaze settled on her face.

"Hi." His tone sounded flat and disinterested. Phoenix peered sideways and Hana watched her jaw flex. Her daughter's eyes narrowed and she gave a low snort of disgust, enough like a snarl to act as a warning. Tiny fingers gripped Wiri's polo shirt until she'd tugged it askew and when his arm tightened around her shoulders, a look of predatory victory turned her eyes into gleaming dark coals. Hana gulped, recognising the sight of pure Du Rose possession when she saw it. Phoenix mirrored her father's tight rein on the things he held dear and it prophesied impending doom heavier than any of them could bear.

Hana let out a breath of exasperation, waved to Libby and walked the children across the busy road to the truck. "We need to talk," she said to Phoenix in a low voice as she leaned across her to belt Mac into his car seat.

"Thought you might say that," Phoenix murmured.

5

The Bad Penny

Logan flipped the last burger on the barbecue and smiled at Hana. "This is nice, isn't it?" he said.

"Perfect." She slipped an arm around his waist and gazed across the horizon. The Tasman Sea stretched out before them like a tablecloth. Wiri's giggles reached them from the tree line as he and Phoenix engaged in a game of hide and seek. Not understanding the point of the game, Mac snoozed underneath the wooden table still waiting for someone to find him. Hana smiled and kissed her husband's firm biceps. Home-grown steak and sausages stayed warm in a tray above the flames and Logan prodded the burgers one at a time. He hadn't mentioned JD's paddock again and she hoped he wouldn't. She didn't want to think about Jacob Du Rose or his cursed legacy near the township. Her talk with Phoenix went nowhere. She'd still claimed her stomach hurt, but her squeal of delight betrayed the lie as Wiri found her hiding place behind a wide totara trunk. Hana frowned at an empty space on the deck. "Did you move some of my plant pots?"

"Nope. Food's almost ready," Logan announced. Glancing across at his sleeping son, he waggled his eyebrows. "Maybe wake Mac before the others stampede around his head."

Hana nodded and stepped up onto the wooden deck. The vibration of her footsteps caused her son's eyes to pop open. Pink-cheeked and bonny, he gave her a beautiful smile. "Dinner time, Macky." Hana lifted her right hand and made the fingers and thumb into the shape of a beak. She tapped her lips and he repeated the action with a lazy, sleep fogged hand. "Come." Hana held her hand out and he rolled onto his stomach and crawled out from beneath the table. Logan appeared around the side of the house with the other two. Phoenix rode on Wiri's back and made a clicking noise with her tongue. Turning aside from Hana, Mac held his arms out to Wiri and the boy stamped up onto the deck with heavy footsteps. Phoenix slid down his back and landed with the finesse of a ballerina. She bore Logan's natural grace and Hana frowned. She needed to get to the bottom of the Holly issue and soon. Wiri squatted down and Mac scrambled up his back like a monkey. After two circuits of the table, he tipped the boy onto the bench and squeezed in next to him.

Three pairs of wide eyes watched Logan's progress from the barbecue to the table, carrying his tray laden with meat. "I'll turn the grill off," he said, setting the tray next to a bowl filled with open bread rolls.

Like the central pivot in a fine mechanism, Wiri held his hands out either side of him. Phoenix ceased clapping her excitement at the sight of the feast and grabbed his right hand. Wiri tapped Mac's leg and the little boy slipped his tiny hand into the offered palm.

"Pray, Papa!" Phoenix demanded and Logan twisted knobs on the barbecue and hurried back. His long legs stepped onto the deck without using the stairs and he clasped his daughter's hand in his. Hana remained standing and reached both Mac and her husband by stretching across the table. She wrinkled her nose as a wasp buzzed near the salad. Logan closed his eyes and bowed his head.

"Ki taku whānau, me nga hua, me te kai, kia ora." He tried to release Phoenix's hand, but she held on with determination and translated the prayer.

"For our family, friends and food, we say thank you." Her eyes blinked open and she smiled at Hana. "For Mama," she said and gave a beatific smile.

"Thanks." Hana felt abandoned as Mac let go of her fingers and knelt up on the bench to reach a bread roll. A tick of sadness began in her chest at the isolation created by the language barrier. She'd tried to learn Māori, listening to the children's bilingual conversations and staring at their picture books. Words and phrases stuck, but nothing enabling her to have a conversation in Logan's native tongue. He squeezed her fingers as though reading her mind and then let go. Hana watched her son slapping sausages into the mouth of his bread roll and felt a kinship with him outside of maternalism. They were both cripples in communication but for different reasons.

"Ka pai, Macky." Wiri gave Mac a beaming smile and praised his skill with the hefty sandwich disappearing between rosebud lips. Mac nodded and a sausage tumbled onto his plate. He rolled his green eyes in exaggerated annoyance and Wiri grinned, a complicit bystander in the battle between tiny fingers and hungry mouth.

"Papa, can we play guitar after dinner?" Phoenix asked. "I need to learn if I'm gonna be a lady vicar when I grow up."

"What?" Logan's eyes widened and he halted in the act of loading a slab of steak onto his plate. His fork poised mid-air and sunshine glinted off its prongs. The horror on his face cheered Hana a little. Her miniature evangelist adored everything about Sunday school and God, challenging her father's upbringing and beliefs with a skip and a smile. The wise kaumātua of the local marae had assured her it would work out okay and the two could coexist. He'd patted her hand and smiled, living proof of the fact. Especially as his grandson served as the local vicar.

Logan frowned. "The guitar is broken. I'm getting the strings replaced. They keep snapping. There's a place in Auckland who reckon they can fix it up for me. I put it in the back of my truck ready for when I go up there next."

"Okay. But please can you be quick?" Phoenix flapped her elbows like a duck. "I'm learning guitar so I can play in church, then I'm getting me long flowing robes for vicaring. And wings."

"Cool." Logan relaxed and sat on the bench next to Hana. She swallowed her disappointment at the evangelist's moment of confusion.

"It's a hood." Wiri prodded Phoenix in the back and she lurched forward. "On Sam's robes. A hood."

"Isn't!" Phoenix's eyes widened to complete the picture of utter horror. "It's wings." Her outrage carried across the table and Hana looked down at her empty plate to avoid being dragged into the debate. She reached over for the salad and scooped lettuce with the tongs.

"Ooh, a burndy one." Wiri snagged a blackened sausage with his fork and waggled it in front of Phoenix's face as a peace offering. She paused a second to make him suffer and then accepted his gift with mumbled thanks.

"Is wings," she whispered and Wiri smirked and ignored her.

Hana lifted her cutlery and glanced around the table at her perfect family and their perfect home. She tensed as though a sixth sense told her she wouldn't get to enjoy it for long.

"This looks cozy." Footsteps accompanied the voice and long legs brought the speaker around the corner of the house and onto the deck. Dark tousled hair hung over his right eye and even, white teeth clamped his lower lip in a look of pure enjoyment. Grey eyes glinted in a once handsome face and Hana shrank back from the look of malice she recognised there. He turned his body to face Logan, not giving him ample time to disguise his dismay. "Hey, bro'," he said with a mischievous chuckle.

6

Animosity

"Get out." Logan rose and dropped his cutlery with a clang. His fork landed without hitting the plate and bounced over the edge of the table.

Kane Du Rose dug his hands in his pockets and Hana couldn't decide if it portrayed peace or nonchalance. He'd lost weight and his jeans hung off him. He swept his gaze around the table and settled on Phoenix. "Nice family," he commented. He gave her a wink and Hana's daughter glanced at her father and pursed her lips. Only Mac continued battling his giant sandwich in happy oblivion.

"Don't let the gate hit you on the way out." Logan straightened his spine and spread his legs in a combative stance. His fists balled at his sides, ready for however Kane wanted to play the game. The old feud reared its head as though only yesterday Kane had slit Logan's side open in a sick, teenage dare. Hana saw hatred flare in her husband's eyes and panicked.

"Would you children like to eat in front of the television?" she offered, breaking every house rule they'd ever made.

"I'm not hungry." Wiri shoved himself back off the bench, tangling his legs in his haste. The ravenous boy of a few moments ago disappeared in a haze of fear.

"I am." Phoenix dropped her chin and furrowed her brow. She picked up the blackened sausage and watched Wiri's retreating back with a mix of disbelief and shock.

"Go, baby." Hana offered her a reassuring smile, ruined by the swallow half way through her sentence. "Take Macky with you."

Kane glanced across at Hana and raised his eyebrows. "This isn't the Du Rose hospitality I remember." He made the words sound wistful and Hana cringed at the lie. Nothing could make Kane Du Rose welcome on Logan's side of the mountain. Her fingers worked fast to toss meat and bread rolls into a plastic container. She pushed it towards her daughter and Phoenix took it without comment. The heavy atmosphere over their comfortable family dinner beggared explanation.

Kane risked taking his gaze off Logan as he observed Hana's frantic movements. She tapped her son's shoulder before sliding him from the bench backwards. He looked up at her in question and she dumped his sandwich into another plastic tub. "Inside," she mouthed.

His delicate brow furrowed and he looked up at the wide blue sky as though expecting to see a rain cloud. His greasy fingers motioned to form a question and devoid of explanation, Hana dropped a kiss on his forehead and told him to follow his sister. They trooped after a fleeing Wiri, but Mac paused at the corner of the house to stare into the face of the man who ruined his fun. Hana saw green eyes meet grey and Mac's narrowed as though he understood more than she believed. He turned, his auburn hair moving in the breeze coming off the sea. He walked into Phoenix twice as he turned to look back at the unusual scene. Hana felt torn in half. She wanted to comfort her children, but dare not leave the men sharing the same air space without supervision. One of them would end up going over the cliff and smashing against the hard rocks below the house.

Logan moved his head in an almost imperceptible jerk, telling her to leave. She pursed her lips and disobeyed, standing her ground and thinking up excuses for the argument later. "My husband asked you to leave." Hana narrowed her eyes and held her hand out sideways, inviting Kane to go out the way he came in.

His gaze roved over her body from head to toe, creating the sensation of having a dead fish dragged across her flesh. "I've got business with your husband, so why don't you just run along?" His lips quirked up in an expression of pure arrogance.

Hana gathered her wits and the Irish grit which mingled with the bloody minded Scots in her veins. "I don't think so," she replied, meeting his mocking gaze with determination. "His business is mine." She resisted the urge to blink and found some deep chamber of pride and courage hidden between chest and stomach.

Kane looked away first and Hana felt victory pour through her nerve endings. Her hands shook and she hid them behind her back, mimicking Logan's iron stance and driving home the message of inhospitality. Kane shook his head and withdrew his hands from his pockets. Logan's eyelashes moved as danger flared in his irises. "You've got something of mine," Kane said and instead of balling his hands into fists, he spread them either side of him as though offering Logan an embrace. Hana stiffened and watched confusion heighten the angry flush in Logan's cheeks.

Then Logan released a laugh, so unexpected it jarred Hana's nerves. Logan settled himself back on the bench and reached for a bottle of tomato sauce. Red fluid squirted from the nozzle as he doused his sandwich. An image of blood filtered into Hana's brain. Half-brothers united through their haemophilia. Sauce dripped from the sandwich as Logan lifted it to his lips and nausea banished Hana's appetite. Every encounter between these men led to injury and bloodshed. She'd lost count of the battles, both legendary and real.

Kane looked wrong footed. He blinked and glanced at Hana, as though seeking solidarity. He found none. "We have nothing of yours," she said, strengthening her voice. "Please leave."

Eyes which matched Logan's seemed to send her a silent appeal before Kane's shoulders slumped. He shook his head. "It's not over," he said through gritted teeth. "I'll make you talk to me."

Logan dropped the sandwich onto the plate and wiped his fingers on a nearby napkin. His eyes flicked up to meet Kane's angry gaze. Hana saw the blackness in his soul she'd foolishly imagined banished. It reared up like an exorcism of horror and she felt herself recoil. An expression of faint amusement settled over Logan's handsome features and Hana saw the bitter root he'd kept hidden beneath. "Good luck with that." His tone sounded dismissive and cruel. Logan pointed towards the corner of the house and jerked his head in Kane's direction. "See yourself out." The words killed all discussion and Hana heard her own heartbeat pounding in her ears.

Kane shook his head and jammed his hands into his pockets. The action seemed necessary to hold his jeans up around his hips. He stepped off the deck in a single stride and glared back at Logan. "You're an ass-hole," he declared. "You always were." Hana listened to his footsteps retreat around the side of the house and a car door slammed moments later. She tried to move her legs and found herself frozen in position.

"Shit!" Logan smashed his fist onto his plate and the crockery snapped beneath it. The shards embedded themselves in the remains of his sandwich. He heaved out an angry breath and stood. Hana saw red liquid staining the heel of his hand and wrist, unable to discern if it was sauce or blood. She swallowed as her husband uttered more curse words and strode towards the fence line. The bush beckoned from beyond, shadowy and dark as the canopy hid its innards from view. Hana swallowed at the abandoned meal and her gaze flicked towards the lounge window. A movement caught her attention and Wiri's grey eyes watched her with an unreadable expression on his face.

And just like that, perfection lifted its hand and the Du Roses plunged into disaster.

7

Kane Du Rose

Bright sunshine warmed Hana's red hair as she strode across the courtyard to the main hotel building. After another disastrous morning failing at raranga, she'd gone for a walk in Miriam's rose garden to clear her head. She blamed Kane's reappearance for the fact that twelve lengths of beautiful flax had turned to stringy rope beneath her fingers and Will's patience had frayed to match. She'd argued with Logan until late over telling Wiri the truth about his father, just in case Kane meant business. They'd gone to sleep without reaching a resolution. The fearful look on Wiri's face haunted her dreams.

The sun beat down on the roses and Hana kicked at the loose dirt beneath her feet. It looked damp and her action uncovered a trickle feed beneath the surface. Droplets of brown bore water oozed from a hose pipe which Will's son had made to administer a steady supply of water to the blooms. She covered it back up with the toe of her boot and looked around, half expecting him to appear from behind a hedge. The damp earth reminded her of something and she groaned out loud. The couple whose photograph she'd just taken looked up from sniffing a white rose and stared at her. "I just forgot something," she said, forcing a smile on her lips. "I forgot to water my mother-in-laws geraniums yesterday."

Hana whirled from the garden and set off back towards the front of the hotel. Guilt made her glance up at Leslie's attic balcony and the pink flower heads peeking through the railings. The apartment was set back into the apex of the roof, the small balcony the only evidence of habitation above the business of the other floors. Instead of crusty, wilting blooms, she saw Logan's back as he pressed his back against the rail. "Oh, thank goodness," she breathed. "He remembered." Hana dodged a bus carrying a large crowd of Spanish tourists going on to their next destination and sighed with relief. The hotel staff had a breathing space of two days for other guests to trickle away and then a conference would start and last for a week. Summer visitors put everyone under extreme pressure but conference bookings proved easier. The rooms didn't require daily overhauls and the kitchen catered a set menu.

Hana's brow furrowed as she remembered Logan saying he'd be mending fences on the bush line for most of the day. Her feet slowed. She recalled him collecting his GPS tracker from the cupboard behind reception as she went to slave over her basket weaving. "Logan!" Her voice sounded a little more than a squeak against the sound of birdsong and the grinding gears of the departing coach. He leaned against the rail, his arms raised in front of him. "Logan!" she called again. Then Hana heard the crack of a gunshot.

His arms flew out to his sides as though to stabilise himself and then his upper body jerked again at the sound of another shot. Hana gasped as the balcony rail shuddered and detached itself from the wall on one side with a grating squeal. Logan's body jerked again as though a heavy blow landed against his chest and the rail gave way, seeming to pause in mid-air before it swung sideways and left a yawning gap.

Hana screamed. Her lips parted and she kept screaming as her legs carried her forward. The body fell with a rushing sound which only stopped with the sickening thud which heralded its landing. The curved metal rail clung to the building by two of its remaining anchors, distended and wrong looking. Hana crossed the sweeping drive at speed. Her breaths came in heaves and her chest locked. She reached the mangled mess of human bones and her ribs strained beneath the pressure as though she might explode.

A car door slammed somewhere behind her. A male voice shouted her name at the same time as another swore. Hana's hand covered her mouth and she heard herself let out a groan with the effort of releasing air. Even with no medical training she could see she possessed no skill that might help. The smashed body leaked precious red fluid from a head wound and blood pooled and seeped into the gravel. Two dark marks sat like emblems on the man's jacket. His head turned at an unnatural angle and grey irises stared at the sky, the life already gone. Gardening gloves covered his hands but one finger stuck out at an unnatural angle from the hand.

"It's okay, Hana. It's okay." Rough hands seized her forearms and spun her around. Strong arms crushed her cheek against a solid chest. Hana forced herself to look at the floor and not the body as nausea bubbled into her throat. A single blue sneaker snuggled a foot stretched at a peculiar angle. The other sat nearby, laces splayed and a bewildered air surrounding its abandonment. A woman's voice screamed, the sound shrill and jarring. Hana closed her eyes against the firm chest and waited for the numbness to give way to an endless pain. The man pressed his lips close to her ear. "It's not Logan, Hana. It's okay. It's not Logan."

She nodded against his chest and kept her eyes closed, not believing him. Then her mind snatched hungrily at the puzzle pieces around her, offering a slither of fragile hope. Logan only wore sneakers in the gym. He wouldn't dispense with his uniform of cowboy boots and work worn jeans to water geraniums. And he shouldn't have been there. "Not Logan," Hana whispered. She tried to purge the image of the broken man on the ground from the inside of her eyelids.

"No, not Logan." The arms tightened around her. "Not Logan, sweetheart. Not him."

"Toby!" Another male voice sounded from behind Hana and she concentrated on regulating her ragged breaths. The fingers of her right hand released her grip on Toby's shirt and fluttered to her left collar bone. The hard edges of the pacemaker comforted her and she kept her eyes closed and counted her breaths. In. A small one out. In. A bigger one out.

"Toby!" The other man's voice grew fractious and Hana recognised Rawhiti's lyrical tones.

"It's not Logan!" The head stock man kept his voice even, as though he expected to repeat the sentence a few more times. "I thought it was, but it isn't him."

"No, but if he sees you wrapped around his wife, he'll tear your soddin' head off."

A ridiculous giggle bubbled up in Hana's chest, awkward, inappropriate but forceful. She made a choking sound which turned into a sob. Toby's grip around her shoulders increased. "I'm not leaving her standing here alone!" he snapped. "Do something useful. Call the cops. See if he's still alive."

"Someone already did." The new man swallowed mid-sentence, betraying his shock. "He's gone. I called an ambulance, but I don't think they can help. The operator said they'll send the local cops too."

Toby dropped one hand to point towards the front of the hotel. The main doors stood open to the glorious summer afternoon. "Lock the front doors and get the receptionist to put a notice inside. She can direct people through the dining room into the courtyard. Thank goodness most of the guests have left." His body shifted as he took another look at the scene. "Put something over him. You'll find a blanket in the stables."

Toby turned his attention back to Hana. He gripped her shoulders as she dropped to a crouch and concentrated on the ground between her boots. "I feel sick," she whispered. Gravel crunched beneath his feet.

"Okay. I'm sorry, Hana."

"I want Logan." His name emerged with a sob and Toby patted the top of her head. He rose and Hana heard him demanding a radio handset from one of the other men. His boots crunched away so she couldn't hear the conversation. She released a held breath as her husband's baritone sounded in the quiet driveway as transmitted crackles and broken words. Her chest ached and her head swam. Giving up on her squat, Hana sat down in the gravel and hugged her knees to her chest. People moved around, an air of reverence hushing their conversation to stilted whispers. Toby's boots remained close to her thigh as he stood guard, issuing orders with a tenseness to his voice. She heard him swear numerous times, the vile words spewing out in waves. Daring to peer through her eyelashes, she saw Rawhiti laying a horse blanket over the body. Straps and buckles clinked as they splayed either side of the man-sized lump. Toby yelled at the new guy for trying to reunite the stray sneaker with its owner.

"Leave it!" he snapped. "Just move away. Go into reception and do what I asked."

Hana scrambled to her feet with difficulty. Toby's hand gripped her beneath the armpit. "Take it slow," he said, his voice kind. The ground vibrated and she sensed rescue coming. Glancing to her left she saw the dust cloud rising on the mountain and her sluggish heart gave a pitiful jump. Orange dust spiralled into the cloudless sky as the hidden riders executed a dangerous downhill gallop. The group of four emerged from the trees. Three halted on a knife edge to open the gate into the top paddock but one didn't. The white horse soared across the barrier as though she flew. A lump rose into Hana's throat and choked her.

"Sacha," she whispered, looking up in time to see Toby roll his eyes.

"Yeah. Like we don't have enough problems."

The mare galloped down the steep slope at a breakneck speed, her head forming an arrow point above blurred and flying hooves. The other riders filtered through the gate, leaving their dust cloud behind them as they switched from the rough bush track to the sweet grass. They cantered at a more sedate pace, far behind the outrider. Sacha jumped the gate into the stable yard and the clatter of her hooves echoed in the valley as she disappeared from view. Logan appeared moments later, vaulting the fence into the hotel garden and wrenching his battered cowboy hat from his head.

"Logan!" Toby shouted and waved, causing Logan to change trajectory. He saw Hana standing in the centre of the driveway and made a bee line for her. She wrapped her arms around herself and hugged the screams of fear, guilt and relief, containing them within her chest wall. Logan halted as a metallic crash sounded from beyond the garden. It echoed around brick buildings and swearing accompanied it. Sacha popped over the fence behind Logan, her lead rope trailing around her legs. She snorted in irritation and followed him at a trot. The stock men backed away, her reputation preceding her. Logan rolled his eyes and shook his head.

"I told you to stay there," he hissed as though reprimanding a child. Sacha snorted again. Seeing Hana, she overtook him and broke into a rocking canter. Toby darted sideways as she arrived, avoiding her snaking neck and lethal, yellow teeth.

"Stupid animal!" Toby spat, shifting again as she turned her bum on him and bent a solid back hock in threat.

"Hana!" Logan gripped her head between his hands and stared into her eyes. He read her mixed emotions and pushed her face against his chest. "It's okay, babe," he breathed onto the top of her head. "It's okay."

Hana shook her head and lifted her right hand to accept the warm breath of Sacha's muzzle against her palm. Everyone kept saying it would be okay, but it wouldn't. How could it?

The mare nibbled Hana's fingers with uncharacteristic gentleness and batted her forehead against her thigh. Demanding attention, she forced her nose into the small space between Logan's armpit and Hana's neck. Her whiskers scraped and prickled the soft skin and Hana allowed her in. Logan took a step back and a glance up at his face showed his jaw flexing as he banished all emotion. He kept a steadying hand against her spine. "Accident?" he asked Toby.

The stock man took a wide route around Sacha's threatening hooves to meet Logan on the other side. "Dunno, mate. But it's Kane and he's dead. It looked like the balcony rail gave out on him. You were right there, Hana. Did you see what happened?" Hana closed her eyes and ignored the question.

"Shit!" Logan breathed. "What the hell was he doing in Alfred's apartment?"

"I don't know. You asked me to take the new stock guy up to the bunkhouse. We just got back."

Hana watched her husband purse his lips and heard the breath he blew through them. He turned sideways to look at the horse blanket spread across the mound of body. "Shit!" he hissed again under his breath.

Hana wrapped her arms around Sacha's neck and buried her face in the scrubby mane. She closed her eyes and concentrated on inhaling the sweet scent of grass and horseflesh. Sweat lathered Sacha's coat with white foam. Steam rose from her midsection and Hana placed a hand against the muscular chest to feel the comforting beat of the massive heart caged inside and ground herself. She still had Logan. He hadn't died. The sounds of muted gunshot sounded in her memory but it seemed too hard to say the words.

"What the hell happened?" Logan's hand shook against her back and Hana turned to look at him. Sacha released a huge breath and damp air and horse snot covered Hana's jeans and boots.

"This is a big mess." Toby frowned. "Sorry mate. I know he's your brother." He reached up and squeezed Logan's shoulder. His knuckles whitened and then released. He gave Hana a sideways smile. "Are you okay now?"

"Yes. Thanks." Hana forced herself to straighten and Sacha ran her hard forehead up and down the sharp point of Hana's elbow to scratch the sweet spot she always struggled to reach.

When one of the hotel staff jogged across and ventured too close, the horse snaked her neck in a wide angle and plastered her ears against her head. She looked terrifying and the man veered away.

"Mr Du Rose." He addressed Logan but watched Sacha, his body tense and ready to dive out of range. "Telephone call." His neat grey waistcoat and slacks identified him as a receptionist and Hana realised she didn't recognise him.

"Yeah." Logan ran his other hand over his chin and the stubble scratched against his palm. "Who is it?"

"Wouldn't say." The man in his early twenties blanched and his complexion paled. "She asked for you. A journalist."

Logan shrugged. "That was fast." He blew out an exasperated breath. "You can see I'm busy."

"Yes, Mr Du Rose. She said it was about the summer fair." His nervousness in the face of Logan's impatience gave Hana cause for sympathy. His gaze strayed to the mound beneath the horse blanket. "I don't think she knows about this yet."

Hana reached out and touched Logan's side for reassurance, feeling the warm flesh through his shirt. He hadn't died. She still had him. Her world had shifted on its axis, but it wouldn't topple. Not today.

"If she calls again, refer her to me," she offered in a wavering voice. She ran the backs of her fingers beneath her eyes and collected her emotions into a neat pile. "My husband will be busy here for a while."

"Thanks." The man smiled, relief flooding his face.

Logan held out his hand and Hana gripped it, despite Sacha's nose appearing underneath and trying to break their linked fingers apart. "Don't waste your time with them," he said. His gaze strayed towards the body again and he swallowed. "Life's too short."

"I can handle it." Hana avoided looking at the blood seeping from beneath the blanket and spreading into the surrounding gravel. Big words from a weak stomach. She didn't know if she could handle anything much.

"Thanks." Logan squeezed her fingers. "What do you think I should do now?"

Hana floundered, not expecting the question. "I don't know, Logan. What do you mean?"

He released an equine sounding snort which could have indicated derision or confusion. She couldn't tell which. "My half-brother just nose-dived off the roof of my hotel. What should I do, Hana?"

8

Silence

"I don't know what you should do here, but I need to get Mac." Hana kept her gaze averted from the body and fought to convince herself it didn't exist. She turned away from Logan as she spoke, sending the words through the side of her mouth.

Logan rubbed his chin and looked thoughtful. He glanced at his watch and nodded. "You know the drill, Hana. The cops are on their way and you're a witness. I'm guessing they've already blocked the end of the driveway. They won't let you out." He tapped his index finger against his lips. "I'll phone one of the aunties. They won't mind fetching them in an emergency. Or the housekeeper. Doesn't she usually go home for lunch to check on her mother?"

Hana swallowed and panic roused in her chest. Worse than the presence of Logan's brother smashed ten metres away from her feet, the thought of Mac's distress sent her heart rate into orbit. "I have to go!" Her eyes widened in horror. "Mac won't understand. The other kids will leave and he'll sit there thinking I've abandoned him."

"He won't." Logan's fingers caressed her jaw and his expression softened. "Stuff happens, Hana."

"I have to get out of here, Logan." She swallowed and broke from his grasp, seeing his irises darken in warning. "My son comes first."

"Phone the nursery. Then I'll organise one of the aunties to grab Mac and then the others. The kaumātua's wife will do it." He dug his phone from his jeans pocket and held it out to her. Hana shook her head.

"No. I have to get him."

Logan's brow furrowed. "Hana, be sensible." His lips parted as she continued backing away, her boots grinding in the gravel. He placed his hands on his hips and took a determined stance. "They won't let you out," he repeated. Hana felt warm breath against her thigh as Sacha sniffed her jeans. Rough lips grabbed at the material and then let go. Logan saw Hana's face change as the idea ran through her mind. He saw the light reach her eyes and took a step forward. "Don't do it, Hana." He moved towards her but desperation for her child made her faster. Logan's longer legs meant the stirrups dangled low enough under Sacha's girth for Hana not to need a leg up. She sprang into the saddle and snatched up the lead rope. It caught against Sacha's chest before reeling into her fingers. Hana preferred to ride with her horses controlled by bit and bridle, but Logan rode on a head collar with a long rope in his right hand. He took a stride across the gravel towards her. Hana lifted the rope against Sacha's neck and the horse backed up.

"You said nobody could leave." Toby's voice sounded laden with accusation as he jogged across the lawn, dodging Sacha's threatening hooves as she whirled her bum in his direction. "Where's she going?"

Hana kept her seat and her eyes begged Logan for clemency. "Please," she whispered.

Logan's eyes narrowed and he lifted his chin. He had trained Sacha from a foal and she obeyed him foremost. With one command he could prevent Hana's journey. He didn't. "Be careful," he mouthed and took a step back. Relief and gratitude filled Hana's expression as she pushed Sacha into a jog.

The horse disliked the loose gravel and trod with exaggerated care. A single stone lodged too long against the delicate frog in her hoof would end her mustering career long before her attitude earned her a bullet. Once on the manicured lawn leading to the main driveway, Hana pushed her into a canter. Hanging left before the driveway snaked through the mountains to the main road, they took the narrow lane leading to Hana's house and then halted. Hana took a moment to alter the stirrup leathers to her height and tightened the girth. Logan rode with a natural seat gained from decades in the saddle, the girth swinging loose under Sacha's gut.

"Sorry," Hana breathed as Sacha complained by releasing a cloud of foul smelling gas. "I want to reach Mac without breaking my neck." She sighed. "I also need to process what the hell just happened."

Hana accessed the many paddocks between the hotel and town by stretching to unlatch the gates. Sacha pushed through the gaps and Hana leaned down to clip them shut. One proved stubborn and she dismounted to fight the rusty catch, led Sacha through and then clasped it shut. "Let's find you some water," she breathed, nudging the horse towards a cattle trough. Sacha dipped her chin in the clear liquid but refused to drink. Hana sighed. "You galloped downhill, girly. Just take a drink to make me feel better." The rusty gate hook had drawn blood and Hana screwed up her face and sucked her finger to dull the pain. Sacha fidgeted and danced on her hooves, straining against the rope with a sense of bottled impatience. Hana used the trough to mount up and checked her watch, dismayed to see the nursery's collection time approaching fast. "Oh, God!" she groaned. "Please keep my baby safe." Her heart felt tight in her chest at the thought of his distress and she pushed Sacha forward. Emboldened by the need to get to Mac, she jumped the next five fences and stayed seated. Kane's broken body and its memory faded behind her as urgency overrode everything else.

A Charolais herd grazed the last paddock, their creamy bodies spread out like flotsam across the lush grass. They seemed a long way from home and Hana watched them scatter aside from Sacha's drumming hooves. Logan's land ended at the boundary with the town. The final paddocks belonged to him by default, awarded in his paternal grandfather's will. The identity of the mysterious JD recalled images Hana longed to forget and she leaned down to release the gate to Jack's land with her lower lip caught in her teeth. "He can't hurt us anymore," she whispered to herself, though the surrounding air chilled and made her shiver. The hair rose on her arms as she shut the gate behind her. Gritting her teeth, she pushed Sacha into a canter and refused to look at the lush green grass which parted to leave a wake behind them.

The catch belonging to the last of the boundary gates refused to budge and Hana dismounted with a grunt of irritation. A hefty padlock sealed it against cattle rustlers, the thick chain demanding heavy equipment to break it. "No, no, no!" Hana groaned. A natural bridge stretched beyond the gate and then the main road. A stream bubbled below the mud covered structure which was suitable for the weight of cattle in single file, but not vehicles. It made stealing from the Du Roses arduous and foolish. It also meant Sacha couldn't jump the gate without risking injury, landing on the thin bridge or running on into the road.

Hana's watch showed her as five minutes late and she cast around for a different exit. Nothing. Her phone lay on the desk in the museum office where she'd left it charging, so she couldn't ask for advice. "I'm sorry, I can't take you any further," she told Sacha. Her shaking fingers unclipped the rope and wound it into a coil. She laid it on the ground inside the gate. Sacha's saddle slipped from her withers and Hana propped it up on its cantle behind the gate post. She placed the green saddle blanket over the top and secured the edges with rocks to protect Logan's expensive tan saddle from nosey Charolais or thieves. "I won't be long," she promised and clambered over the high post and rail fence. Sacha blew out a long breath in reply and pushed her nose into the fresh grass, tearing off long strands and closing her eyes to chew.

A deep ditch met Hana on the other side. Higher than usual, the boundary fence dissuaded opportunist thieves while the gully made it impossible for trailers to gain easy access. Anyone stealing the expensive Charolais needed to come equipped and be certain they could load the herd before someone on the main road saw them. With no other choice and the time slipping past, Hana faced the water. Despite the hot summer, the water still ran from the mountain spring and the mud sucked at her boots like wet cement. She made a giant leap and got over without touching the bubbling flow. Her fingers scrabbled against roots and grass to gain purchase on the other side. Needles scratched her hands and arms as she pushed her way through a line of scratchy totara to the road.

Twenty minutes late. She checked her watch and groaned, but kept jogging. The last few cars left the parking area outside the nursery as children went home. A couple of women acknowledged Hana and she waved back. Someone stopped and called her name but she pretended not to hear, not wanting to delay herself further just to satisfy their curiosity.

The nursery looked empty as Hana crashed through the doors. The reception desk stood unguarded and she barrelled through into the inner sanctum. Toys and books lay scattered across several areas and women's voices sounded from the library corner. Hana kicked off her filthy boots and jogged across the room in her socks, rounding the last shelf to find the staff straightening the equipment ready for the afternoon session.

"Hana!" The leader of Mac's group turned to face her and her brow furrowed, a children's story book clutched in her fingers. "What's happened?" The genuine concern in her blue eyes robbed Hana of intelligible speech and she only managed Mac's name. She put her hands over her face to push the image of Kane's broken body from her inner vision as it surged to the forefront. Strong hands gripped her wrists and steered her away from the knot of staring teachers. "Come to my office," she said, her tone gentle.

Hana ran a hand across her eyes and shook her head. "I need to get Mac." She heard the fear in her own voice and felt the lump rise into her chest. "He'll be upset."

Shirley smiled and shook her head. "He's fine. The vicar came to read a story to the children. Mac spent the whole time sitting on his knee and when you didn't arrive, Reverend Sam took him next door to his office."

"I'm so sorry," Hana breathed.

"One of those days?" Shirley gave her shoulder a squeeze. "Come on." She jerked her head towards the internal doors leading to the adjoining church and smiled. "Sam left it unlocked so you could come straight through. He said your husband rang him, so we didn't worry."

Hana tensed in the church corridor and listened for the sound of violent tears. In their absence, her heart seemed louder in her ears. Shirley's sneakers squeaked on the wooden floorboards and Hana followed. A metal sign asking for donations to support the Anglican nursery leaned up against the wall and it caught on her sock and spun away. "I'm sorry," she whispered, standing it back up as Shirley raised a hand and knocked on the vestry door. Hana heard nothing, but Shirley gave a nod of satisfaction and turned the handle.

Mac sat on Reverend Sam's knee and they shared a packet of sandwiches between them. Sam looked up with a smile and tapped Mac's shoulder. The child tipped his head back and then followed the line of Sam's finger to Hana. His tiny face broke into a delighted smile. He lifted his half of the sandwich and waggled it. A slice of tomato plopped onto the desk. "Luh," he said. "Luh." The sandwich performed a waggle waggle dance and a square of cheese followed the tomato. Mac used his delicate fingers to scoop the pieces into his mouth. His legs swung against the vicar's in a movement which Hana recognised as satisfaction.

"Come in, Hana." Sam nodded to Shirley in thanks and indicated an armchair in the corner of the vestry. A set of black and white robes hung from a peg nearby and Hana felt the softness of the fabric brush her cheek as she sat. "Thanks, Shirley." Sam gave the teacher a smile and she waved to Hana and left.

Hana's eyes widened and she rose again in a jerky movement, her legs wobbling beneath her. "I'm sorry!" she called and Shirley pushed the door open again and popped her head around it.

"What for?" Her brow narrowed. "Hana, you're never late. I know your children come first in everything." She lowered her head to observe Hana over the top of her glasses. Her grey curls bounced. "I knew it must be something unexpected. Just sit here for a moment and catch your breath." The door closed behind her.

Sam pursed his lips to hide his grin as Mac pressed his index finger over the crumbs littered around the desk. The little boy licked them off his finger one at a time without touching Sam's half of the sandwich.

Hana settled in the armchair and bent her body so she could rest her forearms on her thighs. A peculiar lightheaded feeling plagued her and she closed her eyes. "Do you want to talk about it?" Sam asked, his tone gentle.

Hana exhaled and watched her son snuggle against the vicar's chest. Mac pushed his thumb into his mouth and closed his eyes. "He likes you," she said. "He doesn't like many people."

Sam grinned. "He looks like you, but has all the hallmarks of his father." He jerked his head towards the crumb free desk. "Obsessive compulsive and doesn't like people. I think that sums up Logan Du Rose, don't you?"

Hana laughed despite herself, but the image of Kane lying on the gravel wiped the smile from her lips. She sobered and stared at the carpet. "Kane's dead," she said, her voice flat and toneless.

"I know." Sam's brow furrowed but his eyes remained bright. "Logan called to explain. He said I should tell you to leave Sacha and asked me to drive you and Mac home."

"He did?" Hana heard her voice break. She wrinkled her nose. "I left Sacha in the last paddock. She thinks I'm going back for her." She swallowed. "I need to retrieve Logan's saddle. It's expensive."

Sam's eyes twinkled. "Someone will collect it, but I don't suppose he'll get many volunteers to fetch the horse." Hana heard the humour in his voice and glanced up to meet his brown-eyed gaze.

"No. Everyone's terrified of her." She sighed. "She got me here safe though. They just don't bother trying to understand her."

Sam sat back in his office chair and Mac's head lolled. The child's porcelain skin looked like the subject of a painting, his rosy cheeks a stark contrast against the vicar's black shirt. Sam wrapped his arms around the boy and tipped him back a little. Mac released a happy sigh and squeezed his eyelids tighter. His lips made a rhythmic sucking sound and the slender legs protruding from his shorts remained still. Hana's fingers itched to snatch him back, propriety stopping her rejecting the man's kindness. Sam observed her through perceptive eyes. "So, Kane Du Rose died." He said it as a statement of fact.

Hana swallowed and gave a shallow nod. "Yes. It looked like he fell but I know he didn't." She closed her eyes against the image.

"You saw it?" Sam's fingers stroked Mac's head. "That's distressing."

Hana shivered. "Somebody fired two shots from inside the apartment. Then I think they pushed him in the chest and the railing gave way. It's hard to say because I was looking up at the back of him, but I know what I heard."

Slam! Kane's body hit the railing in her mind, over and over again. Like a bad dream, the sturdy rail gave with a pop and Kane was falling. She winced, realising she'd heard the sound of bones breaking on the ground without registering. Nausea threatened and she stopped. "What a mess," she groaned. "What a bloody mess." Realising she'd sworn in front of a vicar she halted and looked up. "Shit, sorry," she said. Her eyes popped as he laughed and she covered her mouth with her hand. "I'm not usually so foul mouthed."

"Not on Sunday, anyway." Sam grinned and Hana's cheeks flushed pink.

"No." She rose. "I should go home. I dodged police questioning by coming here, but I needed to get Mac. I'm sure someone else heard the gun shots but the cops will want to talk to me." She raised a hand as though pleading. "I haven't told anyone I heard the shots yet."

Sam stood and balanced Mac over his left arm. The boy's head rested against his shoulder, arms dangling free and his lips moving in silent speech only he understood. With his right hand, Sam performed a zipping motion across his lips. Hana nodded in acknowledgement, embarrassed she'd felt the need to ask for his discretion. Sam jingled keys in his pocket but he paused by the door and turned to speak to Hana. "Mac's fine," he said. His lips pursed and he filtered the sentence before releasing it into the ether. "You've done an amazing job, Hana. He can sign and read lips. He's intelligent and coherent and in the space of a few minutes conned half my lunch and a play on my phone." His lips turned down in a look of sadness. "Relax, Hana. Let yourself off the hook."

Anger budded in her chest and her jaw flexed as she followed him into the corridor. Good breeding kept the barbed reply locked in her brain for once. She stared down at her sock, seeing her baby toe peeking through torn fabric. "The surgery didn't work," she whispered. "I had such high hopes and it failed."

Sam cocked his head to one side. "But he hears something. Part of it worked."

Hana fixed glittering green eyes on her son's sleeping face. "I wanted him to hear like everyone else. I prayed so hard."

Sam nodded. "I'm sure you did, Hana. But sometimes life just is what it is. We pick ourselves up, dust the crap off our jeans and keep going. We don't always get answers and God doesn't work to our timetable. But there's a real danger you'll smother Mac with care and rob him of the chance to become his own person."

Hana's lips parted and she blew out a ragged breath. "That's what Logan says." She gulped, the sound echoing in the empty corridor.

Sam reached out his right hand and placed it on her shoulder. "Good. Man's got sense." He waited until she looked up at him. "It's my job to say the things nobody else will. I don't mean to hurt you."

Hana felt the tears bubble up into her throat and tamped them down. "Genetics," she managed, the word sounding croaky and strange.

Sam cocked his head to one side. "Mac's?"

Hana inhaled again, feeling her control return. "No, yours. Grandson of the kaumātua and kuia karanga. You have the genetics for speaking the truth."

He raised an eyebrow and then laughed. "Absolutely." He dropped his head to place a soft kiss on Mac's downy red head. Then he faced her. "I hear you're struggling with all things Māori. I wondered if I could help."

Hana's jaw dropped and betrayal made her green eyes sparkle. "Who gossiped this time?" Her tone sounded dismissive and verged on rude.

"I hear things." Sam's smile appeared kinder than she deserved. "And I see things too. You know the words, Hana. You just don't trust yourself to say them out loud."

Hana released an exasperated hiss. "I don't get it. None of it. I've tried and it matters, especially now Phoenix speaks fluent Māori. I feel so left out." Her gaze strayed to Mac and she recognised the root of her anxiety for him. She wanted him to feel inclusion because she didn't. And it hurt.

Sam offered her a sad smile as though he'd seen her neurons fire and understood the moment she made the link. "Let me know if you need help," he said, his tone gentle. He set off along the corridor to the front of the church and Hana trailed behind in her socks. At twenty-eight, the man had more sense in his little finger than most people possessed in a lifetime. Hana wrinkled her nose and remembered her abandoned shoes. "Shirley put them here." Sam jerked his head towards a piece of newspaper near the arched doors. Hana's filthy boots sat side by side on top. "She'll have locked the connecting door." He turned and pushed the wooden front doors open so they could exit, but paused half way through. "Hana, my grandmother is a good weaver. Why don't you ask her for lessons? She can teach you other things too. She also knows how to keep a secret."

Hana bent to collect paper and boots as Sam unlocked the main door and passed through. She clutched them to her chest and slung them into his car boot so she could share her seatbelt with a sleeping child. When Sam looked at her with his head cocked, she cringed. She didn't understand the reservations in her heart and the complicated feelings the thought of immersing herself into Logan's culture dragged forth. "I'm not sure," she whispered.

Sam shrugged. "Perhaps first, you need to work out what you fear."

The cut on Hana's finger oozed pale blood as the vicar started the car and drove towards the edge of town and the scenic hotel turned crime scene.

9

Taking a Risk

"**S**top!" Hana held her breath as Sam screeched the car to a halt.

"What?" He spun around to face her, his eyes wide with alarm.

She swallowed and readied herself to apologise. "I can't do it." She shook her head. "I can't leave Sacha in a field of cows miles away from home. She doesn't deserve that. Pull over just up there and I'll fetch her. I'm sorry."

Sam closed his eyes and paused long enough for Hana to wonder if he counted to ten in his head. His jaw worked in his face and then he opened his eyes and his expression appeared calm. "I'll take Mac home and meet you there."

"No. Thank you, but no." Hana unfastened her seatbelt and Mac roused. "Carrying a child without a car seat is illegal and there will be cops swarming all over the hotel. You'll get a ticket for helping me and it's not fair." She sat Mac upright and he rubbed his eyes. "Just do one favour for me, please? Hold Mac while I climb the first fence and then pass him over to me."

Sam shook his head. "This is ridiculous, Hana. What should I tell Logan?"

Hana pinned her lower lip between her teeth to hide her smile. "I hope you're not scared of my husband, Reverend." Her eyelashes fluttered as she asked the question and Sam let out a loud laugh.

"No, Hana. I'm not scared of Logan Du Rose. I just think he's probably got enough to worry about without adding concern for you to the list."

"Fair enough." Hana opened the car door and pulled Mac out with her. She bent down to his level and showed him the sign for a horse. His eyes lit up and a smile spread across his face. He performed a galloping motion with his legs and clasped her hand with eagerness. His green eyes raked the surroundings for the promised treat.

Hana retrieved her boots from Sam's car and pushed them onto her feet. He waved off her apology for the dirty, balled up newspaper she abandoned and followed her across the road, shielding his eyes with his hand.

"I don't see a horse," he said.

"She's white like the cows." Hana placed two fingers into her mouth and blew. An impressive whistle emerged, a skill taught to her by her husband in the early days. She'd needed it more times than she imagined in the intervening years. A white head popped up amid a sea of cows. Sacha's ears pricked forward, and she turned her body to look for the origin of the sound. Hana repeated it before handing her son over to Sam. She negotiated the bushes and held the branches back for Sam to follow carrying Mac. Sacha started walking, picking up the pace as she spotted Hana.

"How will you get him across the gully?" Sam sounded as though he thought her crazy and Hana grew determined not to prove him right.

"He can ride on my back." She paused to watch Sacha toss her head from side to side, but the mare kept walking towards her.

Sam pushed through the scratchy bushes and teetered at the edge of the gully. Mac's brow furrowed, but he held out his arms to Hana. She pointed to her back and placed his right hand around her neck. "Climb on," she mouthed. Then she signed to tell him they were going home using both hands to make the shape of a roof. Mac cocked his head and replied with the sign for food and she nodded.

Mac lurched behind her and almost throttled her with his tight grip around her neck. She heard Sam hiss as she set off across the gully, picking her way down and feeling the child sway on her back. His legs wrapped around her waist and his heels pressed into the soft flesh of her stomach until it hurt. Hana ventured nearer the trickle of water than before and leapt across at a more acute angle. It left her further to climb but seemed the safer option. Mac gripped like a baby chimpanzee and his cheek bounced against her shoulder. Hana scrambled up the other bank on her knees, hands stinging and wet mud soaking through her jeans. She stood up on the other side and set Mac on his feet. They climbed the fence with ease, Mac popping over the first rung and sliding between the slats with little difficulty.

Sam watched as Hana retrieved the saddle and lead rope. "But he doesn't have a helmet," he said, sounding doubtful. "What if he falls?"

Hana smiled as she lifted the saddle onto Sacha's back. The horse sniffed the grass collected in Mac's outstretched hand. He followed his father's careful instructions, keeping his thumb tucked to the side of his palm to avoid an accidental nip. Hana shrugged. "It's not ideal, but Sacha's fairly bomb proof. We'll be okay." She gave him a wistful smile and attached the lead rope to the loop on the underside of the halter.

Mac widened the gap between his legs as Hana handed him up into the saddle. His fingers clasped around the horn the same second his bottom touched the leather. He beamed and waved at Sam as Hana led Sacha to the fence and used it to clamber up behind him. "Thanks for everything," she called, softening the moment with a smile as she gathered up the rope. Her expression grew serious for a moment. "I'll think about what you said."

With a final wave she pushed Sacha into a gentle jog, feeling the weight of her son against her stomach. With many gates to navigate and no likelihood of going faster than a trot, she anticipated a long journey home.

10

Odering Mark Two

"I presume you know it's an offence to flee the scene of a crime?" The detective sat back on the dining chair and raised a blond eyebrow. Swarthy and good-looking, his perfectly proportioned features defined him as stunning. But he knew it and it gave him an unfortunate air of superiority. An immaculate pin striped suit displayed evidence of a new promotion and his arrogance pinned him as a newbie. A uniformed officer sat to his right, scribbling notes in a hard-backed notebook balanced on his knee. Hana sighed. Odering and Bodie mark two. They'd worked well together, like a well-oiled machine. Which was probably why they'd transferred to the Serious Crimes Unit together.

Logan answered for her. With his backside leaned against the kitchen counter and his arms folded, he dwarfed them all in stance and personality. The detective's pomposity wilted beneath Logan's glare. "She didn't flee," he growled. His tone already sounded piqued. "My wife fetched our son from his nursery." Mana resonated from the force of Logan's presence, the Māori spiritual quality marking him as a leader.

The detective leaned across to examine his colleague's notes and they shared a look. "Yet someone else fetched your other children from school." He turned the notebook towards him. "They're logged as entering the property at 4.10pm with a Mrs Hohia."

Logan gave an irritated huff. "Yeah, that's right. She's our housekeeper and did us a favour. Yet your officers ticketed her for carrying the kids without appropriate restraints. Do you think that's fair?"

"I can't comment on that." Sanders' lips turned upwards enough to show he thought he'd gained the upper hand. "I'm sure you'll pay the fine, Mr Du Rose. So, please answer the question." He spun around in his seat to face Hana. "Why leave the scene of a crime to fetch one child, when the others came home with your housekeeper?"

A vein ticked in the underside of Logan's chiselled jaw and Hana tensed. She needed to give the irritating detective what he wanted and get rid of him. Before Logan did it the painful way. She released a long breath and forced herself to say the words. "Mac's deaf. He wouldn't understand why I didn't pick him up. I didn't think he'd go with anyone else without getting upset." She thought of Mac sitting on Sam's knee in the vestry and snagging his lunch. Tears rose into her eyes and she blinked them back. She couldn't look at Logan but felt his mood darken. He strode towards her and yanked out the seat adjacent to hers. Sanders winced at his sudden proximity. Logan's muscular bulk filled Hana's peripheral vision and a wave of gratitude washed through her as he reached for her hand beneath the table.

As usual, Logan didn't waste words on niceties. "Get to the point, Detective Sanders!" he snapped. "We just lost a member of our whānau here. Show some respect, man. My wife has answered your questions, so now go and find out who killed my brother."

Hana closed her eyes and puffed out her cheeks. She heard the thud and a series of pops as Kane's body hit the gravel and broke. She saw his outline and the seeping blood and her stomach roiled. Logan's fingers closed tighter around hers and squeezed, urging her to hold it together.

"Did you know Kane Du Rose had returned to the north island?" Sanders' chair creaked as he shifted around. His gaze never left Logan's face and his sidekick scribbled an essay in the notebook.

"Yep." Logan told the truth and Hana stared at a burn in the surface of the wooden dining table. Bodie made it a lifetime ago during an accident with a hot glue gun. He'd stuck his fingers together and Vik never managed to sand the brown off the wood. She wondered if Bo still had the white mark between his fingers. "Kane showed up at our house last night." Logan cleared his throat and left the sentence hanging.

"And?" Sanders sat up straighter. "It's no secret you hated each other."

Logan snorted. "You're well informed, Detective. But out of date. I haven't seen Kane for years. I threw him off my property half a decade ago. I've had no contact with him before last night."

Hana gnawed on her bottom lip, admiring Logan's semantics. Half a decade sounded longer than five years and she relaxed against his ribs as he spun a tale for the detective. Not a tale, she reminded herself. The truth. But he laboured it with a cunning born of experience, so the handcuffs remained on the uniformed officer's belt.

"He married your ex-fiancé." Sanders dipped sideways and the officer slid the notebook towards him, perhaps sick of having his knee bumped so he created squiggles in his neat slant.

"Again. Really old news." Logan feigned boredom, but his stillness communicated his wariness to Hana. "She jilted me at the altar and I married Hana months later. I haven't seen Caroline either."

Caroline. The name sent Hana's brain into a spin and her fingers writhed within the safe cushion of Logan's palm. She would return for the funeral, arriving in a hail of expensive perfume with her sights set on Logan again. This time she'd have a child at heel, an innocent who might discover her parents were half siblings if she stuck around too long. Hana tensed and as though he'd read her mind, Logan's thumb caressed the back of her hand.

"Your history sounds a bit messy." Sanders gave a wry smile and Logan shrugged.

"Du Rose means chaos in French."

"Does it?" Sanders' brow furrowed.

"No. Are we done here?"

The uniformed officer popped his head up and a dark eyebrow quirked. Hana detected the hint of a smirk in his full lips. "We need to ask Mrs Du Rose more questions about the moment Kane Du Rose fell."

Logan swallowed and Hana glanced up to see his jaw tensing. He kept his amusement inside though she heard the words, "He speaks," in her mind.

Sanders gaze fell on her face and a sensation like nails on a blackboard ran along her spine. "From the top," he said, then winced at the veiled reference to Kane's accident. Hana sniffed and thought about her disastrous morning.

"As I said before, I worked in the museum with Will," she sighed. "I messed up a basket and felt miserable, so I went for a walk in my mother-in-law's rose garden."

"Did you see anyone?" Sanders leaned forward and the sidekick's pen paused.

Hana stared at the ceiling as she ran the visit to the pretty garden through her mind. "Yes. A group of tourists from China asked for directions to the campground. And I took a photograph by the pond for a couple of honeymooners."

"Can you remember times?"

Hana thought and shook her head. "No. But I wasn't out there long. I wanted to sit and think, but it got too busy. A coach got ready to leave and I couldn't concentrate with the noise."

"You wanted to sit and think?" Sanders took her words and strung them around her neck. He wasn't as green as he looked.

Hana tried not to flounder and nodded. Her voice wavered. "My son had surgery on his ears a few months ago. He still can't hear. I'm coming to terms with the guilt of putting him through a distressing operation for nothing." Her chin wobbled. "They promised me hope where there was none."

"Hana." Logan blew out through his nose like one of his stallions and released her hand to rest his arm across her shoulders. He pressed his lips to her temple. "We both took that decision," he said, his voice lowered to exclude the officers. "It's on me too. We needed to try."

She almost believed him. Staring deep into his eyes, Hana allowed the heady flush of his uncharacteristic and public display of vulnerability to wash over her. For a moment, it united them in a common concern. Her geniality faded at the sight of a glint of manipulation behind his irises and she sensed him playing along. He thought she'd fallen on the most likely excuse for her impromptu walk and backed her up. Hana's jaw clenched and she withdrew her fingers from his hand with a rough motion. Sander's eyes narrowed.

"Okay, Mrs Du Rose. Hana. Back to what we were saying."

"Mrs Du Rose is fine." Logan's low growl warned what might happen if the officer presumed any relationship other than formal. Hana glared at her husband and considered crossing him. A momentary flare of mischief made her contemplate what might happen if she invited Sanders to call her Hana. *Han. Hanipoos.* She pushed the temptation aside with a sigh.

"I left the garden and walked towards the front door of the main building. My mother-in-law asked me to water the plants in her apartment while she and Alfie are away."

Sanders dragged the notebook towards him and the officer tapped his pen against something at the top of the page. The detective nodded. "Alfred and Leslie Du Rose? Kane fell from their balcony."

Hana nodded. "Yes, I looked up and thought I saw my husband standing on the balcony with his back to the car park. I shouted to him but he didn't look down. There were two gunshots and Kane jerked twice. But then he shuddered as though someone hit him in the chest and the balcony rail detached on the left side. It swung open and he toppled backwards." She closed her eyes and the sounds echoed in her mind. Her spine pressed against the wooden chair back and her fingers writhed in her lap. She didn't reject Logan's hand a second time as he laid it over hers and stilled the agonising movement.

"Gunshots?" Sanders tipped forward and the back two legs of his chair lifted off the floor. "Anything else? A shout? A cry? Someone else's voice?"

Hana closed her eyes again. She shook her head. "No, just a rushing sound. Like something moving fast through the air. And then a heavy thud."

"And you say you thought your husband was there?" Sanders' eyes contained a glint of something frightening.

"He couldn't have been, could he?" Hana narrowed her eyes. "Why?"

"Because the man I thought was Logan hit the gravel about ten seconds later!"

Logan's mobile phone vibrated in his shirt pocket and he let go of Hana's fingers to drag it free. His brow furrowed as he read the text message. "The receptionist," he said with a raised eyebrow. "The health and safety people are at the hotel. They want to investigate what happened."

Sanders snorted. "Right." His down-turned lips projected his annoyance.

"They're just doing their job," Logan bit, giving the detective just enough of a stern look to make the man baulk. "I run a business. Chances are they think a guest face planted from a hotel room balcony and they want to make sure it doesn't happen again."

Sanders' lips curved into a smile. "And instead, they'll find a family member who was banned from the property and entered an apartment he had no business to be in. Then according to your wife, someone shot him."

"And your point is?" Logan rose but fidgeted with his phone and then his belt buckle. He looked conflicted, needing to leave but wanting to guard Hana from the threat of officialdom.

"No point." Sanders sensed victory. He'd wanted Hana on her own from the start and she suspected Logan had muscled in on the interview. The tense stand-off prevailed between the men, the uniformed officer continuing to scribble in his notebook. Hana stretched her neck while the attention focused elsewhere and saw the officer's fingers cover an ink drawing of a tui bird perched on a kowhai branch. It looked realistic. She hid her smile behind a cough.

"Remind me of your whereabouts, Mr Du Rose." Sanders smirked.

Logan heaved out a breath of exasperation. "I gave you the paddock number and you can check the GPS tracking on the computer. Two guys rode up with me and can verify what we did and how long we took. I've asked the reception staff not to delete today's data from the tracker software so you can download it." Logan blinked. "I should go and take care of this."

"I'm fine, Logan." Hana gave him a reassuring smile. "Just check on the children on your way past the lounge. Tell them dinner might be late."

"Okay." Logan winked at her. "I'll bring something up from the hotel kitchen on my way back. I shouldn't be long."

A phone chirped and Hana jumped and scooted around on her chair. "That's mine." Her brow furrowed in confusion. "But I left everything in the museum by accident."

"I grabbed it." Logan dug into his tight back pocket and hauled out her phone. He examined it for a moment as it tolled the bell from London's Big Ben. His nose wrinkled. "It's Leslie. What should I tell her?" He directed the question at Hana, but Sanders answered.

"Tell her to come home," he said. "We need to ascertain if anything is missing from the apartment."

Logan gave an audible sigh and lifted the phone to his ear. "Put Dad on," he snapped, not waiting for Leslie to speak.

The look he gave Hana told her he wasn't in the mood to play the inevitable question game. "Put Dad on, or I'll hang up," he repeated. "Hana's busy. Put Dad on." He turned aside and strode towards the hallway. Leslie's voice amplified, sounding disjointed and shrill. The kitchen door closed behind Logan.

"Bit of a complicated family dynamic here," Sanders concluded. He settled his gaze on Hana and she felt like a bird eyed by a hungry cat.

"And completely irrelevant." She inhaled, channelling Logan's refined skills in avoidance. "What else do you want from me?"

"Did you water your mother-in-law's plants every day, or just today?" Sanders nodded to the officer who abandoned his sketch and returned to note taking.

"They left the day before yesterday. She asked me to go every day until they came back." Hana winced. "I forgot until this morning so thought I'd better go while I remembered and give them an extra big drink."

"When are they due back?" Sanders' eyes focused on the kettle as he processed his thoughts.

"Sorry." Hana followed his gaze. "Can I get you a coffee?"

He nodded and leaned back in his chair. "Love one. Black, no sugar. Damian here takes white with two." He relaxed, the absence of Logan Du Rose lulling him into a false sense of security. "Your husband doesn't like cops, does he?"

Hana shrugged and continued filling the kettle. "He likes no one who throws their weight around." She heard the veiled insult in her words and scrambled to clarify them. "Odering and Logan sparked because they had a history. I don't think he has a problem just with cops. I've seen him offhand with lots of other people too."

Sanders snorted and Hana kept her back turned. Every time she opened her mouth, she insulted her husband. She sighed. "You asked me about Leslie and Alfie's trip. They went to Northland to see family there. Alfie's related to the whānau who run the Waitangi treaty grounds. They're both retired, so they didn't give a return date."

She turned with a teaspoon in her hand to find Sanders drawing his lips back into an ugly snarl. "Oh. They're related to them." He spat the statement like a curse. Hana's heart rate increased and she viewed the detective through Logan's eyes, seeing a white man who listened to the media too much. She bridled on behalf of her husband. And Māoridom.

"Also, irrelevant." Hana plonked the mugs on the kitchen table, not caring when the black coffee slopped onto the scarred surface. "What else?" she demanded. "I've told you everything I can remember."

Sanders reached for his drink and drew his fingers back at the heat issuing from the pottery surface. "Why did Kane Du Rose drive all the way up the mountain to see you the night before he died?"

Hana swallowed and kept her gaze fixed on the burn on the wood. Kane's visit flooded back into her memory. They'd assumed he wanted Wiri. He'd said so, hadn't he?

"He said I had something of his and he wanted it back." Logan's voice made Hana jump. She'd missed the sound of the kitchen door opening and closing behind him. He carried Mac on his hip and the little boy held his arms out to Hana with an urgency in his eyes. Logan released him as he dipped forward at a dangerous angle and Mac pitched into her lap. The second he touched down, his fingers formed the sign for food and he pushed the beak shape against his lips.

"Soon," Hana replied, enunciating the words. "Dinner is soon."

"I need to go." Logan snatched his keys off the sideboard. "Tell him I'll bring dinner."

"Wait! No!" Sanders rose to his feet and his chair scraped the tiles beneath with the force of his movement. "What did Kane want? What do you have that's important enough for him to travel across two islands to claim?"

Hana closed her eyes and pressed a kiss against Mac's warm temple to avoid catching Logan's eye. Her son grizzled and made the food sign again. To his credit, Logan kept his cool and waved the question off with a dismissive flick of his left hand. "The same as always," he replied. "The bloody mountain. They ran it dry and when Reuben died, they were ten cents away from complete repossession. He'd mortgaged it to the hilt. I bought it, debts and all." He jabbed his head towards the detective. "Do you want to see the records? Come to the office tomorrow and I'll make them available. Kane didn't love this land. He just wanted the money. It was always about money with him."

Sanders nodded. "A look at the records will be helpful. Thanks." He released a sigh and returned Logan's guise of helpfulness with a nugget of vital information. "Kane Du Rose quit his job two weeks ago without explanation. He just walked out and disappeared. His wife reported him missing a few days later and filed the relevant paperwork at the watch house in Dunedin." He winced. "We can't investigate every missing person's disappearance, but his photo went around the various shifts. Nobody saw him. It's possible he headed here before anyone started looking. What we need to find out is this; what made your brother leave his life and travel across the whole damn country to see you, Mr Du Rose?"

Kane plummeted to earth in Hana's inner vision. She heard his bones cracking and her mind amplified it in the silence of her homely kitchen. She pictured the French doors behind Alfred and Leslie's balcony and her imagination conjured a shadowy spectre which fired a gun, then reached out and gave Logan's troubled brother a hate filled shove.

11

A Fall from Grace

Mac's soft palms against her cheeks brought Hana to her senses. Her son stroked her face and pulled her gaze to meet his. He was hungry and thought she didn't understand. Hana swallowed and nodded, but when she opened her mouth, no sound emerged.

"Hana?" Logan's strong fingers squeezed her shoulder. "Are you okay?"

She shook her head and released a sigh. "I keep hearing him land on the gravel. It feels like it's getting louder in my head."

Sanders met her gaze with a wince. He'd sat back in his seat and gulped hot coffee from his mug like Lawrence of Arabia in the desert. "You witnessed a traumatic event," he said. His lips pursed as he dealt with the burn. "We can organise counselling."

"Maybe." Hana gave herself a shake and wondered where she'd begin trying to explain the many traumas in her life so far to a stranger. In desperation, Mac pointed to the pantry door and then to his mouth. Panic back-lit his sparkling green irises.

Logan sighed and his dark features clouded with a sadness he kept carefully shrouded most of the time. He held out his hand to Mac and the child bounced off Hana's knee and tripped across the tiles between them. He gripped Logan's fingers and stared up at him with innocent hope. Logan nodded. "Dinner at the hotel," he mouthed. He lifted his gaze to Hana. "We'll all go," he announced. "Dad and Leslie are back."

"Back already?" Hana's brow knitted into a series of lines.

"Back?" Sanders leapt to his feet and his offsider jumped and drew a pen line across his neat handwriting. "What did they tell you?" He gathered his wallet and phone from the table and slugged the last of his coffee with a grimace.

Logan glanced at Hana and then at the detective. She tensed at the mischief in his eyes and saw him contemplate dropping Leslie into a big fat hole which might include a pair of handcuffs. His lips twitched as she communicated her disapproval with a glare. "Dad said he's knackered and he wants to hit the whiskey and climb into bed. He also wants to know why there's crime scene tape over his apartment door and a uniformed officer on the landing."

"What did you tell him?" Sanders set off towards the door at a smart pace.

Logan's face remained impassive. "I told him you were on your way." He grinned at the detective's retreating spine, wiping the smile off his face in an instant as Damian rose and jangled the car keys. The two men shared a millisecond of mutual respect. He'd planned ahead, ensuring Sanders couldn't go anywhere without him.

"Mrs Du Rose." Damian gave her a courteous nod. "Thanks for the coffee." He followed the sound of Sanders chasing his shoes around in the lobby, his head held high and his back ramrod straight.

Logan closed the kitchen door behind him with a click and waited for the front door to slam. "Kid's smart," he commented to Hana. "He's gonna be a problem."

She released a long breath. "I think you foxed them with your comment about Kane wanting the land. I'm glad you answered for me. My brain locked up. I couldn't think straight."

Logan winced. "It's not our secret to tell." His voice sounded sad. "I'm not sure it ever will be." He held out his free hand to her. "Come on. Let's take the kids down the mountain for dinner. I'm sure I can find something in the kitchen."

Hana turned off the television while Logan got the children settled in the truck. The sound of Wiri's laughter drifted back to punish her as she closed the kitchen windows. The parallel with Logan's history made her head swim with misgiving. Both had lost their birth fathers before they ever found out the truth. Hana hissed out a breath of regret and anger. Jack started the awful legacy, sleeping with his sister and fathering Reuben. It set in motion a monster which Phoenix Du Rose prophesied would swallow her family whole. Futility washed over Hana. It couldn't be stopped. Not by Logan. Not by her.

"Come on, Mama," Logan called from the front door. "Your son's getting ready to eat his car seat."

"My son?" Hana's smile felt leaden on her lips as she padded into the hallway and pushed her feet into her boots. "Not ours."

Logan cocked his head and narrowed his eyes at her veiled accusation that he might be capable of disowning his imperfect son. He channelled the English teacher beneath his rancher's dusty shirt and jeans. "Don't be pedantic," he chided, grasping the bite behind her words. "You knew what I meant."

"I need to lock up." Hana pouted and Logan shrugged.

"We won't be long," he said.

Tension climbed into the truck beside Hana and rode to the bottom of the mountain uninvited. Leslie greeted them on the front steps of the hotel, arms already flapping and lips struggling to keep pace. "Kane!" she shrieked as though not quite grasping the news. "From my balcony." Her body oozed through gaps in her slinky, azure sun dress. She resembled a large blue bird trying to achieve flight despite the pull of gravity.

"Kane?" Wiri's feet ground to a halt and Mac tugged at his hand with a grunt of frustration.

"Mon. Mon!" Mac leaned backwards and the veins stood out on his neck. The front door led to the kitchen and the kitchen to the fridge. It seemed clear he believed himself starved and seconds away from death.

"He fell off my balcony!" Leslie squawked. "Died right there." A chubby finger pointed to the crime scene tape and the patch of dried, brown blood on the gravel.

"Dead?" Phoenix reached out to grip Logan's thigh. "Papa, who's dead? Who's dead? I don't want anyone to die." Her wide grey eyes sought comfort from first Wiri and then Hana, finding none. "Oh no! Oh no!" Her chest hitched and her right thumb pressed between her lips as a dormant reaction.

"Don't worry about it, kōtiro," Logan soothed. "It's nobody you know. Let's take Macky for some kai." He hoisted her up and let her wrap her legs around his body and cling to him. Seeing Logan as a sure bet for providing his missing dinner, Mac released Wiri's hand and bounced after his father up the hotel steps. Leslie followed, oblivious to the bomb she'd detonated with her mouth.

Hana shook her head and sent arrow curses after her husband's retreating back. She saw what he did there and resented him leaving her to clean up the mess. She hoped Leslie nagged him all the way to the industrial kitchen and gave him a headache.

Wiri remained frozen in place and Hana squatted next to him. She'd learned the child's disposition well enough to know he brooded and then exploded. Encouraging him to deal with things head on seemed to stop the blow ups which often outweighed the minor issues that set them off. A broken shoelace. A spilled drink. A wrong word. When piled on top of his internal agonies of abandonment and rejection, it led to detonations which took Hana weeks to put right. "Talk to me," she said, keeping her voice low. "He was your uncle. You grew up with him in Poppa Reuben's house, so this must be terrible for you. Just say whatever is in your head."

Wiri's chin dropped onto his chest and he balled his hands into fists and then released them. "You wouldn't like it," he murmured. "Is it true?"

Hana nodded and rested a gentle hand in the centre of his rigid back. "I'm sorry, Wiri. Just say it, sweetheart."

Wiri's eyes filled with angry tears which turned the grey irises into fiery, dark powder kegs. His jaw flexed and relaxed, flexed and relaxed. "I'm thinking I'm bloody glad," he hissed. "I'm thinking this is the best day of my life."

Hana swallowed and failed to hide her shock. She drew on every ounce of her faith and thanked God that Sanders didn't hear him say it, sending a quick glance around them just to make sure. Her other prayer of thanks was for Wiri's safe presence at school when Kane fell. Otherwise, she may have wondered too.

12

In Hiding

Wiri ate like a man from death row given an unexpected pardon at the crucial hour. Between them, the three children kept Leslie running from the kitchen to the dining room and back again. The busyness robbed her of the chance to gossip.

Hana blew out a breath as her equilibrium returned, wrapping her arms around Logan's waist. He didn't eat, standing with his back to the room and staring through the long sash window at the front car park. Kane caused chaos even in death, making the front steps inaccessible and forcing the housekeeper to negate the confusion for guests. The health and safety officer from the local council stood on the other side of the car park and stared up at the balcony. A waitress from the dining room loitered beyond the police tape. She swatted at the eager mosquitoes thrilled with their stationary feast. A fake smile wavered on her lips as she greeted another group of visitors returning from a day trip for their late check out. She waved them up Will's wheelchair ramp at the side of the building. From there they walked through the museum to the lobby.

"Will won't appreciate all the foot traffic," Hana whispered, wincing as soon as the words left her lips. "Sorry. I didn't mean that to sound so tactless. There's nothing of any value lying around. I guess it doesn't matter in the grand scheme of things."

Logan's arm slipped around her shoulders and he pulled her close. "No one seems that devastated." His tone sounded laden and strained. "It's such a waste, isn't it? We're always striving and moving on to the next thing. Then one day it's all over and what do we have to show for it? A bit of police tape and a stain that the rain will wash away."

Hana held her breath and kept still, unused to her husband's candidness. Despite schooling Wiri to speak out his issues, she disliked the look on Logan. It struck at a fear reflex deep in her psyche as though his brooding introspection somehow made her safe little world less vulnerable. She closed her eyes and sighed, mindful of an ostrich burying its head in the sand. Tightening her grip around Logan's waist, she kissed his shoulder. "You'll leave much more than that, Logan," she reassured him. "This mountain will crack in two when you depart this earth. And your legacy is bigger than both of us."

Logan glanced back at the children and gave a half nod. Hana followed his gaze and saw Wiri wielding a spoon to separate Mac's peas from his pie. Their son watched with an expression of concentration as though counting each round green pea as Wiri shuffled it aside. Wiri laid his spoon down and spread his hands, pushing his face into Mac's. "See, they're not touching." He shook his head and shrugged. "They're free now."

"Free?" Phoenix jabbed her knife in the air and spun to locate Leslie. "Nonie, are they free? Do we pay for pies but not peas?"

"What?" Leslie wiped the back of a pudgy hand across her forehead. "Your papa pays for all of it. And Poppa Alfie before him." Her gaze strayed to Logan and she narrowed her eyes as though debating whether to say more. Hana dipped her chin and glared at her, gratified when Leslie took the hint. She hadn't yet caught Leslie bad-mouthing Logan to their children but couldn't guarantee she didn't enjoy covert little jabs when the opportunity presented itself. Alfred hadn't paid for anything for decades and needed Logan to rescue him from bankruptcy in the mid 1990s.

"Where is Alfred?" Hana stared at the dining table as though expecting him to clamber out from between the heavy, oak clawed feet. "And why are you back early?"

"So, the peas is not free?" Phoenix persisted. She jabbed the knife towards Wiri again. "You got it wrong."

"Phoe," Logan's rebuke sounded stern and Hana tensed. "Peas are plural. They *are* free, not they *is* free. And don't poke knives at people."

"Oh, they are free, Wiri. You is right." She beamed at Logan and Hana smirked as he released a sound like a low growl in the back of his throat. He opened his mouth again and Hana squeezed his forearm.

"We've got bigger issues right now, dude," she whispered. "Semantics are the least of your worries."

Logan cringed. "She's mangling verbs. On purpose."

Hana glanced at her daughter and noticed a twinkle in her grey eyes. Phoenix used a finger and thumb to squeeze one eye shut in an imitation wink and Logan snorted. The mood lightened until Leslie made a beeline for Hana and the dark shroud of doom settled back over Logan's shoulders. "I need a sit down," she puffed, tugging at Hana's elbow. "Alfie's taking a nana-nap in the old sitting room. I'm not sure why he's tired when I did all the driving." She waved a hand at the feast in front of the children. "There's enough kai to feed an army. I need to show you something." Leslie widened her eyes and jerked her head towards Logan, excluding him from her conspiracy.

Hana winced and shook her head. "I told you I'd feed them." She struggled to keep the pique from her voice. "And I can't leave them here unsupervised. Logan might get called away. There's a lot happening."

"I'm good." Logan sighed and dropped into a chair next to Wiri. He reached for the plate of sandwiches and his fingers twitched over one bursting with cheese and salad. But he withdrew his hand and instead ran his fingers through his hair. "You go. The health and safety people already interviewed me. They've got the maintenance log and the dates someone last checked the fixtures. I'm hoping they don't blame us."

"Okay. I've got my phone." Hana paused, wishing he'd look up at her and see how much she didn't want to leave the safety of the room and her family. She could refuse Leslie's pressing desire to segregate her, but the repercussions would prove endless and Hana couldn't summon the energy for a fight. Mac's pea obsession distracted Logan as his son rejected the rolling objects altogether and hid them on the table under the lip of his plate. "I won't be long," Hana promised, but nobody responded.

Leslie didn't even wait until the end of the corridor to begin her battering ram style questioning. "What happened?" she demanded. She steered Hana into a left-hand turn and guided her past Logan's office. She headed for the family lounge in the private wing. After another left turn, she stopped outside a heavy door. Her chunky fingers pressed numbers into a key code and the lock clicked. "Go inside," she insisted, standing back to let Hana pass through first.

Alfred Du Rose turned on the spot and released the heavy curtain fabric bunched in his gnarled fingers. They righted themselves with a swish, closed despite the late evening sunshine streaming over the back of the house. "Alfie." Hana paused in the doorway and glanced back at Leslie. "I thought you were sleeping."

"The cops are here," he hissed. A shove in her back sent Hana spinning into the room. Leslie followed, closing the door behind her. The lock gave a resounding click.

"I know!" Irritation budded in Hana's chest and she looked from one to the other. "They just want to know if anything is missing from your apartment. Nobody knows why Kane would be up there. The detective is treating his death as a murder, not an accident."

Leslie looked from Alfred back to Hana. "Tell her!" she snapped.

"Tell me what?" Hana groaned. She sank onto a nearby sofa and rested her elbows on her knees. Her palms covered her eyes. "Just get it over with."

"Kane showed up the night we left." Alfred dropped into the seat next to her and Hana felt the cushions sink. His voice sounded lyrical despite the anxiety lacing his steady tone. "He made no sense."

"He'd been drinking?" Hana pulled her hands away from her face. It wouldn't surprise her, although the Kane who visited them looked as sober as a judge.

"No." Alfred waved his hand. "He stopped all that when the wee baby was born. He seemed different, settled. But he talked in riddles. I told him to leave, or I'd get security."

Hana arched her spine to get rid of the kinks and shook her head. "Start again. Where did you see him and what exactly did he say?"

13

A Strange Request

"We'd just finished packing the car to leave," Leslie said. She picked up the story and hurled herself into an armchair. Hana swallowed as a memory rose unbidden of Miriam sitting there with her knitting strewn across her lap. As though he'd seen the same ghost, Alfred dropped his gaze to the carpet. "He parked next to us and got out. At first we thought it was Logan in a borrowed car, but then Alfie spotted the rental car sticker."

"He wanted to know where Logan hung out nowadays." Alfred dragged a palm across his rough chin. "Said he needed to fetch something, but he'd be willing to share. He seemed happy enough and claimed he wanted no trouble. He's lost a heap of weight. Looks thinner than Nev now."

Hana sensed Alfred's reticence. "And," she probed.

"And I told him to leave. Said he wasn't welcome and he should go. He walked back towards the car park and we left."

Hana shook her head. "What were his exact words?"

Alfred scratched his forehead. "I can't remember, Hana. I'm an old man."

"He said he needed to fetch something, but they'd be willing to share." Leslie sat forward. "That's right, isn't it, Alfie?

Alfred nodded and Hana raised a finger and patted the air with it. "They'd be willing, or he'd be willing?"

"They." Leslie nodded with certainty. "They'd be willing to share."

Hana's heart sank. It all pointed to Wiri. Kane and Caroline wanted custody of the little boy, but they'd negotiate access rights. Maybe. For a price.

Hana swallowed. "Why are you hiding from the cops?"

Alfred sucked in a sharp breath and his backside pressed against the sofa as though he wanted to disappear between the cushions. "Because we spoke to him and then he died! You said yourself they know someone killed him." He pointed at Leslie and then prodded his own chest. "He died in our apartment. They'll think we did it."

"How?" Hana rose and paced over to the French doors. She swiped the curtains open in two swift movements and light flooded in from the courtyard beyond. "You'd need really long arms to shoot someone and then shove them over a balcony from Northland. And Kane had no issue with either of you. He hated Logan. Full stop. You're being ridiculous."

Alfred squirmed in his seat and Hana looked from him to Leslie. Dread snaked from her stomach and wrapped its fingers around her heart. "Tell her, Alfie," Leslie snapped.

"We didn't go to Northland," he admitted. He hung his head. "We stayed at a motel in Hamilton so we could catch up with Michael and Aroha. I don't get to see my little moko enough and they won't come here."

Hana sighed and sank back onto the sofa. "You were with your granddaughter. Why let us think you might go for weeks then?"

"Michael said we could stay in Auckland with them." Leslie pouted. "Then he changed the arrangement the night before. He invited us to a nice dinner in Hamilton and then blew us off afterwards. He paid for a couple of nights in a motel then sent us home."

"I got to see my little girly." Alfred's eyes misted. "She's like a wee cherub."

It didn't surprise Hana in the least that Michael had led them on a merry dance. Other people bent to suit his needs and he'd never change, not if the general populace complied. She rubbed her eyes. "That doesn't explain why you're hiding from the cops." She felt her irritation rise. "Or the secrecy. You can visit other people any time you like. What am I missing?"

"You don't like Michael," Leslie said, her tone sombre. "We didn't want to offend you."

Hana groaned and tipped her head backwards. "I have no jurisdiction over either of you." She sighed. "And I like Aroha. They're Tama's parents. It's not his fault his father's a prize dick, but I would never stop you seeing them. It makes me sad that you felt you needed to duck and dive to see your own son." Hana pressed her hand over her heart, analysing every word she'd ever spoken about Michael. She needed to learn to keep her mouth shut around Leslie. She stood. "You can alibi him and he can alibi you. Problem solved. Find Detective Sanders before he calls in the dogs." Hana took a step towards the door and then turned, eyeballing Alfred and searching his face for the truth. "Unless there's something else, Alfie. If you've started a new crop of weed on the roof, they'll find it."

"Nope." Alfred shook his head and sounded confident. "Logan got it cleaned and proper stairs and a door put in so we could both go up there and relax. Only my wife's geraniums live in the greenhouse nowadays."

Hana narrowed her eyes. "You'd better hope so, Alfie. Because linking this hotel to drug growing will bring the whole thing down like a pack of cards around our ears. You throw Kane's death into the mix and you've got a bigger problem than Logan can solve."

Despite her warning, Alfred gave a definitive shake of his head. "All clean," he promised. He bent the arthritic fingers of his right hand into the shape of a wonky scout's salute and held it up to Hana.

She shook her head and left the room with a snort. "You were never a scout, old man," she joked. "Now I'm really worried." And she was. There was something they hadn't shared and it lay between them like a budding cloud of doom.

Hana relieved Logan and walked the children to the play park on the camp ground for half an hour. Wiri ran into the museum office on the way to retrieve her cardigan, emerging with a packet of cookies under his arm. "From Matua kēkē Will," he called, his footsteps pattering against the gravel. Recognising the colourful packet, Phoenix and Mac skipped alongside him with eager sideways glances at the treat.

Hana watched them kick up their heels with excitement and shook her head. "Thanks Uncle Will for giving my kids a sugar high right before bedtime." She contemplated confiscating the packet and doling the cookies out one by one, but Wiri's fingers attacked the seal before she could open her mouth. The play area contained a collection of other families settling into the campground for the weekend and Hana glowed with pride as her generous daughter shared the cookies with their children. Mac followed the packet, trotting behind her with his hand outstretched. He managed to scoff two before the empty plastic went into the trash.

Hana sat on a nearby bench and watched the crowd of small bodies surge over the climbing frame, playing a frantic chasing game. "Now or never," she breathed. Her phone showed a low battery icon and she almost gave up before starting. But the plan seemed too good to let herself fail at the first hurdle. Hana found the number in her contacts and let the call connect. Ringing sounded in her ear.

"Kia ora," a male voice said after the click of connection.

"Kia ora, Matua kēkē," Hana replied, borrowing Wiri's use of the Māori term for an uncle. "Please may I speak to your wife if she's available? It's Hana Du Rose." She halted at the sound of the low chuckle rumbling through her ear.

"Kia ora, Hana," the kaumātua said. "You're the only Englishwoman we know, but you always say who you are."

"Sorry." Hana swallowed down her embarrassment and watched Phoenix growl at the children gathered on the climbing frame. She prowled underneath looking for victims to chase, involving her whole body in the play act. Little fingers bent in claws and she stalked in jerky movements which looked more cute than ghoulish. The green tartan of her school skirt swished around her knees.

"That's okay, but she's not here. Can I help you, kōtiro?"

"It's okay, thanks." Hana faltered and watched Wiri saunter away from the group, hands shoved deep in his pockets and his shoulders hunched. His sandals dragged against the floor. "I just wanted to ask her something, but it'll keep." Wiri looked up and headed in her direction. "I'll speak to her another time." The emotion came from nowhere and Hana heard a catch in her voice. A sense of failure barrelled up her chest and into her throat and she swallowed a sob of something she couldn't name.

The kind voice on the other end of the call showed no hesitation. "I'll tell her you want to speak to her."

"Thank you." The words came as a whisper before Wiri slumped onto the bench next to her. Hana's phone gave a warning beep and the gracious old man ended the call as though sensing her privacy was compromised. Hana's fingers shook as she slipped the phone back into her pocket. Wiri pulled his feet onto the bench and wrapped his arms around his shins. His body language oozed defeat. Hana switched into maternal mode.

"What's up?" She slipped an arm around his wooden shoulders, feeling him pause before sagging against her side.

"Nothing," he lied.

Hana kissed the top of his silky head and chose not to pry in front of an audience. A meltdown at the play park would humiliate him and upset her other children. She'd gained enough experience of navigating the Du Rose men's egos to learn when to pick her battles and when to wait. "Tell me when you're ready," she whispered. "I'll be here."

Wiri snuggled closer but gave nothing away. They sat in companionable silence and watched Phoenix grow bored with rampaging around beneath the climbing frame. Mac clambered after the knot of bodies for a while and Hana felt her heart clench at the number of times he got trampled. He didn't cry or show any signs of distress, extracting himself without fuss. She almost rescued him multiple times, but Sam's advice sent a dart of fear into her mind. Mac didn't need a helicopter mother. So, Hana forced herself to sit on the bench and watch her son make himself comfortable on the rubber matting away from the climbing frame. He placed his palms against the rubbery surface and closed his eyes. His brow furrowed as he enjoyed the stampeding children's play vicariously through the vibrations of their feet, though the matting muted it. Hana pursed her lips and tried not to cry.

Phoenix stopped chasing the children and sought her brother. She hurled herself onto her stomach beside him. Hana saw her lips moving and smiled as she pulled Mac's chin to face her. Whatever she said to him made him chuckle from deep in his throat and they both laughed.

"We should head back?" Hana mused. "It's getting late." Her fingers moved across her phone keys in a text to Logan.

Wiri pushed himself upright and frowned up at her. "Back where?" He sounded guarded.

"Home. Our house." Hana qualified her answer with an exact location. His answering nod gave nothing away. She opened her mouth to question him again and then closed it. Old habits died hard.

Hana's phone gave a strangled beep and she shook it. Wiri smirked. "That won't help," he giggled. "You need to charge it."

"I know Smarty-pants." Wiri stood and straightened his school shirt. A blob of something red and sticky decorated the collar. "Did Nonie Leslie feed you something with jam in it?" Hana asked.

"Might have." Wiri grinned. "She said not to tell you. How did you find out?"

Hana rose and gave him a wry smile. "You're wearing half of it. Bread or tart?"

"Bread."

"So, after dinner, you ate bread, jam and then cookies? I should roll you home." Hana waved to Phoenix and beckoned her to come.

Wiri's jaw hung low. "What? I'm starvin'!" He sounded so hard done by Hana laughed.

Her phone pinged with a reply from Logan. She read it out loud. "Sorry. Got caught up. Toby will give me a ride home." She sighed as the screen faded to black and the phone died.

The visiting children huddled around Phoenix, trying to persuade her to continue the chase game. She shook her head and pulled Mac to his feet with clasped fingers. Her other hand jabbed towards Hana and collective grumbles filled the air. Phoenix waved good bye and kept hold of Mac's hand as she weaved around the other apparatus. "I feel sick," she announced as they arrived. "Cookie sick."

Wiri wrinkled his nose. "Yuk! Cookie sick is the worst!" He took Mac's other hand and they walked ahead of Hana back through the hotel grounds to the car park. She found her truck and unlocked it. The children clambered into their various booster seats and she waited until she saw them belt up before closing the doors.

"When is it my turn to ride up front?" Phoenix grumbled.

"When you're twenty-one," Wiri replied.

"What? That's miles away." Hana saw her daughter's impressive pout in the rear-view mirror and concentrated on navigating the narrow lane up the mountain. "I'm havin' a turn next time." Phoenix muttered.

The landscape dropped away as the truck's diesel engine laboured higher. Native bush covered the view to the left and the hotel disappeared beneath the ridge. At the top of the rise, Hana paused the truck and stared. Wiri unfastened his seat belt, his hand paused on the door. "But I always do the gate." His brow furrowed as he turned to face her. The gate stood wide open, matching the gaping front door.

Hana bit her lower lip and swallowed. "Stay here!" she demanded, raising an eyebrow as Wiri opened his mouth to challenge her. "I mean it, Wiremu. You need to stop just flinging your seat belt off. Stay here and take care of the others."

She climbed down from the truck and closed her door, activating the central locking before putting the keys in her pocket. Her heart hammered in her chest. She skirted the huge front garden by sticking to the boundary fence and staying low. A glance back towards the truck showed her three curious pairs of eyes peering at her movements through the windscreen.

Hana drew close enough to look through one of the bedroom windows. The view showed her Wiri's bed and she heaved in a breath of indignation. Someone had tossed the room, spreading clothing and toys over every surface. Her fingers scrabbled in a pile of building supplies stacked nearby. She extracted a decent hunk of decking left over from the recent addition. The wood felt manageable and Hana hefted it and took a couple of swipes through empty air. She didn't look back at her children, not wanting to see their expressions of horror.

Hana skirted the front of the house, darting past the full-length windows to arrive at the open front door. She raised the improvised weapon in both hands and crept over the threshold. The burglar stood in the kitchen with his hands on his hips, smashed crockery littered around his feet. He screamed as Hana startled him. Then she screeched and he screamed again. "What have you done?" Hana strode across the kitchen with the baton still raised and he backed up as far as the sink unit. Bowls and plates crunched under their feet.

"I didn't do this!" The handsome intruder pulled himself up to his full height and glared at her. "Far out, Ma! I found it this way."

The air left Hana's lungs and she turned at the sound of the hiss from behind her. Then she heard the wailing of her car alarm signalling an open door. Wiri's eyes filled with tears and he skittered across the breakage straight into Tama's open arms.

14

The Dirty Secret

Hana fretted as she twisted flax leaves, creating a loopy looking basket and a trail of devastation. Another morning slipped away from her. She held up her first completed basket with a sigh and furrowed her brow. It didn't look right, but she'd managed it by herself. Will left her no choice, sticking to the other side of the room to avoid watching the drama her fingers created. "I've finished one." Hana turned and waved it in the air.

"You're meant to give the first one away," Will said. He turned in his wheelchair and gaped, staring at the wide gaps and odd corners. Hana poked a stray end through the weave and held it out to him with a smile like a child bestowing a gift. Will shook his head and backed away. "That's nice of you, kōtiro, but I have plenty for now." His arm swept over the pile of baskets and flowers spreading out from the corner and Hana saw him cringe. Her shoulders slumped in defeat.

"Why do you want mine when you have better ones?" she grumbled. Her lips turned down in a pout. "I could fill it with muffins and give it to Logan."

Will laughed. "Not if you bake like you weave." He wheeled across and shoved a gnarled finger through a hole in the side. "They'll fall through the gaps unless you weave more flax through there."

Hana grunted and threw the basket onto the table. "You're fired," she sighed. "With immediate effect."

"Again?" Will raised a bushy eyebrow and his eyes held amusement. He reached out and covered Hana's hand with his. "You're doing fine, girl. By this time next week, you'll be weaving in yer sleep and creating beautiful taonga."

Hana twisted her lips and stared at her basket. "Is that not a beautiful treasure then?" she huffed.

"Not even close." Will withdrew his hand. "That's why you give the first one away. Then you never have to look at it again."

"Oh. I thought the giving of your first fruits had some wondrous spiritual merit."

Will snorted. "Maybe it does. I still don't want yer basket, Hana."

She pushed her chair back and rose. Sunlight scattered glittering shafts across the dark floorboards. "It's a gorgeous day," she mused. "I could almost forget what happened to Kane under that blue sky."

Will masked a frown. "Go. Take a horse for a gallop across the hills. Get rid of some of that pent-up angst."

Hana's brow darkened, but she didn't contradict the old man. "If you're sure," she replied instead. "Can you manage?"

"Yep." Will pushed his wheelchair back from the table and spun it to face her. "A party of sixty is due after lunch. Kids from a high school in Auckland on their way back from Taupo. I'll get them weaving baskets when they've looked around. Where did you put the worksheets?"

Hana pointed to the office. "I copied and stapled enough for the next few months. I won't go far, so send for me if you need help."

Will raised a sceptical eyebrow. "It'll be a sad day when I can't keep sixty kids in order, Hana. Besides, they have that many teachers policing them nowadays, they don't have time to misbehave."

Hana nodded and smiled. Will had curated and maintained the archives of the Māori kīngitanga for decades before losing his legs. He'd dealt with generations of marauding teenagers and possessed a bark loud enough to terrify most people. "I'll take my phone anyway," she promised, lifting it from the table and sliding it into her pocket. She yawned and covered her mouth with her hand.

"Don't do that!" Will rebuked. "Unless you want to spend tonight on the toilet."

Hana sighed. "As opposed to fixing up my wrecked house? It sounds preferable right now."

"Yeah, sorry about that." Will's wheels squeaked against the wooden floor. "What did you lose?"

Hana rolled her eyes. "That's the thing. Nothing. Furniture upended, drawers pulled out and stuff everywhere. But not a single item missing. Detective Sanders came up with some people to take fingerprints and we crawled into bed at three this morning."

"Don't you have a burglar alarm?" Will asked and Hana winced.

"Yeah, but in all the confusion with the cops and then Alfred and Leslie arriving back early, we left without setting it." Her mind played over the moment of discovery. "At least Tama's home for a few days, although he disappeared early this morning and I haven't seen him since." She heard the pique in her voice and hated herself. "I think he rode down in Logan's truck this morning. He left his car in the car park and walked up last night."

"Why?" Will frowned. "That's a killer walk to do by choice."

Hana shrugged. "He told Logan he needed time to process things. He's not sure how he feels about Kane. It's easy to hate someone when they're alive, but you're left hanging on to your anger when they die without warning." She shook her head. "I should know."

"You go." Will patted her forearm and jerked his head towards the main door. "Take a break. I can cope."

Crime scene tape still fluttered around the bloodstained gravel in front of the hotel. It wound twice around a shrub before arcing into the car park, slipping around a road cone and continuing its journey back towards the main house. Hana shivered and looked away, almost missing her footing on the front steps. Dragging her phone from her jeans pocket, she sent Logan a text to ask his location and see if he wanted company. Hearing a beep behind her, she turned.

"Hey, wait up." Logan ran down the front steps and glanced at his watch. He smiled and Hana guessed her text had just scrolled across the screen. "Great minds think alike," he said, borrowing the cliché. He slipped an arm around her shoulders and pulled her close. "I went to the museum but just missed you. Will showed me your basket. He seemed pretty pleased with it."

"Really?" Hana jerked away and her face creased into a sneer. "I recall him using lots of words, but none of them indicated pleasure."

Logan shrugged and his arm stiffened, preventing her shying away from him. "Why don't we go for a ride?" he asked. "I still wanna show you how the maze is doing."

"Where's Tama?" She resented the hunger she heard in her voice. Logan pressed a kiss to her temple.

"Not invited. Am I not enough for you anymore?"

"Idiot." Hana nudged his ribs. "I just worry about him."

"Well don't. He's a big boy. Worry about me instead." Logan winked at her and she shook her head.

Hana fetched the tack from the room above the stables which housed all their gear while Logan rounded up the horses. They'd shifted everything from the old tack room the summer before while builders repaired a leak above the porch. The attic room warmed from the heat of the horses below and the leather relaxed enough for Logan to decide it should stay. The stable manager lived in an adjacent loft and added an extra measure of security. Hana retrieved her Jillaroo hat from its hook and plonked it on her head, before carrying Logan's heavy stock saddle down the stairs and resting it over a rack fixed to the wall. She returned with a head collar and saddle blanket to find Logan already lifting his saddle. "You were quick." Surprise leaked from her voice.

Logan reached out and took the blanket, steadying his saddle over his forearm as he added it on top. "I just snagged two from the paddock next door," he replied. He tipped his wrist over and checked his watch. "We've got a couple of hours to ride. Please can you fetch Sacha's bridle?"

"Oh." Hana paused. "Her bridle?"

"Yep." Logan handed the head collar back and gave her a smile. Confused, Hana returned to the tack room and pulled Sacha's bridle from its peg.

In the stable yard, Hana recognised Sacha's round white rump facing her. A grey spotted station-bred gelding stood his ground nearby, unperturbed by the stamping white legs and dinner plate hooves near his flank. He pressed his nose to the concrete and blew out, sending hay dust and feed husks scattering in a small arc. Sacha strained the rope as she craned her neck around in response to the sound of boot soles. Her ears flicked back and forward in a motion which oozed curiosity and excitement. She whinnied high and loud when she saw Hana. "Hey girl," Hana whispered. She reached out and stroked the mare's wide forehead, feeling a smile tug at her lips. Sacha nudged her hip with the hard bone in her nose and snatched at Hana's pocket with her lips. "Don't tell Logan about the mints," Hana whispered. "You'll get me into trouble." She pushed her fingers through the tufted forelock. "Who's your friend? I hope you've told him to behave for me."

Sacha shook her head from side to side, wobbling the scrubby white mane ridging her neck. She heaved out a sigh of resignation as Logan slipped the saddle blanket over her spine and moved it backwards along her withers. The leather of the tan saddle squeaked as he rested it on top. "Flick me the girth, babe," Logan said, meeting her fingers under Sacha's wide belly.

Rawhiti pushed a wheelbarrow across the yard and raised an eyebrow at Sacha's rump. "I wouldn't stand there while he tightens that," he called to Hana. "She bit the back of my head last week." He rubbed at a sore spot in his hair and steered the barrow wide.

Hana frowned and traced the whirl on Sacha's forehead. It began like a star burst above her brown eye and exploded in different directions until it covered her face. The blue wall eye blinked. "You wouldn't bite me, would you?" Hana whispered.

Metal clinked against metal as Logan tightened the girth and Sacha's head jerked in protest. She snaked her neck towards him and back again, thinking better of it. Logan slipped under her neck and popped up on Hana's side, giving her a sweet smile and reaching for the bridle. Hana puffed out a breath. "Which saddle fits the gelding?" she asked. "Does he have his own?"

"Yep. I'll get it." Logan held the bridle in his left hand and tickled Sacha's tongue to ask her to open her mouth. The metal bit slipped inside and she crunched against it.

Hana scuffed her boot against the concrete. "Why aren't you riding on a head collar? Are you retraining her?"

"Na." Logan fastened the throat lash and gave Sacha's broad shoulder a slap. He caught Hana around the waist and hauled her into his side. "I spend way too much time thinking about you, Mrs Du Rose." He pressed his lips over hers and his breath warmed Hana's cheek. His collar dipped to reveal the hickey on his neck. Satisfaction replaced the knotted feeling in her gut which had settled with Kane's arrival. It had lessened little with his departure.

"Good," she whispered. She teased her lower lip beneath her teeth and fluttered her eyelashes.

Logan jerked as his body pitched forward. He clasped Hana with one arm to prevent her falling. "Sacha!" he snapped. "Idiot!" The horse snorted and shook her head, ears twitching as though his rebuke amused her. "Sorry." Logan didn't let go of Hana and her back arched to expose the soft skin of her neck. His eyes glittered. "She nudged me." His pressed his face into her hair and breathed in, his lips sending tingles through her nerve endings as he placed a kiss on the underside of her jaw.

"Oh, sorry." Rawhiti cleared his throat and turned his barrow around, wheeling it back the way he'd come.

Hana forced herself upright and batted Logan's broad chest. "I thought you wanted to show me the maze," she said, straightening her shirt and checking the buttons over her cleavage.

Logan's eyes glinted in the sunshine like specks of coal. "What?" He swallowed but still didn't release her.

Hana reached up and cupped his cheek in her hand. "You wanted to ride."

"Yeah." A smirk lit his lips and he rested his teeth over his bottom lip. "Can I change my mind? It cramps my style with Tama at home again."

"No, you can't change your mind." Hana pulled away from his embrace and righted herself, watching the battle raging in her husband's mind. A quick glance at her watch sobered him and he released a sigh filled with regret.

"Okay. I'll tack up Blue and you hop on Sacha." His fingers lingered against her waist.

"Oh." Hana jerked her chin back and narrowed her eyes. "But Sacha's yours."

"Yeah. I've looked for a mare for you and every time I think I've found one, I compare her to Sacha and they pale in comparison. I'm giving her to you and I'll bring Blue on as my regular horse. As long as you don't mind if I borrow her sometimes? Just for old time's sake." A wistful look passed across his face.

Hana swallowed. "Really? You'd give her to me?" Her fingers stroked the expensive tan saddle. Embroidery decorated the polished skirt and the buckle dug into the nearest stirrup leather in the same place Logan always kept it. The hole had elongated over time with the constant pressure. "But you'd need to give up your saddle," she breathed. "I can't ask you to do that."

Logan shrugged and his brow furrowed. "You didn't ask. I'm giving it. My gift to you." He placed his right hand over his heart and Hana felt the sincerity of the gesture choking her words.

"Thank you," she said, forcing her lips into a smile. "I don't know what to say."

"Just mount up. I'll be two minutes." Logan stole a kiss before jogging back towards the stables. He disappeared inside and Hana heard his footsteps running up the stairs.

She used the mounting block and climbed onto Sacha's back. The saddle creaked beneath her as she shortened the stirrup leathers to raise the irons high enough to rest her feet in. Logan's gift overwhelmed her and she felt unworthy. The grey Appaloosa nodded his head next to her as though agreeing with her poor self appraisal.

Logan appeared with a saddle and blanket, tacking up the gelding in record time. He fastened a rope onto the ring of the head collar and mounted up. The gelding whirled around and pointed his nose towards the mountain. "We'll take the lane up to our place," Logan called. "Then go off track just above where Reuben's old house used to stand."

"Okay." Hana touched Sacha's neck with the reins, a gentle action meant to wake her up. The horse obeyed with too much enthusiasm and skipped forward at a trot. She shook her head and snorted as though meaning to test her new owner. Hana sat heavier in the saddle, pushing her weight into her bottom and the backs of her legs. Sacha settled and they skirted the gravel car park without disaster.

Calamity came at them as they passed through the hotel's ornate gates and cut left onto the driveway heading up the mountain. Sacha stopped dead at the sight of the red vehicle cruising downhill towards them, black smoke coughing from its rattling exhaust. It kept to the speed limit and the skill of the driver posed no imminent danger, but the sight of Jack's red Jeep sent Hana's heart into free fall. She heard herself give a cry of dismay as the vehicle slowed and pulled onto the verge. The driver leaned out of the window and pushed his cowboy hat higher on his head. His mouth opened in greeting and his right hand formed into a cheery wave.

Sacha rose onto her back legs in a display of terrifying dominance. Taken by surprise, Hana felt herself flying backwards through the air and the ground came up fast to meet her. She held her breath in the final second before she hit the hard surface, but instead found herself rolling onto the grass and down into the ditch behind. Water soaked through her jeans and she lay for a moment, waiting for her brain to run an assessment for broken bones. The brim of her hat pinged back into shape as she pushed her face away from the long grass and she groaned and lifted her right hand, pressing her fingers against the pacemaker beneath her left collarbone. A deafening clang resounded overhead and explained why Logan hadn't followed her into the ditch. Small grunts escaped her lips at every painful movement back up the slope to the road. Hana poked her head out of the ditch and gasped.

Sacha snaked her neck at Logan and her sharp teeth threatened with angry snaps of her wide mouth. The driver's door of the Jeep bent inward at an odd angle and she whirled her rump around and bucked, planting her rear hooves into the same place. The grinding and creaking of metal filled the air and the driver covered his head with his forearms. He disappeared out of view as he crawled to safety via the passenger side. Logan moved backwards, desperate to get to Hana in the ditch. His movement made Sacha's blue eye roll in her white face and Hana saw the imprint of fear there.

Her movements felt laboured as she clambered upright and faced the distressed horse. Ditch weed clung to her soaked jeans and mud caked her left cheek and the back of her shirt. "Sacha." Her breath rasped in her chest. "Stop." Logan's left arm shot out to protect her as the mare squared her feet and advanced. Her reins dangled over one ear and covered the brown eye. With the terror dissipated, she made a sorry sight. Snorts of worry sent damp breaths into the air and for the first time since Hana met her, Sacha looked lost.

Logan tried to shove Hana aside and she resisted, turning her back on him. She held her arms out to the horse and Sacha stopped just short of her. Sweat stood out on the mare's flanks and shoulders, darkening her coat to a dull, matt grey which swallowed the sunlight. Her muscles shook and twitched beneath her skin as Hana approached. "Silly girl," Hana puffed, her chest hitching. She lifted the reins over Sacha's head and let them hang from her shaking left hand. Turning, Hana led her new mare past the dented vehicle and its terrified driver. She didn't look up at her husband, not wanting to see either guilt or defiance in his grey eyes.

Sacha plodded behind her, her footsteps sounding even and rhythmic. The young gelding had run a short distance in fright and joined them, tagging behind as easily as joining a queue. The horses seemed as eager as Hana to escape the chaos induced by the appearance of the old red Jeep. Logan's shout made Sacha trot a few steps forward until her nose bumped Hana's shoulder, but neither of them turned. "Hana!" He raised his voice and tried again. "I need to check you over," he said and Hana heard him following.

She shook her head, wincing as the cord from her Jillaroo hat rubbed against a cut on her cheek. "Leave us alone," she breathed. "Leave me alone."

15

Inside the Wreckage

Hana asked Rawhiti to check the mare's hind legs and he did it from a distance, a frown etched into his regal features. "Run your hand over her fetlock," he ordered, squinting in the sunshine and folding his arms. "Now look at your fingers. Can you see blood?"

"No." Hana peered at her fingers and lifted her palm closer to her face.

Rawhiti scoffed. "If you need to look that hard then she's fine."

Hana rose, her fingers meeting the snout pushed into her hand. "But what about tendons and muscles? What if she's torn something?"

"Then I'll join the queue of guys willing to put a bolt through her brain," he hissed. Unfolding his arms, he stalked away. Logan's grey gelding nosed at loose strands of hay and breathed out a sigh. Rawhiti patted the speckled rump and moved to Blue's offside to tie him up and release the girth. "Where's Logan?" he demanded, giving up with a shrug as Hana ignored his question.

Hana fondled the fluffy ear pushed against her stomach. "Oh, Sacha," she breathed. Her chest hurt from the fall, the physical aches masking the emotional turmoil caused by Logan's betrayal. She made herself busy, removing the bridle, saddle and blanket from a sweating Sacha. Then she groomed her until the white fur glinted in the rays of sunshine streaming through the half door. "I'll turn you loose," she sighed into the downy neck. "Just promise not to get into any more trouble."

Sacha snorted and shook her tufty mane as though in defiance. Hana rolled her eyes and fastened a lead rope into the ring on the mare's head collar. "Where do you want me to take her?" she called to Rawhiti.

Blue shook himself, the motion beginning at his nose and rippling through his body to the end of his tail. His coat held a damp sheen where Rawhiti had hosed him and used the scraper. He snorted and screwed his head round to observe Sacha. He neighed and she snorted back in reply. Rawhiti untied Blue and turned him, the huge hooves scraping against the concrete. "Logan wants them kept together," he replied. "He set up the first paddock, the one behind here." He jerked his thumb towards the gate which kept the stable yard enclosed. "Stupid idea if you ask me." His lips pursed into a thin line.

"I didn't ask you." Logan's gruff voice cut through the awkwardness, hiking the temperature to sizzling point. He materialised with his usual brand of stealth. Hana's heart pounded in her chest and she gritted her teeth and refused to look at him. Logan held out a hand and took his gelding's lead rope from the younger man. "Are the accounts up to date?" he snapped, his left eyebrow rising into his fringe.

Rawhiti gulped. "Almost," he said. His teeth gripped the underside of his top lip in a classic tell and Logan's eyes narrowed.

A passive smile settled over Logan's lips and Rawhiti made the mistake of relaxing. Hana could have warned him it signified more danger than Logan's anger, but his refusal to tend to Sacha disqualified him from her assistance. "I'm doing the tax tomorrow night, so I'll collect the books at lunchtime." Logan completed the effect with a dismissive wave of his hand, knowing it left Rawhiti scrambling. The thought seemed to give him pleasure, lightening his features and allowing Hana to view the Du Rose arrogance hovering beneath the surface of his smoke grey irises.

Rawhiti didn't answer. He picked up the pace, stalking across to the office in the corner of the courtyard. The door closed shut behind him and Logan turned his attention to Hana. She narrowed her eyes. "You don't file the tax until the end of next month."

Logan shrugged. "End of this month, actually. The kid said he could do the job and I gave him training. I even offered to pay for a college course. He lets me down every time."

"Bring Lincoln back." Hana tugged on Sacha's lead rope and the mare started. Her heavy feet clopped against the concrete in obedience. Hana kept her voice even as she reminded Logan of his former stable manager. "Why not? You kept Jack's Jeep and he tried to kill your son. Lincoln just threatened me."

"Hana!" Logan set off after her, but Sacha kept him at bay, swishing her tail in his face and threatening with her back legs. Hana fumbled the gate latch and heard the familiar squeak as the hinges creaked open. She turned right and Sacha trailed her, giving little resistance through the rope and walking behind her in a tight defence. Logan steered a tangent past them and headed for another gate tucked against the back of the stables. A new post was embedded into the ground next to the back wall and Logan released the latch. Hana stared at the pale wood of new fencing not yet treated. The nail heads glinted in the sunshine. The subdivided paddock contained two other horses and Hana recognised them as troublemakers nobody wanted to ride. She swallowed, reluctant to abandon Sacha in what seemed a reject bin. Her footsteps slowed as Blue stepped into the long grass and Logan turned his nose towards the gate. He left the head collar in place but unclipped the rope, standing back as the gelding turned tail and cantered to join the other two. Sacha lifted her head and whinnied. Hana faltered. Her fingers opened and closed around the rope, realising once she released the horse, she'd have to face her husband.

"In." Logan leaned against the gate and jerked his head towards the knot of equine bodies greeting one another with snorts of recognition.

"No." Hana felt rebellion bud in her soul, its influence swelling to obliterate good sense. It invigorated her, telling her to start an argument and distract him. She didn't want to know why he kept the Jeep. Her mind couldn't take the truth.

Logan's eyes narrowed as she unclipped Sacha's lead rope and took a step back. She wanted Sacha to run, to express Hana's sense of outrage as a proxy. Logan's grey eyes studied his wife, reading something she couldn't understand herself. Dismay leaked from her down-turned lips as Logan clicked his tongue to Sacha and the mare plodded towards the gate and sidled past. She picked up a trot and shook her head, moving across to the others at a smart pace. Logan paused to watch her gait before clasping the catch closed. He withdrew a padlock from his front pocket and fitted it through the links of a chain, sealing the troublemakers into their prison. Standing up straight, he fiddled with a key ring in his long fingers, pursing his lips as he withdrew a shiny metal object.

"This is yours." He held it out to her. The key rested against his palm, an unspoken olive branch holding them back from the precipice of destruction.

Hana's gaze flicked behind him to a sign she hadn't noticed. It clung to the gate with cable ties, black writing on red paper sealed inside a laminated pouch. She swallowed and her body regained some of its rigidity. A shaking finger pointed to the notice. "Dangerous horses. Do not approach." Her eyes narrowed. "Really, Logan? That's low even for you."

He flinched as though she'd struck him. "It's the truth, Hana. We can't risk guests putting their hands over the fence or thinking they can waltz through the paddock."

"Because she killed Jack? The others are a smoke screen. That sign relates to Sacha. Just say it." Jack's name sounded forced on her lips and it cut through the air, both familiar and dreaded. She hadn't spoken it for a long while, the gentle old man's memory morphed into the face of a baby-killer. A serial murderer. She shuddered and closed her eyes. Logan's hand on her cheek made her recoil and she took a step back. The long grass snagged her boots and she stumbled. Strong fingers seized her forearms and kept her upright. When she glared up into Logan's face, she saw nothing but sadness. Guilt washed over her like a cold wave.

"Don't do this, Hana," he pleaded. "This hatred isn't who you are."

She struggled against his brute strength and lost, forced to allow his steady grip to reel her closer. His grey irises pleaded with her for mercy, understanding and numerous things she just couldn't spare. "Why?" she demanded, the word echoing off the stable wall and hurling itself back in front of her.

Logan's jaw worked from side to side, but he didn't remove his gaze from her face. "Memories," he replied. Hana saw the smoke grey pale to a glittering, washed out concrete. He sighed and his grip on her arms increased. "I loved him, Hana. He was all I had before you and now he's gone."

His words acted as a whip crack and she struggled. "He wanted me dead!" When she couldn't release herself, she plunged forward, shouting into his face and willing him to recoil. He didn't. Her chest heaved and she heard her laboured breaths sounding suffocated and unnatural in her ears.

"I know." Logan swallowed. "I'm sorry, Hana. Sorrier than you can ever imagine."

"Sorry it happened, or sorry it was him?" The question escaped her lips and took her by surprise. She hadn't realised she even thought it.

Logan jerked back and his thumbs flexed against her flesh. He considered his answer with care and fell on something half decent. "It shouldn't have happened and never him. Not Jack."

His gaze left her face and she watched his eyelashes flutter as he battled unknown demons within his own psyche. "Shit, Hana," he breathed. He released her forearms and ran his palms either side of his face as though desperate to crush his own skull. It frightened her watching him go to war against his own feelings. "I can't do this," he breathed.

Hana's gorgeous husband crouched against the ground and bowed his head, all six feet and four inches of his height curling in on itself like a tangle of crushed metal. His heels touched and his elbows rested on his splayed knees. The fingers and thumb of his left hand squeezed his lips together as though holding in a silent scream. He hauled his hat from his head and let it drop into the long grass where it tumbled to the side. Fear prickled from a hidden nook inside Hana's soul. Logan Du Rose didn't break. He couldn't.

She dipped forward as though seeking reassurance from the brawny arms poking from his folded sleeves. His biceps flexed of their own accord. Logan ran a shaking hand through his hair and looked up at her, his eyes revealing more than she wanted to see. "I'm lost," he confessed. He waved a hand towards the hotel, the action feckless and without direction. "It hurts so much," he breathed. "Everything reminds me, Hana. This place, this life, these people."

Terror paralysed Hana as the cornerstone of her life struggled to stay in place and threatened everything. She kicked against his authority often because she could. It gave her a masochistic pleasure to run at the safe wall he represented and discover it impenetrable. Without its certainty, she felt as lost as he looked.

Logan reached out his right hand and his fingers closed around the loose fabric of her jeans. His eyes implored her to meet him in the wreckage and begged her to make him forget.

16

A Polarising Pain

Hana knelt in the grass and wrapped her arms around Logan's head. He collapsed onto his back and rolled her with him. The long grass hid them from view and the sounds issuing from the stable yard drifted overhead. Logan pushed his arms beneath Hana's and tangled his fingers over her spine. "It's okay," she whispered into his ear. Her rage dissipated on the steady breeze, replaced with an all-encompassing compassion.

"How?" Logan's voice cracked on the single word and he buried his face in her hair.

"I don't know." Hana leaned back and pressed her lips against his forehead. "But we'll work it out."

Logan exhaled and rolled onto his side. He kept hold of Hana and she squeaked as she felt herself falling. Logan's strong arms braced her and she landed next to him, a shower of grass seed dotting her hair and cheeks. He tucked her head beneath his chin and stilled.

Hana closed her eyes and listened to the sounds of the bush canopy half a kilometre away. Birds called, adding their song to the sound of cows lowing in the far distance. It felt as though time stopped, providing a catalyst for changes she realised she didn't want or need. She liked their equilibrium of Logan the authoritarian and Hana the feeble woman needing his protection. It proved enough to make a feminist's lips curl back in disgust, but it suited her as a safe canopy to hide beneath. Logan's heart beat in a steady rhythm, the vibrations reaching through his chest wall and into her ear as a comforting thud. He sighed and she tensed. He'd shown enough vulnerability and she doubted she could cope with more. The scales tipped and the sense of falling returned. Hana dug her fingers into his shirt and her body stiffened.

"I'm sorry I kept the Jeep," he whispered. "The guys got rid of everything except that and some documents from his house. I said I'd deal with it but when it came to it, I couldn't. I left it in the back of the equipment shed and covered it with a tarp. Only Toby knew I kept it."

"So why is it riding around the mountain?" Hana's voice sounded muffled but accusation still leaked from it.

"I don't know. But I'll find out." Logan pulled her so tight, she heard a bone pop in her shoulder. The dart of pain it sent through her arm occupied her thoughts and robbed her of the opportunity to challenge him. She wanted the Jeep gone. Permanently.

Logan lifted his thigh and shifted it across her legs, trapping her beneath him. Every nerve ending in Hana's body relaxed as she recognised a sign of her husband's recovery. The small action reclaimed her, pinning her in the world he'd created and grafted her into. For the first time in forever she realised she wanted to be there, subjugated to his dreams and authority. It threw up other questions. Like what was wrong with her?

Libby's face drifted across her inner vision, a woman not completed by a relationship with a man. Hana pushed her cheek against Logan's collarbone and inhaled his familiar scent of hay and sunshine. Libby's feminism and attractive sense of independence paled before the might of Logan Du Rose. She could keep it. Hana realised she didn't want to swap places. "I love you." She spoke the words and accompanied them with a sigh. "I want this."

Logan exhaled and the sound of his heart grew quieter for a beat. "But what is this, Hana?"

"What do you mean?" She jerked backwards so she could look up into his face. His expression offered little explanation. "Us. This is us." A knot of fear twisted in her gut and rejection threatened. Her voice rose an octave as she tried to process his question and it twisted in on itself until she believed he didn't want her. She wouldn't take it lying down a second time in her life. Her legs thrashed beneath him as the wildfire of terror caught hold and she fought to escape.

"Stop!" Logan pinioned her legs and caught her wrists in one of his large hands. He raised her arms above her head and rolled on top of her to smother her frantic movements. Then he released her painful left wrist, keeping hold of her forearm instead. His grey eyes bore into her soul and he read the doubt burgeoning there as Hana saw rejection in a simple, obtuse question. *What is this?*

Logan pushed his weight into his hips to pin her beneath him and prevent the rising knee making its planned trajectory into his groin. "Please stop."

"You don't want this? You don't want us." Hana's chest hitched.

"Don't put words into my mouth. Stop it!" Logan's eyes narrowed and he pushed a lock of Hana's red hair back from her cheek with a gentle forefinger. He maintained his grip on her arms. His grey eyes dazzled her, the light sparkling off brown and green flecks dotted around his pupils. Hana saw his brokenness recede behind the strong portcullis of his soul as mana and authority stepped up to bridge the cracks. She felt guilty for never wanting to see it again, never wanting to see him on his knees subdued by grief and confusion. "I asked you a question and you answered it," he breathed.

"You're speaking in riddles." Hana ground her teeth in her jaw and bucked beneath him. She slipped back into her role as needy and rebellious and it felt as comfortable as pressing aching feet into warm slippers. Logan's expression remained curious, but his lip quirked upwards a millimetre on one side.

"No. I asked you what you thought this is. You said us. I want that too. What I don't want is something else, something I need to work out."

Hana swallowed. "What don't you want?"

"I don't know, Hana. I need to do some serious thinking and decide." He released her wrists and dropped his hand to her face, tilting to take his weight on the opposite elbow. "But I'm keeping you, so don't get stupid ideas. The way I feel about you isn't up for negotiation."

Hana drew her arms down, taking a moment to stretch out her muscles. The issue of the Jeep's existence on the mountain ticked in the back of her brain like a loaded threat. She could meet it on the driveway or park next to it in the car park. A shudder rippled through her body and Logan jerked his chin down to study her face with his perceptive grey eyes. A tender finger smoothed the soft skin at her temple and his gaze softened. "You don't believe me." Statement of fact, not a question.

Hana sighed. "I don't like change. Knowing his Jeep is here makes me unsettled, like I don't want to be here with it. But I have nowhere else to go."

Logan's brow furrowed and his thumb slipped down to trace the outline of her lips. "It's not a competition. If you don't want the Jeep here, the Jeep goes." He stared at her mouth, his eyelashes flickering and his lips parting as though wanting to kiss her.

"I never wanted the Jeep here." Hana heard the accusation in her tone and Logan sighed.

"But you didn't know it was here, so you didn't have an opinion about it."

Hana scowled, her features screwing up into an unattractive pout. "Making unnecessary distinctions doesn't change the fact you kept his Jeep."

Logan's index finger pressed over her lips, holding in any further tirade. His gaze flicked up to her eyes and down again, the calm restored in his soul. "I also kept Sacha," he breathed. "I knew you'd expect me to."

Hana swallowed and saw his comparison. He'd kept a reminder of his grandfather hidden in the back of the shed because he needed its comfort, but he'd kept Jack's murderer for her because he knew Sacha's death would cause her pain. He'd fought to keep the mare, masking her identity for the police and letting them believe one of the retired trail mares had been destroyed for the crime. Hana sniffed, scenting the grass seed speckled through her hair and clothes. "Are you saying I can't have Sacha if you can't keep the Jeep?" Her chin jutted upward and Logan sighed.

"No, Hana. I gave you Sacha because you love her and because she's too unpredictable for mustering. The other guys fear her and for good reason. You were never meant to know about the Jeep. I'll get rid of it."

Hana reached up and stroked Logan's cheek. The coarse hair caught at her fingers and made a scratching sound which competed with birdsong and plodding hooves as the horses grazed their paddock. Their tails swished and they took random snatches at the long grass. Sacha hung near Blue, tail twitching and her ears flicking back and forth as her lips sought the sweetest shoots. Hana turned to watch them and left her neck exposed, a foolish move in such proximity to her husband.

His nose coasted across the tender skin and she bit her lips to suppress a moan of pleasure. An alarm buzzed on her phone and she sighed. Her fingers plucked it from her pocket and she recognised the number for the school. "I need to make a call," she whispered. She brushed grass from her phone screen and wrinkled her nose when one strand refused to budge. "It's cracked," she groaned. "Must have been when I fell. It's just not my week, is it?"

Logan nibbled her earlobe and his breath warmed her delicate tendons. His fingers trailed along her ribs and slipped into the arc of her lower back, hauling her in closer and resisting the call of reality. "I'll get rid of the Jeep," he promised.

Hana froze at the reminder and swallowed. "Will I see it as I drive out?" She lowered her voice to a whisper.

Logan shook his head and kindness infused his eyes, giving his irises an uncustomary hint of azure. "No. I rang Toby and he's towing it."

"Towing it?" Hana's brow furrowed.

Logan moved backwards and sat up. Hana saw his covert eye roll. "To a scrap yard. Sacha kicked the shit out of it. She bent the front wheel arch into the tyre. He'll get the low loader and tow it. Somewhere."

"What about the man inside?" Her cheeks pinked with the realisation she hadn't stopped to ask how he felt about the incident. She'd claimed Sacha and escaped without a backward glance. The only thing missing from the scene was a sledge hammer so she could join in and knock the last of Jack's memory over the sheer cliff into oblivion. Hana released a sigh and attempted to remove the image from her face. Logan studied her before speaking and she knew he'd seen.

"New guy. He started about an hour before Kane died." He ran a hand across his cheeks and retrieved his hat. In a fluid motion he rose to his feet and offered Hana an outstretched hand. Remembering her question, he shrugged. His fingers brushed across the back of her hand and the connection between them fizzed. "He's not hurt. Toby had asked him to grab a vehicle and run some errands. David Allen backed the bloody truck into the corner of the bunkhouse last week, so we're a truck down. The guy found the Jeep in the shed with the keys still in it and took it." Logan pursed his lips. "I think he quit."

Hana rose and placed her palm against his chest to right herself. "I'm sorry." She found the apology from deep inside herself. "I think Sacha reacted to me." Leaning closer, she rested her cheek against Logan's shoulder and breathed in his familiar, safe scent. "I didn't expect to see it driving towards me and she picked up on my fear."

"It doesn't matter." Logan kissed the top of her head and she felt his lips against her scalp. "I should have known better. There's too much going on to sightsee a stupid maze today."

"It's not a stupid maze. It's a memorial for your parents and I'd like to see it. Maybe after all the stuff with Kane is over. Then we'll ride up together."

Logan nodded. "Okay. The cops are still sniffing around trying to work out what happened. Sanders is using the housekeeper's office to conduct interviews. He's pulled me back in twice."

"Why?" Hana stiffened. "What does he want from you?"

Logan waggled his eyebrows. "A confession, Hana. Sanders asked me not to leave town."

She groaned. "This is a nightmare. You weren't even here when he died."

"Yeah. But I was the last one to admit arguing with him. That other cop took all our guns for examination. Now I'm also a vehicle and a man down." Logan blew out an exasperated breath and closed his eyes. "I agreed to the mid-summer fair for the school but wish I hadn't."

"I wish I hadn't asked you to," Hana grumbled. She paused as Phoenix's dear little face moved across her inner vision. Her lips parted in readiness of dumping the latest issue on her husband's broad shoulders, but the desolation behind his eyes made her steer away. She reached for humour instead. "Will's gone basket mad."

Logan's face relaxed into a smile. "Pity the olds didn't stay away longer. Leslie is doing my head in with her helpful suggestions. The receptionist has taken deposits for over a hundred stalls. It's way bigger than I imagined."

"Could I help by running the errands the new guy should have done?" Hana's finger traced a line along his shirt buttons and Logan covered their action with his other hand. His eyes glinted and she sensed he wanted her to continue even though he stopped her. The conflict creased a line into his forehead.

"Yeah." He drew out the word and his eyes became unfocused. "There's a list. Toby gave it to the new guy and he gave it back. He threw it, just before he shouted his resignation. I think that's what he said, anyway."

"A list." Hana gritted her jaw and tried not to sound as dismayed as she felt. "Can I get it all done before the school run?"

Logan shook his head and fixed his hand tight around hers. "Na, do it tomorrow. It involves a trip into Auckland."

"Auckland?" She whispered the word without enthusiasm.

Logan turned and set off walking, towing her behind him like a trailer. Her steps pattered in the long grass as she jogged to keep up. The glass shard in her left wrist twinged as she tripped and she struggled to snatch her hand back. Logan halted and she read anguish in his expression. It frightened her to glimpse the agonies he kept buried so deep. "Too fast," she puffed. "You forget about my little legs." A smile spread over Logan's handsome face and a breath caught in her chest.

"Sorry." He licked his lips. He kept a firm hold of her, but the fingers of his other hand lifted and stroked her soft cheek. His pads felt coarse from hard work and her face tingled under his touch. "I'm sorrier than you know," he breathed. He swallowed and his lips parted, wanting to say something important. Hana saw it in his eyes even though his lashes kept them shuttered from her. She felt her heart rate rise.

"What's wrong, Logan?" She felt him grow edgy and his fingers snapped back to his sides.

"Nothing." He turned away and began walking again. "I'm just sorry about the Jeep. I'll get rid of it."

Logan produced a handwritten list from his back pocket as they reached the stable yard. Hana tried not to groan at the days' worth of items needing attention. She scrolled down and picked the easiest to tackle. "I'll do as many as I can first thing tomorrow," she promised. "Then I'll take this list back to Toby."

"Thanks." Logan's smile seemed hollow. "Did you want to ask me something? Before. You hesitated."

Hana shook her head and pushed her issues with Phoenix's teacher behind her. The hammer of doom waited above her, eager to fall and crush her skull. "My bag's in the museum. I'll fetch it and get going." She waited for a kiss, her eyes widening as Logan turned aside with a nod. "Logan?" Her voice sounded strained and odd. He turned back to her, his brow furrowed.

"Yeah?"

"Nothing." Hana's shoulders sagged and she gnawed her lower lip. "Nothing," she repeated. She stepped backwards before spinning on her heel, grit scratching beneath her boot soles. Strong hands caught her around the waist and a bristly chin dug into her neck.

"I haven't told you today, have I?" Logan whispered, his voice hoarse. Hana froze in position, not understanding their new dynamic but hating its unpredictability. Logan pressed a kiss to the soft skin, inducing a ticklish reflex. "You're beautiful," he whispered in her ear. Spinning her around, he covered her lips with his before pulling away. He still looked distracted, his eyes glittering as though his mind preceded him to wherever he needed to go.

Hana forced a smile onto her lips and tried to appear reassured by Logan's attempt at normality. But she wasn't fooled, not for a second.

17

Trouble Looming

"The coroner released the body." Detective Sanders stood in front of Hana, blocking her way up the main staircase. "We eventually contacted his wife through a colleague and she's on her way."

Hana paused with her hand on the banister, the stairs blurring as she focused on the lengths of wood beneath her boots. The detective stood at the dogleg to the first floor, his sidekick two paces behind him. Hana swallowed and dug her fingers into the curved oak. Her mind scrambled for a reply, but nothing emerged. She switched it for a question instead. "Did Alfie and Leslie get back into their apartment?"

Sanders nodded. "Yeah. The fingerprint guy finished. I just let them back in. The place has been tossed, but there's nothing else to see. They shouldn't use the balcony though." His brow furrowed. "Don't you think it odd that nobody wanted to identify your brother-in-law's body?"

Hana blew out a pursed breath as the sound echoed in her ears again. Bones cracked and air released from Kane's lungs as he hit the gravel. Her hand reached out for the banister rail.

"Mrs Du Rose?" Damian stepped from behind Sanders, a look of concern etched into his features. "Are you okay?" He tried to touch her shoulder and she stepped back in response, almost pitching down the stairs.

Hana raised a finger to the cut on her cheek and pressed, using the pain to help her rise from beneath the news that the family had exacted their final revenge and Caroline's arrival was imminent. "I just fell off my horse," she said. "You should speak to Logan regarding any arrangements for Kane."

Sanders let his gaze rove over her filthy jeans and shirt and then back to the cut on her face. "I have," he said. "For all the good it did me. And you were correct. The pathologist found two bullets lodged in the chest cavity. No one else heard the shots but you."

Hana swallowed and felt herself sway. "I need to go," she breathed.

Sanders nodded and stood aside. She edged through the gap between the men, one suspicious and the other concerned. Damian gave her a sympathetic smile as she forced her feet to climb the stairs, but Sanders watched her until she turned left and moved out of view.

Hana returned the call to the school from the upstairs landing. She leaned on the windowsill and watched a single cloud scud over the mountain. Phoenix's teacher sounded hurried as the receptionist connected the call. "Holly's mother popped to see me this morning." Mrs Cuthbert gave a huff as though steeling herself to deliver the next volley of shots over Hana's trench. "She didn't realise you owned the hotel."

Hana's head jerked backwards and she blinked. "Pardon?"

"Yes. She'd like to have a little think about what to do next. She suggested involving the principal."

"Wait, what? I don't understand. Involve him in what? Her daughter bullying mine?" Hana heard herself say the words and they sounded harsh.

"She believes your daughter is bullying hers."

The air rushed from Hana's lungs and she snapped upright. The cut on her cheek sent a drip pattering onto the back of her hand. "But that's not true," she protested. "We both know that's not the case."

"I must get back to class but I thought you should know." Mrs Cuthbert ended the call before giving Hana a chance to reply. She remained standing in front of the picturesque view, shaking her head from side to side. Sighing, she lifted her finger and traced the wavering gait of a praying mantis on the other side of the glass.

"How can such intricate beauty live side by side with pure ugliness?" she whispered.

Alfred greeted Hana with a wave as she entered the upstairs apartment. He lounged on an aged sofa with his boots resting on the coffee table. "Hey, kōtiro," he called. He pushed himself upright on rickety legs and moved towards her, arms outstretched in greeting. His hug sent warmth flooding through Hana's bones. "Everything is fine. We spoke to the cops last night. I gave him Michael's phone number for our alibi and told him we stopped to see Alex in his restaurant on the way home. The detective said he'd check and take us off the list." Alfred patted Hana's back and released her. His lips pursed at the sight of the cut on her cheek. "Wahine!" His shout threatened Hana's ear drums as he called for Leslie. "Wahine! Hana's hurt!"

"No, no!" Hana took a step back, not wanting to give explanations or subject herself to the inevitable fuss. She struggled to kick her dirty boots off before Leslie got involved. "I fell off Sacha. I'm fine."

Too late. Leslie emerged from the bedroom with her hair wrapped in a towel. A faded blue dressing gown cord wrestled her body into the folds of her robe as though it fought an escaping sausage. Her heavy brows furrowed into a line of concern. "What's happened?" she demanded.

"It's a tiny cut. It stopped bleeding almost straight away." Hana kept backing towards the stairs, but Alfred looped a gnarled hand through her elbow.

"Nope," he said. "Let her check you over."

The next half an hour passed in a whirl of questions, explanations and daubs of Manuka oil. Hana's gaze slid towards the closed French doors leading onto the balcony. White powder covered the glass and the upended belongings still lay on the carpet where the intruder tossed them. She shivered and Alfred patted her shoulder. "I know, girly. It feels weird knowing he came in here and ended his life through those doors."

"Alfie stop," Leslie warned. "We don't need to talk about it all the time."

"Was anything stolen?" Hana asked.

Through the corner of her eye she saw Leslie's body stiffen and tried to turn her head to see Alfred's expression. Leslie patted her cheek to stop her. "Keep still," she ordered.

"No." Alfred sounded doubtful. "A bunch of random keys to things we don't own anymore. They did more damage than anything."

"Is Logan fixing the balcony rail?" Hana asked. "He said it underwent a routine check earlier this year. Apparently, the Victorians used screws hammered into the brick. David Allen is adamant it was still solid when he signed it off." Leslie stepped back to admire her first aid and snapped the lid shut on the ancient tin of plasters and gauze. Hana watched her expression darken and pressed the point home. "Nobody understands why it came free, although the force of Kane slamming against it three times would probably do it."

"Tell her Alfie," Leslie snapped. "Tell her the truth."

Hana groaned. "What now?"

"Silly old man." Leslie slapped the top of Alfred's head. The remaining few strands of long hair drifted up like smoke. "He thought it felt loose last week. Did he mention it to anyone? No. That could've been me splatted on the ground. Does he care? No!" She waved her arms in the air and Alfred ducked.

"I forgot!" He raised his voice and Hana winced. "I'm an old man. I forget things!"

Hana sighed. "Did you tell the health and safety people? They'll hold Logan responsible."

Leslie pursed her lips. "Alfie can go to court in his place. If he remembers."

"Ha ha!" Alfred grunted. "No, I didn't tell them. I'm not te heahea."

"A fool?" Leslie snorted. "That's debatable."

Hana sought a distraction and found one from the top of her list. "Did Phoenix speak to you last night about fighting with a girl from school?"

Leslie nodded. "She didn't do it."

"Didn't do what?"

"Whatever the lying little brat says."

"Oh." Hana swallowed. "Phoenix is being very vague about it all. What's going on?"

"I'm not sure." Leslie dabbed at the blood on Hana's shirt. "The teacher doesn't listen to her. I told her you would."

"I do." A weight settled on Hana's chest as she began to second guess herself.

"Well, you go careful with my moko's delicate feelings." Leslie made a sound like a grunt in the back of her throat. "She deserves better."

Hana nodded and agreed. She didn't know how to fix the situation, but she'd protect her daughter at any cost.

"Kane looked skinnier than I remembered." She winced at Leslie's rough ministrations as she dabbed the last of the blood off her face with a damp cotton ball. "His shirt hung off him when he came up to the house."

Leslie elbowed her husband in the ribs. She jerked her head towards Hana. "Detective says his wife is on her way."

"Don't." Hana groaned. "I haven't seen Caroline for years. Why do I still feel vulnerable at the mention of her name?"

"Because she's a nasty piece of work," Alfred said and blinked. "I never understood why Reuben and Antoinette took her on. She's trouble. Always was and always will be."

"Yes, thank you, Alfie!" Leslie snapped. "You're not helping."

Hana glanced sideways at Leslie's blushing cheeks and wondered if Caroline's parentage was less of a secret than she'd believed.

"Sorry." Alfred shook his head and sent Hana a grimace of apology. "You've nothing to worry about, girly. If Logan gets his head turned by her, then he's an idiot."

Leslie leaned across and slapped the top of his wispy head again. "Shut up!" She accompanied the action with a glare. "He won't get his head turned because we won't let him."

Hana had a sudden vision of Alfred and Leslie shadowing Logan. He'd understand their motives straight away and resent Hana for sending them to babysit him. "No." She forced a smile onto her lips. "My fears are in my head. She's coming to bury her husband and I mustn't forget that."

"Still won't stop her having a crack at Logan," Alfred murmured and the knot in Hana's chest grew. She rose and her steps felt laboured.

"I need to get the children from nursery and school," she said. Her finger patted the cut on her cheek and the cloth stitches holding the skin together. "Thanks for this. I'm going to look a right mess at the funeral." She groaned at the thought of the long hours sitting on hard, wooden benches. "I hate tangihangas. Do you think I'll ever understand all the cultural references and why Logan yells in Māori at a bunch of strangers like he wants to chop their heads off?"

Alfred chuckled. "He's impressive. Gets all the old aunties fanning their faces."

"Where will Kane's body stay until the burial?" Hana felt her heart rate notch up. "Will people expect him to come here?"

Alfred nodded. "He should. He's family. We don't leave our dead alone. Someone will need to organise shifts for people to take turns to sit with him until Caroline gets here."

Hana groaned. "This is terrible!"

"Logan will take care of everything," Alfred reassured her. His gnarled fingers patted her hand, but he didn't stand. "You worry too much."

Hana shivered and walked towards the top of the stairs. "I hope nobody puts my name on the list to sit with Kane. I can't do it."

"They won't." Leslie enfolded her in a bone-crushing hug. "We've got your back."

Hana laughed, the sound hollow. "That's what I'm worried about," she admitted as she bent to retrieve her boots.

She arrived at school with time to spare and parked in her usual space. Outside the school gates she edged away from Holly's mother, keen to avoid conversation. Wiri found her leaning against the fence on the outskirts of the group of parents.

"Where's Macky?" He bounced across the playground and pirouetted in front of Hana. His library book bag spun with him like a wing. He searched, an expression of concern shrouding his dark features. Then his eyes brightened. "Ah, it's his long day, isn't it? He gets afternoon tea there today, doesn't he?"

"Yeah." Hana leaned down and accepted the customary hug. The bag landed at her feet with a thud.

"Where's Phoe?" Wiri went through the same routine.

"I don't know." Hana frowned. "Year 1s come out first usually."

"Let's break her out!" Wiri snatched up his bag and set off running. After a moment's delay, Hana followed. Her brain performed mental gymnastics as she rehearsed her arguments for Phoenix's innocence ahead of time.

The corridors of the small school bulged with childish bodies and Wiri steered a meandering course through the throng. Several voices rose to acknowledge him and Hana smiled at random faces she didn't recognise. Wiri never asked to bring friends home or mentioned anyone in particular, yet whenever Hana watched him in the playground, he seemed popular. He stopped at the door to Phoenix's classroom and peered in, jerking his head back out to give Hana a look which communicated alarm. She hurried to catch up and arrived in the doorway at the same time as the teacher popped upright. She'd been bending over a child on a tiny chair. "Ah, Mrs Du Rose," she said. Her lips pursed and she waved a hand towards Hana's daughter. "We were just about to come and find you."

Phoenix sat on a child-sized wooden chair with her arms folded. Her small feet looked planted in the fluffy carpet and her spine appeared as perfectly straight as one of Logan's famous fence posts. She kept her misted gaze fixed at a point on the floor, but silent fury oozed from every pore of her tiny body. The essence of Logan Du Rose mingled with Bodie Singh Johal, creating a heady mix of controlled detonation and petulance.

Hana sent up a silent prayer tainted by a curse. The expression on the woman's face rivalled something one of Bodie's long suffering teachers might have channelled. But when her daughter's gaze rose to meet hers, she saw tears fill the almond-shaped eyes and their Du Rose greyness blurred. Hana saw pure hurt in that single glance. Then Phoenix looked away.

Wiri stepped over the threshold and his bag clattered against the frame. He made a beeline for Phoenix and Hana stopped him, grabbing him around the chest and halting his progress. She felt the stiffness of his body and an electrical charge went through her fingers. Like a shining knight, she'd intercepted his rescue charge. "Just wait here, sweetheart," she whispered in his ear. "I'll take care of it."

Wiri's lips pursed and his look of betrayal cut her, but Hana edged him aside with her hip and took his place as an avenging angel. "What's the problem?" she demanded. Her voice remained calm from years of working in a school where parents represented a bigger problem than the students. She walked forward smiling but determined.

Mrs Cuthbert folded her arms to match Phoenix's and Hana resisted mirroring the stance, though her hands twitched. Wiri remained in the doorway despite her raised eyebrow of warning which should have sent him outside. "Phoenix hurt another child," the teacher said. "We can't allow violence in our school."

Hana swallowed and stared at her daughter, willing Phoenix to look up and give her a clue. She couldn't imagine the soft gentle hands raised in anger and some tiny fragment of surety snapped off in her heart and floated free. When Phoenix remained glaring at the carpet, Hana turned her attention to the teacher. She angled her body side on to Phoenix as though demonstrating a silent solidarity. "Why don't you tell me about it?" she asked. "Then I'll take Phoe home and get her version of events. I'm happy to meet you tomorrow to talk about where we go from here."

Mrs Cuthbert's chins wobbled and her jaw hung slack. Unused to decisive parenting, she blustered a little trying to get the story out. "We'd just finished our carpet time and Holly screamed. She said Phoenix pulled her hair and hit her around the cheek." She lifted a hand to her own face to demonstrate. "The slap left a red mark and I had to call her mother."

Hana narrowed her eyes. "Holly? And you called her mother but not me?"

Mrs Cuthbert's stance relaxed and she looked more apologetic. Turning to face Hana, she shielded her lips with a cupped hand. "She's very demanding," she whispered. "She complains about everything."

Hana's jaw clamped shut and she breathed through her nose. "Okay. Well, I'll take Phoe home and get back to you."

"I'd rather talk about it now." Mrs Cuthbert's fingers wrung together and she shot a look towards the door. "Holly's mother will call me to find out what happened."

"What happened with me?" Hana's eyes narrowed. "That's not her business. Tell her you spoke to me and together we'll deal with it. If I feel Phoe needs to give an apology, that'll happen. But not before tomorrow." A movement in her peripheral vision showed Phoenix squirming on the wooden seat. Her grey eyes implored Hana for something she couldn't comprehend and she renewed her determination. The sigh she released sounded impatient. "I'm not a helicopter mother, Mrs Cuthbert, but I'm not a pushover either. My daughter and I will speak in private and I'll come back to you with my conclusions. We'll go from there."

Hana curled her fingers at Phoenix and her daughter shot off the seat like a bullet from a revolver. Her library bag dangled between her legs and she almost tripped, righting herself at the last moment. Wiri's dark eyes studied her face as she clasped Hana's hand and he reached out to take her bag. A silent communication moved between them and Hana failed to intercept it. She whirled around and left the teacher gazing after her, taking the children with her as she swept out of the school.

Phoenix stayed quiet all the way to Mac's nursery. Hana glanced into the back as she pulled on the handbrake and saw her daughter gripping Wiri's fingers across the seat.

18

Surprise Attack

Phoenix refused to leave the car while Hana fetched Mac and remained sullen until they reached the hotel. She lightened up in the apartment where Leslie fed the children more of her baking.

"We should get back and do some homework," Hana said as she finished the last of the washing up. It looked as though Leslie had used every pot and pan in the kitchen to create the delicate fairy cakes.

Leslie nodded and showered kisses on the upturned faces at the table. "Come on," she said with a grin. "I might make cinnamon cookies for tomorrow's treat."

Hana held Mac's hand as they descended the main staircase. He took the steps one at a time, leading with his left foot and his bare toes flexed against the smooth wood. Hana walked at his pace, but when she tried to step properly using one foot and then the other, he tugged on the leg of her jeans and waved towards his feet. He signed for her to walk the same way as him and Hana relented. She led with her left and it felt odd.

Logan sat opposite the staircase on one of the expensive couches. He bent forward with a hand tugging at his left boot.

Phoenix clattered ahead carrying her library bag. She picked up speed and ran across the rug, enfolding Logan's head in her arms. He looked up and blinked in surprise before his face creased in a smile. "Hey." He held his head still as she kissed his forehead and cheeks, a routine they'd shared her whole life.

"And one for the chinny chin chin," she said with a giggle, squeaking at the sensation of his bristles on her soft face.

Leslie walked with Wiri and she halted at the bottom of the stairs with a frown on her crinkled face. "Logan Du Rose!" She raised her voice as though chastising a small child. Hana jumped and her head snapped up. Oblivious, Mac kept his rhythm going on the stairs. A guest checking in at reception turned to stare. Leslie fixed her hands on her hips and pointed to a trail of dirt leading from the front doors to the couch. "Look what you did!" she snapped.

"Oh, my days!" Hana breathed. The receptionist handed a conference guest a key card and ran around the desk to show him to the lift. She glanced over her shoulder at Leslie and hurried the man forward, even grabbing his hand luggage to hustle him faster. Hana froze and Mac twisted on the step to tap her thigh, his delicate heart-shaped face turned up like a daisy. He hunched his shoulders and spread his fingers, palm upwards, asking her why she'd stopped. Following her gaze, he watched his father rise from the couch and square his shoulders. Whatever he saw in Logan's expression made him pop a finger into his mouth.

"Papa, sit." Phoenix patted his leg and looked up at him with disappointment in her narrowed eyes. "I haven't done all the kisses yet." She screwed her head back on her shoulders and winced at the dangerous look in his eyes. "Uh oh," she breathed.

Logan kept his voice lowered and Hana marvelled at his self-control. "Don't tell me what to do in my own house," he snarled. He shifted and Hana spotted the dustpan and brush from behind the reception desk and guessed he'd requested it when he noticed the mess he'd tracked in. He looked tired, dark shadows beneath his grey eyes and he hadn't bothered shaving.

She noticed a blue line high on his right cheekbone and clods of thick mud clinging to his sleeve and the side of his jeans. Experience told her he'd fallen and her heart clenched in fear.

Leslie lifted a chunky finger and jabbed it towards Logan. She didn't leave her position at the bottom of the stairs. Her mouth opened and Hana cringed at the words pouring forth. She grabbed Mac and hoisted him onto her hip. "Your mama never let you stamp around inside in your boots!" she squawked. Her voice rose and Hana clattered down the stairs.

"Shut up, Leslie! Please, shut up!" Desperation laced Hana's words and she jabbed the old woman in the arm as she pushed past her. She lowered Mac to the parquet floor and made sure he had his footing. Then she rose and turned on Leslie. "Just leave it!" Hana's brow furrowed and anger burned in her green eyes. "You don't get to rebuke him like this."

Leslie jerked back in surprise and went on the offensive. "Look at the mess he's made." She jabbed a finger at the clods of mud. "His mama will turn in her grave. It's not like the old days. They knew to take their boots off outside."

Hana cringed and glanced at Logan's face. Dark and brooding, he'd failed to pull the usual mask over his emotions and she saw pure agony radiating from his smoky irises. Hana took a step towards him and he shook his head. She faltered for a second before realising he hadn't even noticed her approach. "Get out, old woman," he hissed, his tone dripping with uncharacteristic disrespect. His gaze burned bright enough to sear holes in Leslie's face. "Isn't it enough that you crept into my mother's bed and stole her surname?" He took a step forward and Hana's eyes widened at the sight of blood on his lower lip. Logan jabbed a finger at Leslie, mimicking her action to him. His face creased into a snarl. "Your days are numbered, wahine. I owe you nothing. You might have feathered my mother's nest in your old age, but you'll get nothing else from me. I tolerate you for my wife's sake." Logan lowered his arm and Hana spotted the tell-tale wince of pain. "Get out of my sight," he breathed.

Leslie blustered and pressed her fingers into her hips. Her knuckles showed through the skin as white knots. Hana shot her a warning look and dug in her pocket for her car key. "Take them," she said, holding them out. "Please, put the children in the car and I'll be right out."

Leslie's eyes narrowed. "I'll do it for you," she growled. "And them. But not for him."

Hana held her breath. The anger in Leslie's eyes revealed something she'd never noticed before and she opened her mouth to cancel the request. But Leslie snatched the keys and waddled towards the front door, her hips swaying beneath her voluminous dress. "Go with Nonie." Hana swallowed and directed the order to Wiri. "Take Phoe and hold Mac's hand across the car park."

He nodded, his eyes dark and his face blank. Phoenix's head bobbed up and down as she wielded the dustpan and brush. She sang to herself and played house, spreading the mud further afield from its origins. "Let's go, Phoe," Wiri said. When she pouted in protest, he picked up her library bag and dangled it in front of her face. "I'll read to you in the car." Bribery. Hana heaved a sigh of relief as Phoenix dropped the tools and skipped alongside Wiri.

"Hairy Maclary," she demanded. "With Scottish voices like Poppa Robert does." They followed Leslie through the wide front doors.

Hana waited until their footsteps pattered down the steps and then she walked towards Logan. He remained rigid, his gaze fixed on a point above her head. His eyes appeared unseeing and every muscle in his chest looked chiselled from stone. "Logan." She touched his arm and he jumped. "Did you fall?"

"What?" His grey eyes settled on her face and he dug his teeth into his lower lip. He swallowed once and a crease appeared in his brow. "It's Ma's birthday today," he said. His eyelashes fluttered. "The Miriam rose in her garden is flowering."

"Oh, Logan." Hana tightened her grip on his forearm and he blinked. "Sit down." She edged him back towards the couch and waited for him to sink into it. The receptionist exited the lift and retrieved the dustpan and brush. Hana gave her a smile of thanks as she swept up the mess.

"She's talking shit." Logan ran a hand over his chin and Hana heard the bristles scratch against his palm. He snuffed out a sad breath. His knees bent and he eased onto the cushion. "Geez, Hana. We didn't own a pair of boots between us. Ma couldn't tell us to take off what we didn't have."

Hana shifted onto her knees in front of him and looked up into his face. Experience told her to wait. Logan heaved in a heavy breath and exhaled. Her fingers gripped his knees and she watched as he settled. His eyes lost their darkness and his stormy irises settled into a flat, Pacific calm. Grass seeds hung from his wavy fringe and his eyelashes flicked them free to flutter onto Hana's knees. "Did you fall off the gelding?" Hana kept her voice soft.

Logan shook his head. "No."

Hana waited, but he offered no further explanation for his injuries. She cocked her head, but her patience earned nothing more. "How does the other guy look?" she asked, forcing a smirk onto her lips.

Logan shrugged. "About the same." His voice sounded croaky. He blew out another breath. "I think I'll give up for today. I'm not achieving anything."

"Okay." Hana rose but wrapped her fingers around his right hand. It looked uninjured and she held fast. "Come home with me. Leave your truck here."

Logan swallowed, but seemed distracted. "Ma didn't hit me or Barry." His gaze grew distant. "She knew we bled and she couldn't do it. That bitch out there acted like an unofficial enforcer. She said Ma spoiled me and she made up for it." His teeth grazed his lower lip and he shook his head.

"She hurt you? And you still let her look after our children?" Hana's brow furrowed and she jerked backwards. Alarm back-lit her green eyes. "Why didn't you say something, Logan?"

"She won't hurt the children." Logan's jaw clenched in his cheek and his eyes took on a dark wildness. "Just me, Hana. Any and every opportunity. Don't tell me you never noticed."

Hana gaped and her brain scrambled for an answer. Discomfort began in her chest and spread outward, heating the tips of her shoulders. She floundered. "I knew you didn't like each other, but not the reason." Her gaze strayed to the open front door and then back to her husband's face. He seemed calmer, as though her belief in him caused a soothing effect. "What should I do?" she asked. "I'll speak to her. This can't continue."

Logan ran a hand over his face, the contact sounding scratchy. "It's just me. Keep her away from me."

Hana nodded and pressed her lips to the end of his regal nose. "Okay, babe. You've got it." She wrapped her arms around his neck and cradled his head. A familiar masculine scent rose up and she inhaled it, soaking in Logan's hay and sunshine fragrance. She glanced up as Wiri stood in the doorway, his slender frame casting a long shadow across the lobby. He raised an eyebrow and she forced a smile onto her lips. "Come on." She pushed herself upright and squeezed Logan's shoulder. "Let's go home."

The stiffness in his body roused a wince of pain as Logan rose from the sofa. He carried his dirty boots and waited until they reached the steps outside before pushing his feet into them. Hana noticed his knuckles as he turned his left hand over, the skin red and sore. Her heart gave an involuntary clench as she realised the truth. He hadn't fallen. He'd been fighting. Heat prickled up the back of her neck as two mysteries demanded her attention. Who got Logan so riled up he'd risk hurting himself to punish them? And what was the real history between her husband and her opinionated mother-in-law?

19

Old Wrongs

"We need to talk." Hana blew out a breath and folded her arms across her chest. She'd delivered the children to school and nursery and her nerves jangled as she faced Leslie. The list of jobs she'd promised Logan she'd do burned a hole in her back pocket. Her blouse parted to reveal a long hickey over her left breast. She sighed with exasperation and lowered her arms to let the fabric cover it. Forcing her ageing body into positions worthy of the Kama Sutra commentary without Logan realising, turned her muscles to jelly. He always took over, making their lovemaking into his private worship of her and frustrating her efforts to please him. Hana yawned and pondered the idea of kinky underwear, her mind already raking the bedroom closet for something suitable. She just needed to take Logan's breath away for long enough to get in first.

"What about?" Leslie bent to check the muffins rising in the oven and looked at Hana from her stooped position. "Want one of these?"

"No thanks, yes, no, no thanks." Hana winced and sucked in her stomach. "I shouldn't."

Leslie rose and wrinkled her nose. "You look great, kōtiro. Too skinny. You need some fat on yer bones."

Hana shook her head at the distraction technique, not wanting to go down a well-trodden road to a dead end. "No, we need to deal with this."

Leslie slumped into a dining chair and rested her elbows on the table. She waited until Hana pulled out a chair and joined her. "Last night?" She swallowed. "I just forgot my place. I'll apologise to him."

Hana sighed and twisted her lips, not sure how to start the conversation. She frustrated herself, always dodging issues and skirting the knotty subjects. It seemed easy to think of showing Logan the eBook until she stood there in front of him with her phone in her hand. Then it felt like an insurmountable wall and a chasm of inadequacy opened at her feet. What if he assumed she'd grown bored with him? What if he believed her motivation hinged on getting more instead of giving? Hana gritted her jaw and spoke, forcing herself into the situation head on. "What happened between you and Logan, Leslie? Why do you dislike him so much?"

Leslie groaned and her forehead thudded against her wrists. She kept her head just inches from the table and her eyes closed. "I tried to help him, Hana. I promised Reuben I'd look out for him and I did. But the other kids resented Logan. They knew what his birth cost them and it was the root of Kane's hatred. Life was different back then. Hitting yer kid was a normal way of giving them discipline. Do you understand?"

Hana nodded, remembering the threat of her father's slipper across her backside in punishment. The slipper was just footwear until he commanded her to fetch it from the bedroom so he could slap her bum with it. Then it morphed into something different. "I remember," she whispered. "Not better or worse, but different."

"Yeah." Confidence filled Leslie's chest and she sat up, running her fingers over stray hairs escaped from her tight bun. Grey mingled with brown hues left over from her youth. "I saw

Miriam making him into a pussy and knew Reuben would hate that. She coddled him, like one of her delicate roses. Yet she'd give Michael and Liza a slap when they crossed her. Barry was evil to the core. He played Miriam, but Logan just turned those soulful grey eyes on her and she turned to putty. The other kids hated him. I thought if I disciplined him and they saw it, they might back off." She shook her head. "I saw it in his eyes last night. He hates me."

Hana frowned. "I think he just doesn't understand why the rules were different for him. And you've carried it on. He's a grown man, Leslie. He doesn't need your chiding."

Leslie nodded and kept her eyes closed. "It's a reflex. We spark. Do you think he meant what he said last night?"

"I don't know." Hana shrugged. "You push him to the absolute limit and he doesn't know why. Do you even understand what you're doing?"

Leslie kept her head down and her eyes closed. "No. It's a bad habit. It got me into big trouble once."

"What kind of trouble?" Curiosity burgeoned in Hana's soul. "Who with?"

Leslie winced. "When Kane and Barry split Logan open with a machete, I got a visitor. He told me to lay off. He said if I didn't, he'd bury my body where nobody would find me."

Hana closed her eyes and a huge exhale deflated her body. "JD."

"Jack." Leslie's steady gaze fixed on Hana's face as she said the name. She watched Hana recoil and reached a chunky hand across to grab her writhing fingers. "Yeah. Logan's grandfather. I didn't know that back then, but I should have. He looked out for Logan. He said my efforts made no difference, not when the others knew who his father was. Reuben's boys hated Logan just for drawing breath and there weren't no way to alter history. Jack side-lined him after that. Took him with him on rides, taught him about horses and cattle, how to muster and break them in. Nobody got near him, he made sure of it." She swallowed and squeezed Hana's hand in a tight grip. "He loved the boy. It makes sense now I know why."

Hana inhaled and stared at the ceiling, searching the white surface for an answer. Stained wooden beams soared into an apex overhead and she released the breath in a long sigh. "You need to stop now, Leslie. I won't support you if you continue to harass him." She shook her head to remove the doubts and niggling memories. "You've made a fool out of me."

Leslie pursed her lips and her dark irises flashed. Her motivation unfolded like a tablecloth shaken out in a strong wind. Hana sighed. "It's guilt, isn't it? That's why you've kept it going all these years."

Leslie snatched her hand back and her lower lip turned down. "Just leave it, will you? Why do you always need to prod at the past?"

"Ugh." Hana shuddered. "I know you had a crush on Reuben, but please tell me that's all it was."

"It was nothing! It was nothing!" Leslie's gaze darted towards the bedroom where Alfred still slept. "Please. Just let things alone."

"Then stop antagonising my husband." Hana tilted her chin up in defiance. She sensed victory and Leslie backed down at speed, but only because she'd seen another loose thread in Hana's armour.

Her brow furrowed into long lines. "Something else is worrying you, isn't it girly?"

"Yeah." Hana wrinkled her nose. "Logan's being secretive. It makes me uneasy. There are things he's not telling me. I can feel it." Her gaze flicked towards the French doors leading to the balcony. An image of Kane's blood sent a shiver along her spine. "Not just Kane's death, but something else."

Leslie shook her head and followed the direction of Hana's gaze. "Do you think he's sorry Kane's dead?"

"Who knows?" Hana withdrew her hand and ran it over her face. "Logan is covered in bruises. I think he got into a fight yesterday."

"A fight?" Leslie's irises sparked to life at the prospect of gossip. "I assumed he fell off that white hōiho."

Hana shook her head. "No, his knuckles are bruised and he kept getting up in the night to use his medication." She yawned and felt the flush begin in the centre of her chest and spread outward. He'd apologised for waking her and then made it worth her while. She pursed her lips as the blush spread into her cheeks.

Leslie grinned, a movement involving all her facial muscles and her false teeth. "Reuben Du Rose was like that." The grin spread and a gap appeared between her top gums and the dentures as they threatened to part company. "Randy all the time. His first wife walked like she just got off a hōiho."

"Stop!" Hana closed her eyes against the image of her elders engaging in wrinkly night time activity. She gave an involuntary shudder and Leslie released a girlish giggle. The oven timer pinged as though designating the end of the conversation and Leslie rose to rescue her muffins. Hana felt spiteful for bringing the subject back to its origins. "So, no more baiting Logan."

"No. I'll try. But it's an old habit." Leslie cocked her head to one side and paused. Her irises flashed. "And very entertaining." The worn oven gloves allowed the heat from the muffin tray to percolate through and she winced and dumped it onto the bread board. "I'd like a truce with him, for Alfred's sake."

"Good." Hana rose and forced her way through the heavenly scent of chocolate cake. She dropped a kiss on Leslie's plump cheek before her tone became serious. "You're on very shaky ground, Leslie. You've won a few battles, but it's time to stop before he makes sure you lose the war."

Leslie nodded, her expression sombre. Her fingers reached for Hana's shoulders to prolong the embrace and her keen eyes spotted the hickey peeking from beneath Hana's blouse. She wrenched the fabric wide and gaped at the line of love bites. Her eyes sparkled with humour and Hana cringed, knowing she wouldn't keep her mouth shut on something so personal.

"Like father, like son," she said with a chuckle and slapped Hana's escaping backside.

20

An Unwanted View

Hana sat in the truck and used the lever to draw the seat closer to the steering wheel. A button next to the seat could have done it with a single press, but she'd messed up the process when she first asked it to record her preferred settings and couldn't work out how to change it. Logan had reversed the truck into its usual parking space and Hana drew the seatbelt around her before looking up. The windscreen framed the balcony of Alfred's apartment and Hana rose up to view Kane's landing area through its perspective. A row of hedging screened the staff cars from the guest car park nearer the hotel and blocked her view of the gravel in front of the kitchen windows. She felt grateful. It seemed hard enough to keep walking past the crime scene tape, knowing he might have laid there dying if the shots didn't kill him first. Hana contemplated the agony of his landing and prayed he'd passed out long before he met the ground. She pressed the starter button for the ignition and gave an involuntary shudder, forcing her mind to turn to the list of neglected errands.

Hana reached Rangiriri before realising the dashboard camera screen looked dark. Joining the queue to merge onto the expressway, she pressed the button to start it recording and waited for the device to start. Nothing happened and she tutted in frustration. Taking her turn to join the four-lane expressway, she settled into a steady speed and headed north towards Auckland. She pressed the button one more time and then conceded defeat. Logan had bought cameras for all the fleet cars after an unknown driver smashed into the side of Toby's truck and drove away. Hana maintained that theirs was faulty as it didn't turn on and off in response to the ignition. Wiri often took responsibility for pressing the button from the passenger seat but when Hana forgot to turn it off and nobody used the vehicle for a while, it drained the camera battery. Once, it produced a night's worth of footage of the side of the house. She gave up when the third press did nothing to bring the screen to life. Her fingers fiddled with the plug in the cigarette lighter but the green light on the screen showed it had power. A truck cut in front of her from the inside line and she growled in exasperation. "And today will be the day I get sideswiped and have no evidence," she complained to herself. "Bloody typical!"

The truck's satellite navigation system took her to a wholesaler on the outskirts of an industrial estate. She picked up the supplies Toby wanted. An assistant helped load the heavy bags of feed into the truck's flatbed. "Sorry," the man said with a wince. His nose dripped and he made no attempt to wipe it, as though resigned to his sinuses misbehaving. "I'll deliver the rest next week as usual. Truck should be back on the road by then." He jerked his head towards the stacked bags. "Toby said that would be enough until then."

Hana gave a smile and resisted the urge to shrug. He could have filled the bags with gravel for all she knew or cared. When he asked her a specific question about the chaff mix, she winced. "I'm just the driver today," she said. "But you can call Toby."

The man rubbed his eyes as though they itched and then wiped his nose on his sleeve. Hana felt relieved, no longer forced to watch the dangling snot get nearer his lips. "What's it like working for that Du Rose guy?" He leaned closer to induce a sense of conspiracy. "I've heard he's a real hard ass."

Hana widened her eyes and hid her amusement by opening the truck door and climbing onto the running board. "Oh, yeah!" she exclaimed. "Total hard ass." She slammed the door and fired up the ignition, waving through the open window with a grin on her face. Thoughts of her husband's backside kept her smiling until she reached a saddlery near the Papakura off ramp. A repaired Western saddle and numerous lengths of buckled leathers took up the remaining space in the truck's flatbed and she slammed the lid with difficulty. A glance at her watch showed she'd completed two of the tasks in record time. She rang Toby. "Hey, I've done the feed place and the saddlers," she said. "I can't fit any more in and I need to pick up the children. Is there something on this list you'd consider urgent?"

Toby blew into his phone and Hana picked up a hint of exasperation. "All of it really," he grumbled. "That horse of yours has caused chaos yet again. It's kicked two of the fence rails clean off. I'm shooting it." Hana gritted her teeth and stared ahead through the windscreen, her eyes concentrating on the road ahead while her mind formed a suitable response. Nothing ladylike presented itself and so she left him hanging. It upset her hearing Sacha referred to as an inanimate object. She wished the mare would stop drawing attention to herself. Toby cleared his throat and changed the subject. "If you put all the kids in the back seat, can you fit in just one more thing?"

Hana considered refusing out of spite but resisted. She huffed out a sigh and accompanied it with a groan of frustration. "Depends what it is," she snapped.

Half an hour later, she headed south on the expressway with a huge box balanced on the floor of the passenger side. It stretched from the foot well to lean against the back of the seat. The warehouse assistant had helped her wind the seatbelt around it to keep it in place and she had to duck forward to use her side mirror. "Bloody Toby!" she grumbled. "Getting me to run his personal errands on Logan's time."

Despite two more pleading calls from Toby, Hana refused to collect anything else and tore him a new one for using her to pick up his online purchases. When he rang again, she sent the call to voice mail, hoping it punished him. She felt tempted to hide his new tent in the back of the hay barn and deny all knowledge.

The traffic thickened as the sun lengthened the shadows of buildings in its way. Hana sped south, wondering how the city dwellers coped with spending so much of their lives in exhaust fumes and frustration. Rural Waikato drivers thought more than three cars at an intersection constituted a traffic jam. She made good time and arrived back in their small township with half an hour to spare before picking up Mac.

Parking outside the nursery, Hana considered driving home to unload. She imagined Wiri's expression of disdain at losing the front seat to an uninteresting cardboard box. Her lips twisted as she pondered her dilemma. "Na," she whispered to herself. "Finding someone to help me unload could use up more time than I can spare." She tapped the steering wheel and chose a different way to kill time. Pulling into the empty road, she pressed the gas pedal and heard the diesel engine obey with a seasoned roar.

The truck covered the few hundred metres and came to rest outside Libby's house behind the main street of the township. Lofty oak trees lined the wide road, creating an attractive leafy avenue suitable for a postcard scene. The houses were modest but pretty, simple structures clothed with wooden slats and a tin roof. No two looked alike in a cornucopia of New Zealand eclecticism. Hana locked up the truck and left it on the main road, yawning and stretching her arms above her head. She strode along Libby's narrow driveway with her hands shoved into her jeans pockets. The elderly lady in the front house waved from her kitchen window and Hana pulled a hand free and returned the greeting. She continued past the high camellia hedge and salivated at the thought of the luxurious coffee Libby would make her in the coveted espresso machine.

A silver car sat by the side of the house, screened from the street by a section of the elderly neighbour's garden wall. Hana's steps slowed until she halted. Then she changed direction. The BMW matched her son's and she shook her head in confusion, deciding a closer examination might reveal her error. The registration number had her holding her breath even before she spotted Hope's spare car seat in the back. A discarded Action Man lay abandoned on the seat next to it. "Oh, Bodie! What are you doing?" Hana gasped. She pressed her fingers over her lips and knew the answer. Libby's married boyfriend was her son.

21

A Chip on his Shoulder

Leslie waved to the children from the front steps and Hana held her breath at the sound of seat belts clicking open. "No!" She whipped around in her seat to glare at the three guilty faces behind her. "You don't do that."

"Sorry." Wiri swallowed. "I started it."

"No, I did." Phoenix stuck her bottom lip out and pouted. Hana's neck complained at the unnatural angle and she gave up trying to get eye contact with her daughter. She sighed.

"Why did you hide from Phoe's teacher?" Wiri demanded. He cocked his head and his grey eyes demanded an explanation.

"Let me reverse into our parking space and then I'll walk you across the car park." Hana avoided the question, tears springing into her eyes. She blew out a pursed breath and tried to concentrate on not dinging her truck.

"You did hide." Wiri flattened his chin and jutted it upwards in defiance, displaying his Du Rose ego. "You looked like you just robbed a bank."

Phoenix gasped. "Did yer, Mama? Did yer rob a bank? What's a bank?"

"No, I didn't!" Hana glared at Wiri and lied about hiding from the teacher. She didn't feel able to cope with Bernice Cuthbert's excuses without slapping her. Collecting Mac early, she'd steered through the primary school like a battleship and snagged her other children. She'd spoken to no one and avoided all eye contact. Hana breathed in a fortifying breath and cranked the gear lever into reverse. "I'm sorry. I'll speak to Phoe's teacher soon," she promised. She half turned in her seat. "Has anything else happened?"

Phoenix shook her head and her gaze flicked to Wiri. "No. Wiri fixed it."

Icy fingers curled around Hana's heart and the shiver ran up her spine. Her foot slipped on the brake pedal and the branches rustled on the conifer behind her parking space. "What did you do?" she demanded.

"Nothing." Wiri smirked and Phoenix's cheeks flushed pink.

"He just told Holly to stop it," she whispered. "So now Jordan's upset at her too. She wants Wiri to be her friend." Phoenix winced and her chin pushed outward so her bottom teeth made her resemble a bulldog.

"Okay." Hana yanked on the parking brake. "Please, do nothing else. Let the grown-ups sort this out."

Wiri shrugged. "It's what Uncle Logan would do."

Hana suppressed the ready groan. "I don't want this getting out of hand. Holly's mother already went to the principal. Please, just leave it now. I'm not convinced Logan's problem-solving skills are always the best."

"I could slap her with a fish," Phoenix suggested. "It's what Jesus would do."

"I clearly haven't read that bible verse," Hana sighed. "It doesn't sound right. No slapping, no threatening, no fish. Please." She glanced in the rear-view mirror and caught Wiri's shuttered expression. Instinct told her she was missing something, but Bodie's infidelity occupied all the firing parts of her brain. Wiri's Du Rose mask of indestructibility sat securely in place and Hana muffled her groan of resignation.

Leslie kidnapped the children off the front steps and waved Hana away with a slicing action from her meaty hand. "You empty the truck," she said with a grin. "I made muffins for my mokopuna. Come up later."

"But I need to speak to Phoenix." Hana lowered her voice but saw Wiri's ears twitch and knew he eavesdropped. "Something happened at school and she won't talk to me about it. I need to go back to her teacher."

"She'll tell Nonie Leslie about it then." Leslie waved her hand in dismissal and they filed away, leaving Hana alone on the front steps. At the sound of a suitcase bumping up behind her, she turned and picked her way through the new arrivals to the truck.

"Where do you want these bags?" Hana demanded, sticking a finger in her ear to drown out the air brakes of a departing coach.

"Ah," Toby replied from his end of the call. "Didn't think about that."

Hana wished she'd kept Wiri with her as she got out three times to open and close gates on the way to the new feed shed she hadn't known existed. Toby's complicated directions led her through numerous paddocks and around the outskirts of a corn field. The new shed loomed up ahead, made from corrugated zinc and painted matt green to match its surroundings. Rounded like an old fashioned hay barn, it blended into the backdrop of corn undetected. Hana reached for the hasp on the final gate and groaned in irritation. A shiny new padlock barred her way. She pulled her phone from her jeans pocket and paused. A text message from Logan flashed on the screen and she pursed her lips, wondering how she missed hearing it arrive. She opened the envelope and read his concise statement.

"*Moving the mob from the fortieth down the hill for water. Home late. We need to talk.'*

Hana sighed. "Yeah, we need to talk about your daughter." Thoughts of Bodie rose unbidden and she swallowed the ball of tension rising in her chest. The ramifications seemed bigger than she dared to contemplate and facing them insurmountable. Her son kept a mistress. He lived a lie.

Hana closed her eyes and imagined Amy leaving him and taking Jas. The thought of never seeing her grandson again pushed the lump higher into her throat and forced her to swallow around it.

"Ah good. You made it." Toby's statement made her jump and Hana clapped a hand over her squeal. He smirked and dismounted from the speckled Appaloosa gelding in a single bound. Taking a moment to loosen the horse's girth, he unclipped the rope from its head collar and gave the rounded rump a slap. "It's an all-you-can-eat-buffet, Red," he said with a grin. "Your time starts now."

Red bent his nose to the ground and sniffed at the corn stalks surrounding the barn. He shook his tufty mane and let his hooves carry him towards the grass bent down by Hana's tyres. Munching and walking, he snatched at the long stalks and closed his eyes to chew.

Hana looked around her and shrugged. "Why build a feed barn in a corn field? It makes no sense."

Toby leaned down to grab the padlock on the final gate. He produced a sizable bunch of keys from his pocket and selected one. The catch released with a click and he unhooked the clasp and pushed the gate open. "You're asking the wrong question," he replied. "You're assuming the corn came first." He leaned on the gate, his muscular biceps flexing beneath his tee shirt. Hana remained immobile, her hand covering her mouth and her feet concreted into her boots. "What's wrong?" Toby touched her shoulder and the flicker of kindness which shot through her heart made her eyes water. The angles of his tanned face grew harder. "Hana! Tell me what's wrong." A radio crackled on his belt and her eyes widened. She took a step back, not wanting him to call Logan. Not wanting him to call anyone.

"Nothing. Everything." Her voice sounded frayed around the edges. She pushed the gate open and heaved in a breath. "Do you have time to help me unload?"

"Sure." Toby's expression softened and a dark ring showed beneath his left eye. A cut across his cheekbone still looked raw. "Want me to ride shotgun?"

Hana glanced back at the truck. It sat in the mouth of the gate, its diesel engine mumbling away to itself like a rhetorical conversation. Toby's tent stuck up from the passenger foot well, the cardboard box leaned back against the seat. Hana shook her head. "No. You drive. I just need to clear my head a little."

Toby narrowed his eyes and then clamped his lips closed. Hana felt a wave of gratitude, understanding why Logan liked him so much. A distant cousin, Toby's responsibilities extended each year as Logan pushed the land to its limits. She knew by the company truck Toby drove that Logan made his loyalty worthwhile.

Toby whistled to his horse and Red lifted his head. His ears flicked as he saw the open gate and spotted the even longer grass beyond. Lush but dried by the sun, it looked like hay on the stalk and he turned his feet towards it. "Far out woman!" Toby grumbled. "Look how far forward you have the driver's seat. You're like a pea on a drum." He cranked the mechanism back to accommodate his long legs and revved the engine. Hana ignored his insults and waited by the gate for him to roll the heavy vehicle through. She reached out to touch Red's warm flank as he passed and then closed the gate behind him. Toby's long right arm dangled from the truck's open window and he paced the vehicle to Hana's walking speed. She cringed as he joined her, wishing he'd go away. The urge to run overwhelmed her as they steered a straight course over the deep grass to the barn her husband had kept secret.

The truck crushed the foliage beneath its tyres and bumped over the uneven ground. Hana sent out a relieved breath as Toby drew to a halt, the tension returning as he hauled on the handbrake without pressing the button. The unhealthy ratcheting sound grated against her fragile nerves. The smirk on his face when she turned suggested he did it on purpose to rile her. "Open it up," he called, pressing the button to pop the boot lid and dropping his feet onto the gravel.

Hana's jaw flexed and her teeth ground until they ached. "If I'm not responsible enough for a paddock key, I won't have one to a barn I didn't know existed," she bit. The retort sounded snippy and she hadn't meant it to. Logan didn't do things without good reason and Hana regretted maligning her husband and painting him as the bad guy in her muddy picture. She closed her eyes and swallowed, desperate to make it better. "That's not true." She turned, finding Toby fixed in place with his hand still on the driver's door.

"Then you do have a key?" He looked confused, his blue eyes narrowed.

"No. But only because I never asked for one."

"Oh." Toby dug into his jeans pocket and pulled his jailer sized bunch. "I figured you probably knew about this place, anyway." He shrugged. "Keys won't matter soon. David Allen's gonna fit one of those other locks he makes. The number codes are genius. He just thinks up this clever shit."

Hana walked back to the truck and held out her hand. Toby threw the keys into her palm and she almost dropped them. "Thanks." She stepped up to the lock and realised she didn't know which key to use.

"Yellow sticker," Toby grunted. He hefted one of the forty litre sacks onto his shoulder, making the action appear effortless. He strode towards her and Hana fumbled the door open. She rolled it back, hearing the gentle hiss of new mechanisms as it slid aside. Toby dumped the bag onto a depleted pile and rolled his shoulder. He winked at Hana as he passed. A beeping sounded from a panel next to the left of the roll doors and Toby strode over to it. "I keep forgetting about this," he grumbled. Quick fingers pressed numbers into the keypad and his shoulders relaxed as the beeping ceased. "Burglar alarm." He waggled his eyebrows at Hana before striding back to the truck.

It took little time for him to unload. Hana carried the smaller items and let the day's events wash over her. She still couldn't process the body blow it had brought. Bodie's unexpected infidelity added itself to the pile of other problems. She'd failed to fix Phoenix's issue with Holly, hadn't known about the secret barn and couldn't discuss any of it with Logan without feeling like a failure. Their distance seemed to extend with each passing day and she felt like a navy wife standing powerless as her husband sailed on the ebbing tide. She'd lost her right to object to anything. And Caroline was coming.

Waiting for Toby to dump the last bag onto the pile, she sank onto a hay bale and rubbed the base of her spine.

"Bad day?" He slumped down next to her and Hana nodded. "Yeah."

"Anything I can help with? You did me a solid favour fetching this stuff. Things are pretty crazy here at the moment."

"I'll be okay." Hana watched a native hawk rise on the air currents above the mountain. "Just send any simple jobs my way if it helps."

"It does." Toby grinned. "And I enjoy bossing you around."

"Don't get used to it." Hana rubbed the base of her aching spine.

Toby frowned. "How long have we known each other, Hana? You can talk to me."

A memory of Robert Dressler rose into Hana's mind and she jerked backwards. She'd shared confidences with him and given him completely the wrong impression. Making the same mistake twice would be stupid. She shook her head. "I can't, Toby. I'm sorry." She scratched around for another topic and settled on something easy. "How are things going with you and Leslie's daughter?"

Toby winced, scrunching his dark features into a mask of discomfort. "We broke up. She's a nice girl but her mother's a nightmare. No wonder the rest of the family high-tailed it over to Australia. Leslie just can't help herself. The woman interferes in everything. Isla doesn't want to get married again, but Leslie started demanding wedding dates and nagging me to buy a ring."

"Oh my!" Hana covered her mouth with her hand but failed to keep the biting comment inside. "Welcome to my world. So, what's the plan for the mountain's most eligible bachelor now?" She side stepped Toby's desire to talk smack about Leslie, but her poor choice of a replacement led to an awkward silence. Hana cleared her throat and covered her embarrassment by standing. "It's none of my business, Toby. You don't need someone else to make you happy. Contentment comes from inside here." She patted her sternum.

"Did you?" Toby squinted up at her, the lowering sun turning his irises to a sparkling blue. "Did you need someone else to make you happy?"

Hana's fingers fidgeted against her belt and she swallowed. The question contained a weight which pressed down onto her head as though forcing her to answer. "For a long time I thought so. When my first husband died, I let myself feel incomplete and it tainted everything."

"Because you loved him?" Toby's whole body appeared rigid and unmoving. "You couldn't live without him?"

"No." Hana spoke before the thoughts were fully formed in her mind. "Because I relied on him too much. He took care of all the important stuff until I didn't know what was happening and didn't really care. Then he cheated on me, died and left me to piece things back together again. I'd become pathetic and didn't realise."

Toby's lips parted until his jaw hung slack. "I didn't know. Did Logan rescue you?"

"No." Hana shook her head. "But he woke me up. He showed me what I could achieve. We broke up for a while and I bought a car and a house in the time we weren't together. I realised I could cope and it's the most empowering feeling in the world."

"So, you don't rely on Logan in the same way?"

"Definitely not. I adore my husband and I don't want to live without him. But wanting and needing are two very different things. I know I can cope. I just don't want to have to."

"Is his money a lure?" Toby gasped at the sound of his own question, perhaps reacting to the horror in Hana's eyes.

"No!"

"I didn't mean it. It just popped out!" He rose, arms outstretched and his cheeks flushing red.

"Is that what you all think? That I married Logan for his money?" Hana backed away, horror widening her eyes. Horror and anger. She'd always known they thought it, but to hear Toby voice the accusation deepened the injury.

"No, I don't." Toby grabbed her forearms and his fingers closed around the painful scar over Hana's left wrist. He released her when she gasped and covered his face with his hands. "Hana, please," he begged. "Please."

She shook her head and strode back towards the truck. "I can't blame you for thinking the worst," she bit. Her heels ground against the dry earth as she spun to face him. "I'd married Logan and fallen pregnant with Phoenix before he told me he owned the hotel. And for what it's worth, I was and still am independently solvent."

"I'm sorry, I'm sorry!" Toby covered the ground between them and his arms seized Hana in a bear hug. He smelled of earth and sweat and his muscular chest and biceps engulfed her head until she couldn't breathe. "I didn't mean it," he whispered. "I'm sorry, Hana."

She felt tears building in her chest and throat and swallowed them down. Almost six years of marriage to Logan should have proved her sincerity and it pained her to think it meant nothing. Hana ground her teeth in her jaw and pushed Toby's chest to make him release her. "Forget it," she snapped. "You only said what everyone already thinks."

Toby kept hold of her right wrist and his eyes glittered in his face. The embarrassed hue still mottled his olive neck and stole through the faint beard growth on his cheeks. The livid cut rose like an affront on his good looks. "They don't, Hana. I'm sorry."

"I never know where I stand with you." Hana snatched her arm free. "You're always looking for a reaction and now you've got it. Are you happy now?"

Toby's arms hung loose by his sides. His eyes widened and his gaze darted back towards the barn's open doors. He lowered his voice as though avoiding an unseen listener. "I give you crap because I know you can take it. I like you and respect you. Please don't let this ruin things."

"It won't," Hana lied. "I need to get back to my children. I'll leave you to lock up."

"Are you gonna tell Logan what I said?" Toby edged closer and the corners of his lips turned down. He glanced backwards again, his cheeks flushed and fear back-lighting his irises.

"I don't know," Hana replied, the answer true. She hated how everyone deferred to Logan and her irritation rose higher. The truck door opened beneath her fingers and she climbed onto the running board. Toby had altered the seat position and she almost fell into it. Her hands grappled to find the button to return it to her settings.

"Please Hana," Toby pleaded. "I'm sorry."

Hana felt the seat rise beneath her backside and clasped the steering wheel. The sense of powerlessness pressed down on her head. "Fine!" she snapped. She glanced back at the open shed and frowned. "But in exchange, you can tell me why Logan built a new barn and why you're keeping feed and equipment this far out?"

Toby shrank from her narrowed gaze and Hana experienced a flicker of triumph. He'd backed himself into a difficult corner. "We just are," he replied, his eyes darting to examine a cricket crawling across the scorched earth. Hana waited for him to look up again, steeling herself to keep her patience. His shoulders slumped in defeat. "I thought you knew. Someone's interfering with the equipment and the feed. We moved it all out here a few months ago. Logan organised it to avoid raising suspicion, so we bring the new stuff out here while using up the older stock in the barn nearest the stables. But we have to check everything. They put engine oil in the molasses for the mares and nails in the oats. Logan's getting cameras installed everywhere." His gaze flicked back towards the barn again and Hana heard the groan come from low in his throat.

"Right." She gave a slow blink to control her redheaded temper as it flared and sent a rush of heat through her spine. More secrets. She pressed the ignition button and the truck fired to life. If Logan wanted to freeze her out of his business affairs, he was doing a fantastic job.

22

Pressed into Service

The hotel looked busy when Hana returned and someone else had parked in Logan's spot opposite the main doors. A tiny hatchback occupied the space, its back seat laden with cardboard boxes and junk. A sticker from a local garage clung to the rear window by one corner and the owner had ignored the sign which marked the car park as staff only. Already irritated, Hana spun the truck into a space on the grass and hoped Will's son didn't come after her for ruining his neatly mowed verge.

Running up the front steps, Hana dodged a group coming down. She almost didn't hear the woman's voice as she called her name. "Mrs Du Rose?" She raised it to a shout and Hana spun around.

"Sorry, yes?"

The kuia from the marae stood on the step below her, static in a sea of suitcases and visitors flowing onto the gravel. Her smile oozed confidence and a steady self-assurance Hana envied. A dark moko tattoo decorated her chin and culminated in lips dyed black. The art embodied her genealogy and anchored her in the roots of her heritage. "Busy day?" she asked.

Hana nodded and stepped down to meet her. The woman had sung the karanga to welcome her onto the marae as Logan's wife and they'd shared passing conversations since, which the older woman managed to fill with nuggets of wisdom. Hana felt the tension release from her spine. "Yes," she replied. "Chaotic is a more accurate description."

"I imagine so. My tāne tells me you called and Sam said you could use my help." She raised a hand as Hana winced. "He's not telling tales. I took some of my baskets to Will and he mentioned you were trying to learn. I asked Sam if I should offer my help and he thought you might like that."

Hana blanched and her nose wrinkled in dismay. "You saw my baskets and knew straight away I needed help. Are they that terrible?"

The kuia grinned and shook her head. "No, kōtiro." She lifted a gnarled finger and wagged it at Hana. "But I could see he hadn't taught you to find your ara. That's the key."

"My ara?" Hana sighed. "Will doesn't teach. He just shouts. I don't remember him yelling anything about an ara."

The old woman chuckled. "I thought so." She reached out and patted Hana's fingers. "Come to my house tomorrow and I'll teach you. Then you can do your shift before the school run."

"Shift?" Hana's eyes narrowed. "Shift where?"

"At the marae." The woman navigated her way down the remaining steps and turned her smiling brown eyes on Hana. "Just two hours. We take care of our own, Mrs Du Rose. You just need to keep him company."

Kane. Hana held her breath, unable to say his name. She stood on the steps and watched Sam's grandmother stride across the car park. The old woman weaved between knots of conference guests waiting for their departure bus like a battleship in full sail. She walked into the staff car park and unlocked the tiny hatchback occupying Logan's space. Gravel spat from behind her reversing wheels like sea spray.

Hana ran up the steps and stomped through the lobby. She veered right and skirted the kitchen and rear entrance to the dining room. A left turn took her to Logan's office. Her jaw flexed at the stress of wondering which major issue to raise first. Her heart sank when she saw how busy he looked.

Hana rattled in the doorway as Rawhiti took his time gathering paperwork and a mobile phone from the desk. Logan glanced up at her and his body took on a stillness she knew well. His scrutiny assessed her jerky footsteps across the antique rug. Strong fingers slipped his glasses from his nose and he placed them on the desk with exaggerated care. Rawhiti continued to fluff around and Hana's fingers bunched and released by her sides. She let out a huff of irritation and he turned to face her. "You want rid of me or something?" His dark eyes flashed amusement and he lifted a hand to his olive forehead. "I'm devastated, Hana. I thought we had a thing." The hidden plea behind his tense expression begged her to play along but Hana faltered, not sure why he seemed determined to press the self-destruct button. Flirting with her in the dragon's den might prove beyond foolhardy.

"You'll get a thing with me in a minute," Logan's voice growled from behind the desk. He rose and Rawhiti shook his head.

"And I'm guessing it'll be your boot up my ass." A paper fluttered from the pile in his arms and swayed back and forth through the air current before resting on the carpet. Hana bent to seize it and recognised the name at the bottom of an official-looking letter. She paused, confused.

"Oh," she mused, peering at the signature. "Where do I know that name from?"

"Chuck it on here." Rawhiti dipped his shoulder so the stack of paperwork met Hana's wrist. She released the letter onto the top, her heart yammering in her chest. A nasty sensation crawled up her spine, leaving her feeling stained and dirty. The name held a bad association but she couldn't understand how its owner related to her husband.

"Shut it behind you." Logan rose from his chair and jerked his head towards the open door. Rawhiti turned and strutted across the rug until his boot heels thudded against the floorboards. Logan folded his arms and observed Hana. "What's up?" he demanded as soon as Rawhiti finished manoeuvring himself through the doorway. It closed with a heavy click and the sound of a whoosh followed it. Then swearing as Rawhiti crawled around the corridor outside retrieving more dropped paperwork. Logan's eyes glanced once at the door and then back at Hana's face. "Hana?"

She swallowed and felt herself fold inward. The reason for her visit seemed less urgent against the wall of Logan's impassive mask. She stared at him for a second and then hesitated. Her righteous indignation cooled. "You didn't tell me the sabotage had started up again. I've just seen the new barn. When did you think you'd mention it?"

Logan jerked his head upwards once as though both issues gave him no cause for concern. "Okay." He said the word with deliberate slowness and cocked his head. "But that's not what's bothering you, is it?"

"Please may I have a hug?" Hana felt the muscles around her chin tense and gritted her jaw to stop it wobbling. Logan dropped his inquisitorial stance and nodded. He held out his arms and they promised her salvation.

"What is it, Hana?" His chin rested on the top of her head and she felt his chest deflate as he released a tense breath.

"Sam's grandmother rostered me to sit with Kane's body at the marae." Her bottom lip protruded in a pout. "I don't want to."

"Yeah." Logan's breath released the word. "You and me both."

"You must do it too?" Hana's head tipped so she could look at his face. Logan's expression didn't change, his eyes soft and his long nose giving him a regal air. Then he grinned and Hana furrowed her brow. "What's funny?"

"I'm guessing she bullied me the same way she did you. She's a smiling assassin."

"She didn't bully me." Hana sank into Logan's lap as he sat back in his chair and pulled her with him. "She just announced it as she walked away. How can I get out of it? I don't want to sit next to a dead body, Logan. Especially not when I saw him die."

Logan tipped her face up to look at him and his thumbs stroked the soft skin beneath her eyes. "That's why you should do it," he whispered. "To banish the monsters. I'm doing it. He's my half-brother and we never got on. But it's not our way to leave our dead alone, Hana. He's whānau and it's what we do for family. Death brings its own treaty."

Hana made a sound like a childish grumble. "But I don't want to," she whined. "Please, don't make me."

Logan shook his head and shrugged. "I've never made you do anything and I won't start now. You make your own decisions." His eyebrow quirked upwards. "Just be prepared to stand behind them."

"What does that mean?" Hana's tone sounded sharp. "What will happen if I back out?"

"Dunno." Logan's dark eyes flashed. "The people in this town have accepted you so far. Are you willing to test it by rejecting our customs and protocols?"

Hana gasped and jerked backwards. "That's dirty, Logan Du Rose! Even for you!"

Logan snorted. "It's not a threat, Hana. I don't want you to start something you can't finish. Kane's just a man. He had no power over you. It's me he hated. There will be people around the whole time. You just need to sit with him at the wharenui for a while until someone else arrives to take over. It's up to you, but I strongly suggest you do it."

Hana groaned. "All I have to offer him is an hour of bad juju."

Logan's laughter filled the room. "It's two hours and that's really funny." His left hand strayed to her collar and he tweaked it to reveal the love bites. His eyes darkened and a smug smile pressed his lips into a line. Hana squeaked as his arms wrapped around her waist like a vice and he hauled her against his chest. "Do you have somewhere you need to be?" he demanded.

23

Adult Intervention

Hana accepted a seat opposite the desk's owner at the start of school the following day. She fixed a smile on her lips and refused to allow the tiny chair to make her feel inferior, though it set her lower than the teacher. The woman opposite dropped the hard look from her face and she blinked in quick succession. "Call me Bernice," she said with a sigh. A deep furrow lined her brow and the slope of her shoulders betrayed extreme defeat.

Hana smiled and nodded. Her gaze flicked to Bernice's hands and she noticed she'd bitten her nails. The chill of unease settled over her as she sensed their conversation mattered as much to the teacher as it did to her. She leaned forward and her knees tensed, ready to propel her away if she needed them to. "You start," Hana said, opening her palms to reinforce the instruction. "Then I'll tell you what Phoenix said."

Bernice sighed and ran a hand over her face. It smudged the red lipstick into a line across her cheek. "Phoenix attacked Holly on the carpet. She pulled her hair and slapped her. I dealt with it at the time, but Holly's mother wants to take the matter further."

Hana frowned. "But Phoenix told her grandmother she didn't do it. We believe her. Yet she apologised, missed her playtime and lunch hour because that's the punishment you chose. We both know Holly has picked on my daughter since the start of term." Her eyes narrowed and she experienced a tremor of satisfaction as Bernice shifted in her seat. The teacher oozed discomfort.

"Yes, we've spoken about the situation. I acknowledge that."

Hana shrugged. "So what have you done to keep Phoenix safe? I'm still waiting for you to come back to me after my initial complaint."

Bernice squirmed in her seat and Hana saw a light sheen appear on her forehead as guilt induced a sweat. "It's rather difficult."

Hana cocked her head and her eyes narrowed. Phoenix avoided talking about Holly and hadn't enjoyed school since the other girl arrived. Hana's insides twisted at the notion she'd failed her daughter. "You promised to deal with this weeks ago." She inhaled a fortifying breath. "I trusted you. Phoenix trusted you."

"Holly's father is funding the new gym equipment."

Hana's jaw dropped. "You let money influence your decision in a bullying case?"

"Oh, Holly isn't bullying her." Bernice frowned and flapped a hand in dismissal. Hana felt her temperature hike towards boiling point.

"So, what do you call it?" She folded her arms to stop the visible shaking of her hands sabotaging her confidence. "My husband's donated a lot of money and resources over the past year. Does that mean my children get a license to make others miserable with no recourse? No, I didn't think so." Hana rose, her sense of righteous indignation shooting her blood pressure higher. Her heart pounded in her chest and the fingers of her right hand fluttered to the pacemaker beneath her collar bone. The urge to escape compounded how Phoenix must feel each day, facing aggression without adult help. Anger flared. Hana felt her chin wobbling and clamped her teeth shut. She rose and the chair scraped the floorboards beneath it.

Turning, she walked away from the floundering teacher and kept her footsteps light and purposeful. Hana crossed the room and stopped in the doorway. She raised a finger in warning. "Sort this out, Bernice. Or my husband will." Her heart pounded as she closed the door behind her.

Wiri held Phoenix's hand and they faced her from across the corridor. Mac sat on a chair and had already made himself at home. He clutched a black crayon in his fingers and Hana lurched for it as he lifted it towards the wall. Wiri's brow furrowed. "What happened, Ma?" he demanded. "Have you made it okay for her?"

Hana swallowed and held her breath. She shook her head, containing the vitriol and aggression inside. She prided herself on keeping her opinions to herself and not colouring her children's view of others through her. Sometimes it felt like an impossible task. She hoisted Mac onto her hip and confiscated the crayon. "No, but I will." Striding towards the playground with the silent children weaving behind her, Hana wondered how she could avoid making the awful situation worse.

She expected Phoenix to make a fuss about going to class but she didn't. She lifted her tiny face for a kiss and gave Hana a smile. "Love you Mama," she whispered. "Thanks for sticking up for me."

Hana nodded and gave her daughter two kisses. The movement gave her time to blink away the gathering tears. Mac wriggled to escape and Hana set him down as she kissed Wiri, though she kept hold of her son's arm. "Have a good day," she told them. She winked at Phoenix and turned towards the gate.

Mac ran into the nursery and headed straight for the sandpit. He didn't stop for a kiss and Hana felt naked as she stared at the back of his head, willing him to turn around. He didn't.

Hana drove to Sam's grandmother's house and parked on the road. Her heart pounded in her chest and she inspected her hands. "Here goes nothing," she breathed and crooked her index finger. "Watch these digits turn flax into a basket."

The front door opened before she reached it and Hana accepted the gentle kiss to her cheek. The old woman's dark hair ran to grey at the front and created an attractive salt and pepper effect which framed her soft features. She'd always reminded Hana of her paternal grandmother and a spirit of affection bubbled in her chest. The woman's body contained no hint of fat and she wore dark jeans with class despite her seventy-plus years. Hana pulled her boots off and left them under the porch, padding across the floorboards in her socks. She'd heard Logan call her Whaea, meaning Aunty, but Hana faltered. It seemed presumptuous and overly familiar without years of history behind them. She paused, unable to pronounce the kuia's last name, despite practising in the mirror. It sounded okay in the privacy of her bedroom earlier, but she held back in fear of ridicule or pity. The woman showed nothing but kindness, but the block in Hana's brain oozed inadequacy and a sense of feeling out of place.

"I don't bite." A strong grip fixed around Hana's right wrist and tugged her towards a dining area beyond the kitchen. Coloured flax lay in neat rows on a dining table and Hana gasped at the bright hues.

"How did you do this?" Her fingers reached out as though by a desire of their own to touch the perfect strips. "It must have taken you hours."

"Whaea." The woman touched her sternum. "Call me Aunty, Hana. It's okay, I feel your hesitation."

Hana swallowed. "You've gone to a heap of trouble, Whaea." Her brow furrowed. "I didn't mean to inconvenience you."

Whaea shook her head. "No trouble, dear. I love weaving and it's good to have a willing student." She inclined her hand towards a seat and Hana slumped into it.

"I don't know about willing." She sighed. "It's like ballroom dancing. Looks awesome until I get on the floor and then remember my two left feet."

Whaea put her head back and laughed. Her smiling lips brought forth a joyous, tinkling sound. "You're not peaceful and the flax knows it. We don't push the flax into a shape, we ask it to bend into something useful or decorative. It's the same in life, Hana. Pushing and shoving creates ugliness, not beauty." Her crinkled fingers rested over Hana's. "First, we say an inoi, a prayer to ask God to bless the work of our hands and to thank him for his provision of the haraheke flax for our use."

Hana heaved a sigh of relief. "Finally, something I understand." She flipped her hand to clasp the old woman's, feeling hope for the first time.

"Te harakeke, te korari, he taonga whakarere iho. O te rangi. O te whenua. O nga tupuna homai he oranga mo matou tihei mauri ora. Āmene." Whaea squeezed her fingers as Hana repeated the amen. "The plucking of the flax is a treasure given to our ancestors. It's a blessing as are all things containing the breath of life. We promise to look after it and it will look after us." Her dark eyes stripped all fear from Hana's heart and she felt herself relax. Her gaze caressed the even strips of flax, already prepared for weaving. Vibrant green, blue and red lengths hung together like a rainbow and the niggle of doubt began again in the back of her mind, threatening to ruin the moment. Whaea kept hold of her fingers and she fought the urge to get up and run away. The woman's kindness radiated through her as though pulled from a deeper source of humanity than she'd ever accessed. Hana floundered.

"I'll mess it up," she whispered. "I'll take those lovely pieces and make something ugly that nobody will want."

Whaea replied with a smile. "Are we speaking about weaving, or something else?" she asked.

Hana's head shot up and she inhaled. Something clicked in her mind and nothing but honesty would do. "I don't know," she breathed.

Whaea gave her fingers a final squeeze and let go. Hana looked down at her hand as though feeling the warmth recede. "No matter." Whaea picked up the blue strips and placed them in front of Hana. "We'll find out, won't we?"

It took Hana two hours just to make the base of her first proper basket. Using twenty-four thin strips, she wove first one way and then the other until a perfect square formed beneath her fingers. Whaea wove her own masterpiece next to her, leaning across to direct Hana's fumbling into a decent example of raranga. She demonstrated how to use clothes pegs and hair clips to hold the leaves in place. An alarm sounded in Hana's pocket as her phone reminded her of the roster for Kane and her place on it. "Wow! That went quick." She held up her neat square and pursed her lips at the flush of pride which coursed through her. "I hate to admit it, but I'm enjoying this."

Whaea chuckled, a low, mischievous sound. "It's just patience, Hana. And a ready heart. We'll get you there. The others would be here but they're finishing the casket for Kane."

Hana swallowed. "Others? Casket?"

Whaea nodded. "Yes. The weavers in our little township get together once a week. We're harmless." She raised an eyebrow. "Our skills become necessary at a time like this. Logan allowed us to collect flax from the slopes below Reuben's old property. My husband remembers Kane's mother planting them. It's a way of enfolding him with loving arms in death. We all need that."

Hana nodded, unable to conjure up the right words in response. She sensed he'd needed it in life too and hoped he'd found it with Caroline. Her fingers worked the flax into neat woven lines and she relaxed. They didn't speak for a long while as though sound might disturb the gentle peace invoked by the rustling of the moving leaves as they encouraged them into submission.

"So, this will be a rourou?" Hana whispered the traditional Māori name and Whaea nodded.

"That's right. A rourou was woven to hold food and when you've done that one, I'll teach you to make a pūtea, which is a special basket used for gifts."

"Kete." Hana said the word for basket and Whaea patted her fingers.

"Now, you have somewhere to be, so I'll put the flax in the freezer for next time. Then it'll stay malleable and won't dry out before we can finish."

Hana lifted her fingers and twinkled them in front of her face. "I'll just wash my hands at the sink." She rose and then paused. "Will you have time one day to teach me how to prepare the flax? Will always does it before he gives it to me. I think it might help."

Whaea rose and stepped into the kitchen to run the water until it warmed. "It does help. It's a process from start to finish and every small decision you put into it comes out in the beauty of the basket. It's a relationship. The finished kete is a snapshot of something much bigger, just like a photograph is only a momentary reflection of a life." She moved away so Hana could spread soap over her fingers and run them under the tap. "Don't try so hard, Hana." She said the last words in a whisper and Hana pursed her lips and nodded. The wisdom of it touched her soul deeper than she anticipated and little pricks of pain began in her heart as the wires holding it together unravelled. She sighed, accepting the towel from Whaea's outstretched hand.

"It's the cost of marrying Logan Du Rose," she admitted. "I feel there's so much against me."

"Like what?" Whaea's question surprised her and she fumbled for the truth, instead of the usual words she used to gloss over it.

"Other women stare at him because he's beautiful. They size me up as though wondering if they can move me aside and it makes me afraid. I can't speak his language or do any of the things he feels passionate about and I get myself into a mess trying. He's clever and I'm not. People listen when he speaks and my squeaks get lost in the noise."

"You don't feel worthy." Whaea's words hit like a body blow and Hana jerked backwards. The urge to run returned. Whaea steadied her with an arm around her shoulders. Her smile never faltered. "You don't see what we see, Hana Du Rose. We see a formidable woman with the ability to make a very unhappy man wear a smile on his face. The power of life or death rests in your hands and you don't even know it. You defend your tāne emotionally and physically." She raised an eyebrow and it soared above the bifocals resting over her regal nose. "I've heard the rumours, Hana. There are as many legends about you as there are of those who went before you. No woman in this town would dare come between you and Logan. They'd fear what you would do to them." Her hand reached up to stroke Hana's cheek and her fingers felt warm, the scent of flax sap rising up to dull her fears. Whaea moved her fingers and they coasted across the uneven scar on Hana's left wrist. It didn't hurt, but she fought the need to pull back, anyway. "You would die for him and he knows it. We all know it. Stop doubting your place, Hana. I can teach you tikanga and kawa, but I can't teach you what you already possess. You have a clear path. Walk in it."

She dropped her hand and shock radiated through Hana's body. Her brain scrabbled for clarity, unable to process the wisdom Whaea offered. As the older woman turned towards the door, Hana lifted the envelope of cash from her back pocket and left it on the counter near the kettle. The koha intended to compensate Whaea for her time collecting the flax, preparing it and teaching Hana, seemed redundant in the light of the other knowledge she had imparted. Hana left the envelope anyway and followed her to the door.

Whaea waited for Hana to pull on her boots before speaking. "How many weeks until the summer fair?" she asked.

Hana rolled her eyes. "Two weeks for me to create something passable." She drew her car keys from her jeans pocket and shrugged.

Whaea cocked her head. "Is that the only reason you're doing this?" The question sounded loaded.

Hana seemed to recede before her perception. "No," she admitted. "I feel judged because I'm a white English girl with no understanding of my husband's culture. I can't connect here and I need to."

"Need to?" Whaea didn't give up, forcing Hana to question her own motives and she felt exposed and stripped bare.

"Want to." She whispered the words and turned away.

Whaea stood on her porch and watched Hana walk towards the gate. "Same time tomorrow," she called. By the time Hana turned, the door had clicked shut. Whaea gave her no opportunity to decline, trapping her into something she'd started but now doubted she could finish.

Hana climbed into the truck and her fingers fluttered over the lead weight in her chest. "What the hell just happened?" she whispered to her ashen reflection in the rear-view mirror.

24

Settling a Score

The marae buzzed with activity as a group swept the stairs and tidied the dining hall ready for the upcoming funeral. Hana halted on the steps of the wharenui, remembering Logan's careful instructions to head straight to the sleeping house and not eat until afterwards. He'd confiscated her toast that morning and her stomach growled. "Why me?" she murmured to herself as she pulled off her boots and stowed them next to a pair of men's shoes.

The door creaked with the pressure of Hana's fingers and she stepped inside the room. A vaulted ceiling soared overhead, every post and exposed beam carved with images of faces. Hana promised herself she wouldn't stare at the figure representing Logan's great great grandfather as it presided over the room from a beam to her right. She failed and her cheeks flushed at the sight of the three fingered figure clutching an oversized erect penis. "Yep, that's about right," she breathed. His eyes formed from paua shell glittered in the light coming through high windows, reminding her of the grey Du Rose irises. The chief had married into the family and allowed his grey-eyed wife to keep her French surname. The smirk on the wide face revealed the root of Logan's arrogance.

"Hana." The whispered voice made Hana jump and she clapped a hand over her mouth to stop her crying out. Whaea's husband walked from the other end of the room with a smile on his lips. Rotund and jolly, he'd headed the marae for decades and Hana relaxed. She'd dreaded being alone with Kane.

"Hi," she whispered back. Her gaze flicked to a trestle table set up at the end. Bright green kawakawa wreaths lay piled up either side, but the table remained empty. "Oh," she said and her brow furrowed. "I'm rostered to sit with Kane."

"He'll be here soon," the kaumātua said. His voice remained soft and reverend. "The women worked through the night to make his casket and they're dressing him now."

Hana swallowed. "Your wife helped them?"

"Yes. She took a break this morning as she had a prior arrangement."

Guilt prickled up Hana's spine. The old woman stayed up all night and then helped her. She pursed her lips and nursed admiration and gratitude within her chest. "Did his wife arrive yet?" she whispered instead.

The kaumātua shook his head. "We haven't heard from her but she has a long way to travel. I imagine she'll get here later today. Come." He took her hand and led her to the trestle table. Bunches of flowers covered chairs stacked nearby. "Let's get this ready," he said with a smile. "My wife will finish the display when she arrives in a couple of hours."

"She's coming here?" Surprise leaked through Hana's voice. "After weaving all night?"

"Yes." The old man bent his large body in half to retrieve a fallen rose. The deep red petals clashed with the scruffy blue carpet. "She's the kuia karanga. It's expected."

Hana jabbed a finger towards the main door. "Miriam and Reuben stayed outside on the porch. I assumed we'd be there." She'd hoped. Out in the open with the blue sky and the mountain for reference. Out in the open where she didn't need to think of anything but escaping in one hour and fifty-seven minutes.

"There's a storm coming." The kaumātua stood up, dangling a bunch of wild daisies in his hand. "We need the rain, but they forecast high winds. It's no fun to sit outside when it's like that." Hana cringed, wondering how much fun anyone could have with a body in the middle of their conversation. She gulped and wished herself elsewhere. Anywhere but there. The old man thrust a vase and a bunch of roses into her hands. "There's a tap on the wall outside. I'm sure you can arrange these with more dignity than I'll manage." His brow furrowed at Hana's blank expression and he reached to touch her forearm. "I know this seems strange. You'd just given birth when Logan's parents died which exempted you from the preparations. And you didn't attend Jack's." Hana hissed through her teeth at the mention of his name and the fingers of her right hand gripped the rose stems so hard the thorns pressed into her fingers. The kaumātua withdrew his hand, a spark of understanding in his dark irises. He gave a nod as though satisfied.

Hana's body turned with the finesse of a plank of wood. Her spine felt locked in an upright position. She fumbled with the door handle and navigated her bundle onto the porch before allowing herself to breathe. "You can do this," she coached herself under her breath. She tipped her wrist to glance at her watch and sighed. "One hour and fifty-five minutes and you're done."

Hana spent the next half an hour creating a decent floral display at either end of the empty trestle table. The kaumātua popped back, struggling with a cardboard box filled with empty frames. He set it on the carpet at Hana's feet. "I asked our community for photographs," he said. Bending, he sifted through the box until his fingers pulled out a wad of paper. "I got one of the teenagers to photocopy the ones of Kane. I knew the fire took all Reuben's family copies."

Hana held her breath as he sifted through the papers and laid them on the table. Her fingers itched to touch the second-hand snapshots of Du Rose history. The kaumātua chuckled at the sparkle in her eyes. "Please may I, Sir?" she whispered.

He shook his head and disappointment drifted across Hana's face. She dropped her arms to her sides. The kaumātua raised his hand. "I meant don't call me Sir," he said. He took her right hand and pulled her towards the table. Then he patted the photos. "Call me Matua kēkē. It means Uncle. It's what everyone calls me."

Hana nodded, her gaze not leaving the table. "Thank you," she said. But the photographs had captured her interest and she wanted to see them more than she believed possible.

"These are generic frames." Matua kēkē pointed to the box. "Put the copies in them where you can and then we'll take them out after the tangihanga."

Hana nodded and stepped forward, an insatiable hunger already devouring the historical feast on the table. "Thank you, Uncle." She didn't notice when the kaumātua left and forgot about the imminent arrival of a man she'd detested in life and feared in death. Reaching for the first of the black and white copies, Hana prepared to step back in time.

Shared by people from the local township, the photographs showed more than just Kane. They told the story of a community, stretching as far back as the late 1960s. Hana recognised faces she knew and experienced a strange sense of belonging as she recalled their names. Some of them she only knew through photographs. They looked younger, but their features had remained the same. "Oh my!" she exclaimed. Her fingers stroked a grainy black-and-white image featuring a dark haired woman, her hair pulled back in a severe bun. Phoenix Du Rose smiled at the person behind the camera and held a small boy on her hip. The child wore just a pair of shorts and nestled against her collarbone. A taller boy with tousled hair stood next to them. He'd kept his shirt on although unbuttoned, it flapped loose in the grip of the breeze which moved Phoenix's heavy skirt. His gaze stared off to the left. The photocopy had captured the white rim around the original and Hana narrowed her eyes and angled the paper to read the words scrawled there. "Reuben's boys," she whispered. The copier had slashed the location written beneath, halving the words and making them difficult to read. "Cattle market?" Hana mused. She ached to hold the original photograph and turn it over in her hands, suspecting it contained clues on the other side. "We need a photo amnesty," she sighed with a shake of her head. "We could copy them for the museum." She reached into her jeans pocket for her phone, leafing through the photographs on the table.

"What now?" Will sounded sharp and Hana released a slow groan.

"Please be nice to me," she grumbled. "I'm waiting for Kane to arrive."

"Ah. That's where you are." Will's tone lost some of its bite. "Then why are you ringing me?"

"I'm looking at an absolute treasure trove of photographs." Hana's index finger sifted through the photocopies. "I think we should hold a bring-and-scan event. What do you think? I can ask Logan if we can host something at the hotel. A glass of wine and a canapé in exchange for lending us their photos for long enough to scan them."

Will released a sound like a blustering wind. "You can't have artifacts near food and drink!" His voice rose.

Hana sighed. "We won't do it in the museum, Will! I'll ask Logan if we can borrow one of the conference rooms." She bit her lip and leaned closer to examine an image of the original Anglican Church. "Oh, wow!" she exclaimed. "I didn't think there were any photographs of St Michael's."

"St Michael's?" A hunger crept into Will's gravelly tones. "I've heard about the original building from Alfred. He said it had a weird spire that leaned at an angle until the whole church burned down one summer."

Hana nodded and then realised he couldn't see her. His rasping breaths sounded amplified through the phone. She smiled, knowing she'd hooked him. "Yeah. It leaned over like a banana. It's quite bizarre."

"Can you get a copy?" Will sounded desperate. "It's the era I'm missing for the collection."

"I can't today." Hana glanced towards the door. "Probably not appropriate. I'm creating a display for when Kane arrives."

Will tutted and Hana imagined him staring at the ceiling for a solution. There wasn't one and she smirked. "Okay. I'll talk to Logan." Will blew out an exasperated breath. "Now, get off the phone, I'm busy." He disconnected the call and Hana released a wicked giggle. It felt good to have the upper hand for once.

As she shoved her phone back into her jeans, another photograph captured her interest. An image of a smiling Logan stood with a rugby ball between his bare feet. Hana lifted the photocopy from the table and shook her head. "He played rugby?" she breathed. "You kept that quiet my darling." Peering closer identified the location as the marae, the picture taken on the grass in front of the wharenui. Hana glanced back at the door again. He'd stood thirty metres from her current location. The photographer had scrawled a date on the bottom right-hand corner in a slanted hand. *July 1967*. Hana's head jerked back in surprise. Logan wasn't born until 1970. She lifted the paper until it almost touched the end of her nose.

The boy's lips looked less full and a cow lick at the front of his head made his hair stick up at the fringe. "Kane?" Hana dropped the picture onto the table and swallowed. He looked so much like the photos of Logan in the museum. She'd liberated them from a rusty biscuit tin in Alfred's apartment.

Hana closed her eyes and released a ragged breath. The photograph showed her who Kane could have been. The sunny, smiling eyes and the mischievous grin reflected hope and promise. It never occurred to her that the spiteful man who'd maimed Logan and ruined Tama's childhood might have once possessed a different future. "You did this." Hana opened her eyes and met those of Phoenix Du Rose in the other photograph. The matriarch stared back, her influence remaining long after her death. She had prophesied in a moment of desperation that the Du Rose sons would be the ruin of the family. Hana shook her head. "You started it." She raised her voice and the silence of the wharenui seemed to mute the volume. "Not the sons, but the daughters. These boys are the victims of the women's poor judgment." The weight of the Du Rose family's sins hung over her head. Phoenix and Jack, Antoinette and the blond drover, Miriam and Reuben. They all shared responsibility for tainting the generations who followed their awful example. In that moment she hated them.

Anger burgeoned in Hana's soul and she set to work, finding scissors in the box and slicing the photos to fit the assorted frames. She built a monument of smiling, happy images filled with hope, her heart heavy with the knowledge of the rottenness which lay beneath. Kane stopped being a monster somewhere between the first snip of the scissors and the last click of the frame which encased his innocence. And Hana honoured her brother-in-law for the first and last time.

25

One Fall too Far

Kane arrived with quiet reverence, carried by four strong undertakers. They lifted him from the hearse, revealing an intricate flax casket. Hana remained barefoot in the background, hiding on the porch of the dining hall. A woman's voice wavered in the still air, the sound eerie and filled with the power of tradition. The lilting words of the karanga sounded haunting, delivered by Whaea. Hana stayed in the shadows, her emotions mixed and confusing. Her fingers gripped the rust red pillar Logan painted with Tama the year before and she grounded herself in the memory of his wide brush strokes. The photos had shown her a different view of Kane. A sunny child with the world at his feet, a succession of selfish adults robbed him of hope and security.

"Haere mai, haere mai," the kuia urged in her wavering voice. She welcomed home a lost son. *Come to me, come to me.* Hana watched as the undertakers filed past on unhurried steps. It seemed wrong to imagine Kane's once powerful, hate filled body squashed into the flax casket which tugged at the men's muscles and bowed their spines. A stretcher supported the body and Hana watched with morbid curiosity as they settled him on the table near her makeshift display. Gentle hands slid him from stretcher to table with exaggerated care and smoothed the weave covering his body. The harakeke casket resembled a sleeping bag, leaving only Kane's face on view. Hana's heart clenched at the sight of his profile. The stillness and peaceful aura of death had shaped it into a mirror image of Logan's.

"Hana?" Uncle called her forward, dispelling her faint hope he'd forgotten her. He jerked his head towards the wharenui and gave her a sad smile. "Come," he said and held out his hand. His palm felt calloused as she placed her fingers into it. Her feet shuffled as though encased in concrete and he urged her forward into the dark embrace of the sleeping house. Uncle squeezed her hand and patted her shoulder, pulling her towards the table. Every nerve in her body resisted. "The women did a beautiful work," he whispered. "The waka kawe is stunning." His eyes twinkled with an emotion Hana couldn't name. "Will you help them make mine?" he whispered and she withdrew her hand in horror. Her gaze darted towards the intricate casket and then back to the expression of sincerity on his face. She sensed he bestowed a great honour on her head but didn't know how to answer. He patted her shoulder. "Death is a stepping stone for us, Hana. You'll understand one day."

The undertaker nodded to Uncle and withdrew from the room behind his men. Uncle turned to follow them and Hana felt terror snake through her heart at the prospect of being abandoned with Kane. In life the thought seemed ridiculous. In death it represented an obstacle too great to endure. "The whānau members are on their way," Uncle whispered in her ear, reading her anxiety through the wideness of her eyes. "Then this place will explode with life and voices. It will turn out okay, Hana."

She nodded, his reassurance offering her less comfort than he intended. The room emptied and the sound of hushed male voices moved away, the door shutting behind them with a dull thud. Hana held her breath and moved forward. With great reluctance, she sat in the chair to Kane's right, keeping her head bowed so she didn't have to look at him. Her fingers reached out to admire the neat basketwork. She traced the line of the weave, whispering under her breath, "Over, under, over, under." She sensed the ara in the strong lines, the weave which travelled left catching her eye. For a moment it seemed obvious but when she blinked, it disappeared into the pattern again. Hana sighed and glanced at her watch. "Fifty minutes," she whispered. "I'm sure I'm the last person you wanted with you. Fifty more minutes and then you'll never have to put up with me again." The finality of her statement hit her and she gasped. "Not that I wanted you dead or anything," she admitted.

She lasted forty-three more minutes of sitting in the chair before her legs complained and her backside formed the shape of the uncomfortable wooden seat. Hana stared at the side of the casket and shook her head. "This is stupid," she breathed. "I can't make something as important as Uncle's casket. Why would he even ask me? I can't even make a basket!" She forced her rigid legs to stand and her feet to turn. The power of the pivotal moment hung in the air before her as she surveyed the women's work from above.

It looked as stunning as Uncle promised. The thin lengths of flax bent around Kane's still body to form a snug shroud which encased him from head to toe. His expression looked impassive, the eyes closed and a delicate dusting of makeup masking the bruising around his left eye. Hana held her breath. A neat white shirt collar poked from within the casket, the creases clean and crisp. A flood of emotion surprised her as she recognised the tie, a cream paisley pattern threaded through a bottle green fabric. She squeezed her eyes closed and pressed her fingers to her lips. "Logan gave you his tie," she whispered. "He gave you his tie and let the women collect flax from the mountain, so you'd be close to your parents." She gulped as a lump rose into her throat and choked her. "Oh, Kane." Her voice broke. "It could have been so different between you."

She remembered the night Reuben died and the look on Kane's face as he'd sought Logan. He hadn't come looking for retribution, though it appeared that way at the time. He'd wanted his brother, seeking solidarity in a shared grief. Hana shook her head in dismay at the pattern of behaviour which always reared its ugly head. It had tainted another generation.

She forced herself to study Kane's pale face, desperate to comprehend the inner workings of a complicated Du Rose male who might hold clues for her understanding of Logan. The undertaker had performed miracles with the broken body, banishing the horror of the fall enough to allow the customary viewing. Kane Du Rose looked at peace for the first time in his life. Marriage to Caroline had worked for him. Fatherhood had turned him into an honest provider. Hana hadn't noticed the subtle differences when he gate-crashed their peaceful dinner because he'd dropped straight back into character. She saw them in death. His resemblance to Logan pained her as though age accentuated the reality of severed relationships and brothers divided. The men were an example of genetics defying humanity's deceit.

Hana shook her head. "All you had to do was ask," she whispered. The cry of her husband's heart seemed to travel across the mountain to her. She sensed him riding through the wide paddocks checking the stock and shook her head. "He would've accepted you if you'd said different words that night, not just picked up the battle where you left off. You're blood. Blood calls to blood. That's what he says, Kane." Hana felt her chest tighten and the fingers of her right hand touched the pacemaker beneath her collarbone. Then they dropped to clasp the healed wound over her left wrist. "What did you want from us, Kane?" she demanded. Her voice rose above a whisper. "Why did you come back? Was it Wiri? Money? What did you want?"

Kane's corpse remained silent, frustrating Hana's ridiculous notion that she might at last find answers. She closed her eyes and stood there for a while, head bowed and shoulders slumped. The futility of it all washed over her like the breaking waves at Port Waikato which spent winter attacking the flimsy sea wall. He was as much a victim of his father's sins as Logan, perpetuating them through the next generation and a child who may never understand his complicated heritage. What did it matter? What did anything matter? All that hatred and bitterness leaked into the gravel after one crazy second of madness and drained away with the next rains.

Hana battled thoughts of Bodie and Libby. A blockage in her heart stopped her processing it further. She thought of her daughter-in-law's imminent misery and the disruption to her grandchildren. To tell or not to tell? Hana didn't know. And Logan. He wanted to sell up, she could sense it eating away at him. She realised she didn't want him to. The mountain and surrounding whenua had wrapped her in its embrace and trapped her as it once did him. She couldn't imagine herself raising the next generation anywhere else on earth. Her fingers reached forward as though to spite her and she rested her palm against the soft flax casket, feeling the stiffness of Kane's chest beneath. "We must do better than this," she whispered. "We need to. Logan's right. We borrow from our children. Look at the mess we've made of everything."

A sound disturbed her and Hana jumped as the kaumātua's wife touched her shoulder. "This is beautiful!" Whaea exclaimed. Her outstretched arm took in the flower arrangement and the photographs dotted in between. Her eyes widened in surprise as though Hana's meagre efforts could eclipse the beauty of the casket. "You're a credit to your husband."

"Thank you," Hana stammered. She glanced back at Kane's sleeping face and tried not to imprint her husband's image there instead. The threat rose like an evil spirit in her mind. "I don't know what to do next."

Whaea slipped her arm around Hana's shoulder. She gave her a squeeze. "I'm here now. You're free to leave," she whispered. Her black lips pressed against Hana's temple, the tattoo seeming to infuse her with courage. "You've done well, kōtiro. It's hard to take our place as the backbone of our family, our whānau. No one doubts you, Hana Du Rose. No one. You must remember that."

Hana nodded and emotion bubbled in her soul. It threatened to spill out through her eyes and she blinked, unable to speak. Acceptance soothed the ache in her heart like a balm. Hana gathered her courage and channelled it through her lips as she bent over the casket of her estranged brother-in-law and pressed a kiss to his cold forehead. "Goodbye Kane," she whispered. "I pray you find peace."

26

The Widening Gap

Logan spent the night at the marae and Hana didn't question him. But she drew the line at letting him take the children and they argued before he left.

"I grew up sleeping by caskets," he protested. "It's how we manage death, Hana. We don't fear it. Wiri should be there even if you won't let me take the others."

"No!" She shot a glance at the closed kitchen door and blanched. "Absolutely not." Giggles emanated from beyond it as Phoenix performed a song she'd learned at school. "It's not appropriate!"

Logan turned his face to the ceiling and closed his eyes. A pulse ticked in his neck and Hana held her breath. He said nothing, but the look of accusation and disappointment in his silent expression cut her to the bone. He slammed from the house and didn't return.

Hana got the children ready for school the next morning and tried to ignore the hollowed out feeling in her chest. The chasm between their cultures opened into an insurmountable void no matter what she did.

Phoenix trapped her fingers in the hinge to the shoe cupboard. Oblivious, Mac gave the door another shove, unaware of his sister's distress. With his head in the cupboard, even as a hearing child, he may not have heard her yelp and Hana allowed that thought to bring her comfort. He looked startled as she hauled him out and released the door, jabbing her finger towards a tearful Phoenix. His eyes widened and he gnawed his lower lip. His fingers moved fast to sign an apology.

Phoenix stood on a chair while Hana ran the cold tap over her fingers to numb the pain. Wiri packed his library bag on the kitchen table behind them. "Build a bridge and get over it," he remarked as Phoenix wiped her nose on her school jumper.

"I can't," Phoenix replied with a sniff. "I'm too little."

Wiri shook his head and slid the bag from the table. He'd borrowed an old Encyclopaedia Britannica from the school library and its weight stretched the seams on his bag and made him huff while carrying it. "Na, that's rubbish. Uncle Logan says bridge building is nothing to do with physical strength," he replied. He looked so sure of himself, Hana held her breath and willed the tears to dry before they fell. Kane's smile glimmered behind his son's eyes and the regrets lined up inside her chest cavity. Her efforts at building a bridge to Logan involved demolishing her husband's ready-made structures. She closed her eyes and swallowed. Logan was right. His culture managed death far better than hers and she'd overridden his desires. She saw how her refusal to face Jack's demise had hindered Logan's healing. The marae would fill with family and their offspring as they visited to pay their respects to Kane. Her children should be among them. Hana swallowed. "You don't have to go to school today," she said, pursing her lips. "Papa's at the marae with Uncle Kane. If you'd rather go there, I'll drop you off. You must promise to stick close to him though. I don't want you running around creating mayhem."

"Mayhem." Phoenix performed a disgusting sniff which originated from her boots and nodded. Hana grimaced and tapped her daughter's bare leg.

"That's not ladylike. Don't do it."

"Can I do it then?" Wiri copied her and Hana felt nausea bubble into her throat at the sound of hawking. "I'm not a lady."

"Nobody does it!" Hana snapped. "Do you want to go or don't you?"

"Yes please." Phoenix nodded. "I do." Her gaze strayed to Wiri and disappointment stampeded across her face as he gave a definitive shake of his dark head.

"No thanks. I'll go to the tangi because I have to, but I don't want to go to anything else."

Hana nodded. An inexplicable surge of relief prickled along her spine and she questioned her own motives. She loved Wiremu Du Rose. Was her gratitude at not having to share him with a dead man selfish? She pressed a kiss to Phoenix's sore fingers and helped her off the chair. "Let's get a wriggle on then. I'll drop Phoe at the marae first and then head into town."

"Is Macky coming with me?" Phoenix demanded. She snuggled into Hana's shoulder, sending a waft of her scent into her mother's nostrils. Hana closed her eyes and inhaled, smelling Logan's familiar aftershave where he must have kissed her upturned forehead before leaving. He'd slammed out on Hana but not his daughter.

"No." Hana shook her head and her red ponytail tapped Phoenix's shoulder. "He won't understand what's happening. He'll get bored."

Phoenix shrugged. "Okay. Please will you tell my teacher why I'm not there?"

"Yep." Hana pursed her lips and contemplated her forthcoming conversation with a woman who'd caved under duress. So far, Bernice had been silent on the Holly-issue. Hana felt for her usual vein of compassion and discovered it missing. The teacher was trapped between a sense of duty and a practical need for funds, but no compromise existed for Hana concerning her children's safety. She leaned down and pressed a kiss against Phoenix's head and drank in the vicarious contact with her husband. "Come on," she said. "Hurry up."

The marae car park buzzed with activity and the gates stood wide open. Logan's motorbike sat alone on a nearby stretch of grass and Mac jabbed an index finger at it and beamed up at Hana with excitement in his eyes. Wiri sulked in the truck, wriggling in the passenger seat in Hana's peripheral vision. She walked across the gravel car park, holding her children's hands and picking her way through the parked cars. Her shoulders tensed as she prepared to once again reach across the chasm into her husband's culture.

"Tēna koe. Kia ora." Uncle greeted her at the gate, his car keys jangling in his hand. *There you are. Be well.* He leaned in and placed a kiss on her cheek. Hana smiled at his greeting and tried to ignore the three carved faces staring at her from the covered porch. Their red painted tongues and paua shell eyes seemed to judge her with less harshness than she did herself.

"Phoenix wants to stay with Logan today." Her voice caught as she swallowed. "If it's okay with you."

"It sure is." Uncle grinned and held out a hand to Phoenix. "You can help me set up the wharekai. I borrowed extra cutlery from the church for our guests." Phoenix transferred her hand from Hana's to Uncle's without a backward glance and Hana's heart clenched. "She has her lunch in the backpack." She tapped the bag slung over Phoenix's shoulder. "I'll just find Logan and tell him she's here."

Uncle nodded. "He's eating breakfast. He slept by Kane all night."

"Thanks." Hana fixed a wooden smile onto her face and let her footsteps carry her towards the wharekai, the huge dining hall which formed the heart of the marae and its community's hospitality. Mac trotted alongside, his eyelids blinking against the bright sunlight. He clutched a tiny metal car in his right hand. It looked old and faded, like something Alfred had dug out for him. He'd taken his sandals off in the truck and skipped across the gravel as though it didn't hurt him. Free spirited and silent, he channelled the irrepressible innocence and invincibility of Kiwi children.

Hana kicked off her boots on the deck of the wharekai and took a fortifying breath. She squeaked as a hand snaked around her waist and pulled her back from the doorway. Logan's lips brushed the underside of her jaw from behind. "Hey." He sounded tired and Hana relaxed.

"I thought you were mad at me." She winced at the pique in her voice.

"Yeah, I was." Logan sighed. His lips curved into a smile. "But I can't stay mad at you, Hana." The tension in her spine eased as he encircled her and spun her to face him. His right knee hooked around Mac's small form and tugged him into the embrace. Mac wavered before he slid a soft palm along Logan's thigh and hooked his tiny fingers into his father's front pocket. He laid his cheek against Logan's leg and fixed his gaze on Phoenix as she skipped back through the gate. The toy car turned over and over in his fingers.

Logan's gaze moved over the cut on Hana's cheek. She'd filled the healing gaps in the skin with foundation but felt Logan's assessment laying it bare. An image of Jack's Jeep rose to haunt her. Jack. Always Jack.

"Hey, Papa!" Phoenix shouted across the meeting ground. A shopping bag filled with clanking cutlery dangled over her right wrist, making her sound like a marching band. "I'm helping Matua kēkē."

"Awesome!" Logan's face broke into a grin and his grip tightened around Hana's waist. His grey-eyed gaze settled over hers, but the grit coloured irises softened. "Thank you," he whispered. His right hand ruffled Mac's red curls. "I'll keep them with me." Phoenix clanked closer and gave her parents a beatific smile before bending to loosen her shoes. Uncle followed her onto the porch with a cardboard box gripped in his hands. He slipped off his shoes and the pair disappeared through the wide front door.

Maori warriors and chiefs watched with carved faces as Hana battled with herself. Her words stuck in her throat. She wanted to correct Logan and extract her vulnerable son but having reclaimed the lost ground between them she didn't know how. Logan placed a soft kiss against her temple and she saw the dark circles lingering beneath his eyes.

"I need to run some errands," she whispered. "Then I'll come back for the children. If you need me sooner just text."

"What errands?" Logan's eyes flashed and Hana chose her words with care.

"I fetched some gear for Toby. I promised to check if he had any other jobs I could do while he's a man and a vehicle down." The lie wrapped around her tongue and almost choked her.

Logan studied her for a moment too long and then released her. "Okay. We'll be fine. The cousins arrived in the night with all their kids. They're just eating breakfast." Hana's mind performed somersaults. She wondered if the label included Caroline and her child too. Jealousy surged and she tamped it down with an effort just as Logan's eyes narrowed. "Where's Wiri?"

"I offered, but he doesn't want to come, Logan. We shouldn't force him."

Logan's jaw clenched. "You know why he should be here. He'll regret it one day."

Hana sighed, the sound filled with sadness, confusion and exasperation. It emerged as a hiss. "He promised to come to the tangihanga tomorrow. I'm not pushing him and I don't want you to either."

Logan shrugged. With his own children secured in his care he cut his losses. "Okay. Fair enough." He dropped another kiss on her temple and stood back, dragging the clinging Mac with him. The action looked effortless as he lifted his son and sat him on his hip. "Have a good day," he said.

Hana watched Logan's broad shoulders flex as he skipped down the steps, his boots clicking across the wood. He stopped before making the turn towards the dining hall and faced her. "This is your marae too, Hana," he said. "Come back later."

Hana seethed as her husband took the stairs up to the wharenui in a single stride. He kicked off his boots on the porch and disappeared inside. Countless unspoken swearwords railed inside her head and she pressed her fingers against her lips to hold them in as her son faced his first corpse without her assurance. Logan's extension of welcome acted as a reprimand. She'd sat next to Kane, her inclusion in the rota both painful and alien. She'd delivered her children and put aside her concerns about their emotional welfare to bow to his greater experience. It wasn't enough. Nothing she did would ever close the gap. It would yawn between them like a beacon of their differences. "Bloody hell!" she hissed at the empty porch. "And bollocks to match!"

Hana chased her boots around the porch and stamped back to the truck. Her right hand felt empty without Mac's fingers clutching hers. She found Wiri sitting in the passenger seat with the dashcam in pieces in his lap. "What did you do?" she groaned. "I left you for five minutes!"

"Ten actually." Wiri fiddled with the camera's innards and clicked the back on the casing. "And you lost a kid."

"I didn't lose him." Hana fired the engine and gravel sprayed behind them as she stamped on the gas pedal. "Get your seatbelt on. And put that camera back."

Wiri pursed his lips and the light went out above the speedometer as his seatbelt clicked shut. "You went in with two kids and meant to only leave one. Did the taniwha keep Macky?"

"No!" Hana snapped. "There's no such thing as a water dragon. It's a myth."

Wiri blew a raspberry. "The word also means chief. I meant did Uncle Logan keep him?"

Hana nodded and grimaced at Wiri's reference. "Yes. He'll text if they get bored and need picking up."

"He won't text." The finality of Wiri's statement stabbed Hana's heart. He was right and so was Sam. Perhaps she needed Mac more than he needed her. Logan wouldn't text her to retrieve her children and she'd backed herself into a lonely corner.

Wiri fixed the camera back together and waited until she parked to mount it back on the windscreen. "There's no SIM card. That's why it won't work."

"What? Where did it go?"

"Dunno."

Feeling mentally drained already, Hana visited the school receptionist and informed her of Phoenix's absence and the reason behind it. She asked to see Bernice. "I've checked the classroom and she isn't there. Is it possible to make an appointment?"

"No." The receptionist shook her head. "It's parents' evening soon. If it's urgent, you can email her." She didn't look up as she tapped notes into a computer program.

Wiri wandered away after accepting the obligatory kiss from Hana. A growing gaggle of girls followed behind him, swelling in numbers with every extra metre Wiri covered. They giggled and whispered in undertones, desperate to catch his attention and already bowled over by the familiar Du Rose magnetism. Confident and oblivious, he bounced his football on the smooth concrete of the playground and had already gathered another six boys for a game before Hana turned to leave.

"Bloody bollocks!" she hissed, spinning away and liking the sound of the rude words on her tongue.

"Oh, wow! Gosh!" Libby held onto her forearms as Hana cannoned into her. "Bad day already?" she asked.

Hana's chest hitched and she fought the urge to scream into the other woman's face. "Something like that!" she snapped. She disengaged her arms and forced a weak smile onto her lips, knowing it wouldn't fool Libby. But Kane's death and her issues with Logan consumed all her available energy and Hana knew she'd need to deal with Libby and Bodie's affair another time.

"Are you avoiding me?" Libby cocked her head to study Hana's hostile expression and took a step backwards. "I've been texting you. It must be crazy up at the hotel with the cops and everything." She paused. "I'm happy to go for coffee. Whatever helps." Libby swallowed as an uncharacteristic awkwardness overtook her. She pursed her lips and waited.

Hana inhaled. "Not coffee at your place then?" Her jaw flexed and the skin pulled taut across her cheeks.

"Not at the moment." Libby licked her lips. "The coffee shop in town is great if we avoid the gossips. Mid-morning is a good time."

Hana's green eyes flashed. "That's a shame. I called at your house before school a couple of days ago. I wanted to talk, but you seemed busy."

"A couple of days ago?" Libby frowned and Hana watched as she sifted through a range of calendar appointments. Then her lips pursed and a pink hue rose up her neck and into her cheeks, leaving blotches of colour in its wake. She did the maths and Hana saw guilt in her eyes.

Hana spun on her heel and stamped away. Misery and fury pressed down on her shoulders like a lead shawl.

27

Ara - a Path, a Way, a Line of Weaving

Hana raised a hand to knock on the front door and gasped in shock as it disappeared before she'd readied a suitable expression. She felt as though her face screamed my-son's-having-an-affair-with-my-friend, but Whaea stood in the gap with a broad smile stretching her lips from ear to ear. "Welcome," she said before stepping aside. Hana made a strangled noise which emerged as a mewl and kicked her boots off on the porch. The sound of female voices and loudly spoken Te Reo stopped her in her tracks. She almost hadn't come, her mood indicating she wouldn't find her ara today. The thought of meeting new people filled her with misgiving. It wouldn't take a genius to spot the gaping holes in her enforced calm.

"I'm sorry," she breathed. "You're busy. I'll come back."

Whaea snatched at her forearm as Hana forced her feet into reverse. "Oh no you don't!" Her tone held the upward lilt of a laugh. "But an impressive attempt to escape. I told them you'd bolt."

"Told who?" Hana's voice wavered as the older woman towed her over the threshold and closed the front door behind her to bar her exit.

"The flax weaving group." Whaea responded to the terrified widening of Hana's eyes and maintained a grip on her forearm.

"Oh, I'm not ready for that." Hana tugged on her arm, finding her opponent's fingers surprisingly strong. She leaned closer. "I'm rubbish at this. I'm not having a good day and I won't find my ara."

"Cut it out, Hana," Whaea whispered. "We're helping you find it today, even if it kills us. It's not missing my dear. Everything you need is in here." She tapped Hana's chest and ignored the dismayed whimper she released.

Hana's feet followed her host through the lounge and under the archway into the dining room. It felt as though she left her brain on the doormat to wait for her. The scent of flax sap rose up as a heady fog of earthiness. Long stalks covered the table, sideboard and parts of the floor. Two women knelt on the carpet and two more sat on chairs leaning forward to watch the drama unfolding on a large blue tarpaulin.

"I got it!" one shouted. She raised her arm in victory and the slender legs of a brown cockroach waved from between her fingers. Hana stood back to watch with a shudder as the woman jogged past her and disappeared through a back door set into the wall of the kitchen.

"I hate those little buggers." The woman in the chair nearest Hana gave her a sideways look and her many chins swung backwards and forwards with the action. "Kia ora," she said. Forcing her flaccid body into a stoop, she shuffled towards Hana and puckered her lips. Hana's eyes widened, but she bowed her head to accept the gentle kiss the woman placed on her cheek. "Ko Rui ahau. Nice to meet you."

"Hi." Hana replied in English, cursing herself for not repeating the simple greeting. She compounded her misery by raising her free hand and performing a ridiculous little wave. "I'm Hana."

"I know who youse are," Rui replied, but the retort held nothing more than a statement of fact.

"Let me introduce you properly." Whaea gripped Hana's arm as though sensing her desire to run away screaming. Hana suspected she wore incompetency on her face like a tattoo. Her heart rate hiked and Whaea's grip prevented her seeking reassurance by running the fingers of her right hand across the raised skin over her pacemaker. It was a bad habit, but something in her subconscious ached to double check its presence. It seemed the only thing in her life right then which worked for her alone. No agenda. No expectations of a return on investment. The irony struck her soul.

Denied her usual expression of fear, Hana fidgeted and her left hand fumbled with the side seam of her jeans. "This is Hana, ladies," Whaea said. She used an open palm to name the women one by one. "This is Kora. She's on drying duty." Whaea smiled at the slender woman still on her knees on the carpet. Kora held a tattered towel in her hand and smoothed it up and down the leaves. The action ceased as she rose to kiss Hana's cheek and then stepped back. Rui slumped onto her chair with a grunt. Whaea turned to the woman seated in the other chair. "And this is Betty. She's just finished making a baby basket for her granddaughter's first child."

Hana swallowed and it turned into a gulp. "Wow," she whispered like a pale echo. "Baby basket?"

Betty struggled to her feet on rickety legs and tottered around to Hana. Her palms felt soft against Hana's forearms as she clasped her before placing a soft kiss against her cheek. "Kia ora," Betty said. A deep and mischievous chuckle rocked her delicate body, incongruous and unexpected.

Whaea grinned. "We'll have you kitting out your house in no time. Baby baskets, table runners, shopping bags and a nice korowai for your husband's shoulders next time he speaks at the marae." She squeezed Hana's arm and then let go. The sudden lack of physical contact allowed the unwelcome sense of isolation to flood back.

Kora waved her dirty towel towards the back door. "That's Noelle who just ran outside with the cockroach," she said. "She's on the slug and bug patrol."

"Slug and bug patrol. Got it." Hana remained standing and Whaea nudged her in the spine.

"Sit down, Hana. I've taken your basket from the freezer and dampened it enough for you to continue." She turned and stepped towards the sink. "Chloe couldn't make it today, but she'll come next time. She's our local raranga harakeke expert. She supervised Kane's casket."

Hana acknowledged a frisson of relief at Chloe's absence. She didn't want to let herself down in front of an expert. Betty crooked a finger at her and patted the seat between her and Rui. "Sit here," she instructed. "Queenie said you struggled with finding your ara."

"Queenie?" Hana looked around for someone else and faltered. Who'd already inspected her dreadful handiwork and deemed her struggling?

"My nickname." Whaea appeared with Hana's basket wrapped in a wet tea towel. She placed it on the dining table and the stained plastic tarpaulin made crinkling sounds. "Betty will help you with the sides." She winked at Hana and moved away, the sound of running water and clattering crockery beginning as soon as she reached the kitchen.

Hana smoothed out the weave of her perfect square and tightened a few edges. Her fingers fiddled with the clothes pegs holding everything in place until she felt happy. Betty leaned across and stilled Hana's movements, her grip firm. "Let's say our karakia first," she said, her voice as soft as her palms. Hana bowed her head and the woman's words washed over her. The other women joined in, their prayer an edifying murmur of female voices. "Te harakeke, te korari, he taonga whakarere iho. O te rangi. O te whenua. O nga tupuna homai he oranga mo matou tihei mauri ora. Āmene."

Hana echoed their amen and paused, her gaze studying the neat flax square in front of her. "I'm going to mess it up," she said, her voice faltering. "I can just feel it."

"You won't." Betty sounded confident. "You'll find your ara and it will be amazing. Is this your first basket?"

Hana sighed. "Not my first attempt, no. I've started a few, but Will or the children always finish them."

Rui waggled her eyebrows. "They shouldn't. It won't help you."

"I've heard of an ara, but please can you explain it? Where do I find one?" Hana lowered her voice and leaned sideways. Noelle reappeared without the cockroach.

"Sorry, Hana." She halted next to her and bowed her head to kiss Hana's cheek. "Nice to meet you."

"Likewise." Hana's grin felt genuine. "You're braver than me picking up cockroaches. I get Logan to bug bomb the house every few months while I'm out. I'm never convinced Mac wouldn't eat one."

Noelle tittered and lowered herself back onto the floor. Her slender hands resumed teasing the lengths of flax through another towel. Her movements matched Kora's and they worked in unison as though performing a well-choreographed dance.

"This is an ara." Betty slid her basket in front of Hana. A neat weave had formed four sides of a shallow basket. It rounded at the corners and the remaining green lengths waved above it like corn stalks.

Hana peered at the basket and then shook her head. "I'm destined to have flax envy," she said with a defeated sigh.

Betty stirred the loose ends with a finger. "Look closer," she ordered. "As you weave, the flax strands poke up to the left and right in diagonals. When we want to cast off, we use everything which points right. The left strand forms our ara. The ara is always uppermost. See?" She prodded at the strands rising towards the left and Hana frowned. The pattern appeared to demystify before her eyes and she gave a shallow nod.

"I think I see it." Her gaze fell to her own square and her fingers itched to try with an enthusiasm she hadn't felt before. "Where do I start?"

Betty led her through a sequence which left Hana feeling as though she had far too many thumbs and not enough fingers. She'd assumed they'd begin at the corners, confused when they didn't. "It's not as strong," Betty assured her. "We form the corners along the lengths of our square, so the original corners help to form the sides of the basket. It just works."

"It's mental gymnastics." Hana paused to shove a peg into the last of her loose weaves and held onto the rest of her basket for dear life. "When do I find my ara?"

Betty chuckled and her olive face creased into a mass of wrinkles. "It will come," she promised. "Just follow the rules and it will come."

Hana sighed. "You sound like Logan. He's always telling me to chill out."

Rui snorted and her many chins wobbled. She shifted in her seat and it creaked beneath her weight. A bun sat on top of her dark head like a cherry crowning a muffin. Dark chocolate eyes completed the illusion of homeliness and comfort. "I'd need to hear that for myself," she snickered. "Because I can't imagine it."

"Maybe he's different at home." Betty frowned as she defended Hana's husband. "You only know what you hear."

Noelle rose with a length of flax in her fingers. Her dark hair escaped from a loose ponytail and she appeared around Hana's age. "My boys are terrified of him," she said. "Dylan is friends with Tama, so that's no surprise. He's probably only seen Logan angry. I think Tama made an art form out of pushing your husband's buttons." With a deft movement of her fingers she snapped the spine of the flax and tore it from top to bottom. The two halves obediently separated but remained held by the stem at the bottom.

"Dylan?" Hana's interest piqued. "I've heard Tama mention him."

Noelle nodded. "Yep. We've heard lots about you too. You've done miracles with that kid." She dug a fingernail into a point near the smooth edge of the leaf and removed the whole thing in a strip. Then she repeated it on the other side.

"Tama's done it himself." Hana pursed her lips, not willing to betray his private agonies. Not just out of loyalty, but because his evolution seemed irrevocably tangled in hers. "He's awesome. Is a korowai a cloak? Could I really make one for Logan?" She changed the subject and chose something she wanted the answer to.

"Yep, sure can." Betty patted her hand. "Let's get you weaving baskets and then we'll move onto other things."

"I always wondered why Logan didn't wear the family korowai," Rui chipped in. "It's a taonga, a treasure. It belonged to the chief."

Hana's eyes narrowed. "Phoenix Du Rose's father?" She cocked her head and her mind ran through an inventory of the museum's contents. "I haven't seen anything like that. I'm sure if Logan had it, he'd wear it."

"Maybe the other one took it and it burned in the fire." Rui waggled her bushy eyebrows. "Who knows?"

"Reuben?" Hana sighed. "Maybe."

"Did you get to meet him?" Betty's smile appeared genuine as she leaned sideways to deliver her question.

"Once," Hana replied. She thought of the handsome giant who'd laid his hand over her pregnant stomach and remembered the involuntary lurch of Phoenix inside her. His features, his mannerisms and his smile were pure Logan.

Rui's eyebrows waggled themselves into a frenzy of activity. She smacked her lips and the sound echoed around the room. "A fine man, Reuben Du Rose. That man was so fine you could stand and watch the traffic stop on the main street when he walked down it. Oohee!" She fanned herself with a meaty hand. "He kissed me once. Best night of my life." She closed her eyes and Betty snorted.

"You were six year's old, wahine! You played Mary and Joseph in a nativity! It's not like he used his tongue."

"He did in my dreams." Rui's eyelashes fluttered and her face split into a grin. "He still does."

Whaea coughed and dumped a tray on the counter. Mugs jangled against each other "That's Hana's father-in-law you're defaming, Rui! Stop it right now."

"I'm not sorry," Rui grumbled. "Is it time for kai? I'm hungry."

Betty patted Hana's hand. "Stop for some tea," she said. Her gentle eyes crinkled upwards. "We don't eat or drink near the flax."

Hana nodded and thought of Will's constant warnings. She rose and took her turn washing her hands under the kitchen tap and allowed herself a moment of triumph as she glanced back at her basket. The weave appeared loose and shapeless, but she'd got further than ever before.

"We'll tighten it once you find your ara," Betty said, following Hana's gaze. "You're doing well."

Hana felt herself blossom under her praise and straightened her spine. She followed the women into the lounge for morning tea.

28

Raranga Harakeke – Flax Weaving

The break lasted half an hour and the women mulled over everything from the state of the economy to the fundraising at the primary school. Nobody mentioned Kane Du Rose and the subject seemed to hang over them and suck the oxygen from the atmosphere. The promised storm arrived, unleashing its anger on the small house and shrouding it in greyness and gloom. A dull headache ticked in the back of Hana's brain as the air pressure decreased. Electric lights fizzed in response to the storm moving overhead. The women restricted their conversation to matters relating to flax and curiosity made Hana prod the elephant in the room and break her silence. "The casket you made for Kane looked beautiful."

Kora's head bobbed up and down as though spring loaded. "We all worked on it." Her gaze strayed towards Whaea. "He was a good boy once. Before."

"Before Reuben's indiscretion?" Hana held her breath, grateful Logan couldn't hear her gossiping about his family.

Betty nodded and winked at her. "Yes. Reuben was hot. But he was also a hot mess."

"All those Du Rose boys were." Rui hunched over her plate and slapped butter onto a cheese scone. It turned into a yellow puddle in the heat and she frowned and spread more on to compensate. "Until now." She acknowledged Hana with a raised eyebrow. "Youse doing good, girl. They needed a firm hand. You're a little wee thing but youse got them under control."

"Doesn't feel like it sometimes." Hana nibbled at a cracker and contemplated the intricacies of her husband's family. She'd held it in tension within her mind through balancing a series of compartments which allowed her to concentrate on what mattered. Michael, and Kane had gone into the box for 'screw-ups' while Reuben remained in the 'don't know' category along with Nev. Logan, Tama and Alfred occupied an unlabelled spot close to her heart, although the latter two had a tendency to slip into the 'screw-ups' box occasionally. It confused Hana that Kane's history tugged him towards a no-man's-land somewhere closer to the 'don't know' category than she thought possible. She needed him to stay in the box with all the other 'screw-ups.' Otherwise it messed up everything.

Jack's name brought her out of her reverie with a thud and she stared at Rui without blinking. She'd buried Jack's memory in a category far below the surface of her consciousness. It languished in a place she chose not to visit, although it seemed determined to shrug free of late. "What?" Hana whispered. The cracker crumbled beneath her fingers and crumbs missed the plate and landed on her jeans.

Rui waved her scone. "I said it was a shame about Jack dying. He kept as many of those boys in order as he could. Wasn't he a distant cousin? My mother remembered him arriving up at the Du Rose place. She said he was quite the ladies' man for a while there."

Hana swallowed and Rui narrowed her eyes. Butter dripped from her chin and pooled on her plate. They didn't know about Jack and Phoenix. If they knew he'd tried to kill Mac, they wouldn't discuss him in such a casual manner. Hana's heart sent blood pounding through her ears. They didn't know and her world hung in the balance, a void opening before her. She imagined herself blurting the truth and undoing the care with which Logan had wrapped them both in a veil of anonymity and safety. She could rip it off like a Band Aid and expose the wounds. If she wanted.

Rui shrugged and answered for her. "It's all ancient history. It happened long before your time on the mountain, Hana. I don't suppose you saw him much. He kept to the stables, didn't he?"

Hana struggled to soothe her hammering heart. She nodded but summoned no words. The other women poured tea and ate without breaking their stride. The subject moved away from the Du Roses and onto the new development in town. Rui used another scone to mop up the butter pooled on her plate. "Ugly town houses," she mumbled over a mouth full. "Full of Jaffas." She winked at Hana. "Just Another Fer...fer..." She glanced at Whaea's raised eyebrow and thought better of it. "Flamin' Aucklander," she concluded, leaving out the swearword.

Hana gave a nervous laugh, but her mind stayed on Jack. The other women tittered in response to Rui's antics and Whaea shot Hana a look which contained concern. Hana's sense of anonymity crumbled. One other person in the room knew.

Whaea sent them all back to work and Hana's fingers followed Betty's methodical directions. Her blue basket rose from the ashes of her distorted memories and formed a thing of beauty in her hands.

"Ooh, this girl's cookin' on gas!" Rui shrilled from across the table. The other women crowded round to admire her work.

"You just need to cast off now." Noelle tapped the strands protruding over Hana's bunched fingers. "Find your ara and then finish."

"Find my ara?" There it was again, like a dousing of cold water over Hana's head. As though an unseen hand flicked a switch, the sense of fulfilment and pleasure ceased.

"Yep." Betty sounded confident as she tugged at a strand. "The ara gives the weave balance and indicates the health of the basket. A neat ara shows a neat mind and a mastery of raranga. If you don't find it, the top edge won't flow. Come on girly, you can do this."

Hana released a long breath and her fingers shook. "Can I finish it another day?" she asked. "I have errands to run before I fetch Wiri from school." Her eyes glittered with unshed tears as she recognised she'd reached the same impasse as before. Her efforts were neater and less frenzied looking, but she still fought the need to complete the work. She'd played a dangerous game of avoidance and it threatened to catch her up and force her to face her issues. In that moment, Hana sensed what finding her ara really meant.

"I'll put it in the freezer again." Whaea leaned over and whipped it from under Hana's nose. She almost didn't let go in time.

Hana stared at her fingers. "I look like a Smurf whenever I leave here," she commented, reaching for light-heartedness as an antidote for her true feelings.

"Blue on the outside but golden within." Kora spoke the words with a smile. She'd said little during the morning and Hana fought the urge to put her straight. She felt as blue on the inside as ever and didn't know how to get past it.

Hana left after washing her hands and reducing the vibrant blue stain to a ghoulish looking hue. She parked the truck in the layby leading to the hotel and thought about her morning. Hunting for her ara had become more than just looking for a pattern in her weaving. She felt as though she hunted for her own sanity amid the tangled strands of her life. She rang Toby for two reasons. Running errands for him stopped her thinking. She'd also detected something in Logan's expression earlier which revealed he suspected her of lying. She didn't want to confess to her flax lessons just yet, fearing he'd expect something amazing from her to show for it. Hana glanced down at her blue tinged fingers. She'd need more than the ability to mimic a Smurf.

"Do you have any more jobs for me?" she asked when Toby answered. "I've a little while left before I need to get Wiri from school."

Toby sighed and his voice sounded distant. "Yeah, you can find a new stable manager," he replied. "Rawhiti hates the book work. He's threatening to quit. I warned Logan he wasn't up to it but he thought the kid had promise."

"I thought he was great in the stables." Hana frowned. She forced herself to practice speaking the name she'd avoided for over three years. "Jack taught him."

A pause gave way to Toby's low hiss. "He did, Hana. But not the book stuff. I don't want to lose him from the stables, but I have no one else to do it."

"What about David Allen?" Hana mused. "He's clever and adaptable. Have you asked him?"

"Yep. Tried that." Toby blew out a breath loaded with exasperation. "He's more useful as an engineer at the moment. He's a whizz with the mechanical stuff as long as I let him ride out with the stock men a couple of times a week. Sitting behind a desk isn't his thing."

Hana blew out a pursed breath. "I could do it."

"What?" Toby spat the word as though she'd offered to paint the sky forest green. A bud of irritation began in her chest.

"Don't worry. If you've nothing pressing, I'll run some errands of my own." She disconnected the call and tapped the steering wheel with her fingernail. "Oh, thanks for the put down too," she grumbled. "Mustn't forget that." She restarted the engine and executed a messy turn on the narrow lane. Dust blew up under her wheels. Her phone rang, the gleeful tone echoing from the truck's speakers and Hana reached forward to kill the call. Toby's name flashed up and then disappeared. "Keep your fake apology," Hana murmured. "I don't want it."

It wasn't the best idea to drive to Libby's house, but Hana did it, anyway. Bodie's car still peeked from its hiding place and Hana's fingers shook as she opened her truck's door and stepped onto the running board. It felt overwhelming. Anger and panic locked up her chest. She wanted to hammer on the door until they answered and then rage at them until she'd exorcised the venom in her heart. But she feared what might be expelled in the process and doubted she'd ever be the same again. Her relationships wouldn't.

Feeling a complete failure, Hana climbed back into the driver's seat and slammed the door. She started the engine and drove for an hour until the diesel light flashed on. Hana pulled up at a pump at the local garage, not remembering the journey or anything along the way. And no nearer to finding solutions to her most pressing issues.

29

Edin

Hana halted at the sight of the child toddling around beneath the climbing frame. Dark curls tumbled around her elfin face and her tiny feet moved in a staccato rhythm as though drumming the ground. She chattered to herself and moved her head from side to side as she touched the slide and then ran to the struts. She repeated the action over and over in a loop. Hana swallowed and her eyes raked the park for the child's parent. Surprise parted her lips as the little girl glanced up and grey eyes twinkled in the sunshine. The child possessed the classic Du Rose colouring, her genes mingling with another's creating a thing of beauty.

Mac released her hand and Hana's gaze fell on a woman sitting on a nearby bench. The long blonde hair ruled out Aroha and Hana felt her shoulders relax. Logan said both Michael and Liza declined their invitation to Kane's tangi, but she didn't trust either of them not to just show up and expect star treatment. Hana took a deep breath and readied herself to meet another Du Rose wife of indeterminate origin.

Mac ran across the rubber matting towards the climbing frame and the little girl. He'd spent most of the day at the marae eating something that came out purple and gave him belly ache. Logan admitted defeat at tea time and texted her to fetch him. The truce between them strengthened with each small compromise.

Mac's courage failed and wariness halted him at the first of the metal supports. He clasped it and placed one bare foot over the top of the other. His body language radiated uncertainty. The little girl saw him waiting there and her face opened into a radiant smile. She toddled over without reservation and slipped her fingers into Mac's hand. He looked back, sending his mother a vibe of confusion and her heart stilled in her chest. Hana heard herself swallow and her footsteps halted as the perfect mirror image of Phoenix babbled sentences Mac couldn't hear.

The blonde woman rose from the bench and shoved her mobile phone into her jacket pocket. "I guessed we'd meet eventually," she said. She glanced at the floor and then back up at Hana. "I'd hoped for a little longer before you threw us out."

Hana swallowed and forced air into her lungs through a pure act of will. "I'm glad of the opportunity to speak to you before it gets busy." She pursed her lips, regretting her crass choice of words to describe Kane's burial. Her bottom slid onto the bench and she pressed her hands over her shaking knees. In her peripheral vision, Mac helped the toddler onto the bottom of the slide. "I wanted to tell you I'm sorry for your loss. In private. Just the two of us." Caroline sank onto the bench and she gripped the metal arm to support herself. Her face muscles worked through myriad unreadable emotions. Hana forced herself to face her. "I also wanted to apologise. Last time we met I said some horrible things. No excuses. I'm just sorry."

Caroline looked up to meet Hana's steady gaze. By inheriting the strong Du Rose genes, the elfin princess on the slide had missed out on her mother's stunning azure irises. "Thank you," she whispered.

Hana trapped her trembling fingers between her knees and watched her son walk around beneath the apparatus with

Kane's daughter. He took special care of her, the familial bond already fixed in time and awaiting the opportunity to spark and connect. "I know what it's like." Hana heard the waver in her voice and turned to see Caroline looking at her with a quizzical expression on her face. "To lose a husband. I know what it's like. You have my sympathy."

The old Caroline returned long enough to release the scornful scoff. It sounded sharp in the quiet campground. "Did you tell your dead husband how much you hated him the last time you spoke to him too?"

Hana sighed and closed her eyes. She shook her head. "No. But it might have helped with what came afterwards. I ended up feeling powerless for too many years." Logan's wedding band on her finger glinted in the sunlight and the diamonds of her eternity ring sparkled like tiny stars. "I've said it plenty of times since."

"The perfect Hana Singh Johal. Somehow I can't imagine that." Caroline's barbed tone and the use of her former name put Hana on notice. She rose.

"You're welcome to stay here, Caroline," she said. Her feet took two steps towards the climbing frame before she turned to face her old nemesis. "The first hint of trouble means you find somewhere else. Stay away from Logan. Do you understand?"

"Edin." Caroline's eyes filled with tears and she pursed her lips.

"Sorry?" Hana allowed her feet to turn, so she faced her.

"Edin Du Rose." Caroline jerked her head towards the stunning girl in the floral dress. It fluttered around her chubby knees as she held both Mac's hands and practiced jumping. The children both laughed as she managed to get airborne. "I gave birth to her in Dunedin, so Kane called her Edin."

Hana nodded and her lips turned upward in a small smile. "She's beautiful."

"Miss Marsh! Miss Marsh!" The women jumped as the shouts reached them and they turned to see the receptionist from the campground walking towards them. She held a sheet of paper in her hand and a key dangled from a wooden keyring. "Your room is ready now," she said with a smile. "You asked me to let you know. Would you like me to help you shift your gear in?"

Hana smiled at the girl and inwardly commended her on her dedication. "Hi Paula," she said.

"Oh, hi Mrs Du Rose." She waved and the booking sheet fluttered from her fingers and danced in the light breeze. "Oops."

Hana caught it beneath her boot and bent to retrieve it, scanning the printed words for Caroline's location. She'd chosen a motel unit at the edge of the grounds near the bush. Had Reuben's house remained, it would have overlooked it. The booking sheet listed one adult and a child and Hana baulked at seeing her own surname linked with Caroline's. She forced down any ill will and corrected Paula. "This is Mrs Du Rose," she said, holding out an arm to include Caroline. She held the sheet out and Paula took it. Confusion burgeoned and her brow knitted into thin lines. She peered down at the sheet in her hand and turned it the right way up. Her eyes widened.

"Oh, sorry." Her cheeks pinked with embarrassment. "My mistake. I'm really sorry." She glanced at the women and shifted on her feet, aware she'd just slighted a member of her employer's family.

"It's fine." Caroline seemed keen to brush it off. "I can manage by myself, thank you." She held her hand out and fixed a fake smile onto her face. Paula dropped the key into her palm and offered her the booking sheet.

"Sorry again," she murmured. "It does say the right name. I'm not sure why I said the wrong one."

"It's fine." Caroline sounded agitated and Hana gave Paula a reassuring smile. Logan wouldn't hear about it from her. If she had any sense, he'd hear nothing about his ex from Hana. Not a peep.

Deciding to cut her losses and take Mac back to the museum, Hana stepped onto the play matting and walked towards the children. Paula walked back to the campground reception and Caroline sat back on the bench. Mac looked up as Hana cast a shadow across his vision and he smiled. He released Edin's hands and the child stared up at Hana. Grey irises sparkled and black eyelashes fluttered. Hana squatted down next to her. "Hello," she said. "I love your dress."

"Mummy buyed it." Delicate fingers grasped the hem and yanked it high for Hana to see. It exposed a rounded belly and a pair of sagging training pants. "Mine."

"It's very pretty." Hana felt her chest tighten. If Kane Du Rose did nothing else of worth with his life, then Wiri and this elf might prove enough. She swallowed. "I need to take Mac home now."

"Mac." Edin repeated the name and reached up to pat Mac's chest. "He's free." She held up five fingers and closed down the extras. "I'm free at my next birfday."

"Wow. Congratulations." Hana rose and collected her son's hand in a single fluid movement. He shot her a frowning look of disgust. Hana made the beaked motion for food and he wrinkled his nose and tried not to let her sway him with promises of food for his empty stomach. His willpower failed and he gave Edin a cute wave and a smile, allowing Hana to tow him off the rubber matting and onto the pavement.

They left the playground and headed across the wide lawn to cut through Miriam's rose garden. Mac trotted next to her with a furrowed brow. Hana looked down as he touched her thigh. "Peen," he said, spreading his hands in confusion. "Peen?"

Hana nodded, tamping down a raft of rising emotion. She forced a smile onto her lips, stopping so Mac could see her face. She put her right thumb under her chin and brought her hand down to knock on the top of the other. "Yes," she admitted. "She's very like your sister."

Mac jerked his head up and down in agreement. He linked hands with her and skipped through the rose garden. His head tipped from side to side as he registered vibrations Hana couldn't even distinguish. Dread snaked its fist around her heart and closed, sealing her into a bubble of fear.

Toby spoke to her as she crossed the front car park, but she didn't acknowledge him. Her mind galloped through endless worries she couldn't name and Mac bounced alongside in his silent, carefree world. It didn't occur to her to question how Edin Du Rose learned her son's age in a matter of minutes. The threat of Caroline's presence overwhelmed her and she missed the clues of a transformation taking place at her feet.

/ 30

Tangihanga – Funeral, Weeping

Hana sat beneath the canopy of the marae with the rest of Logan's family as the visiting mourners waited for their invitation to step onto the marae. She hung near the back with the other women, the males forming their barrier of protection against any potential visiting enemy. An ancient ritual enforced by time and practice, they re-enacted it every time they held an event. Her British heritage squirmed beneath the rituals of Māoridom and she'd never felt more alien. Phoenix wriggled on the bench beside her and the delicate wreath of woven kawakawa leaves tilted on her dark curls. Hana reached out to take her hand and Phoenix pursed her lips and plopped her fingers into the open palm. She frowned at the coded maternal message to sit still. The peppery scent of the kawakawa leaves filled the air and drowned out Hana's floral perfume.

"Mama, Papa's got a hairy face." The child projected her observation into the hushed silence and Hana cringed. Leslie rescued her, hauling the child into her lap in a fluid motion.

"Hush now. He's been here with you for two days. When did he get time to shave?"

A titter moved around the gathered crowd and Alfred glanced back from the front row with amusement in his eyes. Hana stared at her grey skirt and sympathised with her husband's silent protest. With no one else available from Kane's dwindling family the elders insisted Logan speak for him. It seemed the cruellest of injustices, forcing him to eulogise for a man who hated his existence from the very first breath. The irony stung that Kane should resent Logan's entrance into the world, find himself farewelled out of it by him.

Hana swallowed and watched her husband's rigid spine. He'd dressed in his usual clipped manner, but she'd noticed the lack of a shave, the greying stubble giving his angular face harsh, uncompromising edges.

Hana pursed her lips and the chasm between her culture and Logan's yawned wider. She battled thoughts of unworthiness and failed as she wondered why he hadn't worn the family cloak which came to light just the previous day. Glancing up, she caught his eye as he turned to face the outer gate. His expression morphed from unyielding to the hint of a smile as he offered her comfort across the distance. Hana allowed her lips to curve upward in reply. She forgave his recent shortness and pondered on the impossibility of his situation.

Kane's flax casket rested on the porch of the wharenui, ruining any happier times she'd had in the building. Designated as a place for sleeping visitors during overnight stays, Hana had taken many turns at cleaning it with Leslie. Mac, Phoenix and Wiri always made a beeline to bounce on the mattresses piled in the corner, their muted giggles filling the vaulted ceiling with joy.

Hana leaned sideways to glimpse Mac and her brow furrowed. Her son sat on the bench between Alfred and Toby and his body moved with the motion of swinging legs. She waited for Alfred to lean sideways and stop him, but he didn't and the child's head continued to dip and rise. Glancing at

Leslie, Hana saw her roll her eyes in exasperation at Alfie's oblivion. Hana experienced a flicker of relief as Toby's left shoulder dipped and Mac looked up at him. Rosebud lips parted in a grin and he raised his left hand to jab a finger towards his father. Toby nodded and slipped an arm around Mac's shoulders. The boy snuggled close and settled. Hana felt her limbs relax and squeezed and released her fingers. Logan often quoted the African proverb, "It takes a village to raise a child." Hana watched her son rest his head against Toby's chest and bowed her head in agreement.

She knew Caroline stood across the meeting ground from her and refused to allow herself to look. Edin slept in the arms of an aunty and the woman rocked the toddler with practiced ease. Hana banned herself from watching Caroline when Logan stepped up to speak. She couldn't bear to see the longing she fancied still lingered in the other woman's eyes. Whaea stood behind Kane's casket, her feet bare and her fingers fluttering next to her skirt. She readied herself to call Kane's immediate family and friends onto the marae and Hana tensed. Her shrill cry would fill the airwaves with a haunting sadness.

"Look, Macky! Tama's bootiful!" Phoenix broke the uncomfortable silence with a shriek fit to raise the dead and Hana's heart rate hiked again. But a glance at her husband found him stifling a smirk behind his hand. Tama strode up to him wearing a stunning cloak. She recognised the fuzzy outline of hawk feathers and gasped at how it came alive on the young man's broad frame. Will arced back in his wheelchair and caught her eye, frowning at her bewilderment. Logan had honoured Tama beyond measure, allowing him to wear the cloak belonging to the Māori chief who formed an alliance with the red-haired French settler in their ancestry. It wasn't lost. Alfred had produced it from inside a forgotten box in the apartment's airing cupboard.

Hana's gaze strayed to Will's profile and she smirked at the twitch of his fingers as he coveted the heirloom. Will had corrected her earlier when she referred to it as a korowaī, his tone short as he shook his head and said, "No, it's a kahu huruhuru, a kākahu with feathers. It was handed down to the Kuia Phoenix. It's been in the bloody airing cupboard all this time. And it's not going back there!"

Hana felt tears well up and forced herself to swallow. The gulp sounded loud beneath the wooden canopy and the women nearest her glanced sideways, their kawakawa wreaths rustling on their heads. A gentle hand squeezed her shoulder and then another and the chasm reduced as the gathered women welcomed her into their solidarity. Hana breathed in through her nose and avoided the sight of the two handsome men waiting to address the mourners. Her ready tears flowed for Tama, not Kane. And Wiri, the real son nobody knew about. She willed herself not to look at Wiri's glossy curls on the other side of Toby as he studied the marae's clipped green lawn. They'd tell him one day. But not yet. Kane terrified him. Hana blew out a slow breath and pushed the thoughts away, not wishing her mind to go down a track she dreaded.

The eerie, beautiful strains of the kuia karanga's voice cut through the slow footsteps of the visitors as they shuffled onto the marae. Whaea's voice wavered and Hana saw a side view of the elderly woman's fingers fluttering in the traditional movement taught to her by her mother and grandmother. Hana glanced down at her fingers clenched together in her lap. The visitors moved forward in unison, a tiny knot of women proceeding the males as an ancient act of contrition. During the years of tribal dispute and wars, it signified peace when the women of the visiting manuhiri entered first. They filed to the back of the guests' stand and the men sealed them in with a gentle pincer movement, placing themselves in harm's way. Whaea continued her call. "Haere mai, haere mai."

Hana listened to the lilting, lyrical song. She felt the kuia weaving the past and present together as she blessed Kane Du Rose and welcomed his mourners. The strains cut through Hana's brain, healing her failed attempts to create anything worthwhile from the springy flax until now. Whaea wove the song together with as much ease as her fingers created baskets and wall hangings. Hana's sigh echoed and she pursed her lips and stared at her husband's stunning profile.

Logan stepped forward to greet the mourners in both Māori and English, his speech eloquent and his hands moving as though he taught a literature class. Hana recognised the familiar words of his mihi as he stated his twisted genealogy for the benefit of those gathered. He named the mountain behind them as his origins, claimed the Waikato River and traced his heritage back to the Tainui canoe which landed at Kawhia bringing his ancestors. Hana waited for him to elaborate, entwining his whakapapa with those seated around him through citing the eldest of each male line. He left them out, listing his connection to the Waikato tribes through the female generations. It re-established his credentials. His female ancestry hadn't changed. Hana swallowed and watched Logan's capable hands gesticulate. She'd heard his mihi often enough to know it by heart and this wasn't it. Several of the men in front of her frowned and shot sideways glances at one another as Logan rewrote his own history through the energy of the women who went before him.

He stepped back and the veiled whispers grew as he touched Tama's elbow. Hana watched the young man stride towards the gathered visitors. He wore the cloak over his formal fire service uniform and held his peaked cap in shaking fingers before him. Hana saw his jaw working through his cheek as though he mouthed something to himself and the realisation came with a sickening jolt. He'd avoided her because he was in pain. His eyes looked dull as though he'd stayed out drinking from the moment he landed in the town. Hana released a sigh and wondered how she'd allowed herself to drop the ball with such ease.

He straightened his broad shoulders and planted his shiny shoes on the meeting ground to face the visiting mourners. Hana longed to see more than the back of his head as he fumbled through his own mihi, nerves leaking through his voice. It followed Logan's by generation until he jerked a shoulder back towards the host's seating and she heard Alfred's name. Like a beacon, the diversion revealed where it all went wrong for them both, caught between the tainted branches of Alfred and Reuben Du Rose like feathers trapped in barbed wire.

Hana darted a sideways glance at Leslie, but the woman avoided her gaze. The old woman kept her face straight as Phoenix leaned against her large bosom and fingered the edges of the jade koru dangling around Leslie's neck. Hana swallowed and dropped her gaze to her fingers. Logan condemned his male ancestry as though they'd committed the sins alone. She thought of Libby and wondered who would come off worse in that situation. Every generation appeared tarnished and peppered by the errors of their people, male and female. Did they ever see beyond their own suffering? Kuia Phoenix Du Rose had. But too late. Much too late to reverse the damage.

Tama departed from Māori and spoke in English, perhaps his subconscious reaching out to Hana as she clenched her teeth behind him. "Kane Du Rose is listed as my father on my birth certificate," he said. "I suspect he did his best with what he knew at the time. I never loved him, but I didn't hate him either. It's the hope of our whānau that he finds the peace in death I believe he spent his life seeking." Tama turned and sought Caroline in the stands. He gave her a decisive nod and his words sounded sincere. "Sorry for your loss, Aunty," he said. Instead of re-joining his relatives under the canopy, Tama walked towards the casket and touched the gentle slope of the flax as it arched around Kane's shoulder. Hana masked her shock as Tama sank onto the top step next to Kane and placed the smart cap in his lap. He bowed his head and his shoulders slumped.

She looked away, realising this tangihanga contained too many moments she didn't want to witness. Opting out hadn't been a choice offered to her, but as she considered the silent, gathered crowd she knew she needed to stay. For Logan. And for Tama. Her boys.

31

A Blast from the Past

"Kai time!" Phoenix clapped her hands and swished her flounced navy skirt around her legs. Mac beaked his little fingers and Hana nodded to confirm the imminent arrival of dinner.

"I need to help in the kitchen." She tugged the cuff of Logan's shirt and leaned close enough to keep their conversation private. "Can you mind the children?"

Logan snaked an arm around her shoulders and kissed her temple. "Sure." He located each of them in turn and performed a mental head count. "You don't have to help today," he whispered. "You're exempt on a technicality."

Hana swallowed and hid her dismay at his harshness. As the sister-in-law of the deceased she didn't need to help with the food, but as the wife of Logan Du Rose she felt she should. "It's fine." She covered her misgivings with a smile and slipped away as a tall man intercepted Logan and pressed his nose and forehead against his. She skirted the wharenui on her way to the cavernous dining hall. A crowd sat on the front steps enjoying the sun. Kane's casket lay in the baked ground of the town's cemetery with the charred remains of Miriam and his father.

Phoenix had fidgeted during the slow procession through the urupā gates and Wiri halted Hana's progress by refusing to go inside. The haka the men performed as Kane departed the marae for the final time left her nerves feeling frayed and tender. Uncle had served the role of the leader, rousing the other men into a resounding war cry. But Hana couldn't forget the sight of tears rolling down Tama's cheeks. She'd needed to turn away.

Her high heels clacked against the path on the way to the dining hall and several mourners turned to watch her. The northern branch of the Du Roses eyed her with suspicion and curiosity, though they'd pressed noses with her following the tangihanga as she waited in line. Some of the women kissed her cheek instead as though making allowances for her lack of culture. Hana gave a tight smile and moved away. A familiar shadow crossed her path and Detective Inspector Odering fell into step next to her, reducing his stride to match hers. "My money's on the wife," he said, his air casual.

Hana frowned and shook her head. "No. I don't think so. Caroline seems broken by Kane's death." She glanced across to see Logan's ex-fiancé standing aside from the throng of people. Hana's step faltered and Odering grinned.

"And yet you still worry about her around your husband?" His eyebrow quirked upward and his serious face creased in a victorious grin. "Perhaps she's not as devastated as she appears."

Hana stopped and faced the tall policeman. A sigh passed her lips. "She possessed too much power over me for a long time. It's hard to see beyond that." He nodded in response and followed her gaze. Edin held onto Caroline's dark skirt and ran around her legs. Her mother reached down to stop her as the child tripped over her own feet, unbalanced by the swathe of fabric binding her knees. Caroline kissed the little girl and gave a shimmy which released the skirt and allowed it to flow back into place. Hana shook her head. "She's definitely still got sex appeal." She sounded wistful. "Logan says he's not interested. I need to take him at his word."

Odering's eyes narrowed and he cocked his head as though trying to assess the damage. He frowned. "Du Rose never struck me as the straying type. Are you saying otherwise?"

"No!" Hana's voice rose and she felt a flush of embarrassment. Colour rushed into her cheeks. "He's never cheated and promised he wouldn't. But doesn't everyone say that?"

Odering cleared his throat and looked away. "I should head back to Hamilton," he said. His eyes raked the azure sky above like a farmer seeking rain clouds. "I popped in because I was passing." He jerked his head towards the wharenui. "I'm picking up vibes that your official detective doesn't want me here."

"I'm disappointed. You've given up sooner than usual." Hana followed his gaze and saw Detective Sanders trip up the steps on his way to intercept the knot of mourners. They moved away as though herded. She sighed.

Odering gave an undignified snort. "I haven't given up," he retorted. "It's not my case. I'm here in my own time. I like the Saturday burial thing though. Very convenient for people to attend."

"Don't you work weekends anymore?" Hana heard the clatter of crockery coming from the kitchen and winced. She took a step towards the sound.

"No. I work eight until five on weekdays unless something big blows up and then we all pitch in for as long as it takes. I do the odd on-call now and then. Happy wife, happy life." The phrase jarred as it crossed his lips and Hana frowned.

"You remarried?"

"No." Odering's irises flashed a strange, glittery blue and Hana sensed she'd missed something important in their conversation. She couldn't grasp it and the sensation abated. "Same wife. We patched up our differences and I made some changes to my work-life balance. We bought a house in Hamilton and the children settled well." He smiled and the darkness left his face. "My son is applying to your old school for next year. Do you think your husband would give him a reference?"

Hana shrugged. "I think so, although I'm not sure it'll have any influence. A lot of the management staff left after Angus retired. The person handling enrolments might not know who Logan is, or that he taught there."

Odering jutted his chin upwards. "It's worth a try. It's still the best private school in the north island and the waiting list is a mile long."

Hana wrinkled her nose. "Won't you need a second mortgage to pay the extortionate fees? Bodie got in because I worked there. Half fees were a staff perk." Her eyes lit up. "Ask Bodie for a reference. He's alumni, so it counts for more than an ex teacher nobody remembers."

Odering gave a satisfied nod. "Great idea. It saves me trading favours with your husband, so it's an all-round win."

Hana sighed. "Stop. You and Logan act like you hate each other when your relationship is based on mutual respect. I think your sparring days are over."

Odering's lips curved upwards in a delighted grin. "He respects me?"

"I should remind you this is a funeral," Hana retorted. She kept her face expression solemn with down turned lips and a look of feigned piety. "Mind your head on the way out."

Odering laughed, a melodious, tinkling sound. He leaned forward and brushed Hana's cheek with his lips. "Good bye, Hana," he said, his voice low. His gaze slid sideways and Hana sensed her husband's attention. Logan's grey eyes left scorch marks in her right cheek. Odering straightened, gave her a grin filled with mischief and strode towards the marae gate with a definite spring in his step.

Hana forced herself not to turn around and meet her husband's veiled jealousy. Instead, she pushed her way through the knot of female bodies and busied herself in the kitchen.

32

Kai – to Eat

The younger men dug up the hangi while the older ones supervised. Tama hung back, not wanting to get his best uniform stained. Hana stood next to him and watched the baskets retrieved from the ground, the scent of chicken and sweet potato filling her nostrils. "There's no other smell like it, is there?" she mused, her tone thoughtful. "When we travelled Europe, we sampled all sorts of smoked delicacies, but I need to be right there whenever a hangi is dug up.

Tama smiled and nodded. "It tastes of home to me. Every time."

Hana's brow furrowed and she took a step back to allow the men to pass. Their biceps bulged with the weight of the food laden baskets. The vegetables emerged first and the meat last, liberated from their smoking pit. "You don't sound settled, Tama," she said, her tone gentle. She slipped her fingers around his elbow. "Is something wrong?"

"Nope." He brushed off her concerns with a casual air, turning his body to follow the food. Wiri appeared and fell into step beside him, reaching out to twirl the hem of Tama's smart jacket beneath his fingers.

Hana leaned around to speak to him. "Hungry, darling?" she asked.

Wiri shrugged and shook his head, changing the action to a nod at the last minute. Her heart seemed to clench in her chest at the deception and she toyed with the thought that perhaps the little boy knew he'd just buried his father. She glanced around at the nearby faces in alarm, but reason gave her reassurance. Only four other people ever knew the identity of Wiri's father. One was a lawyer, one a fugitive, one struggled through a mental relapse in a secure facility and the other she'd just seen buried six feet under fresh earth. Hana shivered. Wiri couldn't know.

"Where's Logan?" She spun around and her heels ground into the dirt. The plain grey skirt felt odd in place of her usual uniform of jeans and boots. It trapped her legs and prevented her walking properly. She wondered how she ever managed in suits and dresses when she worked at the school.

"Dunno." Tama smiled and shrugged off the dark spirit resting on his shoulders.

"Please don't freeze me out." Hana's voice wavered as the portcullis slammed down between her and her men.

"Sorry." Tama snaked an arm around her neck and pressed a kiss to the top of her head. "I'm fine, Ma. Today's been hard because it's made me think of all the lost opportunities." He heaved out a breath and screwed his face into a grin reminiscent of his teenage years. "I'll shoot off as soon as we get home. My next lot of assessments are due at the end of the week."

"Hmnn. And that's not code for a woman, is it?" Hana raised an eyebrow and Tama laughed. He tapped the side of his nose in an expression of mischief Hana recognised. She groaned.

"Don't make me lie to you." His grey irises flashed and Hana shook her head. Tama clasped Wiri's fingers and led the child towards the line forming into an orderly queue outside the dining hall. Hana watched as Sam sprang up onto a chair and raised his hands for silence.

"I'll just perform a blessing over the food," he said. A hush settled and heads bowed with eyes closed. Hana squinted from beneath her fringe and continued her search for Logan. She heaved out a breath of relief at the sight of him standing head and shoulders above everyone else. Then she recognised his companion. Lincoln Haines stood with his blonde head bowed and his hands clasped in front of his belt buckle. He looked smart in black trousers and a white shirt ironed so that creases showed along the arms like bones. Hana tensed at the sight of Logan's former stable manager and a shiver ran up her spine. Phoenix held her father's hand and watched Sam from beneath her lashes. A sense of awe shrouded her and Hana's lips twisted into a reluctant smile.

Sam concluded his blessing and a rumbled, "Amine," gave the gathered crowd permission to join the line for kai. The tantalising scent of smoked chicken, pumpkin and taro mingled with potato and the peppery foliage of the women's wreaths. Hana's hand snaked to her head and she remembered discarding hers in the seating area. She glanced around to find many of the other women had done the same. A sigh escaped her lips as she felt like a soldier picking her way through a series of land mines, never sure which unobserved custom might detonate in her face and ruin everything.

Logan sensed her staring and sought her out as bodies surged around her. He jerked his chin upwards in acknowledgement and his lips parted in the smile he kept only for her. He saw her gaze flick to Lincoln and back, knowing in that split second she'd formed her own conclusions. Logan gave a slow shake of his head to put her straight and she forced herself to trust him. Though she'd used Lincoln as a stick to beat Logan with when the Jeep's existence came to light, she didn't expect to see the man ever again. She mustered her courage, pointed her feet in their direction and took a step forward.

A vibration came from the small bag slung across her body and Hana jumped. Her fingers fumbled to retrieve her phone. She peered at the screen and saw the number for the school. Confusion knitted her brow into a series of creases. "Hello?" She jammed her right finger into her ear to cut out the sound of the hungry masses and turned away. Logan didn't follow, but his gaze bored into her retreating back.

"Mrs Du Rose." The school principal's clipped tones changed her confusion to curiosity and Hana steered herself away to a quieter spot.

The marae backed onto a creek, drawing water from the same source as her house. Hana found a rock and sat down. The flow tinkled by with dead leaves bobbing along on its surface. Too little rain had sapped its energy and made it appear half hearted and lazy.

"How can I help you?" she asked.

"Apologies for disturbing your weekend," he began. He paused, as though waiting for Hana to grant him permission to continue. She opened her mouth to speak and he ploughed on, regardless. Just a nicety then. "Bernice has spoken at length about the issue between your daughter and Holly Golding. It's a complicated situation." Hana sensed the capitulation in his voice and she closed her eyes and ground her jaw as he delivered his solution. "I've had a chat with her parents. We think it's best if we move your child into the other composite class. She's a bright girl, so Bernice thinks she'll excel with the older children."

Hana's breath hissed from between her teeth. The township's tiny primary school boasted only three teachers and a principal. He intended to move Phoenix into an older, mixed age class instead of dealing with the real issue. "No." Hana's reply sounded sharper than she intended. "Why should Phoenix move? She says she didn't hit Holly and I believe her. Now you're talking about shifting her into Wiri's class. He's much older than her. And what happens when those children move up to the intermediate level and high school?"

The principal dodged the question with ease. "It's more realistic to move your daughter than the other child." He paused and Hana sensed him considering his words with care. "We believe Phoenix will cope better with the work."

"This is so unfair," Hana gasped.

"Not really. She did hit the other child."

Hana exhaled and watched a lone brown leaf flutter against a rock. The current kept it pinned in place while battering its fragile stem. "Damned if you do and damned if you don't," she breathed.

"Pardon?" The principal's voice sounded snippy. He wanted to deliver his bombshell and go back to his Saturday morning paperwork. "I didn't catch that."

"This is about money, isn't it?" Hana said. She sat up straight and smoothed a palm along her skirt. "Holly's father offered to fund the new gym equipment and dealing with her bullying jeopardises that."

The principal's voice took on an aggressive edge. "I'm not sure where you're getting your information," he bit. "I don't run my school based on blackmail threats."

Hana ran a hand across her forehead and found it damp. The sun beat on the back of her neck and her feet ached in the high-heeled shoes. She wanted to scream and smash something. "I'll speak to my husband," she snapped. "You're not penalising my daughter for another's bad behaviour. I'd rather move both my children elsewhere." Hana issued the ultimatum without decent thought. Wiri seemed happy at the local school and Logan had rescued their annual fair from the depths of failure. She sighed and shook her head. "I'll come back to you on Monday." She pressed the button to end the call and frustration shot through her. The principal had disturbed her at a family burial to deliver the news of his feeble solution. His motivations extended far beyond the welfare of his students. Hana imagined cancelling the fair and saw only spite in the action. Besides, Will would never speak to her again. The pile of baskets occupied one corner of the museum with more promised. He'd kill her.

Gravel crunched behind her and Hana jumped. She turned to find Lincoln Haines picking his way down to the water. "Hey." He jerked his head upwards and raised his hands in front of him. "Don't get up. I just came to say hi."

"This day just gets better and better," Hana growled. She straightened her skirt and watched Lincoln perch on a larger boulder to her right. Her fingers shook as she slipped her phone back into her bag. "I don't think we have much to say to each other." Her gaze flicked towards the marae and she pictured Logan's face and tried to send him telepathic messages of discomfort.

Lincoln nodded. "I know. I'm still sorry, Hana. Threatening you wasn't my dumbest move ever, but it came close."

"Why are you here?" Hana narrowed her gaze and focussed on the water. She identified with the frustration of being tossed around against her will.

"Saying farewell to a friend." Lincoln dug his hands into his pockets and pursed his lips.

"Right." Hana hugged her knees and wished he'd leave her alone. She needed to process her thoughts.

"How are things?" Lincoln ignored the hint and his shoes scraped in the gravel.

"Great," Hana lied. "You?"

"Not bad. The compensation came through and gave me the opportunity to quit my job and think about what I really want to do." He sighed. "The guy I worked for wanted me to fiddle the accounts. I needed to leave there, anyway. I don't want to waste any more time. The wrongful imprisonment payment sounds like a fortune when other people hear the numbers, but it can't make up for a lost decade of my life."

Hana shrugged. "You're not completely innocent in all this, Lincoln. We both know that." Her mouth hardened and the toe of Lincoln's right boot scuffed against the gravel.

"I've paid for my stupidity in other ways, Hana." He lowered his voice. "Your husband's my friend. I'd like to think we could at least be civil."

Hana blinked. "Logan sent you away."

Lincoln chuffed out a laugh. "Away from you, Hana. He'll always be like a brother to me. He stood by me twice when nobody else did. I'd take a bullet for him."

"Then let's hope you never have to." Hana closed her eyes and hoped when she opened them, he'd be gone. He took the hint at last.

"Okay. See ya." Lincoln straightened and Hana squeezed the bridge of her nose between finger and thumb as his footsteps moved away.

She knew she'd made a mistake as she poured the bitter cup of unforgiveness and drank it herself.

33

Dignity

Hearing nothing but silence, Hana went in search of her children. The whispered conversation from the laundry promised nothing good. "I hope you're not putting Mac in the tumble dryer again," she snapped, barrelling into the room. Phoenix jumped back with wide eyes and a nervous titter left her lips.

"No, Mama," she said. Her gaze moved to Wiri and then slid back to Hana. "He asked us, but we promised we wouldn't do that again."

"Urm. Urm." Her son beamed at her from the tiled floor. He sat with his legs spread apart and a worm wiggled in his outstretched fingers. Hana cringed.

"You said worm! Good boy, Macky. Good boy!" Phoenix squatted next to him and pushed her face into his. Mac blinked and accepted the wet kiss on his button nose.

Hana forced a smile onto her lips. It faded as he brought the creature closer to his face. "Don't eat it!" She held a hand up in the universal stop motion and Mac burst into a peal of tinkling laughter. His speech transitioned back to gibberish with such seamlessness, Hana wondered if he'd ever attempted to name the worm or if her desperation had played a game with her.

"He said worm." Phoenix rose and skipped on the spot, reviving Hana's faith. Faith in the doctors. Faith in God. Just plain old faith that her son would one day hear her voice.

"He did." Hana dipped and lifted child and worm off the floor in a fluid movement. Mac dangled the worm in her face and Hana shrank back. "Wiri, help me," she begged, her tone containing urgency.

"I can't." His mumbled response conveyed a deep reluctance so unusual, Hana spun round to look at his face. Wiremu leaned over the washing machine. White powder poured from the scoop onto a heap of bedding. Hana leaned closer and caught the unmistakable scent of ammonia. She floundered, sensible answers abandoning her for a moment. The worm bounced in front of her nose, its crusty back end suggesting the creature had somehow entered the house months ago and died beneath the washing machine. Wiri refused to catch her pointed look, unscrewing the lid of the fabric softener and dripping it into the cup at the top of the machine.

Hana almost cried with relief at the sound of Logan's footsteps. Her handsome white knight stepped into the laundry and summed up the situation with a practiced eye. Phoenix caught hold of Mac's dangling ankle. "Papa, Macky said worm!" She kept her teeth together as she smiled and her eyes widened in delight. "He's so clever." She kissed her brother's shin and Logan forced an expression of wonder onto his face. In the same moment, he held out his hand and Mac dropped the offending object into his palm. The little boy screwed up his face and brushed his hands together in a clumsy movement.

"Urm," he whispered through pursed lips. "Urm."

Logan's smile looked genuine and he leaned forward to kiss the boy's cheek. "Well done," he mouthed into his face and Mac beamed. With a magician's sleight of hand, Logan flipped the worm into the sink and leaned across to twist the tap. Liquid spurted free, taking the worm to its watery grave in the depths of the septic tank hidden beneath the lawn. "Wash hands," Logan said, grabbing the soap and rubbing foam onto his fingers.

"Ooooh! Ooooh!" Mac's legs swung against Hana's thighs as he spotted his favourite two objects on offer; gushing water and slippery soap.

Logan hauled a wooden step across the room with his foot and kicked it into place in front of the sink. Mac's eyes bugged and he dipped forward, eager to feel the tantalising sensations against his hands. "Get your shoes on for church, Phoe." Logan jerked his head towards the hallway and Phoenix gave Mac's leg a final pat before slipping past and skipping into the bowels of the house.

"Are you coming, Papa?" she demanded over her shoulder. "Your soul could use a good scrub with Reverend Sam's scratchy communion wafers." She made a sound like a gag and Hana's eyes narrowed, wondering when she'd got her hands on one.

"No thanks." Logan dried his hands on a towel and swapped places with Hana so she could set Mac's running feet on the step. She held onto his shoulders until the child got his balance and watched him plunge his fingers beneath the spray. His eyes closed in an expression of bliss.

"What are you doing, son?" Logan's tone made her tense as he turned his attention to Wiri. Hana closed her eyes and forced misgiving from her expression.

Wiri swallowed and pressed buttons on the machine's high-tech dashboard. "I spilled a drink in my bed." He pursed his lips, hating the lie as much as the soaked patch on his sheets. "I'm sorry."

Logan's jaw clenched and he gave a decisive nod. "You know the rules. No food or drink outside the kitchen or dining room."

"Yes, Uncle." Wiri dropped the lid of the machine into place and water gurgled into its cavernous innards. Mac blinked his eyes open as the pressure lessened against his hands. The soap leapt skyward as he squeezed it and he giggled. "I'll empty the bins in the kitchen and bathrooms for a month," Wiri offered, his eyes wide and his tone earnest. "Is that fair?"

"I think so. It's a rotten job." Logan kept his expression blank and jerked his head toward the hallway. "Get ready for church and don't let it happen again."

"Yes, Uncle." Wiri fled and Hana heard his sigh of relief as he passed her. She pushed the laundry door closed with her heel.

"He wet the bed." She lowered her voice and spoke to her husband as though he hadn't realised.

Logan reached across and turned off the tap. Mac gasped in shock and drummed his feet on the stool. Hana patted his tiny hands dry and stood back while Logan caught him up in his arms. He blew a raspberry on the child's neck and Mac giggled, frustration and tantrum forgotten in the moment of closeness. "I know." Hana watched her husband's handsome face crease in concern. "But I left the kid his dignity."

Hana nodded and conceded to his wisdom. He seemed to have a solution for every situation. She wished some of the trait would rub off on her. It hadn't yet. "Do you think he's upset about Kane?" Her teeth gnawed on her lower lip. "He hasn't done this for ages."

"Maybe." Logan shrugged. "Kane's reappearance. His death. Pick any one." He shook his head and smoothed water droplets from Mac's forehead. "I'll make time to ride with him and see if I can get him to talk."

Hana nodded and released the sigh trapped in her chest. "You're a great dad, Logan. I don't deserve you."

"Maybe not." Logan grinned. The scarred fingers of his right hand released Mac's waist and he reached out to stroke Hana's cheek. The muscles bulged in his left biceps as he supported the child on his hip with effortless strength. He dipped his torso and his lips pressed over hers. Hana closed her eyes and basked in the sense of security he gave her. Logan rested his forehead against her fringe. "But then I don't deserve you either," he whispered. "So, perhaps things are as they should be." He smiled and Hana pushed herself into his body.

"But what about Kane's death?" she said. Logan shook his head. "We need to know who killed him."

"Not our problem, Hana." His tone held a warning and she blanched, sensing he meant it. She needed to stay out of it. Mac yawned and twisted his fingers through a hank of Hana's red curls. "Want me to load the kids into your truck?" Logan offered. Mac poked a pink thumb between his lips and Hana nodded.

"Thanks. If your boy sleeps for a couple of hours after church, I can practice making those damn flax things."

Logan snuffed out a laugh. "Raranga, babe. My ancestors are rolling in their graves right now at your disregard of their heritage."

"They can roll all they want," Hana retorted. "I still can't do it."

Logan sat Mac in Hana's truck and covered him with his favourite blanket while she sorted out the rest of Wiri's bed. She removed the stained duvet inner and snagged a spare from the airing cupboard. "I'll finish it when I get home," she said as Logan returned, inspecting the mattress. "Thank goodness for mattress protectors."

"Okay. Mac's in your truck snoring and I've got the others. Phoe wants you to hurry."

"Logan." Hana caught hold of his sleeve and worry settled like a shroud over her head. "What can I do about Phoe? She's too young to move up to Wiri's class. It will create a huge gap in her learning and she'll spend years treading water."

Logan lifted his fingers and stroked her cheek. His gaze misted as his brain worked through the various options and Hana closed her eyes and leaned into his comforting touch. Leaning down, his kiss infused her with a sense of hidden promise. "I'll fix it," he whispered. "Just say the word."

"How?" Her eyes flicked open.

Logan's right eyebrow quirked upwards and he bopped the end of her nose with his index finger. "You don't need to know that, babe," he replied. Turning, he strode along the hallway towards the front door.

Hana followed, a nervous beat dancing in the back of her head. As a man with untold resources at his fingertips, it seemed doubtful Logan Du Rose would allow the principal to remain standing against his might and influence. The fact that he wouldn't tell her his solution suggested it involved an after-hours visit to the man's house and Hana cringed. The rational part of her mind told her the ends justified the means. Her conscience told her otherwise. "Don't Logan!" she called after him. She searched in the hall cupboard for her shoes, listening to his gentle tone as he spoke to the children.

By the time she'd locked up, Logan had fitted both trucks beneath the covered porch at the front of the house. The rear doors of both stood open. Mac's head lolled against his car seat and Phoenix's puckered lips leaned from the front seat. "Kiss, Mama," she called, closing her eyes.

"Funny girl, I'm coming with you." Hana breathed, placing her lips against her daughter's soft cheek. She glanced up to find Logan watching her. A memory surfaced and she seized it while it hovered in front of her. "Please can you take a look at the dashcam?" she asked him. "It keeps playing up and Wiri said the SIM card is missing."

Logan's brows furrowed. "It's fine. It's working. Look."

Hana leaned past Phoenix to see the image of the driveway reflected in the camera's screen. "Weird," she breathed. She turned back to him and her eyes narrowed. "Please don't do anything to the principal," she whispered. "Let me try to fix it."

"You're sure?" Logan's right eyebrow quirked upwards and Hana saw doubt cloud his grey irises. "I just meant I'd speak to him, Hana. What did you think?" His head jerked backwards on his shoulders.

"Nothing." Hana shook her head. "Please, give me the chance to fix this."

"Wiri wants a kiss too." Phoenix's eyelashes fluttered and sadness flooded her grey irises. Hana delayed, her footsteps heavy as she waited for her husband's word.

She was still waiting as she opened Wiri's door and leaned in. He pursed his lips and avoided meeting her gaze. "I love you, Wiremu Du Rose," she whispered. "Thanks for letting Phoe have a turn in the front." She felt his jaw flexing as her lips touched his cheek. As she withdrew from the car, he reached out and snagged her hand, squeezing her fingers in a death grip.

"Things will stay the same, won't they?" he whispered. "You won't send me back now?"

"Send you back where, darling?" Hana's eyes narrowed in question, but she saw him already slamming the portcullis on his fears. "No, Wiri." She ground her teeth and issued the stark promise, hoping above every other tumultuous thing in this child's world she could keep it. "You belong to us. We have papers to prove it." Her fingers shook as she pulled his face towards her. "Things change all the time, Wiri. We can't help that. But we will fight for you with everything we have. Do you believe me?"

Wiri nodded and turned away. Hana took the hint and closed the door against his sadness and unbelief. Her teeth worried at her lower lip to halt the tears ready to fall in sympathy at the boy's fate. She met Logan at the side of her truck. He wrapped his arms around her waist and pressed a kiss to her forehead. "I heard," he said. "Wonder what that's about."

"We need to find out." Hana sighed and shook her head. "He might tell you."

"He's a Du Rose, so I doubt it. We learn to keep our emotions hidden in the womb."

"Not Mac." Hana let her gaze rove over the pink cheeks of her sleeping son. "Not him."

"Good luck with that." Logan's lips curved up in a sexy arc. His eyes widened. "It's genetic." He wrinkled his nose and slapped Hana's backside, making her squeak in surprise. "Lots of things are."

She shook her head and laughed as he sauntered back to his truck, admiring his fine ass moving beneath his work jeans.

"My son will be different," she vowed, meaning it.

34

A Sickening Visitor

The possum lay on the doormat without moving. Its fur looked bloodied and matted. Hana spun on her heel to send the children away before they saw.

"Asher didn't do it." Wiri missed nothing. He set up an immediate protest. "My brother didn't do that. I know he didn't."

"Do what?" Phoenix pushed at Hana's hip and tried to squirrel past.

"Please, go and play in the garden," Hana pleaded. "You really don't want to see this." She forced a calming breath into her chest. Fear stampeded through the peace which the church service had given her.

"I do want to see it! Wiri saw it." Hana jerked sideways to stop Phoenix poking her nose through the gap between her and Wiri.

"But I don't want you to see it." She turned the child, placing her hands on the thin shoulders and bodily moving her. "Do as you're told and take Mac to the swing."

"But I want to hang Jesus on the fridge!" Phoenix flapped a stick-man drawing in her hand and pouted. "He'll get creased and Pastor Sam said it's the best Jesus he's ever seen."

Wiri snorted. "Is that a pizza on his head?"

"A halo!" Phoenix peered at the bright yellow oval suspended above the stick-man's head. "Or maybe a pizza would be useful in case he needs to do another forty days and nights without eating. I might put a fizzy drink on top. What do you think, Wiri?"

Wiri shrugged. "Dunno. Did they have pizza and fizzy back then? What if he doesn't like pizza and fizzy?"

"The decibels could have it for their last supper." Phoenix frowned. "What do you think, Mama?"

Hana sighed. "Disciples. They'll love it. Now go."

Phoenix grumbled but obeyed. Hana regretted not being quick enough to protect Wiri from the inevitable nightmares. She faced him, flushing confidence through her system and giving him a smile. Wiri lowered his head and gave her the side eye. "So now you're gonna give me a speech about how it came to visit, knocked on the door, got tired waiting for us to get home and fell asleep forever on the doormat."

Hana gaped. "I hadn't got that far. But that'll do."

"I'm not a baby." Wiri screwed his handsome features into a scowl. "And someone killed it and let it bleed out on the doormat."

"Maybe don't tell the others?" Hana's fake smile wilted and she glanced at her daughter pushing Mac down the slide. Stick-man Jesus floated across the lawn on a gust of wind.

"I won't tell. It looks like roadkill, Ma. Want me to grab a rubbish bag from the kitchen?"

"Yes please."

Hana stood guard as Wiri unlocked the front door and hopped over the stricken bundle of bloody fur. He returned with a black sack and a fistful of cookies. Hana accepted the sack and raised an eyebrow at the cookies. "I don't think it's hungry," she murmured.

"Distraction technique." Wiri grinned. "I learned that from you."

"Where did you learn your sass from?" Hana rolled the furry body into the scratchy doormat and wrestled it into the sack. The heavy material sprung open as soon as she released it and a metallic smell hit the back of her throat. She tied the bag tight and met Wiri's coy smile. "Tama." She answered her own question. "You learned it from him."

"Mostly you." Wiri's nose crinkled and a dimple appeared in his right cheek. He looked like Kane in that split second. Hana convinced herself it was Logan, the shift easy because of their strong sibling likeness. But the spark of devilment in Wiri's eyes channelled pure Kane Du Rose, no matter how she spun it.

"Wiri?" Hana paused with the question on her lips. He'd already suffered so much in his short life and the possum's appearance wouldn't help with the bed wetting or nightmares. "Would you like me to phone the hospital again and ask if your mother can see you for a visit?"

"Why?" His irises morphed to a stormy grey and his body stiffened.

Hana shrugged and the force of his angst took her breath away. The body dangled in the bag at her side and she floundered. "No reason. We haven't seen her for a while. Shall I ring them?"

Wiri nodded, the action wooden. "Yes, please. I'd like that. I need to ask her something."

"Okay." Hana forced a smile onto her lips. "I can do that. Just keep the little kids busy while I mop up the porch first?" She darted a glance at the slide as Mac pushed himself up backwards. Phoenix sat at the top, a dreamy look in her eyes and her mind elsewhere.

"Okay." Wiri moved away, his body already turning. "Ask Uncle to check the cameras."

"Wait! The what?" Hana spun to face him.

"The cameras." Wiri waved the cookies towards the porch roof. "I know they're there."

"How?" Hana's voice squeaked. "How can you know something like that when I don't?

Wiri turned and raised a dark eyebrow. "Pee in that plant pot and see if he shouts at you."

"You peed in my plant pot?" Hana looked down at the spray of colourful blooms taking pride of place either side of the brick porch supports. "Wiri!"

"I know, I know. Sorry. I was on my way to pee on the lemon tree and didn't make it. I saved up a big one because it was raining but it was too big."

"You pee on my lemons?" Hana whispered.

"Yep. Poppa Reuben taught me. Citrus trees love man-pee. Not girl-pee though. I'm helping."

"Great. Thanks. Maybe ask before you help anymore." Hana eyed the last of the phenomenal lemon crop hanging from the young tree. She forced herself to swallow. "Wiri!"

"Yeah?" He stopped walking and turned. Biscuit crumbs dotted his lips where he'd scoffed a crafty extra cookie before he needed to share.

"Why cameras?" She spread her hands out to her sides, the mental leap making no sense.

"Uncle wasn't at home when I did it. It's the day he and Toby trucked the steers to market and they got into a fight. He wasn't even near here. And he told me off hours later."

"They got into a fight?" Hana's chin jerked forward in shock. "How do you know this stuff?"

"I listen. A lot." Wiri tapped the side of his nose. "And I learned that from Uncle. Oh," he turned again, "and the fight was over you. Toby loves you and it makes Uncle Logan real mad."

"What?" Hana raised her voice at the retreating child and Phoenix looked up. Wiri wafted a hand behind him in dismissal before distracting Phoenix and Mac with the cookies.

Hana used a mop and hot soapy water to clean the porch, washing the spilled blood into the drainage pipe at the side of the path. Then she stood and looked at the front of the house with a more critical eye. If there was a camera, he'd hidden it well. "Are you spying on me, Logan Du Rose?" she demanded. Her phone rang in her jacket pocket.

35

Cloak and Dagger

"Cameras Logan! Really?" Hana fixed her hands on her hips and shook her head. "Why do you feel the need to spy on me?"

"I don't." Logan sank into a kitchen chair and fixed his hands behind his head. The chair rocked backwards on two legs and defiance back-lit his grey eyes, turning them the colour of grit.

Hana turned away and watched Wiri and Phoenix play on the slide. Mac sat underneath and ate a plate of sandwiches, oblivious to the thudding overhead. Hana saw him pick out the cucumber and lay it on the ground in a pile. "He's feeding that hedgehog again," she sighed.

"I'm not watching you, I promise." Logan lowered his voice and his tone changed to one of placation. His arms stretched higher and revealed his toned abdominal muscles. Hana turned in time to see a small scar above his tummy button grow and shrink with his movements as he dropped his arms.

"Then why do it and say nothing?" She spread her hands to emphasise the plea behind her question and Logan let the front chair legs crash onto the tiles. He straightened his shirt and peered at her from beneath his dark fringe.

"I didn't want to worry you. We've increased security over the last few months and I didn't want you to feel unsafe. I can see you're struggling with Mac's operation not working. It didn't seem fair to pile this on top."

Hana gave a slow nod and her shoulders slumped. "I found out about the new equipment and feed shed you've set up miles away."

"Toby?" Logan sat up straighter in the chair and his eyes became gimlet hard.

"Remember the errands I ran for him? I picked up the specialist feed from the wholesalers and it needed to go in the barn." Hana clicked her fingers. "The rest should have arrived by now. Do you think I should check or just leave it to him?" Logan's shoulders gave the slightest uplift and Hana felt herself on shifting sand. She squared her feet and leaned her backside against the kitchen counter. A sigh escaped her. "Do you think it's Asher again?"

"No." Logan's breath exhaled in a tired rush. "He caused casual vandalism, if there is such a thing. Irritating stuff meant to annoy or inconvenience me."

Hana snorted. "Apart from mating your prize winning Charolais heifers with a black and white bull!"

"Yeah." Logan grinned. "I don't think he thought that one through." He steepled his fingers in front of him and stared at them. "Last I heard he went to Northland to work with a whānau member."

Hana shook her head. "That means you got him a job in the family so you could keep tabs on him." Logan stared at her without replying and Hana's shoulders slumped. "I almost wish it was him, Logan. Otherwise, who is it and what are they doing? I want details this time, buddy. Don't freeze me out."

Logan listed the catalogue of mishaps on his fingers until he ran out. Hana slumped into the chair opposite with disbelief pulling her lips into a grimace. Some of the occurrences sounded minor. Others less so. Broken pipes, cut fences, smashed water troughs, adulterated feed, farm vehicles tampered with, brake lines cut. The list went on far longer than Hana imagined when she'd demanded details. She rolled her eyes. "Now the burglary and a dead possum," she said with a sigh. "What did the cameras show?"

"That's the problem." Logan reached for her hand. "The footage captured two different people. The one who came into the house entered through the laundry door. I can only see their shadow as they climbed over the fence from the bush. The camera doesn't reach around the side of the house and the sun might have lengthened the shadow to make them seem taller. It means very little, but it looks like someone of slight build. He knew where he was going and there's no external damage, so they had a key. The person who delivered the possum wore this weird tracksuit and I'm fairly sure it's a woman. She drove up as far as the gate, walked right in and knocked on the door before pulling the carcass out of a plastic bag and dropping it on the mat. She wore this striped hat thing with a peak. I think her hair went into the hat."

"Why would a woman do something like that in a house where there are children?" The shake of Hana's head contained indignation. "That's sick! Wiri saw the bloody thing."

"Yep. But not as sick as David Allen will be when I kick his ass into next week."

"You think he broke into the house?"

"No." Logan's eyes narrowed. "But I gave him locations for the cameras and he didn't finish installing them. I wanted one at the gate and more around the side of the house. He's left us wide open and that annoys me. I asked him four times last week to finish the job."

Hana closed her eyes and summoned up an image of the resident handyman turning up unexpectedly the week before. She pursed her lips and glared at her husband. "It's your fault, not his. You made him duck and dive to keep this from me. He came back up to finish the job that day I kept Wiri home with a cold. I thought David behaved a bit weird." She sat back and folded her arms. "He said you thought you'd forgotten to turn the outside tap off and sent him to check."

Logan gave a slow nod of approval. "You believed him though."

"Can I watch the footage?" Hana narrowed her eyes. "The woman might be Caroline up to her old tricks."

Logan's expression clouded. "Na. It's not her. Too tall and not skinny enough. She's made no attempt to speak to me and I think Caroline's got enough on her plate right now without harassing us. Besides, she hates blood and that thing was oozing as the woman pulled it out of the bag."

Hana shuddered. "Can I see the footage?"

"Nope." Logan shook his head. "I don't want you involved, Hana. I gave Sanders a copy. The possum was roadkill, but it's still not okay. Stay out of it."

"How do you watch the cameras when you're at work?" Hana probed for answers and knew the moment Logan conceded. The warning vein ticked beneath his jaw.

"On my phone." He said it as though it was normal. "The cameras connect to the WiFi at the house, but I need an Internet connection to log in. I tend to check in when I'm at the hotel. It's harder in the hills."

"And you're telling me you didn't take stills of the footage and keep them on your phone?" Hana held out her hand. "I want to see."

Logan huffed and dragged his phone from his jeans pocket. His index finger scrolled through a picture gallery and Hana rose and looked over his shoulder. Photos of the children mixed with images of broken fence wires and a close-up injury of a hairy white fetlock and a deep gash. Hana pointed. "What's that?"

"Methuselah. I'm not sure when he did that injury, but it isn't healing. I took the photo and emailed it to the vet." His finger pushed the broken fence wire back onto the screen. "This is just some of the niggly damage we're seeing. It started about three months ago, just after Mac came out of hospital. I can't get to the bottom of it." Logan's finger shoved aside more pictures of the children including one of Bodie's son, Jas. His finger froze at the image of a figure moving along the boundary fence. Hana tapped her temple in frustration.

"They stayed on the bush side. It's amazing they didn't fall down the cliff. Show me the other vandal. Are you sure it's not the same person?" Hana released a breath at the female shape wearing a large tracksuit. A Rastafarian hat encased her hair, its rainbow coloured peak covering her face. The pixelated image blurred the colours into a hazy effect.

Logan raised an eyebrow in question. "See, it's too hard to see her features because of the hat. But it's a woman, isn't it?"

Hana nodded. "I need to see them both moving though. The walk might give her away. I'm not convinced they aren't the same person. It's too hard to think of more than one vendetta against us."

Logan shrugged. "Let's see what Sanders comes up with."

"Okay. What about the hotel cameras? Won't they show who went into the apartment with Kane?"

Logan wrapped his arms around her waist and hauled her onto his knee. "No. We already checked. The only camera to catch Kane on the property is the one over the front doors when he spoke to Alfred and his bloody wife on the driveway. He goes nowhere near the main doors but walks out of range into the car park."

"Oh." Hana winced. "So how did he get inside their apartment a few days later?"

"Easy. He's used the private entrance and the spiral staircase. The private areas still have the old number code system Alfred's father created decades ago. He engineered the boxes and we don't know how to change the codes. I installed card access to all the hotel rooms years ago but avoided changing the family areas. It's expensive and nobody carries keys out here."

"Ahhhh." Hana tutted. "And Kane lived here as a child before the family split."

Logan nodded. "Yeah. It's a stupid oversight and on my list of improvements. David Allen is creating a similar thing from scratch, but we'll be able to change the codes on his. He's made the prototype and it's working. We've concentrated on installing cameras in the public areas and Kane avoided them all. The next time he appears in any footage, he's leaving the property feet first in a hearse."

Hana frowned. "How could he know where the cameras were? He's been living in the South Island since you sent him packing after the fire."

Logan shrugged. "Maybe he's in contact with Nev. He was here when we installed the camera in the main building."

"No." Hana wrinkled her nose. "Nev has no reason to do that. We've never wronged him. And we've kept Wiri safe. As far as he knows, we still believe Wiri is his son."

"Maybe." Logan shrugged. "None of this makes any sense."

"Did the camera over the front doors pick up anyone you recognised going into the house? And did Kane leave fingerprints anywhere?"

"No." Logan gave a slow shake of his head and accompanied it with a sigh. "I checked the camera and so did the cops. They dusted Alfred's apartment, the lift and every set of stairs for prints. I don't think they got anything decent. They ruled us out from the ones we gave them, but the kids' little fingerprints were everywhere."

"Oh." Hana winced. "I noticed Kane had gloves on when he died."

"Yep. I'm guessing the person with him wore gloves too. They were tossing Alfred's place, so went equipped."

"What does the camera show about Kane's death?" Hana asked.

Logan pursed his lips. "You come into shot and then jump back, as Kane falls out of shot. Then it's just chaos." His body stiffened and Hana felt him distance himself from her. A blank mask crashed down over his expression, leaving her cold inside. Something else about that camera footage upset him. Hana gave herself a mental shake and attributed it to his half-brother's death.

"When will Sanders get back to you about the footage?" she probed. "If I can see moving film, I might be able to identify both our visitors."

"Dunno." Logan patted her hip to indicate he wanted to stand. "Until then I want you to stop worrying about it. I've got this."

Hana nodded and pressed her lips against his before rising. She decided not to mention the phone call she'd taken earlier. Libby wanted to meet.

36

Libby

The barista tapped the metal scoop against the counter to dislodge the used coffee grinds. The sound echoed off the walls and ceiling, jarring Hana's nerves. Libby was late and Hana twisted the endearing trait into an annoying trigger. Sitting back in her chair, she forced herself to calm by staring through the wide windows at the mountain range. She pinpointed the location of her house on one of the lower peaks though the bush canopy blocked it from view.

A light rain dusted the ground and offered relief to the earth's baked crust. The weather forecast promised another period of drought which would negate the effects of the last few days of storms with one kiss of the sun. Hardened earth had repelled the few minutes of heavy rain they brought. The hotel roof collected what it could, perhaps delaying the need for water trucks for a few days. Logan monitored the stream near their house daily and fretted.

Hana contemplated the last few years of living on the mountain. Mostly she'd felt happy and secure. Logan had mentioned selling again and the conversation hung between them like a veiled threat. Perhaps he needed freedom from the whims of nature, a release from worrying about lack of water, cattle diseases and dwindling grass reserves. He loved teaching and could go back to it.

"Thank you." Hana smiled as the barista delivered her coffee. The girl frowned as she balanced Libby's chai tea on the tray. "She shouldn't be long," Hana promised. "You can leave it here." A little liquid slopped into the saucer as the girl laid it down. She paused as thought wanting to say something. Losing her nerve, she turned and hurried back to the counter.

Hana reached for a newspaper on an adjoining table and frowned at the headline as she held her phone to her ear. A grease spot bisected the by-line, but it still made her cringe. *'Murder halts school fair!'* the headline screamed. She groaned and read the loose copy. The writer knew less than her but had fished for drama, none of it accurate. It claimed police overran the hotel and put it at risk of closure. "Just what Logan needs," Hana breathed. "Fantastic."

"Pardon?" The call went through and Hana jumped.

"Sorry. I wish to make an appointment to see Anahera Du Rose. Her son is missing her."

The woman on the other end paused. "I'll check with the nursing staff monitoring her condition and come back to you. She went out somewhere the other day and she's been quite buoyant since."

"Out by herself?" Hana's nose wrinkled. "If she's going out, then we could take her for coffee. I think her son might enjoy that."

"I'll check. She went out on an accompanied visit, not by herself. Please can I take your phone number and phone you back?"

Hana finished the call as Libby blasted through the outer door. She stood on the doormat and shook water droplets from her hair. Her shoulders stiffened in an uncharacteristic tension and Hana guessed she'd been putting off the meeting until the final moments. Hana caught her eye, smiled and pointed at the waiting drink. Libby's steps seemed slower than usual as she navigated the chairs and tables. She stripped off her waterproof before sitting and Hana waited for her to stop fiddling around. She hadn't discussed the matter with Logan, choosing not to burden him further with her trivia, but as she watched Libby dig in her handbag, she wished for his straight-shooting brand of wisdom.

"I couldn't find my car keys," Libby said. She pursed her lips and blew an upward breath which mussed her damp fringe. Sighing, she took a sip of her tea. "Thanks for this. Today's a crazy day. I'm teaching a class in Pokeno over lunchtime, then Darren has an orthodontist appointment in Manukau at three. I need to find my car keys." She jerked her head towards the newspaper as Hana folded it and lay it back on the next table. "I saw that. Terrible thing to happen."

Hana nodded, listened to Libby's garbled itinerary and absorbed the hidden message behind it. *Hurry up.* She placed her elbows on the table, but the words wouldn't come. When she reached inside her mind, she found it devoid of sensible sentences. Her silence acted as a catalyst and forced Libby to speak first. "I realise this is hard for you, Hana. You see why I couldn't say anything."

Hana nodded. "Where did you meet?"

"I spoke at a conference a couple of years ago. The convener asked me to talk about the benefits of relaxation techniques." Libby shifted in her seat. "I like him, Hana. We know what we're doing."

"This has been going on for a couple of years? But he's married! He has children!" Hana raised her voice and Libby glanced at the barista. The girl frothed a jug of milk and the hissing of the machine covered Hana's cry. "Sorry." She raised her hands to placate the fire in Libby's eyes. "I don't mean to spread your business far and wide." She sighed. "This is a tiny town. I'm amazed I haven't found out before now."

Libby nodded. "So am I. But we are where we are."

"And where's that?" Hana leaned forward. "Where does that leave our friendship and his marriage?"

"That depends on you." Sadness clouded Libby's eyes. "Will you tell his wife?"

Hana blew out a breath and sat back in her chair with such force, the front two legs raised an inch off the ground. "I don't know," she admitted. "She should hear it from him."

"Or what? You'll tell her?"

Hana shook her head. "I'm not threatening you, Libby. I hate this. We've become good friends and I wish I didn't know." Hana swallowed. "I've been here before. A good friend started an affair with a relative of Logan's. We broke up for a while over it. Things got messy and I lost her friendship." Hana pushed a sugar sachet around the table with shaking fingers as memories of Anka and Tama flooded back. She exhaled and shook her head.

"Leave it with me." Libby sprang up and gulped the last of her tea. Her waterproof scattered droplets as she snatched it from the back of her seat. "I'll talk to him. Please don't do anything until I get back to you. I'll need to wait until he calls me next." Hana nodded and forced a smile onto her lips. But the smile fixed in place like a grimace at Libby's final parting shot. "You know, Hana, it's interesting. I told you the truth a few weeks back and you seemed fine with it. You're only upset now because you know who he is and it's a bit too close to home. I think that's a little hypocritical, don't you?"

Hana sat with her head in her hands until the barista returned to collect the crockery. She rattled the cups in their saucers and apologised as Hana jumped. "You look like you've got the weight of the world on your shoulders, Mrs Du Rose," she commented. Hana felt an expression of wariness crash down over her private agony and failed to hold it at bay. Perhaps hypocrisy weighed more than she imagined.

"Yeah, it's a hard time." Hana rose to leave and saw the girl's olive cheeks flush.

"I heard Tama came home for the tangi," she said. She lifted one foot from the floor and placed it over the top of the other.

Hana recognised the hall marks of infatuation and exhaled. "Is he still here?"

"Sorry." Hana burst her bubble without enjoyment. "His crew needed him back at work. He left straight afterwards."

"Oh." Disappointment ravaged the girl's expression. Hana fought the urge to warn her off and left before the words tumbled free.

Outside in the car park, she gave in to her craving to hear Logan's voice. She dialled his number half expecting to hear a voicemail message. A tingle shot through her when he followed the answering click with, "Hey beautiful."

"Hey. It's raining."

Logan's laugh warmed her. "Yep. Is that what you rang to tell me? Because I kinda got the message the second time my pants got soaked."

"Sorry. I wanted to hear your voice and prepared myself to get your voice mail. I don't have anything to say, really."

"Is something wrong?" Hana heard the power in his voice and imagined his broad shoulders squaring for a fight. She headed off further questions.

"No. Can't I just miss you?"

"Yeah. You can." His words betrayed the smile behind them. "Hey, do you wanna come somewhere with me? I just took a call from a dude in Rangiriri. He asked me to stop by."

"Yes please." Hana's face brightened. "As long as we're back in time for the school run. I nipped into town for coffee with Libby."

Logan paused and Hana heard him speak to someone else in a low voice. His tone sounded decisive as he came back on the line. "David Allen said he can drop me at the cafe near the school if that's where you are. He's got an appointment in Hamilton. I'll be about fifteen minutes. Wait there and we'll take your truck."

37

Breakfast with the Dead

"This is a very delicate matter." The Englishman ran a hand over his smooth chin and frowned up at Logan. "But I knew you'd rather we spoke in person."

"What's this about?" Logan sounded irritated and Hana felt the muscles in her neck tense. "I don't have time for guessing games, Paul."

The man raised a dark eyebrow and released a heavy sigh. He spread his hands in placation, dwarfed by Logan's height and mana. "I can claim on the insurance, but it's your reputation, mate. It's your good name."

"What is?" Logan dipped forward and Hana saw the warning vein begin a steady pulsing just under his jawline. His eyes flashed and Paul took a step back. Hana checked her watch and saw the hands moving closer to Mac's nursery finishing. She refused to arrive late and harried again.

"We don't know what you're talking about." Her tone sounded impatient and she tapped a frustrated toe on the glossy tiles of the hotel lobby. Her romantic honeymoon night spent at the expensive golf lodge seemed a lifetime ago. Logan glanced sideways at her and the sparkle of his grey irises mirrored her thoughts. "Please just tell us," Hana insisted.

Paul looked relieved at the opportunity to interact with Hana instead of the terrifying man next to her. He side-stepped, emboldened by her English accent. "He arrived ten days ago and he's run up quite a bill." Paul swallowed. "Now I hear he's passed away and I'm left with a large debt which won't get paid. I can tell my insurance, but they'll head straight to his widow and I didn't think you'd want that."

Logan tipped his head back and released a groan. Slower on the uptake, Hana paused for a moment before realising the implications. She frowned. "He stayed here? And you want us to pay Kane Du Rose's hotel bill?" Impatience budded in her chest as the minutes ticked by. "This is the important thing you've dragged us to Rangiriri for?"

Paul winced. "Not just that. His stuff is still here. I didn't want to throw it away."

Logan shook his head. "Didn't the cops take it?"

"What cops?" Paul blinked and his eyes widened. "Why would the cops come here?"

Hana heaved out a sigh and checked her watch again. "Someone murdered him," she bit. "The cops searched everywhere to find where he stayed before he died. They assumed he drove down from Auckland. I don't suppose they checked here." She glanced up at the glittering chandelier and suspected she knew why. "Did he have a car?"

"He arrived here over a week ago. No car is registered to his room." Paul stalked back to the reception desk and leaned over to lift something from beneath the counter. He stood on tiptoes to reach and withdrew a sheaf of papers bound with a staple in the top left corner. "I just heard he died." He shot a nervous glance at Logan and licked his lips, adding, "Sorry for your loss." Hana detected very little sorrow in his face as he pushed the papers into Logan's hands.

Logan's fringe bounced against his eyelashes as he scrutinised the contents. Hana drew close enough to recognise a lengthy invoice totalling over ten thousand dollars. She inhaled in shock at the cost of the room, movies and meals. Her shoulder bumped Logan's biceps as she snaked a comforting arm around his waist and jammed her fingers into the back pocket of his jeans. Bloody Kane, managing to stick the knife in even after death.

To her surprise, Logan smirked. He flipped to the back page and tapped an item listed near the bottom. Then he shoved the papers into Paul's chest. "Nice try!" he snapped.

"What?" Paul caught the crumpled invoice before it fell, searching through the listed items like a drowning man. "What am I looking at?"

Logan slipped an arm around Hana's shoulders and turned them both towards the front doors. "I don't know who you had staying in Room 14, but it wasn't Kane."

Paul winced and looked ready to concede the point. Then he shook his head. "He didn't register in that name, no. But I remember him. If he wants to call himself Kyne Smith, who am I to argue?"

"Not that!" Logan snarled. "I buried my brother in the ground on Saturday and put the soil over him myself! He sure as hell didn't eat scrambled eggs on toast for breakfast on the day of his own tangi."

Paul blanched and the papers shook in his hand. "But he did! I saw him." He swallowed and shot a frantic glance at Hana. "I wouldn't lie about this."

Hana looked up at Logan, watching him shake his head in disbelief. She took up his corner of the fight. "But you were happy to phone Kane's grieving brother to settle his bill as soon as you heard about his death. What do you want us to think?" Logan raised an eyebrow and rolled his eyes. Perhaps referring to him as a grieving brother stretched the truth too far.

"I know, I know." Paul's shoulders slumped and he appeared deflated. "I'm sorry. It's tacky. Times are hard." He waved the papers at Logan. "Don't worry. I'll talk to my insurer."

"Wait!" Hana held out her hand. "We'll settle the bill if you prove Kane ate that breakfast." Logan turned his body enough to give her an approving look, his eyes narrowing and one eyebrow raised high. "Do you have security cameras?"

"Yes." Paul grinned and Hana sensed him stepping back onto safe ground. "Let me get it organised." He jerked his head towards the busy restaurant. "Grab a coffee on the house and I'll be right back."

They sank into a leather sofa in the sumptuous room and Logan stretched an arm behind Hana's head. His fingers performed an irritating tap on the surface behind her. "It's changed since we came here on our wedding night." His lips quirked upward and he gave her a sultry sideways look laden with promise. "Remember?"

Hana snorted. "Parts of me will never forget."

Logan reached his other hand across and smoothed her soft cheek with the side of his thumb. "I love you, Hana Du Rose." His lips brushed hers. "I never tire of hearing your name linked to mine."

"Ahem." Paul stood in front of them. He hopped from foot to foot in an awkward balancing act. "I'll have your coffee brought to the office. We've found the relevant footage if you'd like to view it."

Hana glanced at her watch and groaned. "I can't arrive at the nursery late again."

"This won't take long." Logan rose and jerked his head to tell Paul to lead the way. Hana followed, dragging her feet along the corridor as she checked her watch. She walked into the office to see her husband shaking his head.

"What?" she asked. "It can't be Kane. I sat with his body."

"But it is!" Logan turned to her, his eyes wide and a quizzical expression on his face. "Look" He stood back so Hana could step in front of him.

The screen showed a pixelated view of the restaurant from above. Two images bisected the screen, both from a vantage point near the ceiling. A nerdy looking man ran the footage from both cameras at the same time. Hana watched as a grainy Kane Du Rose leaned over his breakfast. The black-and-white picture dulled the sumptuous food Hana remembered from her honeymoon and the image of the man looked blurred. She held her breath as Kane moved, seeing his head swing left and right as he surveyed the room. He looked nervous, any sudden noise causing him to jerk his head towards it. He stared at his breakfast without eating it, his fingers turning the pages of a complimentary newspaper. Then he rose to leave. His long-legged gait took him across the restaurant and through the open doors into the lobby.

The office remained silent throughout the few minutes of film. Then the tech killed the footage rerun and a hazy reception area filled the screen.

"See." Paul sounded triumphant. He spoke to the man sitting at the keyboard. "Can you find the feed from the first floor, please? We should see him going back to his room."

He nodded and Hana's brow furrowed to painful lines as she watched Kane Du Rose stride along an upstairs hallway and stop outside a room. He glanced left and right as he put the card into the door access reader and both cameras captured the darkness of his expression, thought it didn't show clear features. She shook her head and sighed. "It's him, isn't it?"

Logan nodded. "Yeah." He stared at Paul. "Your cameras are old. The picture is so bad, it would never stack up in court. But I'm an honest man, so show us the room he used and then I'll settle his bill."

"Thanks." Paul's expression took on a brightness absent before. He led them to the reception desk and handed them over to a man behind the counter. "Sorry for your loss," he reiterated before shaking Logan's hand. He didn't even bother to offer Hana the same courtesy and she sensed his interest waning after Logan's promise to pay the bill. He strode back into the restaurant and Hana heard Logan mutter an insult under his breath.

They followed the receptionist into the lift and up to the first floor. He didn't relinquish control of the card, slotting it into the reader and standing back for them to enter. "Paul had the room cleaned this morning," he said. His tone sounded apologetic. "He gave instructions to collect his luggage together and told the maid put it all there." He pointed to a luggage rack next to the bathroom and then blanched. "Oh. It's gone." He shook his head and whipped around to face them. "There wasn't much, but it was there. Just a couple of plastic bags. That's what Paul said, anyway." He peered into the empty dustbin as though it might hold clues.

Hana peered around Logan to see the empty luggage rack. She watched her husband walk across the room. She noticed how he touched nothing and pressed her hands behind her back to mirror his caution. A double and single bed occupied one wall facing the dressing table. A wall-mounted television filled part of the opposite wall next to an air conditioning unit. Logan poked his head into the bathroom and shrugged.

"It's been serviced." He sounded thoughtful. "They wipe every surface at our place, vacuum and mop the floors. Is there somewhere they might not have cleaned that the cops can use for prints or DNA?"

The receptionist's head jerked back on his neck. "Not at five hundred dollars a night," he scoffed. "They wouldn't dare."

Logan shook his head. "So, where's the luggage?" he demanded.

"I don't know. Paul gave the maid clear instructions." The man squirmed in discomfort. "Does that mean you won't pay the bill?" He gnawed on his lower lip and Logan sighed.

"It means you need to call the cops," he replied. His footsteps looked heavy as he trudged towards the hallway without looking back. Hana trailed behind, an air of finality in the situation. Confusion cast a pall over the elevator as they rode down to the lobby. Logan's knuckles showed white on the hand rail on the ride to the ground floor and Hana used his credit card to settle the bill while he waited for her on the front steps.

"I'd like a copy of the invoice," she said, holding out her hand in expectation.

The receptionist printed off a fresh one and gave her a practiced smile as he folded the papers in half. "Thank you for your custom," he said and then faltered, realising what he'd said. "Oh, sorry." He pursed his lips and Hana turned away and left him blustering. He called after her and his cheeks pinked at the glare she administered. "There's a key card outstanding for the room. We'd like it back please to avoid an additional charge."

"Help yourself," she called over her shoulder. "I can give you directions to the cemetery."

Logan climbed into the truck and sat with one hand on the steering wheel as Hana reached back for her seatbelt and clipped it into place. Logan remained frozen, the keys still in the cup holder between them. He made no move to press the brake and activate the button to start the ignition. Hana sat in silence for a moment, giving her husband time to collect his thoughts. When he looked at her, she felt a flicker of alarm at the hopelessness in his eyes. The darkness in his soul seemed near the surface and frightened her. "What is this?" Logan shifted in his seat to face her. "I saw his body, Hana." She heard a catch in his voice. "I hated the guy but never imagined I'd see him smashed to pieces like that." He heaved out a sigh and shook his head. "Shot by a jealous husband, getting into a bar fight or drunk driving off a cliff. That's how I imagined Kane Du Rose going, not this way." Logan held his hands out, scarred palms facing upward. "How can a man die one day and eat breakfast the next? What am I missing?"

Hana shook her head and reached for his fingers. She caught his left hand and lifted it to her lips. "I don't know," she replied. "Let's leave it to the cops for a change like you suggested, shall we? If it's an error with their tech, Sanders will find out. They might show the wrong date on everything."

Logan exhaled and started the engine. "Okay." He slipped his hand from her grasp and reversed out of the parking space. "But just so you know, Sanders doesn't fill me with any confidence."

38

The Orphaned Calf

Hana checked her watch and directed Logan towards Mac's nursery. He drove the mountain roads with expertise and familiarity, allowing her to relax enough to broach her latest issue. "Do you think I'm a hypocrite?" Her question startled Logan and his face creased into a mask of confusion.

"No. Why?"

Hana exhaled. "What if you knew someone was having an affair but rationalised that it was okay because it didn't affect you? Then you realised you knew both the people having the affair and it really mattered. Is that hypocritical?"

Logan swallowed and had more difficulty with the question than Hana anticipated. "I don't know, Hana. That's a messed-up question and I can't answer it." His words emerged as a growl.

Hana peered sideways at the hard expression on his face. She pouted. "But you always have answers. If you don't know then nobody does."

Logan exhaled. Then he opened the side window enough to make the air freshener dangling from the rear-view mirror dance. The violent breeze also killed the conversation.

Hana climbed onto the running board of the truck as Logan pulled up to the nursery. She looked back to see if he would come with her, but he picked up his phone and dialled a number. Hana shook her head and walked towards the low building, her shape disappearing amid the throng of other parents rushing from nursery to school to collect children. Some of the women glanced at Hana and then across at the car, making silent appraisals of her husband. She gritted her teeth and forced a smile onto her lips.

Sam greeted her with Mac in his arms. Her son played with the pastor's dog collar, fitting it around his own neck and grinning. He held it in place with one tiny hand and sucked his other thumb. Hana snuffed out a laugh. "Don't give him ideas," she warned. "Logan's already wary about our tambourine banging daughter. I don't think he's ready to lose his son to the priesthood."

Sam threw his head back and laughed. Mac mimicked the action, then popped his thumb free so he could fit the ends of the white plastic back through Sam's collar. He leaned away to admire his handiwork and satisfied, pushed his thumb between his lips and rested his temple against Sam's collarbone. Then he closed his eyes. Hana envied him the simplicity of his touch-based world view. "Ah well," Sam mused, "I'm sure my grandmother could offer tips if it happens." He waggled his eyebrows and Hana nodded.

"Yeah, thanks. I'll remember that. And thanks for sorting out my flax lessons. I'm actually starting to enjoy raranga."

"I don't know what you mean." Sam feigned innocence and Hana wagged her finger.

"Isn't lying a sin?" Her smile drooped as she remembered Libby's accusation. She contemplated asking Sam the question Logan wouldn't answer. When the words refused to form on her tongue, she found her own conclusion. She was looking for absolution where there wasn't any. It was hypocritical and so was she. Libby spoke the truth.

Sam carried Mac to the truck and settled him inside. When the little boy puckered his lips for a kiss, Sam offered his whiskered cheek. Logan killed his phone call and offered Sam a handshake. He seemed less tense and Hana hung nearby, his refusal to vindicate her both painful and strange.

"How goes it, Logan?" Sam asked, his tone casual. "How's life on your mountain? Did the rain earlier help your drought?"

"A little." Logan blinked and his nose wrinkled. "I just rang the vet. One of my best dams died giving birth this morning. We worried she might be a victim of the drought or the vandalism, but he did a post-mortem and said she died from natural causes. Her heart gave out."

"Sorry." Sam clicked his tongue. "That sucks. I guess it's about more than just lack of water or the quality of the grass, isn't it? Do the cops know about the vandals?"

Logan nodded. "Yep. And now I've an orphaned calf to find a substitute dam for."

Sam winked at Hana. "I'm sure your wife would love two hourly feeds and a baby cow in her kitchen."

"No, she wouldn't," Hana retorted. "But Phoenix would."

"Ah, Phoenix." Sam rolled Hana's daughter's name on his tongue. "What a little trooper she is. How did you two spawn such delightful offspring?" His lips creased into a grin and he turned away with a wave. "See you around Du Roses."

Hana climbed into the passenger seat and gave Logan a look of sympathy. "You didn't tell me about the cow," she said, her voice soft. "What will you do with the calf?"

Logan shrugged and started the engine. "What I always do, Hana. I'll sort everyone else's shit out."

Hana reached out to touch his hand as he spun the steering wheel. "Have I done something wrong?" she asked.

"No." His reply sounded sharp and his jaw tightened as he ground his teeth. "Just leave it."

Wiri seemed subdued on the ride home after school and Phoenix chattered to herself in the middle seat. Hana glanced around once and saw her daughter slip her hand into Wiri's without looking at him. He squeezed her fingers and kept hold of them as though the tiny girl provided a lifeline Hana didn't understand. She sighed and rested her head against the seat. "Are you going back to work?" She lowered her voice and spoke to Logan.

He offered her a nod. "Yeah. Need to sort this calf out now." He ran a hand through his hair and sighed. "Hana, we need to talk about some things. I just don't know where to start."

Hana stiffened. "Bad things?"

Logan's smile lacked reassurance. "Just things," he said. "But not now. Later."

Hana opened her mouth to reply but ringing issued from the car speakers. Mac slept on but the other two children stared with interest at the dashboard screen. Wiri leaned sideways for a better look, his nose crinkling in recognition of the number for the hotel reception. Logan accepted the call. "Du Rose," he answered. "What's up?"

The male receptionist's voice echoed around the vehicle. "Hi, Mr Du Rose. Your four o'clock appointment has arrived early. I've put him in the restaurant and offered him a drink."

Logan groaned and pursed his lips. Hana's brows furrowed as she watched her husband's clever brain go into action behind his grey irises. He shot a sideways glance at her and winced. "Thanks. I'm five minutes out. Give him whatever he wants on the house." Hana's lips parted in surprise, but her expression clouded as Logan raised a hand to silence her questions. His finger moved to kill the call. He wasn't fast enough.

"How do I pronounce his name again?" the receptionist asked. His tone sounded contrite as though Logan had given him copious instructions earlier. "Is it Chee or Chay?"

Hana gasped at the name of the Triad commander as Logan responded. "Che. How many people did he bring with him?"

"Four," the receptionist replied. "Men. I gave them drinks too. Is that okay?" He lowered his voice. "Two refused. One is walking around the hotel and the other is standing by the front door."

"It's fine," Logan snapped and his index finger ended the call. He turned to Hana before she could begin her ready tirade and he shook his head. "Don't!" he ordered. "Just don't!"

Hana swallowed her curiosity and a reflex action in her heart locked the betrayal away. Logan had promised to drop his association with the Triads and she'd believed him. She worried at the tag on her fleece until fluff came away in her fingers. Logan refused to look at her, his lips pursed into a thin line and the vein beneath his jaw pulsed like it might burst.

39
Old Wounds

"Hi." Hana nodded to Caroline as Mac escaped to the play area with Phoenix hot on his heels. Wiri sauntered behind them with his hands shoved deep into his pockets. His gait looked stiff and odd, his legs kicking out sideways as his hands dragged his trousers down around his hips. He shot a glance back at Caroline and though he'd spent time with her in Reuben's house, he ignored her. Hana watched him make the conscious decision not to speak and her brow furrowed. He was pure Du Rose to the marrow.

Logan had refused to discuss the presence of the Triad commander on his home turf. They'd parted with animosity between them. Logan had stalked towards his office in the hotel and left her standing in the car park. Hana worried at a thumbnail and gave herself a mental shake. She needed to keep her wits about her.

Caroline shifted sideways on the bench and left Hana no option but to sit. She offered a watery smile with just a hint of sincerity. "When do you head home?" Hana asked, desperate to know the answer.

Caroline shrugged and a blonde curl slithered over her shoulder. "I don't know. I might not."

Hana forced her face into a blank mask, but her heart rate hiked. "Where will you go?"

Caroline turned towards her and rested an arm along the back of the bench. She leaned forward and lowered her voice. "Can you ask Logan to let me stay here?"

"What?" Hana's voice rose, all pretence at cordiality abandoned. "No, I can't."

"Can't or won't?" Caroline released a sigh and watched Edin greet Mac. Her lower lip trembled. "I have nowhere else to go, Hana. Logan and I are history. You won."

Hana shook her head, rational thought replaced by panic. Caroline's words meant nothing in the face of desperation. "Logan won't allow it."

"He might if you ask him."

"No." Hana cringed and closed her eyes. "You jilted him at the altar. He won't forgive you." She yearned to state the obvious, but it sounded too cruel. *I don't want you here.*

Caroline blew out a breath. She lifted her fingers to her lips and worried at a nail. "I didn't want to jilt him," she whispered. "I loved him."

The play park grew too small to contain Hana's distress at hearing Caroline's profession of love for Logan. The bench and Caroline's proximity seemed to constrict her breathing. Hana rose in a jerky movement. "This is why you can't stay," she hissed. "It drags up too much of the old stuff."

Mac held hands with Edin and they giggled like conspirators. Wiri leaned a sloped shoulder against the climbing frame and watched. Phoenix shouted to him from the swings. "Push me, Wiri!" She let go of the swing to wave and Wiri's eyes widened in concern.

"Don't let go," he grumbled. "I'm coming."

"Sorry about Kane," Hana said. "I'll give you a couple more day's grace and then you should head out. You can't stay here." The old Hana would have added an apology and taken on the weight of guilt for Caroline's situation. With an effort of will, she knocked it aside as the mantle tried to settle on her shoulders. She wasn't sorry.

"Reuben went crazy." The unexpected words cut through the fog in Hana's mind and she stared into Caroline's blue eyes in confusion.

"What?"

Caroline waved her hand, the fingers fine boned and delicate. "When I left Logan at the altar. Reuben went crazy. He thought the marriage would give him access to his son. He started the land deal as a project for them both to work on after we married. Reuben was a dreamer and had big plans for the future once Logan got to know him. He nurtured this stupid father and son illusion. But it all went wrong. I missed the wedding, Logan skipped town and the developers turned nasty and took more land than they agreed. Reuben ended up in court, in debt and devastated. I'm sure you know the rest."

Hana paused and took a step towards the bench, her escape forgotten. The noise of the children's laughter faded. "Reuben wanted the marriage?" Her voice croaked as her throat dried and her tongue stuck to the roof of her mouth. Caroline's version of Logan's father went against everything Hana believed.

She nodded. "He did. Reuben raised me. He loved Logan and our marriage offered him an unlimited free pass to see his son. I'd never seen him so excited." Her eyes filled with tears. "I never knew my parents, Hana. Reuben was my father and mother. Marrying Logan was the one thing I could do to thank him for a lifetime of loving me when no one else did. He never forgave me for letting him down and now he's dead. Kane too. There's no one left who gives a damn about me and Edin."

Hana put a hand up to her forehead and felt the clamminess there. Sweat beaded at her hairline and edged along her spine. "Reuben didn't want the marriage." Her voice sounded strained and odd as she repeated the facts as she knew them. "He couldn't."

Caroline shook her head and Hana pressed her fingers against her lips to keep the secret from spilling out in her anguish. It wasn't hers to tell. Maybe Reuben hadn't known about his wife's infidelity, or that she birthed Caroline as a result. Caroline couldn't know she'd married her half-brother. Could she? Hana's gaze strayed to Edin as the child gripped Mac's fingers and practiced jumping again. His eyes lit up with a curious green fire as though the little girl sparked a hidden life within him. Caroline released a heavy sigh. "Reuben wanted it," she reiterated. "I let him down."

"Why?" Hana breathed. "Then why did you jilt Logan?"

"She made me." Caroline's eyes darkened until her blue irises shone like gems. The wariness returned to her face and five years of happiness fell away to leave the familiar hard mask. She rose and collected a child's cardigan from the seat next to her. "I don't want to talk about it," she spat. "Give me a week to find somewhere else. Then we'll get out of here."

40

Taken

Hana spent the evening helping Leslie wind a mess of skein into balls neat enough to knit with. Its representation of her messy situation silenced her on the matter of Che's visit. Leslie had curbed her opinion of Logan as promised and Hana wanted to do nothing to stoke the latent fire again. The children played a board game with Alfred and dined on food filched from the hotel's industrial kitchen. Hana wound the wool and listened to the children's giggles.

"Ooh, Macky, no! Don't eat that." Phoenix tussled with her brother and winced as Mac spat the black counter into her palm. When he glanced across at Hana with a mischievous glint in his eyes, she gave a slow shake of her head in reprimand. Mac clambered into Alfred's lap and contented himself with sucking his thumb and watching Alfie bounce his counters around the board. An emotional paralysis descended over Hana's head as the sadness since his operation caught up with her and compounded the other issues in her life. Her hands kept busy winding the wool, but her mind engaged her elsewhere in myriad worries both tumultuous and minor.

"You're quiet, girly," Leslie mused, her voice low. "You okay?"

"Yeah, fine thanks." Hana tucked the last end into the ball and rose. The darkening sky heralded doom and she stretched her arms above her head and heard the tiny bones in her back click. "It's later than I realised. I should get this lot into bed."

Phoenix wrinkled her nose. "But I'm winning, Mama! Can you let me finish?"

"Sorry, no." Hana stepped around the room collecting discarded school clothes and bags. Mac snoozed against Alfred's chest and Hana felt a wave of guilt for staying out so long. She sensed herself avoiding the dark, empty house and the ensuing argument with her stubborn husband. They made an agreement and he'd broken it.

"I haven't done my homework." Wiri rolled his eyes and stared at Hana as though expecting her to fix it. She shook her head.

"Tough, Wiri. You played games instead."

"I didn't do my reading." Phoenix's eyes widened like saucers.

Hana shrugged. "Then you both need to do detention. I'm not responsible for everything. I wish people would learn that."

Leslie frowned and eyed her sideways. Hana almost heard the alarm bells going off in the other woman's mind as her intuition put in overtime. She opened her mouth to speak but Hana derailed her with a request for help putting the children into the car. Wiremu grumbled all the way up the mountain and Hana ignored him. Nobody fought over the front seat, choosing instead to keep a distance between them and Hana. When Phoenix made whimpering noises, she turned in alarm and almost drove them over the cliff. "Stop!" she snapped. "I can't do this!"

Hana heard the click of a seatbelt and felt a hand on her shoulder. A knot formed in her chest as the whisper tickled her ear. "You're not gonna take tablets and die, are you, Ma?"

She shook her head. "Belt on Wiri and no. I promise." Her voice wobbled at the reference to his mother and the weight of the child's expectations added themselves to the heavy pile. "I'm just tired," she lied. "We'll finish homework in the morning over breakfast. Everything will be okay."

The front bumper of an expensive SUV came into view as Hana's headlights bounced over the narrow lane. It didn't quite block her route through the gate, but she slid to a halt and engaged the hand brake. The gate stood open behind the strange vehicle, indicating the owner had turned around in the driveway beyond to ensure they faced back down the mountain. It bore the hallmarks of planning for a hurried escape. Wiri's belt clicked free again and he stood. "Whose is that?" he demanded.

"I don't know!" Hana snapped. "Stop undoing your bloody seatbelt!" She turned to glare at him. "The little kids copy everything you do, Wiri! Sit down and fasten it." His grey irises gleamed and Hana turned to face the children on the back seat. "Sit here and do not move or there will be big trouble!" She climbed from the truck and used the key fob to engage the central locking. Mac remained asleep, but two curious faces peered at her from the rear seat.

Hana used the light on her keyring to pick her way through the open gate and along the drive. Logan's unhealthy obsession for solar lights helped strengthen the effect of the weak beam, although two lay smashed on the ground where the visiting truck had driven over them. Whoever owned it hadn't gone as far as the house to use the turning circle.

An odd scraping sound came from the back of the house and Hana froze. A distant smash sent her moving off the driveway and onto the grass. Grappling in her jeans, she dug for her phone and groaned as she remembered it charging in the truck. A return to the vehicle would herald endless questions and risk Wiri wanting to take a look. Hana turned towards the house and kept moving.

"So that's where my plant pots are going." After navigating the building with an impressive stealth, Hana stepped out from the darkness beneath the eaves. The figure froze at the rail, the next potted victim already raised in outstretched arms. Hana's favourite gerbera dropped out of sight and she heard the thud and then smash as the pot broke against the jagged edges of the ridge below. She took another step which put her on the deck. White hot temper flared behind her green eyes. "Nice hat." Hana's head cocked to one side and her fingers shook. Fear mingled with anger. "Not really your thing though."

The figure turned towards her, but the expression remained blank. The Rastafarian hat covered her hair and the wide peak shrouded her eyes in shadow. Hana opened her mouth to speak again as the woman's lips curved into a flat smile. "Oops," she mouthed.

Hana heard her laugh, a tinkling backdrop against the sharp crack which reverberated within her skull. She experienced an explosion of pain. The nothingness pulled her into an embrace filled with sickness and confusion.

41
A Very Real Danger

Hana heard the children moving around in the room next door and sighed. Her body ached and she groaned as she tried to push herself upright on jelly arms. With a head that felt filled with cotton wool, she turned enough to push her feet free of the covers and find the floor. A soft rug met her bare skin and she let her toes wriggle against the texture, not recognising it from home. Hana raised a hand to her face and her fingers contacted a lump over her cheekbone. She felt roughness and a stab of pain shot into her eye like a needle pressed through her pupil into her brain. "Ow!" she groaned. Dipping forward increased the pressure in her head and she battled with the desire to sink back into the oblivion of sleep. Nausea bit deep inside her stomach and she rubbed a hand over her ribs. "Not my bloody head again!" she groaned.

Straightening her legs, she forced herself into a standing position. She recognised nothing. Dark curtains swathed a window next to her bed. Hana flicked at the fabric and it moved enough to reveal a brick retaining wall a few feet from the glass. The strange room spun and she lurched sideways. Her hands grappled for something to hold on to and she connected with a cabinet. The clink of a glass preceded running water and as she fell, Hana felt a wave of guilt mixed in with fear. She'd knocked something over. A glass containing liquid.

"Mama?" Running feet pattered over bare floorboards and then light spilled across Hana's face. She leaned up on one elbow and shielded her eyes, blinking from the glare. Phoenix appeared through an interconnecting door and her wide eyes channelled anxiety.

"Ma." Wiri reached her first. His small hands grasped her upper arm and he tugged.

"Hold on." Hana's voice croaked from lack of use. She dropped the hand from her face and saw Mac standing in front of her. His green eyes studied her with open curiosity and a furrow lined his brow. "I'm okay." She tried to smile and felt her lip crack in the corner of her mouth. "Just give me a minute."

Scooting back, she pressed her spine against the bed and curled her knees into her chest. Pyjama bottoms clothed her legs and she didn't recognise the pattern. She smoothed her hand over the matching pyjama shirt. "Who dressed me?" She looked up at Wiri for answers. "Where are we?"

"Holiday." Phoenix pushed a finger into her mouth. She chewed it and balanced on one leg, the bare toes of the upper foot pressing over the others. Her eyes sparkled with pleasure and curiosity. She liked the idea of a holiday, but Hana's distress took the happy edge off it and left her confused. "Do you want the bathroom? It's just there. We can share it, but Mac's hidden the soap."

"Holiday." Hana repeated the word and forced herself to calm. "Do you know where?"

"Secret." Wiri put a finger to his lips and pressed, a subconscious demonstration. Hana inhaled, sensing they didn't know and the facade made it into something mysterious and exciting. Wiri's old blue robe hung like an overcoat, tatty and worn next to his newer pyjamas.

"Oooooh!" Mac took a step towards her, his green eyes round with concern. He lifted his hand and moved to stroke her cheek, recoiling at something he saw there. Hana mirrored his movement, identifying the slickness of oozing blood. She caught Mac's hand and squeezed his fingers with her other hand, infusing him with fake reassurance.

"I'm okay," she mouthed. Forcing a smile, she felt her lip crack in the opposite corner. "Just tired. I'm fine."

"Mama, you bleedin'. It's hurtin' you." Phoenix's grey eyes filled with concern. "What happened to you?"

"Don't worry, Phoe." Wiri snaked an arm around her shoulders and she nestled close, still chewing her finger and eyeing Hana with jerky, frightened movements. Mac caught the atmosphere and his fingers reached out to clasp the fabric of the older boy's pyjama pants. He bunched it in his fingers and held on. Hana forced herself to focus on something familiar to chase away the fog in her brain. The children wore their spare nightclothes from Leslie and Alfred's apartment. Mac's favourite nightshirt looked too short. It didn't meet the waistband of his pants and left a gap where his pale tummy peeked through. She'd replaced them but he refused the new ones after sniffing the fabric. They looked the same but apparently weren't.

Hana inhaled and sat up straighter. She forced her body to uncoil. "Who put you in your pyjamas?"

"Papa and Nonie Leslie." Wiri pouted and tugged on his dressing gown cord. "Poppa Alfie stopped her throwing my favourite gown away."

"Right." Hana gave a shallow nod that didn't threaten to make her head fall off. "So, where's this holiday then? Somewhere nice?"

Phoenix brightened and her eyes resumed their sparkle. "There's a beach," she said. She unfurled her legs and dropped down next to Hana on the floor. Shuffling closer, her cool feet pressed against Hana's thigh in a search for comfort. "Wiri saw it."

Hana's gaze flicked to him. He nodded. "There's a beach outside our window. It got light about half an hour ago. The sun is rising above the sea, so our room faces east." His lips pursed as though he knew something. He jerked his head towards Phoenix and crouched down to speak to her. "Take Macky to see it, Phoe. He loves the beach."

Phoenix lit up from the inside and excitement opened her face like a delicate bud sensing warmth. "Okay." She bounded to her feet and snatched up Mac's hand. "Beach," she said and nodded her head with emphatic movements. "You wanna see a beach and the sea?"

Mac squinted but allowed her to lead him back through the connecting door. Hana heard them clambering onto a mattress. Wiri waited a beat before dropping to his knees next to Hana. "There's nothing to worry about," he whispered. "Something happened to you at the house. I called Uncle Logan on your phone." He swallowed and his eyes widened. "I know you said not to undo my seatbelt again, but you didn't come back. A lady with a stripy thing on her head ran towards the car so I covered us with the black blanket from the parcel shelf. She looked in but couldn't see us in the dark. She drove away and Uncle arrived soon after. The lady nearly drove him over the bleep bleep cliff on her way down." Wiri pursed his lips and gave Hana a smug smile. "He didn't say bleep though, Ma."

Hana raised her hand to stop him finishing the tale with a hail of expletives. "I can imagine," she sighed. She sent her hand to her cheek and touched the raised cloth stitches. "That sucks. It's in the same spot I cut before when I fell off Sacha. It had almost healed." She squeezed her eyes shut and the action hurt. It gave her time to think, so she didn't alarm Wiri further. "Is Logan here, Wiri? Where is he?"

Wiri pursed his lips. "Why don't you remember, Ma? You told us to get in the car." He pointed at her cheek. "And that's worse. Way worse than before." He dragged out the syllables for emphasis.

"I told you to get into a car?" Hana shook her head and winced. "I got hit over the head and woke up here."

"No. You were talking. Uncle Logan wiped the blood off your head and talked to his friend. We went down to the hotel and stayed there for a while. Then we got into the big car." He sighed. "Maybe the pain pill they gave you made you forget."

"Pain pill. I don't remember a pain pill. I'd love one now though. Who gave it to me?"

"A man in the big car." Wiri lowered his voice. "A lady keeps checking on us. Phoe and Macky didn't wake until an hour ago, so I told them we're on holiday. Maybe the lady has pain pills."

Hana released a sigh. The boy's earnest expression pained her. He knew too much. Far too much. "What does the lady look like?" She swallowed as Wiri's narrowed eyes told her he didn't understand. "Do you know who she is? Is it the same lady from last night, the one with the stripy hat?" Her mind drifted to Caroline, but she couldn't ask the question.

Wiri winced and glanced at the door to the next room. His bottom teeth trapped his top lip and he grimaced. When he looked back at Hana, his grey eyes held the glint of seriousness. She saw a man trapped in a child's body. "I don't know any of them. There are guards and a lady. This lady is smaller than the one from last night. She brought you a drink of water." He grimaced. "You knocked it on the floor when you fell." Crawling to the side of the bedside cupboard, he reached between the gap and retrieved two halves of a crystal tumbler. Setting them one inside the other, he put them on the cupboard with care.

"Who undressed me?" Hana whispered, not sure why it mattered so much but feeling it did. "Where are my clothes?"

Wiri turned towards the bedroom's main door. It stood between two pine wardrobes. "The lady. I think she took your clothes. They had blood on them." He swallowed and pointed to her face. "You have more blood on you even though Uncle Logan wiped it away. You growled at him for using Nonie's drying towel. Are you sure you don't remember? Are you tricking me?"

Hana released a gasp and tried to stand. Her legs wobbled beneath her and she used the cupboard to haul herself upright. "This is crazy!" she breathed. "I don't understand what's happening."

"I will explain everything." The voice sounded clipped and contained the inflection of someone speaking English as a second language. Hana screwed her head around to face the door and the action sent darts of pain into her temple. She held her breath as the gap widened to reveal a slender woman with dark hair. She'd pulled the long straight tresses so tight against her head, they appeared painted onto her scalp. An olive complexion added to her stunning appearance. High cheekbones and almond-shaped eyes finished the delicate face, but the mouth remained in a straight line. She pushed herself into the room and closed the door behind her. Then she bowed. "My name is Annalise Che," she said. "I believe you know my mother."

42

Safehouse

Hana opened her mouth to speak and Annalise Che raised a hand to stop her. The movement of the delicate fingers held a hidden command for silence and Hana's spine prickled with irritation at her immediate compliance. She exhaled, recognising her old nature and hating it. Pushing herself up and backwards, her legs settled on the mattress and she straightened her spine. "Don't shut me up," she bit. "I have questions."

Annalise Che inclined her head and a small smile found her lips. "You do. But your children are hungry. Breakfast is served in the dining room if you'll follow me."

Hana swallowed, hearing a meal invitation from her captor and experiencing momentary confusion. The sound of Wiri's stomach growling tipped her hand and made her compliance assured. "Okay." She forced her legs to obey and wobbled upright. Wiri wrapped an arm around her waist and she braced herself against his shoulder, surprised at the strength in his young body. Her tentative mass pressed harder as she realised he could take her weight. Hana held her breath, sensing his childhood slipping away from her. She had so much still to teach him and the hour glass conspired to rob her. His upturned look of encouragement made his eyes sparkle as though he'd plugged into her soul and understood. His fingers flexed and tightened against her ribs. "Thank you," she whispered.

They followed Annalise along a dark hallway and she steered towards a door at the end. Phoenix followed Hana, her fingers clasped around Mac's. She chatted to no one in particular, her sweet voice tinkling as a faint echo. A glance back at Mac's face showed pursed lips and eyes fixed on the route ahead. He blinked once and registered Hana's quick smile with a slight jerk of his head. Fine-tuned to her moods, he'd tasted her reticence and disliked it. Hana brightened her face and faked a certainty she didn't feel, determined to keep her concerns off his thin shoulders.

Light flooded the hallway as Annalise turned the door handle and Hana gasped. She raised her left hand up to protect her eyes at the same time as Wiri breathed out a curse straight from Logan's banned list. He halted and released a grunt as Phoenix barrelled into his back with her head down. A small hand pressed against Hana's thigh and Mac saved himself from the same fate. He snaked his arm around to clasp her leg, his contact solid and determined.

"Breakfast is served." Annalise stood aside and offered a short bow of her lithe body. Black eyelashes fluttered in pleasure as the ragtag group pressed into the room.

"Whoa!" Phoenix exclaimed. She released Mac's hand to clap hers together in delight. Her eyes sparkled as she beamed up at Hana. "It's a princess palace," she whispered. "I love it."

Annalise's smile grew broader, though she kept any comment to herself. Hana stared around at her sumptuous surroundings. A wide sitting room gave way to an open plan dining room and then a kitchen. Windows covered every available space and the absence of walls created a greenhouse effect. Heat filled the rooms and a light breeze kissed her cheeks. It took a second for Hana to realise the windows were doors flung open to the sea view. It appeared as though the ocean lapped at the foundations of the house.

"Please. Sit and eat. Your husband knows you're here." Annalise waved her hand towards the huge table and the children edged forward. She raised an eyebrow at Hana in silent communication and she nodded.

"Up table." Hana forced a smile on her face as she issued the familiar command and the children surged onto the ornate wooden dining chairs. Shades of red and gold shrouded a dark wooden table in a sparkling fabric. The expanse of windows displayed blinds at ceiling height, but nothing obscured the incredible view. Mac clambered onto a chair and sat, his eyes only just at table height. A mountain of fresh fruit blocked his view of Wiri opposite. Hana watched him chew on his upper lip before shifting sideways to maintain eye contact with the older boy. Waiters in white uniforms appeared as though from the walls, sliding across the parquet floor like silent automatons. Mac jumped as one arrived by his elbow. His green eyes widened in shock and Hana saw him turn to search for her. She offered him a reassuring smile forced from the depths of her being. Her right hand formed the sign for eating and he turned back and accepted the slice of pineapple placed on his plate with gold tongs.

"Thank you for your hospitality," Hana said. She licked her dry lips at the sight of fresh orange juice poured into gold goblets by a waiter with a cloth draped over his left forearm. All young and male, the staff resembled the waiters Hana once saw at the Triad's Chinese restaurant. Triads. Lost for words, she fought the anxious ball rising into her chest and wondered what Logan was thinking. What favours would this cost him in the distant future? His fortune, his freedom or his life?

"Prayers!" Phoenix chirped. She elbowed Mac and his slice of pineapple missed his open mouth and plunged to the floor beneath his chair. "Prayers!" Phoenix mouthed and clapped her hands together.

"Thank you, Jesus. Amen." Wiri spoiled her moment and offered a sardonic smile over the top of the fruit mountain.

Phoenix's face clouded and she whipped around to seek justice from her mother. Hana sighed. "It's fine, Phoenix. Just eat darling," she pleaded.

"You have questions." Statement. Annalise's accent contained a hint of the clipped staccato of her mother.

Hana nodded and forced herself to face the woman. "Many." She waved a hand towards the trappings of paradise through the window. "Where are we?"

Annalise's eyes studied her with a cool intensity. Her scrutiny made Hana feel uncomfortable and her fingers clutched at the fabric of her pyjama pants. She felt outclassed in every respect. Gold rings adorned Annalise's fingers although no wedding band graced the slender left hand. Immaculate clothing shrouded a perfect hourglass figure and Hana folded her arms across her stomach and tried to suck everything in. Annalise's smile morphed into something more genuine. "Your husband asked for protection for you and your children. You will remain here."

Hana shook her head and her fingers strayed to her cheek. "Why don't I remember anything?" Her green eyes searched Annalise's face for lies. "Wiri said something about a pain pill."

Annalise's nose wrinkled. "I'm sorry. We felt it best to subdue you. You'll feel groggy for a few hours, but it will wear off."

"What did you drug me with? And why? Will it interfere with my heart medication?" Hana raised her voice, regretting the three concerned faces which whipped around to stare at her. Her body trembled and fear tied up her tongue. She leaned forward and hissed at Annalise. "My husband wouldn't sanction you sedating me. This makes no sense." Her voice rose again, matching the heightened colour of her cheeks.

Annalise's gaze remained cool and she stood her ground. "He would if your lives were at stake," she replied. "And they are. Just not in the way he imagined."

43

A Peculiar Agenda

Annalise refused to answer any more of Hana's questions. She offered veiled promises of a discussion later, but Hana mistrusted her. She reminded Hana of Mrs Che with her darting gimlet eyes and the wariness of her wiry frame. Hana forced herself to believe in Logan's solid judgement. He'd sent her to safety, yet she felt more vulnerable than she did when her assailant knocked her unconscious.

Accepting a bowl of fruit, she watched the children eat. They sampled the mango and pineapple, laughing at Mac's face screwing up with every bite of the fruit. He grinned and returned his fingers to the bowl for more. Hana stared at the delicious slice of melon, unable to make her fingers pick it up. "What about my heart medication?" she asked. "I need it."

Annalise cocked her head, an elegant twist of her lips heralding a change of subject. "Logan married you in secret." Hana swallowed, not sure how to answer. The lack of inflection made it sound like a statement more than a question. She shifted in her seat and a grape rolled around in the bowl.

"I need my heart pills."

Annalise lifted her hand in a regal wave. "Why?"

"Because I have a pacemaker." Hana dipped forward and hated her body with a vehemence which took her by surprise. She felt her pulse speed up and struggled to get control.

"No, why did you marry without me knowing?"

Hana gasped. "How should I know? I never met you before today."

Annalise lifted a perfect eyebrow and appeared sceptical. "Logan's bride jilted him on his wedding day and then I discover he's married you a few short months later. An unknown. Where did you come from?" Her pupils dilated like a lioness readying for the hunt. Hana felt her poised to strike and placed the bowl on a low coffee table.

"This isn't relevant." She rose and her gaze darted to the children. "It's my business." Every nerve ending in her body twanged with alarm and her tired brain tried to formulate an escape plan. Annalise's probing questions led down a route she didn't wish to revisit. They jarred like nails on a blackboard, out of place and disturbing. "I need my heart pills."

Annalise stood and her grip on Hana's wrist caused pain. Her slender fingers tightened over the glass shard embedded in her artery and the gritty sensation sent an ache cannoning up Hana's arm and into her shoulder. She yanked her wrist away, but Annalise held on. "I want to know why Logan married you."

"Ma?" Wiri's chair scraped as he got down from the table. A waiter stepped up to block his view and wordlessly urge him to take his seat. "No!" Hana heard the panic in his voice. "What's happening? Let her go!"

"Let her go!" Phoenix added her voice to his plea, although it sounded lacklustre, like she joined in just to please Wiri.

Annalise let her gaze drop to Hana's wrist and her lips quirked upwards in recognition of a weak point. She released Hana's arm and took a step back. "Answer my questions," she hissed. Her head turned towards the children and something dark flared in her eyes. The man dressed as a waiter picked Wiri up and sat him on the chair, holding him still until he stopped wriggling.

"I'm fine," Hana called, though her tone conveyed the opposite. Annalise waved her hand at the sofa behind them and Hana sank into it. She blinked away defeat and forced herself not to give the woman the satisfaction of seeing her cry. "What do you want to know?" she breathed.

"How you got Logan Du Rose." The question sounded simple, but the answer wasn't.

Hana licked her lips. "I met him when he was fourteen. We reconnected six years ago and married soon after. We have three children." Her lungs closed and she swallowed and took shallow breaths.

Annalise Che shook her head and jabbed a finger in Hana's face. "Liar!" she hissed. "Your time line doesn't work. The older two are his, but not the younger boy." Her beautiful face creased into a snarl. "You'll tell me the truth, eventually. I didn't buy off one delusional fool just to let him go to another." She rose and whirled around, leaving the room and slamming the door behind her. The waiters tensed and then seemed to relax as one.

Wiri fidgeted on his seat and peered around the man next to him, not satisfied until his gaze locked with Hana's. His perceptive grey eyes begged her for an explanation she didn't possess.

Phoenix chased a slippery segment of orange around her plate, but Mac sat with his hands in his lap. His delicate fingers stroked the plush red fabric of the seat cushion between his thighs as he watched Wiri's face with interest. The child missed nothing.

Hana joined the children, taking the seat pulled out for her. She thanked the waiter and he released the back of her chair to allow her to slide it closer to the table. Wiri reached out to clasp her fingers in his hand and Hana offered a watery smile.

"Try this, Mama." Phoenix waved a slice of pineapple at her across the table.

Hana shook her head and pointed to her cut lip. "I can't sweetheart," she said. "But thank you."

"Where did the lady go?" Wiri leaned sideways so he could whisper without the others hearing.

Hana shrugged and her gaze flicked to the waiters. They stood like statues, their eyes facing forward at a point above Hana's head. Their cookie cutter uniforms fitted over identical bodies. Hana counted six men in the room. Five encircled the table and one clattered around in the wide kitchen to her right. She licked her lips and tried not to panic.

Wiri studied her expression and then pushed his glass of juice towards her. "Drink," he whispered. "You'll feel better."

Hana nodded and lifted the glass to her lips. The citrus stung the cuts and she realised she had more tiny wounds in her mouth. Her fingers pressed against her cheek to dull the pain and she sighed.

"When can we play in the sea?" Phoenix curled her legs beneath her and rose up to peer across the loaded fruit bowls and a platter of pastries. She snagged a croissant and dropped it onto her plate. Crumbs fluttered in a wide arc around her and Hana winced.

"Pick up your mess, sweetie. I'm not sure about the beach. It might not be safe."

"Yeah, might have a rip." Wiri waggled his eyebrows. "You don't wanna die, do you?"

"Rip." Phoenix licked a delicate finger and prodded at the crumbs. She gathered one and popped it into her mouth, making a game of picking up the debris from the glitzy tablecloth. "Rip." She savoured the word and Wiri rolled his eyes at Hana. Mac watched his sister, his gaze flicking from her face to her finger and back again. His hand poised half way to his lips, an orange segment clutched between his forefinger and thumb. He glanced up at Hana and held the segment out to her, eyebrows raised in a silent question.

"No, thanks, baby. I'm not hungry." She signed for his benefit and spoke for the others. The nearest waiter shot her a curious glance and then raised his eyes to face forward again. Wooden, they resembled identical items of furniture dotted around the room.

Hana turned as Annalise appeared on the balcony outside. She wore form fitting track pants and a sports bra. Her elfin figure looked wiry and toned and Hana tugged at the pyjama shirt hiding stretch marks and freckles. Phoenix faced the windows and saw her, clapping a hand over her mouth and squeezing her eyes closed. Fingers crusted with flaky pastry reached out to cover Mac's eyes. "That lady's rudey dudey!" Her horrified tone sounded straight out of Leslie's mouth and Hana pursed her lips and stifled an inappropriate giggle. Wiri turned to look and wrinkled his nose.

"She's too skinny," he commented, darting a look at Hana. "I like mine with more meat on their bones."

Hana raised an eyebrow and jerked her head towards him. "Do you now, Tama?" she replied. It comforted her, hearing intonations of the people she loved from the mouths of her children. The fattist, sexist, arrogant comment should have drawn a rebuke but instead, it made her feel less alone, less isolated.

One of the waiters appeared on the balcony, his white shirt replaced by a black outfit. They bowed to each other and then Annalise attacked him. Phoenix inhaled in shock, choking on the loose pastry and coughing. Her grey eyes widened in a plea for help and Hana rushed to her side. The surrounding waiters stiffened and one took a step forward, correcting himself as she shot him a warning glare. Hana snatched up Mac's glass and pressed it to Phoenix's lips. She coughed and the action blew a bubble into the liquid. The resulting laugh dislodged the flake and she swallowed, covering Hana's fingers with hers as she pulled the glass closer for a sip. Hana patted her back, offering more reassurance than assistance.

Mac leaned sideways around his mother to watch the display outside. A sandy eyebrow quirked upward and Hana held her breath as pure Logan radiated from his unimpressed expression.

She kissed the top of Phoenix's head and pressed herself into the seat next to her.

"I'm okay." Phoenix sounded hoarse. "It went down the wrong hole."

"I know. Drink some more." Hana rested her wrist on the back of her daughter's chair and watched Annalise spar with the slender male. He dodged and feinted, taking some hits and avoiding others. She pursed her lips and tried not to feel impressed. Phoenix nudged her elbow.

"I wanna do that," she said. Her grey eyes concentrated on the view through the window as her lips rested against the rim of the glass. "Not ballet."

"Kick boxing?" Hana watched Annalise raise her leg and spin sideways, catching her opponent in the shoulder. She sighed. "I did ballet. But you do what you want." The more she considered it, the idea of her brawny husband strutting up to collect his daughter from a dance class seemed ludicrous. She pursed her lips to smother a smile. He'd do it, but he'd hate every second of the oestrogen dominated environment. Yet when she thought of his tender moments with her children, she felt herself relax. Logan Du Rose had hidden depths. He worked hard on the land and harder still at home. His scarred fingers had secured the multiple fiddly ties into his daughter's hair when she insisted she wanted a head covered in tiny ponytails. And he'd spent hours communicating wordlessly with his son. Teaching Wiri to ride had soothed the older boy and given him an outlet for his confusion.

A heavy knot formed in Hana's chest and she missed her husband. The tangible ache spread out across her torso and landed as a weight in her stomach.

The slender male continued to play the choreographed game, a substitute for Annalise's real opponent. Hana. She performed her stunning display of strength for Hana's benefit but wasted her sweat and energy. Hana's mind strayed elsewhere to a handsome man with fierce grey eyes and an attitude more formidable than the craggy mountain he loved.

Hana's clever brain formulated a plan and as it did, a smile slipped across her lips and the faraway look remained.

44

The Test

"I need to speak to my husband."

Sweat dotted Annalise's forehead as Hana joined her on the balcony flanked by two of the waiters. Annalise dabbed her face with a towel and gave her opponent a sharp nod. He bowed and moved away backwards, spinning on his heel to enter the house through a doorway further along the deck. "He knows you're safe." The towel slipped from her fingers with ease and slumped on the wooden slats. She didn't give it another glance. Hana's eyes narrowed at the overt display of arrogance and her jaw tightened.

"I speak to him every day," she replied. "He'll know something is wrong if I don't call him today. If he knows I'm here, it won't be a problem, will it?" Two dots appeared on the horizon, a dog bounding between them on the sand. Hana gave them a pointed look and then let her gaze track back to her captor's face, the threat implicit.

Annalise pursed her lips and her delicate nose wrinkled. She nodded at someone behind Hana before turning her serious brown eyes back to her face. "If you're lying, I'll make you sorry." Her voice lowered and Hana sensed she meant it. She gave a nod of concession.

A waiter Hana hadn't noticed stepped forward and presented a black phone to Annalise. Her long fingers took it and she flicked through contacts on the screen. She activated the speaker so she could listen. Hana reached out for the device, but Annalise shook her head. A ring tone cut through the air and Hana held her breath.

"Yeah." No fuss, no airs and graces. Pure Logan Du Rose. His voice stirred a primal need in Hana. She must get this right.

"Logan?" Her voice wavered as she said his name. She wrapped her arms around her stomach and pressed, desperate for his strong embrace. His breathing sounded loud as though he'd halted his horse to answer. Hana heard outside sounds, birds, rustling trees, the cackle of a tui. Tack clanked and she imagined him riding the gelding.

"Hey, gorgeous." He smiled through his voice and Hana pictured his soft lips curving upwards. "How's your head? Are the kids okay?"

"Fine." She swallowed. "You're on speaker, babe. Annalise is right next to me." Annalise jerked her head towards the window and Hana followed her gaze. A waiter stood with his back to the glass, overseeing Wiri as the small boy chased a chunk of melon around his plate. As though receiving some telepathic message, the man lifted the back of his neat jacket to reveal a handgun nestled in the waistband of his pants. Beyond him, Phoenix's dear little face scrunched in concentration as she fed Mac a grape.

"Ah, okay." Logan sounded doubtful as though the name meant nothing to him. Annalise narrowed her eyes and held the phone up higher, withdrawing her head. Hana saw her internal suffering at the easy brush off. When Hana reached to take it, she raised it in the air and shot her a warning look. She understood. Her freedom didn't extend to holding the phone.

Her heart banged in her chest and her tongue stuck to the roof of her mouth. "Logan," she breathed. Her brain froze on her and she grappled for ways to ask for help without Annalise realising. They needed a code word. They'd never discussed one. What would it be if they'd ever sat down and worked one out? A tremble sounded in her voice and she stammered over her next sentence. "I need to hear you say it." Her breathing hitched. "You promised every day you'd tell me you loved me. Remember?"

Silence. Him saying nothing sounded better than a denial. She prayed he'd understand and not state the obvious, bracing herself in case he corrected her. That wasn't the promise. She'd messed up the wording. He should tell her she was beautiful. That was the promise. The wait seemed endless. "Sorry. It's been crazy today. But you know I love you, don't you?"

"Yes." Her voice sounded wooden and she wanted to scream for help. It didn't seem enough to raise the alarm. She needed him to understand she wasn't safe even though he believed she was. Somehow Annalise had intercepted them and Logan wouldn't find them. "Logan, remember how I felt the day after Vik's funeral?"

"Oh." He sounded unsure and her heart rate hiked even higher. She pleaded with him in her mind. *Just understand me, Logan. Please, just think about it.* The static laden silence continued until hopelessness took root in Hana's brain. He hadn't understood the veiled reference to her former life and the day her husband's mistress visited her home and blamed her for everything. He couldn't understand because he wasn't there. She'd communicated her hopelessness and lack of safety in that single reference and hoped he'd work it out. It didn't seem enough. Hana stiffened as her brain ran through possible scenarios. What would happen if she screamed? A glance through the window at her children's innocent faces stopped her, robbing her of sensible thought. As though sensing her panic, Annalise drew the phone away.

Then Logan spoke, his voice distant as Annalise turned aside. The sound of the waves crashing onto the beach dulled his words. "I'm sorry you feel that way, babe. I'll make it up to you."

The colour drained from Hana's complexion and she felt the slow throb of her heart as it pushed blood through her arteries. He hadn't heard her coded plea, assuming she was harking on about Vik's affair over a decade ago. She wondered if he'd heard accusation instead of a cry for help. Either way, he'd heard her voice and believed her safe.

But she wasn't safe and nor were her children. They'd flown into a gilded cage and she didn't know how to escape.

45

Pure Du Rose

Rain clouds scudded across the sky and occasional showers made the beach scene less appealing. Phoenix stopped complaining as soon as the rain began. The waiters changed out of their white shirts one at a time, only two returning with black jackets buttoned up to the neck. Hana tried to distinguish between them, finding differing features when she stared hard enough. One had a nose slightly kinked, the other a mole near his lip. She gave them unflattering names in her head to remind her and force her tired brain to function. Mole found a battered game of Scrabble in the drawer of a sideboard and set it up on a rug in front of the wide windows for the children. Nose found an English dictionary in another room which upped the stakes from words like 'sit' and 'cat'. Wiri hogged the dictionary, sharing it with obvious reluctance. He grew irritated with Mac, who stole the letters and created a teetering tower on the hearth.

Hana shivered as the air grew chill. Her head pounded and she lay on her back on the rug. She rubbed her arms once and heard a hiss as the open doors slid shut. A blanket appeared next to her face. "Thank you." She took it with a smile and covered her legs. The thin pyjama pants allowed the thick pile of the rug to cushion her and she shook her head in response to the pillow Mole wafted in front of her face. Her neck ached and she lay flat, practicing yoga breaths and subduing her panic to a dull white noise behind her ears. She dozed, listening to the children's muted chatter and keeping her eyes closed.

"Bollocks." Wiri pursed his lips. His finger traced a line in the dictionary and he winced.

"Wiri?" Hana pushed herself up onto her elbows and stared at him. "That's a swear word."

"Bollocks." Phoenix repeated it. "How do you spell it? I think I need two more letters."

"You can't use it." Hana pushed the blanket away from her waist and forced herself into a sitting position. She reached for the dictionary, pausing so Wiri could keep his finger in the page for her. Her eyes scanned the words and she found it, releasing a groan of frustration. "Why?" she hissed. "Why do they let these words in when they know they're bad?"

"I won't use it. Promise." Wiri held his hand out for the book and Hana relinquished it. Her brow furrowed but circumstance left her little choice.

"Bollocks. Is it with an X?"

"It doesn't matter, you can't use it." Wiri answered Phoenix and flicked through a few pages to get rid of the word. He leaned across the board to give her the dictionary. "Choose something else. Bollocks is rude."

"Then stop saying it!" Hana heard her frustration and tempered her tone, turning it down a few notches to mild irritation. A glance sideways found Mole smirking as he cleared the kitchen and she narrowed her eyes and gave him a well-deserved glare. Logan always said information brought power and she focused on collecting more. The waiters-turned-guards understood English. Hana extended the data in her mind to include colloquial English. They understood the swearword. It meant she'd need to be more careful.

Wiri turned his face towards her and smiled. Hana twisted to lie on her side and watched as his fingers flicked to the pocket of his dressing gown. The dark blue fabric had lost its fluffiness through washing and overuse. Patches looked flat and threadbare on the elbows, but he refused to let her replace it. She'd bought it for his birthday two years ago and it had hung almost to his feet then. Hana's gaze followed the line of the hem, seeing it only just covering his knees. Familiar pyjama bottoms poked from beneath. His hand movement caught her eye and he gave the pocket a definitive tap. Then he looked straight at her. He wanted her to know something. Tap tap. Tap tap.

Hana shuttered her eyes so she could peek through her lashes. She felt Nose staring at her from behind Wiri and ground her teeth. Wiri gave her a sly sideways glance and then dropped the top of the pocket lower so she could see what he kept hidden. The dark shape of a phone glinted against the sunlight and then disappeared. Hana forced her eyes closed and masked her emotion with a blank expression. Mole clattered around in the kitchen, emptying crockery from the dishwasher and speaking to someone else on a mobile phone.

"What's that?" Nose materialised behind Wiri and Hana jumped so hard she felt her lip crack. A hand appeared in her peripheral vision. "Give it to me. Now!"

She pushed herself upright and tried to block Wiri from harm. Phoenix dropped the dictionary to watch. "Leave him alone!" Hana snarled. "He's just a little boy."

"Phone!" Nose snapped. "Give." He waggled his fingers and Wiri gave Hana a pointed look she didn't understand.

"It's okay, Ma," he said. "He can have it. I can't make calls. Nonie lets me use it to play games." Wiri pushed his fingers into his dressing gown pocket and pulled out the lifeline. Hana felt like crying as she watched it disappear into Nose's palm. Crawling towards the children, she tried to shield them with her body, anticipating reprisals.

Nose inspected the phone, pushing buttons and cocking his head. Mole joined him and peered over his shoulder. "Code,"

Nose demanded, glaring at Wiri. But before the child could answer, Mole took the device, turned it over and opened the back. He held it up to show Nose and gave a shrug.

"No SIM card," he said. "Useless. Just games." He dropped the phone and case into Nose's fingers.

Nose stared at them with a frown. His gaze darted to Hana and then back to Mole. He seemed unsure. Wiri jabbed a finger at him. "You can play with it," he said in his most generous and gullible tone. "But please don't let my worm die or I'll have to start again."

"Not your worm!" Phoenix gasped and hugged her collection of Scrabble letters to her chest. "But you've loved that worm your whole life." Tears sprang into her eyes and her eyelashes fluttered. Nose hesitated and his jaw shifted under the skin. Phoenix went for the full academy award, rolling forward onto the Scrabble board and scattering the letters everywhere. Her flailing heel got close to destroying Mac's teetering tower. "Not Wormy!" she wailed into her forearms. Her chin pressed into the carpet and muffled her voice. "It's too sad. I can't cope."

Nose looked down at the blank screen and pursed his lips. Turning it over, he slotted the back into place. "Take it," he growled.

Wiri almost missed catching it as the man dropped it without bending. "Thanks!" he gushed.

"Nap time." Hana discarded the blanket across her legs with a definitive shove and Mac's Scrabble tower collapsed. He made a sound like a gasp and then puckered his lips at her. "Sorry," Hana mouthed. "Accident." She jerked her head towards the door. "Nap time now."

Nose glided across to the door and blocked it with his body. He kept his arms behind his back and Hana saw a muscular chest flex beneath the ornate coat. Gold buttons glittered against the light. He lifted a finger in the air and dragged it down in a line. "I check," he said. His voice rumbled low and melodic. It took a second for him to escape through the door and it clicked shut behind him. Hana allowed herself the first genuine smile of the day as she glanced sideways at the resourceful Du Rose in her corner. He gave her a pointed wink and her heart lifted enough to allow a little hope into the gaps.

46

Piecing the puzzle

Hana leaned against the headboard and cradled Mac as he slept. Phoenix snuggled next to her, tender lips moving as she sucked her thumb. The little girl kept her other hand on Hana's thigh, as though the contact grounded her even in sleep. Wiri perched on the end of the bed and tried to get a signal on the battered mobile phone. "This thing's knackered," he concluded with a sigh. "The message won't send. Do you think I damaged the SIM card hiding it in the pillowcase?"

"No. Don't worry." Hana rubbed her spare hand over her eyes and her tired brain ran through scenarios and options. "Just give me a minute to work some things out."

"Like what?" Wiri perked up, the promise of a puzzle lightening his mood. "I can help."

Hana smiled at his willing expression and pushed herself upright. Her back ached in the slumped position and she edged sideways, depositing Mac in the dent she left. A rumble began, making her freeze in shock. A clanking sound accompanied it and Hana recognised the sound of a garage door rolling up beneath them. Crawling towards the window, she lifted the curtain and pushed her face against the glass. By resting her right cheek against the sill, she could just see a driveway beyond the bank in front of her window. She watched Annalise and a guard climb into a sleek white Mercedes. Four doors slammed and she guessed at least three guards had left the property, two outside her limited field of vision. "That means three guards left here that we know about," she whispered. Phoenix stirred and transferred her hand to Mac's waist. He wriggled into her body with a grunt and Hana extracted herself. She used a loose blanket to cover them and jerked her head in the direction of the connecting door. Wiri slipped from the bed and padded into the adjoining room. Hana paused in the doorway with a finger to her lips, watching her younger children settle. Then she pushed the door enough to leave a small gap and stole towards the window seat on quiet feet. "Right," she said. She spoke in a whisper and Wiri joined her on the seat, huddling close as her co-conspirator. "Logan let them take us but doesn't know where we are. That's not his style, which suggests someone intercepted us." Their status had altered from guests to captives in the long walk down the corridor to the bedroom. Annalise ordered them confined there and let no illusion of a holiday remain.

Wiri nodded, his action jerky and enthused. "He wouldn't drug you either." He stared through the rain speckled windows. The weather ruined the beach scene beyond the sad Du Roses as though sympathetic to their incarceration. A thin balcony snaked around the house as a widow's walk. Hana leaned closer to the glass and peered left. She saw the back of one of Annalise's men guarding a set of steps down to the sand.

"I'm trying to remember what happened." Hana turned to Wiri. "I found a woman at the back of our house. I caught her destroying my plants. Someone else hit me from behind."

Wiri pursed his lips while he thought for a moment. "I only saw one person get into the SUV before it left." He tapped a finger against his thigh and closed his eyes. Then he gasped. "Oh! She got in the other side, the one without the steering wheel!" His eyes widened in horror. "I didn't see the other person because I hid everyone under the blanket." His shoulders slumped. "Someone else got in the driver's side and I didn't know. I'm rubbish at looking after everyone, aren't I?"

"No. You're amazing." Hana curled an arm around his thin shoulders and leaned back against the windowsill. It broke her heart to hear him berating himself for failing at something that wasn't his job. She kissed his temple. "Don't beat yourself up for things you can't change. You've already done better than me by protecting the others and keeping hold of the phone." Hana raised a hand to her cheek and fingered the raised, painful wound. She frowned and the action hurt. "Tell me again how we got here?"

Wiri nodded. "Uncle Logan came up and told us to stay in the truck. He carried you across the garden and put you in the front seat. You kept mumbling something I couldn't hear but by the time we got to the hotel, you seemed fine. When Phoenix got scared, you said everything would turn out okay. Uncle drove us to the hotel and met a man in Poppa's upstairs lounge. Nonie gave us cake and mended your face. Uncle Alfie dressed us for bed, but Uncle Logan said we needed to go with the man. He put us all into a car."

"What car?" Hana massaged her forehead and pain shot down the back of her neck. She groaned. "Geez, why do they always go for my head?"

"A very long car with bench seats and a secret hidey with glasses and drinks inside. Uncle Logan kissed us and said we could come home in a few days. He told you to trust him. Some men got in with us, but not the man who owns the car."

"Men from here?" Hana's eyes narrowed. "Waiters from breakfast?"

Wiri nodded and held up two fingers. "The one who laughed when I said the rude word in Scrabble and the one who pretended to play fight with the horrid lady on the deck. The scary old man bowed to the driver and said something foreign to him."

"Then what happened?"

"The one with a wonky nose gave us a drink from the hidey cabinet and we felt tired. He gave you a pain pill. Before I fell asleep, the car stopped and the lady got in. I don't remember too much more, but I heard an argument between two drivers outside and the man with the wonky nose. The new driver got in and they left the first one standing on the street. Wonky nose rode up front after he smashed the other driver's phone on the road. The lady waited until she thought I fell asleep. Then she talked to someone on her phone."

"What did she say? Who did she speak to?"

"Dunno." Wiri wrinkled his nose and failure crossed his furrowed brow. "I didn't understand her language. She sounded like she wanted the other person to believe she made things better. But she didn't, did she? She made it worse."

Hana squeezed his shoulders and felt the weight of responsibility as he slumped against her. His Du Rose bravery faded as he struggled with his inner thoughts. "I'm not sure, Wiri. We know nothing concrete yet." Hana jerked as images flooded her inner vision. A flashback of a blinding pain behind her eyes and the crack of wood on bone. Someone stood in front of her, their features fluid and indiscernible. Hana gritted her teeth. The plant destroyer wouldn't get away with her vandalism. She leaned back against the pillows and groaned at the sudden twinge in her spine.

"What?" Wiri leapt to his feet and his voice sounded loud and jarring. Hana gave a sharp inhale and pressed a hand over his open mouth.

"Shush! Don't wake the others. I remember things but it's foggy." She turned and lifted the edge of her pyjama shirt. The material felt fleecy beneath her fingers. "Please can you look at my back? It hurts."

Wiri's cool fingers brushed hers as he lifted the shirt further and examined Hana's spine. He tugged the hem of the pants down a little and gasped. "Yes! Ouch. That looks painful."

"What do you mean?" Hana spun, but the sight evaded her. Frustration blossomed and she jerked her head towards Wiri's pocket. "Does that phone take photos? Can you take one and show me?" Her gaze raked the bedroom with its minimalist furnishings of a double bed, wardrobe and chest of drawers. "No mirror. Can you take one of my face too?"

"Okay." Wiri retrieved the phone from his pocket and pressed buttons. He tutted as he abandoned the screen containing the message for assistance. "It didn't send. Uncle Logan still doesn't know we're in trouble."

"Don't worry. It might send in the background if the reception picks up for a minute. Just take the photos."

The child fussed around like a professional photographer, displaying an expertise Hana didn't know he possessed. When he turned the phone towards her, she frowned. She tapped the screen but couldn't zoom in to see the black bruises any closer. Wiri snatched the phone back. "It's not touch screen. It's old. You need to use the buttons." He fiddled for a moment before handing it back.

"Where did you get it?" Hana peered at the lengthy bruise and blew out a breath. "No wonder it hurts. I must have fallen onto the corner of the deck. Let me see my face now."

Wiri tutted. "You're not gonna like it," he murmured.

Hana gasped at the cut running along her cheekbone. Fabric stitches butterflied it closed, but the surrounding bruising looked livid and her right eye appeared a different shape from its almond pair. "My modelling days are over," she breathed.

Wiri's fingers fluttered near her face but didn't come to rest. His expression creased in fear. "Your face was bleeding when Uncle Logan brought you back to the truck." He gulped. "It looks like it's stopped now. Do you remember other stuff? Like, you know your name and that you're married to Uncle Logan. Do you know what the year is and the prime minister's name?"

Hana raised an eyebrow and shook her head. "You watch too much television, Wiri. And I bet you don't even know who the prime minister is, do you?"

"Na." His face creased into a bashful grin. "Maybe the American one, but not ours."

"Then that's not very helpful, is it?" Hana sighed. "I remember everything until the bang on the head."

"It might come back." Wiri snuggled closer and twisted the phone over and over in his fingers. "If we didn't go where Uncle Logan meant us to, he'll know by now something is wrong."

"I tried to tell him when she let me speak to him. I don't think he understood." Hana's fingers writhed in her lap. "You need to hide the phone in case someone comes. Or they're watching."

Wiri nodded and slipped the device back into his dressing gown pocket. "They've seen it now. They think I'm a stupid kid with a toy phone."

Hana pursed her lips and smiled. "And you're neither. You're a wily, cunning Du Rose, just like the rest."

Wiri swallowed and dropped his gaze. "About that. I need to tell you something."

Hana stilled, the shiver down her spine like cold water. "About the phone? Whose is it?"

"Nonie's. I stole it as we left. Just in case. Yours is still in your truck. But it's not about that. It's something else."

"Go on. What's happened?" Hana braced herself, but nothing readied her for Wiri's next sentence.

"My dad came back." His grey eyes widened and he turned his face upwards like a sunflower seeking yellow warmth to make it bloom. "I didn't tell you because I thought you'd let him take me."

Hana held her breath and waited. Her heart sank into a pit in her belly and she reached out to pull him close. "How did you find out?" She pressed a kiss to the top of his head and her lower lip smarted.

"I saw him. He talked to me at the tangihanga, but I also saw him a few days before."

"Wait, what?" A throb began in her chest as her heart thudded back to life. He wasn't talking about his real father. He'd seen Neville.

Wiri's face scrunched into a ball of features. "Ma, you're not listening to me, are you?"

Her brain whirred with the effort of processing Wiri's news. Neville Du Rose. They'd watched Nev at the hotel, eating breakfast and unaware of Kane's death. Reuben's boys looked alike, Logan included. Not Kane. Nev. "Tell me what happened," she demanded.

A furrowed brow followed her volley of questions and Wiri shrugged. "I don't want to talk about it, Ma. They came for the ticket."

"Ticket?" Hana's head jerked backwards and the action sent a pain from the cut on her cheek, down her neck and into her shoulder. "Ouch! What ticket?"

Wiri squirmed beneath her gaze. "I dunno, Ma." His voice rose to a whine. "My dad made me promise to look but I couldn't find it. He said it's a ticket with numbers on it. Nonie Leslie took us to play on the swings at the campground and he called me over. She didn't see him because Phoe fell over and she had to cuddle her. My pa hid in the trees and showed me a picture of the ticket. He said Logan will keep it somewhere safe and he wants it. At the tangi, he said he also wanted something with Logan's name on it. He said it had to be his handwriting. I don't know where Uncle keeps things and I told him that. When you got hurt, it scared me in case he did it." Wiri's voice hitched and his fingers fluttered in the air.

Hana closed her eyes to shutter her emotions. Her grip on his shoulders tightened. "What did he promise you?" she whispered. "Did he say he'd take you with him if you did what he wanted?"

The soft touch on the back of her hand forced her eyelids apart. "No. He promised he'd let me stay with you."

"Oh, Wiri." A ball of sadness mingled with relief in Hana's throat and made speaking difficult. She pulled the boy against her and wrapped her arms around his neck. He wanted to stay. With her. "Your mother signed papers, sweetheart. No one can take you without her consent." She didn't add the reason why. A DNA test would remove any rights bestowed by Neville Du Rose's false entry on the boy's birth certificate. The only other person with a valid claim could no longer stake it. "You get to stay with me for as long as you like, or until your mother wants to make a home for you together."

Wiri sat up and shook his head. "I don't wanna go with my real mum. I used to, but I don't anymore."

"But you wanted to see her." Confusion narrowed Hana's brow and she kept her arm around Wiri's shoulder. "I rang the hospital for you."

He shook his head again. "I wanted to ask her about the ticket. He wanted me to steal from you and Uncle Logan and I wanted to ask her to make him stop."

"Oh." Hana's thoughtful expression clouded. "Oh. Do you think he trashed our house?"

Wiri frowned. "I don't know. He wanted the ticket real bad."

Hana tutted. "None of this makes sense, Wiri. Logan said someone's been damaging the property. It's why he put up the cameras. Someone is trying to drive us off the mountain and I thought I'd found out who. I think Logan gave money to Poppa Alfie and Nonie Leslie to go up north for a holiday right before Uncle Kane died. He wanted to keep them safe, but they lied to him and then came back. Now he's sent us away too. That's why he called the Triads for help and I saw Mr Che at the hotel." Her brow furrowed. "Do you think your dad caused all this?"

"No, Ma." Wiri's eyelashes flickered and his face looked utterly sincere. "He doesn't want the mountain, he never did. He just wants the ticket."

47

Reuben's Dream

Hana settled in the spare bed with an arm around Wiri, letting her mind wander through her predicament while he played a game on the phone. She knew the battery would run out without the charger but didn't have the heart to remind him. Its usefulness had ended when it failed to send the text for help. Wiri's dark fringe flipped over his eyes as he tipped this way and that, trying to stop a worm eating counters on a chequered board. "Do you remember Poppa Reuben?" Hana mused. The house sounded eerie and silent with only the occasional clicks of the building settling to break up the monotony. Occasional footsteps reminded her they weren't alone. Or safe.

"Yeah." Wiri's face brightened and his lips curved upwards. "I do."

"Tell me about him." Hana turned on her side and watched his expression as his mind moved through internal images. Wiri twisted to face her and let the phone rest between them.

"He was fun and scary at the same time. Does that make sense?" Hana nodded, not wanting to admit it made no sense at all. Wiri frowned. "He played guitar and sang sad songs. I didn't like it when he drank too much because it made him crazy. Then he ranted and sometimes he cried. There was always blood in the bathroom sink after he cleaned his teeth or shaved his beard. He bled a lot, sometimes for no reason. Uncle Kane did bleeding too. Blood doesn't scare me like it does Phoe and Macky. I'm used to it." Hana smiled and raised a hand to stroke his soft cheek. He gave her a coy Du Rose smile which reminded her so much of Logan. Wiri inhaled and his irises glittered. "He loved Tama best and then me. He took me out hunting and I helped with his garden. Weeding and stuff. He liked growing things. Once, I pulled out a stalk and it had a red bulb underneath. A baby beetroot. He shoved it back in and didn't even get cross. He said we can fix most things in life."

"Your poppa sounds amazing." Hana sighed. "I only met him once."

"He was real cool." Wiri sounded wistful. "He let me play with his tickets."

"Tickets?" Hana's hair swished against the pillow. "Tell me more about these tickets."

"Money tickets. They have numbers on and you get money with them."

"Cheques?"

Wiri shrugged. "I don't understand what cheques is. Tickets are small, about this big." Wiri used his fingers to show something the size of a five dollar note.

Hana's eyes widened. "Lottery tickets! Reuben bought lottery tickets?"

Wiri wrinkled his nose. "Nonie Leslie buys those. Uncle Logan says they're a waste of money. He helped me work out the maths when it was raining one afternoon. It's one in fourteen million based on the different divisions of Powerball and the number combinations. Poppa Reuben was clever with maths too. He wouldn't waste money on something like that either, not if he ran the maths and worked it out like Uncle Logan."

"Did Reuben's tickets look like Nonie's?"

"Nope." Wiri's emphatic head shake showed his certainty. "Not like hers. It looked like money with numbers on. I couldn't read back then because I was a kid." He wrinkled his nose and Hana pursed her lips to contain her smirk. She wondered how he viewed himself now.

"You were three when Reuben died," she whispered. "It seems like yesterday."

Wiri frowned. "We need to find the stupid ticket and then my dad will go away."

Hana sighed. "But first, we need to know what the ticket is. Then we need to know why he thinks Logan's got it."

"Yeah. Poppa Reuben bought lots of tickets. They didn't all fit into my hand. He said one day his number would come up and then he'd buy back everything he lost. Every last piece of stinkin' brown earth. Then he'd make them listen to him once and for all."

$$48$$

One Answer

Wiri fell asleep against Hana's shoulder and she lay awake and listened to his steady breathing. Footsteps passed the bedroom door without stopping. Wiri's memories of Reuben felt close and personal, as though she'd known him herself. Desperate and cast aside, he'd done something to improve his chances of reclaiming his heritage, but what? She knew the thing he'd wanted to say which seemed so important. He'd wanted to demand access to his son. Nothing else had mattered as much. Everything Reuben did pointed to that one goal; seeing Logan. He'd wanted to buy back the mountain, but only for that single purpose. Hana inhaled and closed her eyes.

Hana murmured to herself to alleviate the loneliness and boredom. "Lotto started in the late 1980s," she whispered. "But they're too small for lotto tickets. Unless they were early ones." She pursed her lips and wondered how she knew the date the lottery started in New Zealand. Her mind wandered to a trivia night held to raise funds for the school she'd worked at. She smiled. It was the only question Peter North got right and he mentioned it in the office every day for a month. "1987," she breathed. "So, what else might Reuben have bought and held on to which could convert to cash later? Enough cash to buy back the mountain?" She tapped her thumbnail against her teeth and stopped when she caught her lip. "But he couldn't just cash it in whenever he liked. Something had to happen, like a number coming up."

Hana sat up with a gasp and Wiri's eyes shot open. "What?" he hissed.

"Sorry, sorry." Hana patted his thin chest and shook her head. "Logan was born in the 1970s." Excitement leaked from her voice. "The government pushed this new scheme for people to make savings but also get a chance to win cash prizes. Bonus bonds!" She slapped the heel of her hand against her forehead and then groaned at the painful effects. "Reuben bought bonus bonds." Hana narrowed her eyes at Wiri. "Is Neville good with numbers? Like, would he remember a sequence of numbers if he saw them a few times?"

Wiri shook his head and stifled a yawn. "No. He can't remember his own phone number."

Hana heaved out an exaggerated breath of frustration and slumped back against the pillows. Her excitement trickled away like water down a plug hole. "Damn," she mused. "So, Nev's not like Logan then?"

"Na." Wiri scrabbled between them looking for the phone. His slender fingers clasped it and flicked on the screen. He toggled buttons beneath it to bring his game back into view. "He's rubbish, but Kane's amazing."

"He was?" Hana's enthusiasm made a miraculous recovery. "So, if he saw a winning number once, he'd remember it for a very long time?"

"Yep. Definitely." Wiri frowned and pressed buttons. "I think my worm is gonna die. It sucked up a bad counter."

Hana slumped back against the pillows. "But he'd claim it online, wouldn't he? Nev can't show identification, or they'd arrest him. But Kane could. He could prove Reuben died in the fire and the tickets burned, then claim the money as his heir.

Logan cleared all the debt when he bought their half of the mountain, so they'd keep it. Why didn't they just do that?"

"Dunno." Wiri shrugged. "Why would they look for it in your house if all the tickets burned up with Poppa Reuben?"

Hana gasped again. She clasped Wiri's head between her hands and kissed his forehead. Her lip hurt but the pain dulled against the thrill of her discovery. "Because it's not in Reuben's name. It's in Logan's!"

"Oh." Wiri kept pushing the worm-thing around his screen. "That's nice."

"It is. It's beautiful." Hana sighed and her sentimental fantasy about Logan's father revived in her mind. "You remember Peter North, right?"

Wiri's eyebrows shot up. "Yeah. He got his willy out at my school."

"Not on purpose!" Hana inhaled. "His shorts blew up, but yes, him. He once got this quiz question right about the lottery and he bored me to tears every day for weeks with details about that and bonus bonds. He said it was traditional for fathers to buy one for their children on the day they were born. Just for a dollar. Like a gift. His dad bought him five and he checked them all the time."

"Did he ever win anything? Were his odds better than one in fourteen million?"

"No." Hana shook her head. "He won nothing. But he said the statistics were lower, like one in ten thousand. Only the prizes were smaller, fifty thousand dollars and amounts like that instead of millions."

"So, the statistics make it more likely, but he still didn't win?" Wiri's eyebrows wiggled up and down. "What a loser."

"Wiri!" Hana nudged his arm with her elbow. "Don't say mean things. It's just Pete. You could give him a golden ticket and he'd lose it." She sighed. "But this means that Reuben bought a bonus bond when Logan was born and somehow got it to Logan without him realising. If Kane and Nev burgled the house and then went to the hotel, they didn't find it. Then

Kane went over the balcony when they searched Poppa Alfie's apartment."

"Dad wants it." Wiri swallowed. "He said he won't stop until he finds it." His eyes widened. "Do you think they shot each other?"

"I don't know. The cops will sort it all out."

"So, if we find the ticket it might help?"

"I don't know." Hana sighed out pure sarcasm. "Marvellous! We've moved heaps of times and never come across it. I don't know where it is. Someone wants to frighten us off the mountain and someone else wants something we can't find. Logan sent us somewhere to keep safe, but we ended up where he can't find us. What should we do? And where do we go next?"

Wiri's head jerked and he forced himself upright in a fluid motion. "Dunno." His hand fumbled on the bed for the phone and his eyes sparkled with interest. Hana closed her eyes and left the child to pander to one of his robot pets in the game.

"Other people nurture puppies and kitties. You take care of worms," she sighed.

Wiri cupped a hand around his mouth and leaned in to Hana's ear. "Uncle Logan replied to my text," he whispered. His breath tickled Hana's skin. "He says hold on."

49

Hold On

Wiri removed the SIM card from the phone and hid it. Deft fingers pushed it through a hole in his pocket and he shook out the material until the card nestled between the layers and against the hem of his dressing gown. When Phoenix and Mac awoke, Hana tried the door handle into the hallway and felt it turn under her fingers. One of the austere guards slid from the shadows, making her jump and jerk backwards. "We need clothes, please," she said, hearing the waver in her voice. "We'd like to get dressed and go for a walk."

"No walk." Nose shook his head and kept his expression unsmiling. "You remain in the house."

Phoenix let out a groan behind her. "It's not raining anymore. I wanna see the beach." She dipped in the middle to speak into Mac's face. "You wanna see beach, Macky? Beach? Play in the sea?"

"No beach." The man's eyes flashed a warning. He jabbed a finger at the children gathered behind Hana. "You do as told or we separate."

"What? No!" Wiri's hands reached out and clasped Mac and Phoenix, gripping their tiny fingers and hauling them against his sides. His knuckles showed white through the skin and a dark fury burned behind his grey irises. The house sounded silent and Hana wondered if they'd emerged earlier than expected. She felt her heart speed up and waited for the kick from the pacemaker beneath her collar bone. Anticipating the life-giving jab only increased the tension and she darted a worried glance at Wiri. His eyes narrowed into slits and he jerked his head upwards. Hana swallowed and read the intention in his face. She shook her head.

Wiri took a step forward, dragging the little children with him. They surged around the guard's legs and caused him to take a step backwards. "Ma?" He raised his voice and infused fear into his voice. "What's wrong, Ma? You look pale. Is it your heart, Ma? Is your heart failing again?"

Hana swallowed and her right hand flicked up to touch the pacemaker. "No, I'm fine." She didn't sound sure and Phoenix widened her eyes.

"Mama. Is you sick, darling? Oh no! Mama's sick." She raised her voice into a wail and her face crumpled.

Wiri raised the stakes by releasing the children's hands and gripping Hana's thighs. He gave her a spiteful pinch on the soft inner flesh of her leg and she cried out. Mac's face creased to match his sister's and he began a low keening sound in the back of his throat. The children surged around Hana's legs and the guard took a step backwards. The other doors along the narrow hallway remained closed. "Ouch! Stop!" Hana batted Wiri's hands away as he went in for another pinch.

"It's your heart," he insisted. "You should lie on the ground."

"What?" Nose reached for a mobile phone in his smart pants pocket and stared at the screen to flick through his list of contacts. The claustrophobic corridor seemed to close in on Hana as she contemplated a million reasons why she shouldn't buy into the charade. There were no tears in her daughter's eyes and the unmistakable sparkle of glee back-lit her irises. She wasn't sure when Wiri had schooled them in the finer points of the drama, but they played their part with gusto. Phoenix upped the ante with a blood-curdling scream. Hana chanced a peek at the guard and saw him floundering. Equipped to deal with threats of brute force and skilled in torture and intimidation, he seemed lost at the prospect of a woman suffering a heart attack and three distraught infants.

With no better suggestion, Hana clutched her chest and sank to her knees on the hallway tiles. She cursed herself for validating the mad-cap plan of a child, but the powerful Du Rose nature handed down through the generations won her over and temporarily urged her to play the game. It pained her to summon the memory of her actual heart attack and she pictured the lush grass of Rangiriri Pa coming up to meet her. She forced herself to remember the feeling of suffocation as pain engulfed the left side of her body until it numbed her screaming brain. The groan she released sounded real, the feigned agony enough to alarm the guard further. Nose pressed buttons on the phone screen.

"I'll get help!" Wiri called. He turned and dashed under the guard's arm as the man grabbed for the hood of his dressing gown. Hana distracted him, hissing in actual discomfort as Mac wrapped his arms around her head and squeezed. Pain shot from the cut on her cheek and released the knives buried behind her eyes.

"Medical!" Nose shouted into his phone. The house shook with the vibration of running feet and silent, austere figures appeared as though slipping free of the walls where they'd waited for a summons. Hana slipped Mac's slender arms from around her head, lowering them and drawing him into an embrace. He increased his grip around her neck and pressed his face against her cheek.

Hands appeared beneath Hana's armpits and Mac attached himself to her torso like a koala bear. As they lifted her upright and supported her, the child wrapped his legs around her waist and clung on. Mole moved into view from a room at the end of the corridor and his gimlet eyes flickered with curiosity. "What's this?" he demanded, drawing an invisible line through the air with his index finger. His action took in Hana's upright frame from head to toe and he glared at the nearest guard. "Why is everyone in here?" He switched to a fast Chinese and Hana closed her eyes and breathed in Mac's musky scent of baby powder and sunshine.

Nose raised his phone and replied, his rapid words like a staccato beat. Supporting hands remained beneath both Hana's elbows and she shook them off and wrapped one arm around her son while using the other to search nearby for Phoenix. Her daughter responded, drawing close with a sigh and pushing her curly head under Hana's palm. Wiri hadn't returned and Hana's heart thudded in her chest for real. She forced herself not to panic as the pieces of the ruse fell into place.

"Mama?" Phoenix sounded odd and Hana glanced down at her daughter's pale, upturned face. She opened her mouth to reply as Phoenix bent double and projectile vomited in a three-metre radius. Mac caught the scent of fermented fruit and jerked backwards, his eyes widening in horror. The cogs of his sensitive stomach began their inevitable turn and he clapped a hand over his mouth and made retching noises.

Nose shouted something in Chinese which betrayed a mix of shock and annoyance. He flicked his hands towards the ceiling in pure irritation as Hana squatted to deal with her daughter. In her peripheral vision, she saw a silent communication flash between Nose and one of the other guards.

"You okay, baby?" Hana whispered to Phoenix.

Her daughter rose with a look of disgust plastered across her delicate features. She drew the back of her hand across her lips. "I taste oranges," she replied. "I don't like oranges anymore."

Mole fixed his hands on his hips and glared at Hana. Vomit dripped from an expensive tapestry to his left. "Why are you all sick?" he demanded, his tone harsh. He glared around at the other guards and they shook their heads and shrugged. "This is not good!" he snarled.

Hana frowned. Mole had supervised their breakfast and cleared away afterwards. She detected another agenda humming beneath the current deceit and panic etched its way in. She glanced at Phoenix and her retching son and felt her chest tighten. "We need help!" Her voice rose. "You've poisoned us." Nausea bubbled deep in her stomach, not enough to herald an immediate reaction but there as a reminder of her vulnerability. Hana groaned. "You've poisoned my children."

A door opened from the living area and a guard slipped through the narrow gap. Seven guards, not six. Unless only two left with Annalise. Hana held her breath and waited for him to produce Wiri. Instead, he gestured towards Hana. "Medical coming," he announced, his brow furrowing. "Your heart?" He tapped his chest and Hana nodded.

Her voice sounded croaky and she swallowed mid way through her sentence. "I have a pacemaker. Stress brings on palpitations. There's a shunt. But someone has poisoned us. Just help my children."

"Shunt," Phoenix whispered. She pressed her cheek against Hana's hip. "Shunt rhymes with blunt." She licked her lips and sounded as though she might contemplate running through the alphabet. She shaped the letter 'c' and Hana slipped her free hand under her daughter's chin and clamped her mouth closed.

"Please can you get a doctor?" she begged. "Just help my children."

Phoenix hiccoughed and released a burp which smelled of citrus. Mac's eyes widened and he made a sound low in his throat like he might puke.

Hana knew what it was then to fall into the hands of the Triads. Annalise Che intended to make them all disappear.

50

Help from Strange Quarters

Mole ushered Hana and the children back into the bedroom and dismissed the other guards. He jerked his head towards the bed and his eyes narrowed as he performed a head count. "Where is boy?" he asked.

Hana widened her eyes and clasped her children to her sides. She felt like a hen collecting her chicks beneath her wings. "You will get rid of us, won't you?" Her voice trembled. "This is it."

Mole shook his head and placed a finger against his lips. "Just wait for the doctor," he hissed. "Where is boy?"

"I don't know." Hana sank onto the mattress and took the children with her. Watchful and silent, they didn't complain as her fingers gripped their clothing and held them too hard. "I'll do whatever you want. Please, let the children go. This isn't about them."

"No." Mole glanced back towards the door and shook his head. "Lay on bed." He lowered his voice and jerked a finger towards the pillows. "Look sick," he whispered under his breath.

A grain of hope swelled in Hana's chest and she froze in place. The slight upward tilt of Mole's right eyebrow seemed to suggest complicity with her as though he gathered her into a conspiracy of their own. Too afraid to ask, Hana dragged the children back against the pillows and lay there. Her mind ran through scenarios involving doctors and syringes, knives and guns. Her limited resources offered nothing useful.

"I want Wiri." Phoenix's whine made Hana hold her breath and clasp her daughter tighter.

"Shush," she whispered. She turned her face, so her lips touched Phoenix's ear. "Don't remind them. Play sick."

Phoenix bestowed a look of half-hearted dismissal on Hana and gave a pathetic retch. It sounded fake even to her and she punctuated it with a giggle. "I did pebble dashing," she grinned. "That's what Tama does when he drinks too much beer. Is that pebble dashing, Mama? Did I do it?"

"Yep." Hana didn't remove her gaze from Mole's face.

"You should clear it up now." Phoenix winced. "I'm very sorry for you." She thought about her words and her chin flattened in a look of guilt. "I would help but I've got a bellyache."

"Yep." Hana concentrated on the sounds in the corridor. A doorbell rang, sounding muffled as though deep in the bowels of the house. She heard footsteps, a thud and then a muffled groan. Her body stiffened and Mac cried out as her fingers dug into his thin shoulder. Drawing her knees up, she pressed her bare heels into the mattress and readied herself to spring. Nobody would take her children. Not without a fight. Three guards at large and one in the room. Her brain ran through unrealistic scenarios.

Hana kept her gaze fixed on Mole. Unsure of his loyalties, she'd dismissed him as an ally. He worked for Annalise and double-crossed Mr Che, more than enough evidence of his stupidity. She jumped as Phoenix gasped and her gaze shot to the closed door to see nothing but Mole's rigid stance in front. Phoenix jerked next to her and pointed to the open doorway leading through to the children's bedroom. A dark figure occupied the gap. "Finally!" Phoenix complained. "I sicked up oranges."

Logan Du Rose stared at Hana as though not seeing her. His gaze coasted across her and the two children and he performed a perfunctory head count. His eyes blazed with an emotion which mimicked temper. Alfred's father's war relic balanced in his hands, the M1 Garand's wooden stock pressed against Logan's left shoulder. Its weight tugged Logan's arm muscles and they bulged in resistance. Hana had fired it once, the heirloom both unregistered and illegal. She'd struggled to hold it, caught her thumb in the en bloc clip and almost dislocated her shoulder as it fired. A thing of complex beauty, it represented vengeance and pain.

"Stay there," he growled through the side of his mouth to Hana. He lifted the gun and checked the sight, lining the barrel up with Mole's head. "Choose," he demanded.

Hana slid her hands over her children's eyes and resisted their tugging fingers. The fire in Logan's eyes showed no mercy and she could only guess at what he'd been through to get into the house. His uniform of jeans and cowboy boots looked dusty and his white tee shirt stained with a green substance and dotted by sand. A cut on his forearm oozed blood and clear liquid.

Mole held his arms up in front of him. "Commander Che sent orders," he hissed. "Lady boss left earlier. She took three of her guards. Two are bodyguards and the other drives for her. There are two hostiles in the house and one guarding the roof."

"Not anymore." Logan's fingers flexed on the underside of the gun and Hana saw grazed and bloody knuckles. He raised an eyebrow at Mole. "And I'm not alone, dude. Just so you know."

Mole gave a regal bow of his head. He let his hands drop, pausing as Logan aimed the long barrel at his forehead. "I work for Che," the man said. "Not lady boss. He would have warned you."

"Yeah." Logan nodded. "He did." The gun barrel lowered but only enough to give Mole breathing room. The guard pulled a handgun from a holster inside his jacket, his fingers slipping between the neat buttons with the ease of practice. Hana noticed wider spacing between the buttons above and below. The gun slithered beneath the sleek cloth and appeared from under Mole's left armpit.

Logan jerked his head towards Hana, shifting his gaze towards the door. "Get in the bathroom, Hana," he ordered. "Don't come out until I tell you."

She opened her mouth to argue but Mac's tiny frame shivered beneath her hand. His eyelashes tickled her palm. "Okay," she breathed. The presence of the children made her a hostage to both captors and rescuers.

Hana halted in the doorway of the small, windowless ensuite bathroom. Two little hands occupied hers and she looked for somewhere safe to hide her children. Her gaze took in the vanity unit beneath the sink, perhaps snug enough to contain Mac. Hana dismissed it, knowing he would neither understand his confinement nor stay there.

"Papa's got his mad face on." Phoenix's wide eyes seemed to glow in the darkness. "He's got a bumble bee up his ass."

"Phoenix!" Urgency ticked in the back of Hana's brain and overrode the expression her daughter had appropriated from David Allen. "Shower. In." The door to the cubicle creaked as she hauled it open and shoved the children into the square shower tray. Yanking towels from a heated rail, she persuaded them to sit in the corner and covered them from the threat of shattering glass. Crawling in and shielding them with her body, she sank onto the white plastic and waited as the plug hole dug into her left thigh. The door swung closed behind her with a click.

"I think I need to pray." Phoenix's voice sounded muffled. "What do you think, Mama?"

"Yep, great idea." Hana listened for the blast of Logan's gun and heard nothing. Phoenix began a warbling discussion with God concerning everything ranging from a troubling wart on Mrs Cuthbert's left hand to their current dilemma.

"Dear Jesus, please don't let anyone slip in the sick," she noted. "And I'm sorry for pigging the oranges. I thought that might happen, but their juiciness tempted me real bad."

Hana closed her eyes and said prayers of her own against possible poisons, illegal gun use and for Logan's safety. Mac shifted under her and a tiny hand wiggled free of the towel. He pushed his fingers beneath her shirt and laid his hand against her bare waist, grounding himself in maternal contact. Hana renewed her grip over her babies, hearing Phoenix add a grunt to her rambling prayer. A series of bumps and slams sounded from within the house, dull and without urgency.

Her heart thudded in her breast, but Hana resisted touching her pacemaker, choosing instead to keep her arms around her children. Phoenix murmured through her shopping list of prayer in a steady cadence, asking for Wiri's escape and moving on to Alfred's hair loss and Leslie's unfortunate issue with flatulence. "She just farts, Lord," her little voice chatted. "And sometimes we have to open the windows."

The click of the bathroom door opening sent warning signals through each of Hana's nerve endings. Her spine throbbed from the awkward position and the constant pressure of the plug hole had burned a circle of pain into her thigh. She forced herself to turn, half expecting to see Logan standing there.

Annalise Che looked calm, her expression impassive and her body relaxed. "Three little birds for the price of one," she said, her tone lilting. Hana spun on her backside, spreading her arms out to cover her children. Her gaze took in the other woman's stance and saw no weapon in her hands. Logic told her she didn't need one.

51

A Crippling Spirit of Shame

"You should have just killed us in the first place." Hana struggled to her feet, her joints and muscles complaining as she used the shower cubicle walls to stand. "Stay." She jabbed a finger behind her at the rustling of the towel and Phoenix's face disappeared back behind it. Hana faced Annalise from behind a layer of glass, anger lighting a fire in her belly. "Come on then. What are you doing? Gun, knife, bare hands. What's your plan?" The words emerged unfiltered from her lips and the terrified quarter of her brain panicked at the baiting tone.

"I'll think of something creative." Annalise grinned, her porcelain face a beautiful, horrible mask. Her right hand stretched out and her fingers gripped the narrow ridge which ran from top to bottom of the door and acted as a handle.

Temper and fear vied in Hana's soul and she darted forward, lifting her hands to press her palms against the glass. The door pivoted open on its mechanism and Hana added her body weight to the motion, shoving the door into Annalise and sending her backwards. Her own hand hit her in the face, but the impact robbed the door of kinetic energy and it spun back towards Hana in a feckless swing. She kept going, moving towards Annalise as the other woman caught her balance. Hana slammed into her, knowing she'd lose the battle even before Annalise freed her limbs and flexed her muscles to fight. The woman's display of strength and wiry aggression on the balcony earlier told Hana all she needed to know about her fate. But she'd go down fighting and buy her children time.

Annalise hit the wall behind her. The towel rail made a sickening pop as the screws bent. She gave Hana a gargantuan shove. Hana gasped as the pacemaker pressed against the tight skin of her collarbone and a red mist of pain descended over her eyes. "I'm sick of it!" she screamed, not quite sure what 'it' represented. Everything collided in her mind and exploded outward as a hailstorm of pounding fists raining on Annalise's surprised face. "He's my husband!" Hana heard her voice rise to the hysterical tones of a mythical banshee.

Her advantage ended as Annalise used her promised fighting prowess to flip Hana onto her back. She felt her head hit the edge of the plastic toilet seat as she passed it and confusion descended in a fog. Annalise stood over her, lifting her heel to end the battle. Glancing sideways, Hana saw her daughter's horrified expression as she peeped from behind a corner of the towel.

"Enough!"

Hana rolled her head to the other side and saw Logan's cowboy boots in the doorway. Her gaze tracked upwards, taking in the snugness of his jeans and the way his tee shirt clung to his powerful chest. Dark curls fell over his eyes, masking the darkness within his soul which was best unseen. His left cheek rested against the antique gun as unblinking, he viewed Annalise through the sight. "I still have eight bullets in this clip," he growled. "More than one has your name on it."

Hana looked up at Annalise, watching her melt in Logan's presence like a schoolgirl. The sight made Hana feel sick and she closed her eyes as Annalise capitulated. Che's men flooded the bathroom and Logan stepped aside, keeping the barrel of his gun trained on Annalise until they'd carried her away in their swarm of eager bodies. Logan leaned the gun over his right forearm. He racked the bolt back to eject the clip and unused bullets nestling inside the chamber. He let the clip fall to the floor and waited a moment before bending to retrieve it. Deft fingers slipped clip and bullets into his jeans pocket. They created a rectangular bulge against his leg, the hard edges loaded with threat.

Logan hefted the gun into his right hand and offered his left to Hana. He dipped forward and his biceps flexed as he hauled her upright. She saw the comforting sight of his whakapapa tattoo sneak from beneath his tee shirt as his muscle pulled the fabric tight. Once upright, Hana released a gasp of pain. The impact with her head had cracked the toilet seat and left an egg sized bump on her skull. The pain in her cheek hiked in sympathy and left an agonising jackhammer running rampant in her brain. She clutched her head as Logan released her hand and retrieved his children from the shower. Phoenix clung to his thigh and Mac rode high on his father's hip as they made a silent procession through the bedroom and out into the corridor.

Logan led his family away from the sumptuous kitchen and dining room to stairs Hana didn't remember from her arrival. He halted at a wide front door and Hana released her pounding head long enough to see why he'd stopped. Mrs Che stood in front of the door to freedom, her slight frame encased in its usual black uniform of a straight skirt and neat jacket buttoned to her neck. Sunlight spilled in behind her, creating the illusion of a stick woman with her hair scraped into its tight bun. Hana braced herself for the woman's prickly greeting. But what she saw in the pained expression took her breath away. The formidable woman's gimlet eyes swam with unshed tears and shame left a trail of pink across her high cheekbones. "I'm sorry, Logan ér zi." Her chin wobbled and Hana sensed her holding herself together.

She thought of all the times Bodie had let her down and felt the familiar sense of hopelessness wash over her. Annalise had done more than just kidnap Logan's family, she'd detonated a relationship based on honour and favours which stretched back decades. Empathy flooded through her and as Logan administered a curt nod and ushered his children through the narrow gap in the front door, Hana reached out and gave Mrs Che's bunched fingers a sympathetic squeeze. Pencilled brows drew into a single line across a creased forehead and Mrs Che dipped her head in acknowledgement of the unexpected understanding.

Hana's compliance ended on the front steps. "No! I'm not leaving without Wiri!" She reached for Phoenix's fingers and saw Mac press his cheek against Logan's neck. His thumb found his mouth and his eyes grew misty as he retreated inside his own head.

"Where did you see him last?" Logan's brows drew into a line.

"I want Wiri," Phoenix echoed. "I need him." She tipped her face up towards Hana and her widened eyes communicated her belief in her mother's ability to fix everything. Hana swallowed and wished she possessed half Logan's wisdom and agility. Then she might feel justified accepting the faith in her daughter's grey eyes.

Hana stood her ground and Mrs Che turned on the doorstep to face her. Hana shook her head and fear laced her speech. "He's a little boy wearing a dressing gown. He has dark hair and bare feet. We need to find him." She spun on the spot. "Perhaps he headed for the beach or went to a nearby house looking for help."

Mrs Che lowered her regal nose and surveyed Hana from beneath her lashes. "There is no nearby house," she said. "Your husband is waiting. You leave now."

"Not without my child," Hana whispered. She planted her feet on the steps, aware of her inability to stand against the woman and her army if they carried her off against her will. She gritted her teeth and lifted her chin, tired of feeling like flotsam in the turbulent schemes of others. "I promised him." Hana infused iron into her voice. "I'm not leaving without him."

Mrs Che released a long sigh and spoke to the man at her right shoulder in a lilting dialect. She didn't turn to gauge his reaction and he kept his expression impassive. His shallow bow stirred the air and communicated his compliance. "They will look," she snarled.

"Where did he go?" Logan demanded. His right hand clasped the gun, white knuckles showing through the skin. Mac nestled against him and turned him into a paradox. One side father and husband, the other warrior, chief, defender.

"I'm here." A tiny voice issued from inside the front door.

"Wiri!" Hana spun on the spot dragging Phoenix with her. She saw nothing and jogged up the steps and over the threshold. Back into captivity.

"Here."

Hana heard a click and then something touched the back of her leg. She moved as the door of a cabinet jabbed her again and Wiri's face appeared from beneath a stack of linen. Phoenix squealed with glee and her feet drummed on the spot.

"Wiri's so good at hiding," she gushed. Seizing his wrist, she hauled him from the tiny space.

52

Unresolved

"I didn't invite Che to the hotel," Logan replied. He ran a hand over his eyes. "He invited himself." His eyes narrowed. "As usual, he took ages to get to the point. He wanted drinks and food and all the formal stuff he loves. Wiri called right as he started saying something important. I just left, Hana. It took him by surprise, so he didn't have time to send one of his guys with me. When I got back to the hotel, he was waiting. I took you upstairs to Alfred's apartment and Leslie patched your face. She said you were concussed, but you went nuts when she tried to call Dr Seuli."

Hana shuddered. "I have no memory of that, but I'm glad my subconscious self stopped her calling him. I'd find myself in the bed next to Anahera. He'd enjoy that little victory."

Logan sighed. "Che rang me and came up to the apartment. I thought I could just bluff my way through and arrange another meeting. Then Wiri said he saw a woman in a stripy hat and Che panicked. I asked you what happened and you said she hit you around the head. That's all it took. He said he knew who did it. He offered to take you somewhere safe and you agreed." Logan's eyes implored her to remember. Hana sighed and tapped her forehead.

"I have snatches of memory but nothing concrete. Now you're talking about Che I can see him standing in Leslie's kitchen." She tutted. "That's all. But Wiri said someone gave me a pain pill in the car and I went to sleep. Could it have been one of those drugs that make people compliant and sleepy, but wipes their memory?"

"I don't know." Logan sank into a kitchen chair and ran his hands through his hair. "What a bloody mess." His fingers moved as though he wanted to touch her, but he withdrew them and laid his clasped hands on the table. His gaze glanced at his watch, noticing the hands moving towards the threshold of midnight. "We should get some sleep. That stupid fair starts the day after tomorrow."

Hana's brow furrowed and she felt her shoulders slump. "Mac's sleeping with Phoenix and Wiri is on the floor in a sleeping bag next to them." She closed her eyes in defeat. "They've seen more than is good for them in the last few days."

"Sorry." Logan sounded it. A deep scratch lined his collarbone where he'd squeezed through the window at the beach house. Pure good luck sent him into the children's temporary prison from the balcony outside.

"How did you know where she'd taken us?" Hana asked. She rested her hand on Logan's left forearm and felt his whole body stiffen.

He sighed and withdrew his arm. "It's one of Che's houses. He gave it to her years ago, before he sent her away."

"Sent her away?"

Logan nodded. His fingers turned a box of medication near his left hand. He turned it and then turned it again. "She did something bad that upset him. Mrs Che sent her to China and she's been there about six years. Annalise is the Ches' youngest daughter. His daughter by his first wife is an actuary in Europe. She returned to China recently after an accident that left her needing plastic surgery. She found Annalise gone and alerted Che."

Hana felt sarcasm bubble up her throat and seemed powerless to stop it overflowing into her speech. "Another student of the Logan Du Rose School of Appreciation."

Logan glared across the table at her. "That's not fair!"

"But it's my life." She shook her head and rose. "And it sucks." His refusal to touch her stung and the distance he'd created between them seemed cavernous. Hana looked down at the pyjamas bestowed on her by her captor and shivered. "I'm getting a shower and then going to bed," she said. "I need to burn these things."

Logan nodded and stared at a knot on the table. "Okay."

"Are you coming with me?" Hana hated the pleading in her voice.

"Soon," he replied.

Hana's tired feet dragged her to the bathroom where she washed the last days' dirt from her body. A heaviness settled in her soul. She loved her husband with a bone shaking, overwhelming love and his rejection dug into her flesh like a million wasp stings. He'd given her no opportunity to tell him anything she'd learned and the knowledge burned a hole in her brain. Hana snuggled herself in a soft towel and wrapped her hair up to dry. In the doorway of her bedroom, she peered through the soft light to the four-poster bed waiting for her. Turning away, she padded to her children's room and squeezed herself into the small space behind Mac. The pillow smelled of Phoenix's fruity shower gel and she closed her eyes. Even the pulsing of the bump on her head or the cut and bruising of her cheek couldn't stop her sinking into a welcome oblivion.

Logan didn't look for her. He didn't go to bed at all. A spectre of darkness carved furrows in his soul and he wished he'd broached the burning issue. He just didn't know how.

53

The Big Day

The summer fair promised a continuation of the heat wave as temperatures soared before breakfast. Hana arrived at the hotel early, her back already soaked just from driving down the mountain. She parked the truck in Logan's parking spot and hurried into the museum. "It's baking out there!" she gushed as Will met her in the doorway.

"Tell me about it," he grumbled. He wiped the back of his large hand across his forehead and blew out a breath. "Lock your gear in the office then come out here and help me. I hope your husband's providing water for the poor suckers coming today. It's baking hot and only gonna get worse."

"Yep." Hana gave a definitive nod. "I saw the girls from the restaurant setting up a water station near the front steps. Water is free but if they want anything different, they can buy it from the food vendors."

"It's a money spinner," Will commented. He waggled his eyebrows. "And I bet your savvy husband is taking a percentage of everything."

"Only for the school." Hana winced. "Not that I'm very committed there anymore."

Will gave her the side eye but didn't ask. "Have they found the owner of that red car yet?"

"What red car?"

"The one blocking the bus lane. Toby says it's dusty, so must have been parked there a while. They can't find who owns it." He narrowed his eyes. "Where did you go? I've been texting you for help for the last two days. I thought you'd run out on me."

Hana floundered and remembered Logan's warnings. *Say nothing. Tell no one. It didn't happen.* Hana had escaped to her raranga group the day before for a modicum of sanity and left Logan to deal with Phoenix's fantastical tales of his heroism. He'd resisted all further efforts at communication with her, withdrawing to a dark place where she couldn't reach him. Hana sighed. She hadn't been able to tell him about the ticket yet. She lied to Will. "I went out of town for a couple of days."

If he saw the glimmer of guilt in her eyes, he said nothing. He flapped his hand towards the stack of baskets towering in the corner. "I've weighed out bags of candy and printed a heap of price tags. Sort the candy into ketes according to their size and stick the price tag on the candy bag, not the basket. The glue will melt onto the flax in this heat."

"You're selling them?" Hana frowned. "I thought they were for the mock settlement."

Will shook his head. "Those went across yesterday and these are surplus. Leslie made lollies and bagged them for me. Logan said the museum can keep the profits from the sales as long as I make a notice saying so." He grappled next to his wheelchair and pulled up a handwritten sign. A smile of victory accompanied it. "You think this is okay?"

"Handmade by the family. Profits to the Du Rose Museum." Hana read the sign and nodded. She scanned the higgledy-piggledy pile of baskets and spotted a few of her own. Hindsight showed her straight away she'd failed to find her ara in any of them. She looked down at her fingers and experienced a wave of undefined emotion. She realised she'd learned something and it gave her pleasure. Whaea and the little crowd of weavers had helped her finish her masterpiece, not commenting on Hana's facial injuries or her obvious exhaustion. They'd admired her basket and treated her as one of their own, enfolding her into their family as though she'd always been there.

Turning her hands over, Hana stared at her palms. "Is it a sign of age to wish you could go back in time with what you know now?" she asked, her tone soft.

"Maybe." Will patted her thigh. "But maturity tells us to look forward and do better tomorrow." His pat turned to a slap. "And if you don't fill those baskets, you won't even make it to the end of today."

Hana smirked and stroked the nearest bag of Leslie's famous peppermint delicacies. "I think someone has a tendency to forget who the boss is here," she mused. She glanced sideways in time to catch the grin flit across Will's face before disappearing. He shook his head and busied himself making sure the glass cases on the display cabinets were all locked before the expected deluge of visitors. "Hey." Hana called his attention back to her and swallowed before dropping her bombshell into the ether. Will turned his chair and wheeled back towards her. "You know I love you, don't you?" she said. She pursed her lips and doubted herself.

Will reached her and lifted her writhing fingers into his strong hands. He pressed his lips against her knuckles. His whiskers tickled her skin and she looked down on his bowed head. Sun spots dotted his aged forehead and the bald patch on his crown. A flicker of panic rose into Hana's breast, knowing that time ticked on and the old man would one day leave her behind to cope without him. He raised his head and his brown eyes channelled kindness and returned love. "Right back at you kōtiro," he whispered. Thought he didn't say the exact words, Hana heard them through the echo of his soul. Will turned his chair and wheeled away, concluding the moment with his customary dismissal and Hana stuffed sweets into baskets alone.

The first wave of visitors came on four coaches containing Japanese tourists. They photographed everything and exclaimed in excited voices. Ignoring the signs banning photographs inside the museum, they gathered around Will and nodded as he rebuked them like a schoolteacher. Then they returned to their happy snapping. They were so enthusiastic and genuinely sweet, Will admitted defeat against their flash photography.

Locals arrived in the next rush, eager to tour the hotel but not keen to pay a small donation for access to the private family areas and decadent banqueting hall. Hana left the housekeeper to sell the baskets and wandered away to find Leslie and her children.

Wiri found her first and the panic in his eyes stalled her rebuke at him for wandering amid the strangers alone. "What's wrong?" she demanded. "Where's Nonie and the others?"

Wiri gulped and his chest hitched with the effort of smothering his tears. "You promised!" he hissed. "You promised he couldn't take me."

"What do you mean?" Hana gripped his forearms in fingers which communicated her fear through their clamping action. She held on despite his wriggling. "What's happened?"

"He's here," Wiri gulped. "My dad's here. I need to hide."

Hana searched around her with frantic head movements, seeing another crowd of chattering holiday makers heading towards her. She clasped Wiri to her and stood still like an island as the sea of bodies surged by and tried to carry her with them. "You belong to me," she asserted, leaning forward to whisper in Wiri's ear. "Nobody can take you." The determination in her voice settled him, infusing his soul with peace and confidence. He wriggled his arms to make her release him and linked his fingers around her waist.

"I don't wanna leave." His voice sounded small and plaintive. "Promise I can stay with you, Ma? Promise?"

"You're going nowhere." Hana gritted her teeth. "Show me where he is and I'll deal with him."

Wiri shivered despite the heat and his shoulders felt brittle beneath Hana's palms. "I went to the settlement town with Nonie and I saw him there. He's hanging around the games because he knows the locals aren't interested in throwing gumboots or tossing hay bales."

Hana winced and heard the voice of her husband issue from the child's mouth. He hadn't wanted the games but the rest of the committee demanded it for the tourists. "Is it busy over there?" Hana asked. The last of the new crowd dawdled around her, oblivious to the child's agony as they poked around the craft stalls. "Will he see me coming?"

"It's packed," Wiri answered. "But he wants to see you. It's why he's here."

The colour drained from Hana's face and panic ticked an unhealthy beat in her chest. She reached into her jeans for her phone and groaned when she remembered locking it in the museum office.

54

Neville Du Rose

Hana climbed over the fence behind the settlement town and dropped into the grass with the grace of an elephant. She'd avoided the main thoroughfare to avoid giving Nev the advantage. The makeshift streets buzzed with activity as visitors peered into the buildings. Will's careful direction had produced a museum quality exhibition and Hana already imagined him arguing to keep it standing after the fair. An 1840s English town had risen from the paddock over the last few weeks, set aside enough from a replica Māori stronghold to emphasise the division in cultures. Hana frowned. The original Logan Du Rose who set out from Scotland married the daughter of a Māori chief. Will had overruled her argument for more unity, citing the experience of every other settlement in New Zealand. "It wasn't true of any other town, Hana," he asserted. "Why let tourists think we lived in harmony when we didn't?"

Hana's steps slowed as she approached the back of a mock bakery. Fake loaves nestled in a basket on the porch and she saw the corner of the sack tablecloth blowing in the gentle breeze. Skirting the roped off area, she navigated the narrow lanes between the buildings and followed a crowd speaking

German. They paused near the gunsmith's shop and pointed at an antique musket mounted on a rack. The ropes prevented them getting close and Hana could see the fine thread of fishing line tying it to the wall. Will had insisted on authentic and Logan had thrown his hands in the air. "If someone blows their nuts off with a family heirloom, it's on you!" he'd growled. Enough invisible deterrents existed around the displays to fox most people just wanting to touch and explore the artifacts. For those with more serious intent, the burly security guards offered a mix of intimidation and brawn. Used to working for an exacting and uncompromising Logan Du Rose, they stood on duty in their smart uniforms and missed nothing. Hana made her way towards Big Dan as he surveyed the crowd. Muscles rippled beneath his smart uniform and a dark baseball cap cast shadows over his eyes.

"Do you have anyone in the games area?" Hana asked in response to the upward jerk of his head.

Big Dan's eyes continued to watch the visitors. He fostered an air of a man protecting the crown jewels and it created a tantalising mix of mystique and excitement. It seemed to draw the crowds rather than deter them as Hana had feared. "Yup," he answered. "What do you need, Mrs Du Rose?" He flexed the hands clasped in front of him and the action sent a shiver through his muscles. Hana blinked.

"Just checking," she said. "I'm meeting someone over there and I might need help."

Big Dan lifted his index finger to his ear piece and spoke into a walkie talkie clipped to his front pocket. "Big Dan to Big Ed. White Rose heading your way." He lowered his voice. "Watch for signals for assistance. Over."

He gave a definitive nod and Hana imagined the reply in his ear piece. She held onto the laughter bubbling in her chest. Only Logan could find a security team with names like Big Dan, Big Ed, Big Grant and Big Bob. She wondered if it was an application criterion. She moved away and then turned back, confusion budding in her eyes. "White Rose?" she asked. "Is that me?"

A smile split Big Dan's lips. "Yes, Miss," he replied.

"Why white?" Hana hid her disappointment. She fancied herself as a vibrant red, sultry and romantic. Not plain white.

Big Dan afforded her a side glance before returning to his avid people watching. "White roses signify purity, Miss. Mr Logan calls you that."

"Does he now?" Hana mused. She gave Big Dan the benefit of a raised eyebrow and watched the colour flush in his cheeks.

"Be most grateful if you didn't tell him you know." He kept his head moving on his beefy neck in a slow arc and surveyed the crowd. Hana smiled and placed her index finger over her lips, waiting for his gaze to reach her. He nodded and his smile held relief. "Thank you, Miss. Big Ed is watching out for you now."

"Thanks." Hana turned away without diminishing the man's sense of importance. He took his job seriously and security around the hotel and campsite had improved tenfold since he arrived a few months ago. Free use of the hotel gym and rooms in Jack's old bunkhouse gave a ready incentive to his team to stick around. A free meal after every shift added to the lure. Logan paid a good wage and listened to their more sensible suggestions. Hana moved on and hoped the promise of discretion went both ways. The sad reality dictated that once Logan got on the warpath, neither of them could keep their agreement. Hana hoped she got the meeting over with Nev before Logan rumbled her.

Hana walked through the gate to the games area and dodged to avoid a flying sponge. It landed in a sopping heap at her feet and Toby grimaced from his position in the stocks. "Sorry," he called. Another sponge hit him in the mouth and Hana grinned at his unintelligible, spluttered reply.

"Karma," she mouthed and saw his eyes narrow into thoughtful slits. Another sponge hit him in the forehead and robbed him of the right to reply.

Hana skirted the gumboot throwing and hay bale tossing, approaching the coconut shy from behind. A familiar figure stood watching a mother with four small children. The woman took it in turns to help each child make their throw with varying degrees of success. They seemed oblivious to the tall man observing their fun. Hana held her breath as she walked up behind her brother-in-law, feeling his arm tense as she gave it a light touch on the elbow. "Nev?"

He turned and she jumped back in shock. "Kane!" She spat the word and backed away, ramming into a woman carrying multiple bags of candy floss. Apologising, she extracted herself and grappled for an escaping bag. She handed it over without looking.

"Hi Hana." Kane Du Rose hid his face beneath a wide brimmed cap. A red tee shirt draped over his head helped him blend in with all the other locals outside the games field who kept the sun off their shoulders that way. Surrounded by tourists he stood out as odd amid the floral sun hats and baseball caps. Sunburned necks and shoulders swam around like painful beacons. Dark curls coiled around Kane's eyebrows and the beginnings of a beard shrouded the lower half of his face.

"But I saw you die." Hana raised a hand to her mouth. In her peripheral vision she saw a neat uniform move towards her. "No, no!" she mouthed. She flicked a hand towards Big Ed in the distance and he halted on the spot.

Kane followed the action and his eyes narrowed at the sight of the guard. "There's no need," he said, his voice calm. "I won't hurt you."

Hana blew out a breath and looked around for somewhere to sit. Blood rushed through her ears, muffling normal conversation and the shouts of victory from the coconut shy. Her right hand fluttered upward until her fingers contacted the pacemaker. Kane jerked his head towards a group of picnic tables scattered beyond the games. Food trucks gathered, setting up their attractive wares and touting for business. Hana gave a resigned nod and followed him as he moved against the flow of traffic, head and shoulders above most of them.

Hana sank onto a vacant bench and waited while Kane seated himself opposite. The effort of sitting seemed to drain his energy and accentuate the greyness of his complexion. "You look thinner," she said. With shaking fingers, she lifted her cowboy hat on the cord around her neck and pulled it up and over her head. It protected her eyes from the sun but shadowed her face from Kane's scrutiny. She shook her head in disbelief. "No wonder the dude in the hotel footage looked like you. It was you."

Kane shrugged. "Dunno what you mean." He appeared unconcerned.

Hana leaned forward to avoid being overheard. "The owner of the golf lodge called Logan. He made him settle your bill after he heard you died. We watched security footage of you eating breakfast."

"Sorry." He sounded it and Hana felt her shoulders relax. "Nev went off somewhere with the car and didn't come back. He said it wouldn't take long."

"He came looking for the bond, didn't he? The one Reuben took out the day Logan was born. Did the number come up?"

"Yeah." Kane nodded and his smile held a thousand pinpricks of sadness and regret. "I didn't mind sharing, but we needed Logan's help. It's in his name."

"I thought Nev trashed our house looking for it." Hana shook her head. "But he was already dead. Was it you? And why didn't you just explain what you wanted instead of being so cryptic?"

"Sorry." Kane shrugged. "I don't know anything about your house getting tossed. I intended to tell Logan everything when I came up that night, but we just fell into the same old pattern." He wrinkled his nose. "Sparring with my bro' felt safe and familiar, but it's not why I came."

Hana lowered her voice. "We thought you came for Wiri."

Realisation bloomed in Kane's eyes. The diamond irises transformed to slate grey. He shook his head. "No, Hana. Fathering that kid was a drunken accident. He's better off with you. His mother's a complete head case."

"He knows, doesn't he?" The knowledge lodged like a stone in her stomach. "Wiri knows you're his father. That's why he's afraid of you."

Kane's head jerked backwards. "I did nothing to that kid!" He reacted as though Hana had levelled an accusation. She sighed.

"No, I don't believe you did. I think he's scared you'll take him. It makes sense now." The bed wetting, the anxiety and Wiri's depression ever since Kane showed up and spoiled their dinner. The pieces fell into place. Hana leaned forward. "We can straighten this out. Logan will know how."

"Will he?" Kane tugged the tee shirt further over his hat as the sun beat on his thin shoulders. He snuffed out a sad laugh. "You talk about him just like we used to speak about Reuben. We thought he could fix everything. He couldn't even fix himself."

Hana exhaled. "Come and see Logan with me. He'll be hiding out in the office near the stables until these visitors get off his property. How did you get here if Nev took your car?" She frowned. "Where is the car? It must still be here." Kane's eyes flashed and his lip twitched at the left. A dimple appeared in his cheek. Another Logan Du Rose tell. "Where is it?" she demanded.

"I've seen it in the car park where the buses stop."

"Oh." Hana winced. "Is it the red one that's causing all the commotion?"

Kane nodded and his grey eyes misted in wistfulness. She sensed he didn't care about the car. "I've been reacquainting myself with the bush and reminiscing since the tangi." He smiled. "I like that maze you've planted on the site of our old house. Dad would have approved of the irony. He wasn't a complicated man like the maze though, Hana. He knew what he wanted, but he couldn't have it."

"I know. Believe me, I know." Hana's eyes widened as she recognised Detective Sanders watching the antics at the coconut shy. He stood with his back to her, his casual clothes blending in with the visitors. She looked around for Damian but didn't see him, figuring the detective was attempting to outshine the uniformed officer by attending a weekend function at the crime scene. "Don't look now but there's a cop behind you."

Kane nodded. "Okay. It's time I shot through, anyway."

"No, wait." Hana fished for reasons to hold on to him. "You haven't explained what happened at the hotel. Why did Nev come back here without you? Why was he searching Alfred's apartment?"

Kane thought about his answer for a moment. His hand shook as he straightened his cap and hauled the tee shirt higher. "He didn't stay with me. Nev rented a room at a motel just off the expressway. Said he didn't want any cameras picking him up. He kept the rental car and texted me when we needed to travel together. I always met him on the main road away from prying eyes. I didn't feel so flash the day he died. He said he'd thought of one last place to look and wanted me to go with him. I told him to see Logan and just ask. He promised he'd think about it. When I didn't hear from him again, I assumed he'd got picked up by the cops. I knew he'd find a way to let me know. He didn't. I haven't been well, so I tend to sleep most of the time. During breakfast this one day, I saw an article in the newspaper about a summer fair and how it might not go ahead because of the accident. That's when I discovered I'd died." Kane pursed his lips. Tiny scars dotted the skin, adding white hairline cracks to his once handsome face.

Hana exhaled. "You went back for your bags after they called Logan?"

Kane's grey eyes sparkled. "No. I kept everything in a supermarket bag. I didn't bring much with me. No bags, Hana, but thanks for paying the bill."

"How did you get here if Nev had the car? And why didn't the cops find his phone on his body? That would have helped identify him."

Kane shrugged. "I stole a car from the golf lodge and dumped it in the township. The tracks we made as kids still run through the bush from the town to the marae. I made it to the tangi and hid so I could listen. I overheard Tama's speech about me." He gulped and his voice cracked. "I realised what happened to my bro'. I thought the newspaper just printed my name in error, but everyone mistook him for me." Kane swallowed and Hana waited for him to collect himself enough to continue. He seemed shaken by Nev's death and she sensed the severing of the familial bond causing him untold agonies. It offered an alternate view of the brothers as though the sun had kissed a pane of glass and created a prism. Kane shook himself free of his despair. "His phone kept losing power. It's just a burner phone. Maybe it's still charging in the car."

"I'm sorry Nev's dead." Hana delivered her commiserations with sincerity. She frowned. "If it's any consolation, I even said nice things about you." Her lips curved into a rueful smile. "Ironic you didn't hear."

Kane's smile appeared genuine. The likeness to Logan seemed more striking when he relaxed. Peas in a pod. The same father and a pair of sisters for mothers. Kane wrinkled his nose, reminiscent of Logan's familiar stress tell. Hana looked for discomfort in his expression and found it right where she expected it to be. Just under the surface but masked by bravado. "I never had a problem with you," he said.

Hana's gaze strayed to a jagged scar above his eye and she winced. "Despite wearing the evidence of my left hook?" She snuffed out a laugh. "I'm not sorry for that. You deserved it."

Kane's fingers strayed to his forehead and he hauled the brim of the cap lower. "I respected you for that. Me and you are good."

The creases around his eyes were Logan's. Hana looked at them every morning as she counted her blessings. Impulse made her reach out and clasp Kane's thin wrist between her fingers. Age had matched him with Logan, but his decreased body mass made him thinner than Neville. "Let's go and see Logan. We can clear this whole mess up. You both have regrets, Kane. This could be our chance to make everything okay."

Kane's jaw tensed and he withdrew his wrist, pulling his arm too far across the table for her to hold on. But he did it with forced gentleness. Resistance without aggression. "I can't." He closed his eyes in a slow blink. "I'm leaving, Hana. It's all too hard."

"But Caroline thinks you're dead!" Hana raised her voice and Kane stiffened. His spine straightened and she knew she'd lost him. "Please don't do this. Logan can make it all okay," she pleaded. "What about Edin? There's something else, isn't there? Tell me the truth, Kane."

Kane made a sound like a groan and his chin dropped onto his chest. "This makes no different to Caro. I'll be gone soon, anyway. Edin's the one good thing I did in my entire life, Hana. Take care of Edin for me? Please?"

Hana panicked. "Take care of her yourself!" she implored. "Please, Kane. Don't do this. We can fix all of it."

Kane twisted on the bench and swung his legs free. He stood and Hana fought to untangle her feet. He observed her for a second before speaking. "Can you tell Logan I'm sorry?"

"For what?" Hana pulled herself free and moved towards him, navigating the table between them.

"For everything. I was angry at him because of something he couldn't control. Reuben and Miriam made the mess and me and Nev suffered, but it wasn't Logan's fault. He didn't ask to be born. Tell him I'm sorry for everything I did to him. Promise you'll tell him I don't hate him."

"Tell him yourself!" Hana implored. "Why are you running away? You've done nothing wrong!"

"I'm dying, Hana." Kane's jaw flexed and the pieces fell into place; the thinness which made him appear to switch places with Nev coupled with the resignation behind his eyes. "Final stages mate." He tapped his right side and sighed. "I abused my body for too long and now I'm walking out the consequences." Raising his hand, he pointed at her and spoke as though giving a public service announcement. "Take care of your body and it will take care of you."

Hana closed her eyes and shook her head. "No. This makes no sense."

Kane raised his hands and cupped her cheeks. His grey eyes glittered like diamonds in his pale countenance. "Look after Logan, Hana. He's the last one of us left. And look after Edin. Promise?"

Hana's heart turned into a lead weight in her chest. "Why do I need to look after Edin?"

Kane pushed her hat back and pressed a kiss to her forehead. "Because you already have Wiri," he whispered. "And you're a good person."

He released her face and lifted his hands to prevent her catching hold of them. Hana lurched for him and he took a long stride backwards. She missed. "What about Caroline?" she demanded. "What do I tell her?"

Kane tipped his head sideways and regret oozed from his stunning almond-shaped eyes. "Tell her Karma is a bitch," he replied. "Tell her it gets everyone in the end."

55

The Impossible

"Kane didn't die!" Hana seized the detective's sleeve and tried to spin him towards her. He took a step back in alarm and his expression radiated shock. He pulled his shirt free of her grasp and glanced around him.

"Oh. What happened to your face?" His eyes narrowed. "Is your husband violent with you, Mrs Du Rose?"

Hana heaved out an exasperated breath. "No, Detective, he wouldn't dare."

"Then why do you have fresh injuries every time I see you?"

"Thanks for your concern, but I don't. That's not what I wanted to talk to you about. Kane didn't die. Neville Du Rose fell from the balcony. Not Kane."

Sanders' brow furrowed and created a mask of irritation. "Mrs Du Rose, I realise this whole situation is upsetting for you, but that's ludicrous. Our investigation is ongoing. I'd rather talk about that cut to your face."

Hana's heart performed a flip-flop in her chest and her fingers fluttered over the collar of her shirt. "I know it sounds crazy, but it's true. I just met Kane Du Rose over there." She jabbed a finger back at the games area and watched Sanders' gaze flick behind her and then settle on her face.

"These Du Rose boys are very alike," he said, his tone gentle and placating. "It's easy to confuse them. Is one of the others hurting you?"

Hana's green eyes flashed. "You're an idiot!" she snapped. Temper blazed until a red mist descended over her vision. She moved closer to Sanders' broad chest and tapped it with a stiff index finger. "Kane Du Rose had haemophilia, you moron. Nev Du Rose didn't. Talk to the coroner."

Hana stalked away, aware of nearby knots of people stopping to watch her. She reached the stocks and searched for Toby, seeing one of the newer stock men closing his eyes against the wet sponge flying towards him. "Where's Toby?" she demanded, receiving a spluttered reply as he took the hit straight to the forehead.

"Mrs Du Rose!" Sanders sounded puffed and his voice contained urgency. He grabbed Hana's elbow and whirled her around. Big Ed observed from a position near the coconut shy and moved towards Hana. "There were no medical records for Kane Du Rose!" Sanders snapped.

Hana closed her eyes and shook her head. Logan's hatred of hospitals and Michael's desire to change the world as a doctor drifted through her mind. Wiri never complained about his ailments and grew distressed at suggestions of medical assistance outside Hana's simple first aid skills. Logan had succumbed for the sake of his Factor 8 infusions and Michael became part of the problem. But Reuben had been an intelligent man. He might have fixed his children's minor ills by himself. She heaved out a breath, imagining her capable father-in-law mending everything from stomach upsets to broken bones. "Who identified the body?" she demanded. "And what about the evidence from the golf lodge?"

Sanders swallowed. "We found no hard evidence. Maid service cleaned any fingerprints off every surface. The video footage resolution looked too grainy for a positive identification and taking stills didn't help. Kane's sister-in-law identified his body. Your husband's family refused and it took time to locate his wife."

"Caroline didn't identify Kane's body?"

"No." Sanders blinked, attempting to shutter his awkwardness. He reached into his pocket and drew out a notebook. His fingers leafed through the pages before he tapped an entry. "Anahera Du Rose."

Hana jerked backwards. "You pulled a mentally disturbed woman from a hospital ward to identify a dead man! Is that even legal?"

Sanders squared his jaw. "Everyone else refused. I didn't have time to arrest people, process them and follow the procedure required to force someone to do it. With no medical or dental records, we kept searching until we found someone able to identify him."

"Someone able? That's debatable," Hana spat. She winced at the thought of Logan's refusal. It had aided a disaster. "What did Anahera say? Was she okay afterwards?" Hana put a hand on her hip and waited for the answer.

Sanders radiated discomfort. "The hospital agreed. They signed her off as capable. A nurse came with her." A faint tick pulsed beneath his left eye. "She seemed fine."

"What did she say?" Hana imagined Anahera arriving at the morgue to view Kane's battered corpse and instead finding her husband's.

Sanders' shoes ground the gravel as his feet shifted. "She laughed. She said he got what he deserved."

"And she identified Kane?" Hana's eyes narrowed as she contemplated Anahera's sense of victory.

Sanders nodded. "Yeah. She signed the paperwork."

Hana snorted. "Oh man, you've been Du Rosed." She turned on her heel and stalked back towards the settlement buildings. She saw Big Ed lift his radio to his lips and heard his whispered message.

"White Rose has left the games area."

Sanders called her name numerous times, but she didn't look back. She stiffened her spine and steered a rough course back to the hotel, intending to flush out Logan and lay the whole sorry mess at his feet.

"Hana!" Libby's voice cut through the clamour and Hana paused. Libby appeared next to her with Darren in tow. She jerked her head sideways to indicate her intention to keep the conversation brief and without detail. "He wants to speak to you." Her face remained impassive and though she noticed the healing cut on Hana's cheek and her black ringed eye, she chose not to probe further. Darren tugged on her hand and pointed to the candy floss seller.

Hana looked around the fair, trying to pick out her son in the throng. She shook her head. "I don't see him." Squeals carried across the paddock from the coconut shy as a conquering male claimed the teddy bear prize and handed it to his daughter. Hana watched Holly jump up and down with excitement and her eyes narrowed. Her heart beat a raised tattoo in her chest.

Libby tossed her head and her blonde hair fluttered in the light breeze. "He's waiting for you in the rose garden. Play nice, Hana. He has the greatest respect for you. Try to return the sentiment." She spun on her heel and Hana watched her tiger print yoga pants disappear into the crowd. With heavy steps, she forced herself to walk towards Miriam's rose garden. "Like I need this right now!" she hissed under her breath.

Her daughter appeared like a genie in front of her and Hana skidded to a halt. "Look, Mama!" Phoenix stood on tippy toes and waved a stick packed with candy floss at Hana. Wiri held her other hand and Mac rode up on Leslie's hip. "This is tasty."

"Ka pai." Hana smiled and let the Te Reo words slip from her lips.

Phoenix's eyes widened and she beamed. "It is good, Mama," she agreed. She released Wiri's hand and pressed the centre of her stomach. "But I feel a bit sick."

Hana rolled her eyes and leaned in to speak to Leslie. "Are you okay to mind the children a little longer? There's something I need to do."

"We're grand." Leslie's head bobbled up and down in time with her chins. "My mokopuna have looked at everything now. They want to see Poppa Alfie and eat some brownie." She jerked her head towards Wiri. "He keeps running off."

Phoenix paled at the thought of more sweet food and winced. Wiri caught Hana's eye and smirked. "Eyes bigger than belly," he muttered.

Hana nodded and reached out to stroke his cheek. Wiri pursed his lips and nodded, understanding she hadn't forgotten her promise. "Please stay with Nonie. Everything will be sorted out soon," she whispered. She winked at Mac and turned back towards the rose garden. "I promise this won't take long."

"Mama!"

Hana spun at the sound of the soft voice and her jaw dropped open. Mac held his hand out and opened and closed his fingers. Leslie pursed her lips and stared at the child in her arms as though wondering how he got there. "Well, bless my soul," she breathed.

"Tiss." Mac puckered his lips and closed his eyes. His fingers continued to beckon Hana. "Tiss."

The few steps to his side seemed to take a lifetime and her boots felt filled with concrete. Mac closed his eyes as Hana pressed her lips to his. They felt wet and sticky, the sugary taste of pink candy floss searing itself into her brain as a snapshot of a never forgotten moment. Though her heart tumbled over itself, she stepped through the landmark with dignity and offered a wavering smile and another kiss to his left cheek. "Won't be long," she promised again.

Her body shook as she moved away and she battled the tears which prickled behind her eyelids. Relief vied with sadness and she couldn't sift through the emotions fast enough. How long had Mac chosen to stay inside his cocooned world without interaction, or had he spoken to everyone else but her? She'd missed the signs. Hana beat herself up all the way to the rose garden and rounded the corner unready for battle with her other son.

She froze in the narrow arch and stared at the man bending to sniff a yellow bloom. He looked up at her with a slow smile. "Hi," he said, looking much more wrong footed than she expected. His hands dropped to his sides and he squared himself for a fight.

Hana shook her head in confusion. "You?" she said.

His jaw dropped open to reveal perfectly straight teeth before he clamped it shut again. "She said you knew." He sounded irritated.

Hana placed her hands on her hips and narrowed her eyes. "I should have," she snapped. "It's the real reason you came to Kane's funeral, isn't it?"

Odering tipped his head a little to one side. "I was in the area, Hana. Seemed too good an opportunity to miss winding up your husband."

The sickness of relief and anti-climax roiled in Hana's gut. Her legs felt shaky and she stepped sideways so she could fold onto a nearby bench. "Why are you driving my son's car?" Her voice sounded hoarse and strained.

Odering seated himself next to her and leaned his forearms on his thighs. His head dropped. "I borrowed it for a few days. I'm thinking of buying it so he can get a people mover for his expanding brood. You didn't know at all, did you?" He sighed. "You thought Libby was seeing Bodie." Hana nodded, unable to formulate a coherent sentence in her head. Odering groaned. "Well, this is awkward."

"No." Hana shook her head as relief thudded through her brain. She'd wronged Bodie and it caused a gnawing pain in her gut which vied with the desire to fist bump someone. She made a decision. "Not at all." She stared around her at the brilliant blooms turning their velvet faces to greet the overhead sun. Logan called her the 'White Rose.' He believed in her purity of heart. She figured it was time she exercised it. "This is your wake-up call, Detective Inspector. Libby called me a hypocrite for not caring when I believed her love life couldn't affect me. She was right." Hana stood, her legs shaking under her. "I was married to a man who lived a double life. I'm not sure how long he betrayed me and I probably never will. But I wish he'd told me the truth and not negated the last few years of our marriage. I no longer know what was real and what wasn't. I refuse to stand by and see someone else made a fool of." Hana lifted an index finger and drew a line in the air. Her hand remained steady. "One week, that's all I'm giving you. Get your house in order and let me know what you choose. Seven days from today, I'm having a conversation with your Chief Superintendent. He golfs with a friend of mine and I bet you've stolen work time to visit your mistress." Hana spun on her heel and forced her legs to move with dignity and poise.

Instinct herded her away from the growing crowds circling the many stalls and displays. Her feet took her up the ramp and through the open doorway of the museum. Will gave another half hourly tour, explaining the fascinating history of the Du Roses as he propelled his wheelchair in front of an interested group of tourists. Hana let herself into the office and locked the door behind her. She sank onto a stool and let her gaze coast over the beautiful cloak draped across a manikin's shoulders. Tama had looked stunning at the tangi.

Hana dug her phone from the desk drawer and dialled the number for her brother's partner. He answered after two rings and Hana heard laughter in the background. "Hey," she said to her son's ear surgeon. "Macky can hear."

56

Guilty

Hana smiled through the congratulations, allowing the news to filter from her brain to her face expression. Her son spoke, giving her the thing she'd desired more than any other. And he'd said her name first. The events of the last few weeks paled into insignificance and she let her shoulders relax. "It's amazing," she agreed. "Please, can you tell Mark for me? Oh, do you still play golf with Paul McAndrew, the police chief?" Her smile widened with the confirmation and she set the groundwork to make good on her promise. "I need to go sweetheart," she said, glancing at her watch. "I have some things to sort out."

Hana ended the call and drank from the tap in the washroom, even though the sign over the sink declared the water not drinkable. "So, kill me then," she murmured, straightening her ponytail and squaring her shoulders. She fired off a text to Bodie, saying she was sorry she hadn't spoken in a while and asking if they could catch up for coffee soon. Then she ventured out into the museum after stuffing her phone into her jeans pocket. It vibrated as she pulled the door behind her and she yanked it out far enough to kill the call. She fought the urge to see who she'd just ignored but focused instead on her immediate goal.

Gina followed Will around the museum, listening to his explanations and nodding at various points. A slim man in an expensive suit trailed her. His gaze missed nothing as he studied the family portraits in their gilded frames. A look of distaste settled over his expression at the image of a tattooed rangatira glaring down at the proceedings. The Māori chief's tattooed black lips pulled back in a snarl to reveal neat white teeth. The familiar Du Rose hooked nose lent the man in the oil painting an air of natural superiority. Kuia Phoenix Du Rose's father. He'd married her mother and allowed her to keep her family name. He was a man of honour who loved the whenua, the land. Hana waited until Gina glanced her way and then beckoned to her.

"I can't believe you live here!" Gina stage whispered. "You're so lucky."

Hana smiled and led her into the long office. Gina's heels clattered against the quarry tiles and Hana closed the door behind her. She leaned against it and her smile turned icy. "I do live here," Hana replied. "And I am lucky. I intend to stay here for a very long time and raise my children and grandchildren here. This property is not for sale."

Gina lost her confident smile and removed her manicured fingers from the frame of another Du Rose ancestor who Will had propped up against the wall to await cleaning. "I don't know what you're talking about." Her gaze flicked to the door and she pursed her lips as though she might scream for help.

Hana's jaw tensed. "Do it," she said, her tone threatening. "Scream. There's a detective outside. Shall I fetch him for you? He's got the camera footage of you vandalising our property in your stupid hat. A confession will make his day. I'm guessing Louise hit me around the head?" Hana's fingers rose to touch the space beneath the cut and saw Gina wince. "Sabotaging animal feed is below the belt, Gina. Smashing plant pots and bits of vandalism are one thing but wanting animals to suffer is a whole new level of cruelty."

"I didn't do that!" Gina took a step forward to emphasise her denial and paused as Hana reached for the te rākau Will kept behind the office door.

Hana raised the pole and ran her fingers across the dents and creases in the hard wood. Logan had found it in the attic. It held no value apart from the sentiments coveted by the unidentified Du Rose ancestor who'd worn hand prints along its centre. Hana twisted the long pole in her hands as she'd seen Logan and Tama do with theirs a million times before. The movement felt clumsy but the te rākau obeyed, twirling through a complete circle and whipping the surrounding air. She imagined Logan's great grandfather exacting obedience with it. And the strong men before him wielding it against English guns. She shuddered and allowed injustice to spark through her muscles and provide energy to her nerve endings. "Who did?" she demanded. "Your developer husbands? I've seen Holly's surname on documents, Gina. Louise changed hers after her divorce but not her daughter's. Did you think I wouldn't work it out?"

Gina blanched and she sank into a nearby office chair. It spun a little and her heels scraped against the tiles. "We lost a fortune on that land deal with Reuben Du Rose," she breathed. "The company took deposits for the houses and sold expensive plans. We're up to our necks in debt."

Hana shook her head. "You built on the land near the school. Those townhouses are selling to Aucklanders. The locals can't afford them."

"It's not enough." Gina's hand shook as she brushed her fringe from her eyes. "We took out massive loans expecting to make it back tenfold on the mountain properties. My husband and Louise's paid for the services and roading which your house now uses. It's not fair." Her voice took on a whine which jarred Hana's thin patience.

"Services their company installed on land bought from a man who didn't own it. So, you thought you'd harass us until we left?" Her teeth ground in her jaw. "You'd only just got started, hadn't you? You planned to do much worse."

Gina cringed. "My husband knows nothing about this." She gulped. "Please don't call the police. Louise didn't mean to hurt you." She sneaked a glance at the bruising beneath Hana's eye and the scabbed cut on her cheek.

Hana snorted. "Didn't she? Somehow, I doubt that. Your husband might not know about your antics with her, but he's done a little sabotage of his own, hasn't he?"

"Maybe. I don't know." Gina spread her hands wide and her eyes filled with tears. "Please, Hana. Don't sink us."

"Sink you?" Hana shook her head. She took a step forward and shoved the blunt end of the te rākau under Gina's chin. The other woman reached out and gripped the pole with both hands as Hana braced it against her throat and pressed. Gina's head hit the back of the chair. "I want to bury you!" Hana hissed through gritted teeth. She forced herself to release the pressure, her rational mind pushing away the images of Louise's daughter Holly making Phoenix's life a nightmare. A fire burned in her belly at the incompetence of the school staff as they kowtowed to a promise of funds which would never materialise. Hana lifted the te rākau and held it in sweating palms. The end clunked against the tiles.

"I like to keep things nice and neat," she bit, remembering her threat to Odering. "You and Louise have a week to leave our town. We don't want you here. If you don't comply, I'll go to the cops and a lawyer." Hana reached up to touch her cheek, drawing attention to Louise's stupidity. "I'd quite like damages for assault and battery. Especially as there's a witness." Hana made the bluff, knowing Wiri's testimony wouldn't stand up against scrutiny. "If you think you have financial problems now, just see what happens when I get my sister-in-law involved. I'm sure an intern in her chambers would love to impress her." In seven days, she'd mop up everything if she didn't get her demands met. No negotiation. Odering and the Stamford-Goldings development company would experience the Du Rose side of her nature. It knew no compromise.

"You can't do that!" Gina clattered upright and took a threatening step closer. Her eyes darted furtive glances at the pole in Hana's fingers as she lifted and twirled it again, cutting the air with a whipping sound. The te rākau missed Gina's chin by mere inches.

"I just did," Hana snarled as Gina took a step backwards. "One week. Or the cops pay you a visit. Stop pestering my husband to sell any of his land to you. It's not for sale!"

Hana felt the draught sweep across her back and stepped forward to avoid the force of the opening door. It slammed against the wall and the handle embedded itself in the plaster. She heard Will halt his gentle, echoing tenor in a distant corner of the museum.

Logan Du Rose filled the doorway, his grey eyes flashing like diamonds over a slate surface. "Get out!" he growled at Gina. "One week. You heard."

He stood back and dragged Hana with him, allowing Gina the freedom to totter past on her heels. Then he slammed the door behind her with a force which echoed through the museum. Will's list of jobs swayed on the noticeboard above the photocopier like a lopsided pendulum. It condemned Hana for the urgent scanning task she kept avoiding. Dragging her phone from her pocket with shaking fingers, Hana's heart quailed at the sight of the open call symbol. She hadn't killed it like she believed. She'd given Logan an open line to everything she'd said. The anger, the misdirection and the threats. It all returned to bite her.

Her eyes widened in fear and her lips parted, eager to ply her furious husband with excuses. He glared at her, his lips drawn into a thin line of temper and his fists balled. He shook his head. "Don't," he said. "Don't ruin it, Hana."

Snatching the te rākau from her hand, he dropped it on the workbench with a thud. He lifted her off the ground in his strong arms. She felt the force of his pride and trembling with embarrassment and guilt, buried her face in his neck.

57

The Basket Case

Logan held Hana's hand as they wandered through the many stalls set up in the hotel gardens. The brown grass suffered under the heavy footfall, despite the sections of carpet the professional traders used to line their tents. The sun beat down in a relentless barrage of heat and sunburn and the requests for cool water kept the hotel staff busy at their stations. Logan lifted Hana's hand and kissed her fingers, rubbing his thumb across the back of her wrist. He said nothing, communicating his approval through his actions. Hana still stung from her interaction with Gina, unsure where the courage came from. The woman she'd become in those few moments both terrified and delighted her. The English White Rose had nasty thorns.

Whaea Queenie winked at her from a stall selling local handcrafts and Hana smiled back. The older woman jerked her head at Logan and Hana nodded. She considered their conversation and pursed her lips. Other things seemed more important, like telling Logan that Nev died in Kane's place and that Odering was a cheat. She made the decision to delay the bad news and break it to him later. Sanders hadn't believed her.

Logan may not either. Whaea settled her hands on her hips and raised an eyebrow. Hana cringed, nerves flooding her jittery brain and adding to the mess.

"I've something for you," she said to Logan. Colour flushed into her neck and she dug in her back pocket, grimacing as she remembered leaving her car keys in the museum office. "Damn, do you have the spare key to my truck?"

"Yep." He nodded. He released her hand and hooked his forearm around her neck, pulling her under his arm. "Wanna go somewhere?" His irises glittered and Hana grinned.

"Not where you're thinking."

Logan dug into his jeans pocket and hauled out the key. "Where are we going?"

"Just to the truck." Hana tugged his hand and led the way, picking through the crowds towards the staff car park. The truck sat in its usual space with Whaea's little car next to it and Hana turned and walked backwards between the vehicles. "Close your eyes," she ordered. Fumbling with the key fob, she unlocked the truck and reached in to the foot well behind the driver's seat. Her shaking hand withdrew the perfect little basket she'd finished the day before. A neat plait cast off around the rim and finished with a sweeping fringe. She'd left it with Whaea to let the older woman trim any loose strands and comb out the fringe. It had dried a little more overnight in her cool pantry and the weave had parted to leave open diamonds between the leaves. Not big enough to hold more than a few pieces of fruit, the basket's value lay in what it represented more than in its function. The sunlight caught the shades of blue in the dye and created mottled highlights.

Hana held her breath and repeated the sentence she'd practiced with the women. "I hunga au i te kete." She swallowed, doubting herself as Logan's brow furrowed into harsh lines. With his eyes still closed, his emotions remained hidden and she wondered if she'd offended him by bastardising his precious language. Finding the deep reserves of courage which Whaea assured her she possessed, Hana took a step forward and pressed the basket against Logan's chest. "I made this basket," she repeated in English. "It's the first one I've finished myself. I want you to have it."

Logan blinked and after a second of hesitation, reached up and claimed the offering. He opened his eyes and turned it in his hands, examining the weave and frowning at the way she'd turned the remainder of the plaited end into a tight coil. Rui helped her stitch it to the lip of the basket with a darning needle. He swallowed and his voice sounded odd as he pointed to the coil. "I love the koru." His index finger touched the plait and his gaze flicked to Hana's face and then back to her basket. "It represents new beginnings."

Hana held her breath. She'd known that for years but failed to identify the deviousness of the women as they'd made her force the plaited end into submission despite her aching fingers and futile complaints. They'd known Logan would understand the coded message. She wanted to start again. "Ka pai," he whispered. "This is good." He kissed the basket and leaned across Hana to lay it with care between Mac's car seat and Phoenix's booster. His fingers caressed his son's seatbelt as he withdrew his hand and he transferred the tenderness to Hana's cheek, brushing his thumb over her lips and leaning his forehead against hers. Hana felt his breath warm her nose and closed her eyes, desperate to feel his kiss. She tilted her face up like a flower meeting the sunshine, wanting his affection before revealing Mac's secret. She jumped as a female throat cleared.

"Can I have a word?" The tones sounded jarring and clipped and Hana held her breath. Logan didn't bother looking around, but his body stiffened.

"No."

"It won't take long." Heels scraped the gravel as Caroline held her ground. "In private."

Logan's jawbone pressed through his cheek as a hard line. He released a breath of exasperation and his irises seemed to flicker, switching from a passionate diamond grey to the darkness of grit. "What?" he bit, turning to face her. His hand rested on Hana's shoulder and she sensed him using her to stay grounded.

"In private." Caroline's gaze slid to Hana and then back to Logan. "Please."

Hana stared at the other woman and saw the predatory look in her eyes. The softness the years with Kane had created fell away to reveal the hard underside of Caroline's nature. Her renewed obsession with Logan Du Rose poked holes in Hana's fledgling confidence. It threatened to plunge her back in time and allow vulnerability and weakness to reclaim her. Sickness roiled in her gut as she saw it there. It hadn't gone at all, just remained dormant.

Hana took a step away from Logan, edging around him and catching her arm on the wing mirror of Whaea's car. She glanced back to see betrayal in his eyes and offered him a reassuring smile. Turning her back on Caroline and waiting until she got eye contact with her husband, she stepped into her role with determination and courage. "I trust you, Logan," she whispered. "E aroha au ana a koe."

Logan's eyes flashed and his stance strengthened. Instead of stiff and unyielding, he opened his chest and his shoulders squared. She'd asked Whaea to teach her to say, 'I love you' and the uplift of Logan's lips told her she'd hit the spot. With a nod of acknowledgement to Caroline, Hana strode away from the car park and through the arch into the rose garden.

There her courage failed her. "Damn, damn, damn!" she groaned, stamping her feet in temper. Fury became an aching ball of fire in her stomach.

"Ma?" Wiri sounded anxious and his gentle tap on her forearm followed. "What's happened? Is he taking me away?"

"No!" Hana's reply exited without a filter and the child jerked his hand away. Hana shook her head. "It's not that. Caroline wants to speak to Logan in private and we've been here before."

"She wants him for herself." The lack of inflection at the end of the sentence turned it from a question to a statement of fact.

Hana nodded. "I think so too. I can't believe the audacity of the woman."

Wiri shrugged and he glanced back towards the archway. "I don't know what audacity is, but I do know what we can do about it."

58

Through a Child's Eyes

Hana tried not to squeak in fright as a spider's web splayed itself across her nose and mouth. Wiri reached up to brush it away and pressed a dirty finger over her lips. He took another step forward and Hana followed, tracking his movements through the narrow gap between the bushes. A double layer of conifers provided a thin pathway between their trunks, but the luscious foliage prevented anyone using the route with ease. Which explained why Hana Du Rose followed a small boy through the undergrowth on her hands and knees while he moved ahead in a mixture of crouching interspersed with bunny hops. "How do you know about this?" Hana hissed and Wiri stopped and turned around. He frowned and drew his lips back in a grimace.

"Everyone knows," he whispered.

"Not me," she grumbled, holding her breath as a cockroach skittered over her fingers. She recognised the mud flaps of her truck and rose to a crouch, parting the branches enough to see Logan's back. He leaned his hip against the front wing, arms folded across his chest. Hana winced as her phone vibrated in her pocket. She tugged it free and killed the call, keeping the button pressed in to turn it off.

"Did you know?" Caroline's face twitched and her blue eyes sparkled with uncontrolled mania. "Did you know Antoinette was my mother?"

Wiri leaned closer and Hana bent so his lips met her ear. "No shit," he breathed. "Everyone knew that an all."

Hana frowned at the swear word and then decided she'd tackle his language later. Adrenaline loosened her muscles and weakened enough of them to allow relief to slip through to her nerve endings. The conversation hadn't played to her expectations. She heard Logan's sigh. "Yes, we found out by accident from one of Kuia Phoenix's diaries."

"And no one thought to mention it." Caroline's voice wavered and Hana pursed her lips as pity washed over her. "Not even my husband, who must have known I was his half-sister."

Logan shrugged and his shoulder muscles bunched beneath his shirt. "What was the point, Caroline? You'd found happiness together. Why destroy that?"

Caroline took a step forward and then another. Her palms rested against Logan's shirt. "It could have been us."

Wiri fixed a steadying hand over Hana's right wrist and she shook her head. Fury consumed her from the inside out. Only bursting through the branches and knocking Caroline Marsh flat on her back would assuage its angry burn. Alarm filled Wiri's grey eyes and he stood on tiptoes to clap a hand over Hana's mouth and block her makeshift exit. His other hand gripped her sleeve between clenched fingers. She no longer cared. She'd take him with her on her rampage through the foliage. They struggled and the wily child hooked his index finger over her nose and pulled, cutting off Hana's oxygen. It made her angrier.

"No!" Logan's voice held command and Hana froze. Wiri's hand slipped from her mouth and he scrambled to push the branches aside. "I'm not interested!" Logan squeezed past Caroline and exited the narrow gap between the vehicles. His features creased in a look of revulsion as he turned back to face her. His right hand rested on the bonnet of the truck. "It's too late, Caroline. I've built my legacy with Hana and I'm happy."

Caroline's right hand slipped behind her back and her shoulders bunched. "I wanted to marry you, Logan. That crazy Triad woman stopped me going to the wedding. I couldn't tell you or she'd hurt them all. She said she'd take them away from me, you, the boys and everyone else I loved if I told a soul." She lowered her voice. "I think she set the fire that killed Reuben. It's my fault, Logan. Everything is. I fought with Kane the last time we spoke. He told me to go back to you and I told him I hated him."

Logan paused and glanced down at the ground. His tongue caressed his top lip. "I'm sorry," he said. Hana's heart sank. The threat of Caroline had hung over her for so long, it caused a permanent crevice of doubt to lurk beneath the surface. She watched the conflict filter through her husband's brain and his irises mist in thought. She wondered if he reran the motion picture of his life and wished he'd married Caroline instead.

"You're just sorry?" Caroline's shoulders slumped in defeat.

Logan's voice sounded hoarse. "I'm sorry for not believing you when you tried to tell me later at the school. It sounded ludicrous. But Che came to see me a few days ago. He told me about his out-of-control daughter and what she'd done. I'm truly sorry." Logan exhaled. "But we are where we are, Caroline. Everything happened for the best, despite all the agony. I love Hana. You loved Kane. We both got what we wanted, but not how we imagined. I'm sorry Kane died, Caroline. I am. Even if we could go back and rewrite history, I wouldn't. You and I were toxic and it wasn't meant to be."

He started to turn and Hana heard Wiri's muffled gasp. The fingers of Caroline's right hand lifted her shirt and drew out the weapon she'd concealed in the waistband of her jeans. She shifted in the gravel to cover the movement and Hana's eyes widened. "Listen to me, Logan!" Caroline pleaded. She raised her voice and slid the revolver sideways. It looked faded and old, like something handed down through generations and given no care. Her hand shook and Logan faced her. His eyes narrowed as she settled her index finger over the trigger.

"That's where it went." He sounded calm and jerked his head towards the weapon. "The last time I saw that gun, Kane pointed it at my forehead." Logan's lips pursed and the fingers of his left hand moved up to the ragged scar along his right side. "Then you decided the machete might give me more of a fighting chance. Remember?"

Caroline's hair swished as she nodded. "I didn't mean it." Her voice shook. "I'm sorry for everything. I regret it from the bottom of my heart. There's no one left but us. They're all gone. Reuben, Kane, Nev, Barry. All dead."

Logan's head tilted. "Nev isn't dead. And where's your daughter, Caroline?" His tone sounded gentle, placating. His expression looked blank as though he didn't believe she'd follow through. Concern edged his voice. "What's her name? Edin? Where is she?"

Hana squeezed Wiri's shoulder, anxiety making it more painful than she intended. She leaned sideways and hissed into his ear. "Get the policeman," she whispered. "Get anyone."

Wiri nodded and dropped to his knees. A wood pigeon's sudden flight masked the sound of the scuffle which marked his departure.

"Mr Du Rose?" Hana held her breath as Big Ed lumbered across the car park. "The White Rose is gone." He sounded puffed. "I lost her in the garden. She met a guy in the games area and I lost her."

"What?" Logan's brow furrowed and he turned just a half step to greet the guard.

"Hey!" Big Grant jogged across the grass leading from the rose garden. "One of the kids is missing," he called, urgency in his voice. He tapped his ear piece. "The Black Rose just stopped Big Bob in the main building."

"Leslie lost one of my children?" Logan sounded indignant, as though she'd done it on purpose. "How?"

Caroline's arm moved up through an arc and Hana calculated the gun's trajectory. Her own handgun had no safety and she figured this one didn't either. One definitive press of the trigger and Logan would be dead too, just like the others Caroline named. Except Kane. Not yet, anyway.

Hana glanced at her husband's confusion as Big Ed drew closer. She saw the white knuckles ridged on Caroline's fingers as she took aim and knew she'd shoot Logan in the side without guilt. If she couldn't have him, no one would. And then Logan moved. He turned back to face Caroline and saw the revolver aimed at his chest. Surprise coasted across his features at whatever he read in her expression.

Hana burst through the branches, gasping as spiky, green needles jabbed her face and exposed arms. The seam of her shirt tore as she leapt free with her arms raised in front of her. Caroline started in fright and screamed. The revolver discharged and Hana used her forward motion to force Caroline's face into the side panel of the truck.

She registered a blur in her peripheral vision and heard Logan grunt as he hit the gravel floor and lay still.

59

Taking a Bullet

The gun shot should have caused chaos. In reality, it barely registered amid the noise generated by the crowds, the stalls and the general melee. Hana felt her top teeth bite into her lower lip as her chin hit the back of Caroline's head and they fell without grace. The force of their combined bodies caused a dent in the truck's wing and when they hit the gravel, Caroline lay beneath her, unmoving. Blood spattered the back of her white shirt and spread out in a growing patch and it took Hana a second to realise it came from her. She lifted her right hand to her face and groaned as her fingers became stained. Remembering Logan's spectacular fall to the ground, Hana pressed herself up onto her hands and rolled off Caroline's back. "Logan?" A metallic taste hit the back of her throat with the first swallow and her stomach revolted.

"He's okay, he's okay!" Wiri's voice sounded high pitched and he crouched down to tug on her elbow. "Please get up, Mama?" Hana glanced up to see his grey eyes glittering with tears. A sob rose into his throat and anxiety occupied his flushed expression. "Please be okay, Mama," he begged. "I need to tell you I love you and it's too late if you're dead."

"I'm fine," Hana gasped. She lifted her arm and pressed the sleeve over her lip. "Just a cut."

"It looks bad." Wiri's voice caught and the first of the tears spilled over onto his cheeks. "You're bleeding. Heaps."

Hana shook her head and the action hurt. Pain alerts shot from her neck into her brain. "Whiplash and a cut mouth," she promised. Blood sprayed her sleeve as she spoke.

Caroline stirred next to her and rage filled Wiri's face. "She killed my dad!" he wailed. He released Hana's elbow and stood. His body stiffened like a sentry's. "She killed him. I didn't get to tell him I love him. I didn't get to say thank you. He looked after me when the other one didn't want me. Like Poppa Reuben did for Tama." Wiri took a step backwards and shifted his balance onto one hip. He jabbed a shaking finger at Caroline. "You stopped me telling him I loved him! I never got to say it!" Hana sensed him make the mental decision and saw his foot rise off the ground. She braced herself for the impact of the kick, raising her forearms to cover her head as Wiri aimed at Caroline. The risk of him catching her seemed inevitable.

Wiri screamed in fury as his feet left the ground and Hana blinked as he disappeared skyward. Gravel shifted next to her as Logan's cowboy boots appeared. "Stop!" he commanded Wiri. "This isn't the way!"

Relief flooded Hana's body and a bubble of tension popped in her chest. It turned her to jelly as her brain reassured her of Logan's survival. She looked up to see him towering over her, Wiri clasped in his arms. A livid graze exposed the fatty layers beneath Logan's forearms and he bled from an open wound on his chin. Hana blinked against the blinding sunlight and a hand reached down to her eye level. Logan's hands were occupied with the sobbing child, but the proffered fingers looked familiar. Hana allowed the muscular arm to haul her upright.

Lincoln held on to her fingers until she stood upright and then he let go. "You good now?" he asked, his tone gentle.

"Thanks." Hana nodded and coughed on a mouthful of blood. She looked up to see the security guards gathering and

Big Ed squeezing between the cars to get to her and Logan. He caused a blockage in his haste and Whaea's wing mirror bent at a horrible angle.

"What's going on?" Sanders kicked up dust as he jogged towards the vehicles. His eyes widened at the sight of Caroline attempting to sit up. His gaze moved from her battered face to the blood flowing from the Du Roses and his eyebrows knitted. "What is this? That kid said someone had a gun and then ran away." He raised a finger and pointed it at Wiri.

"I kicked the gun out of the way. It's under the truck." Lincoln straightened his shirt and tucked it back inside his jeans. He ran the toe of his right boot along the back of his left leg, then he jerked his head towards Caroline. "She pulled the gun on Logan. Hana took her down as she pressed the trigger and I put Logan on the ground." Turning, he pointed to the shattered side window of Whaea's little car. "The bullet went through here and smashed the back window too. It's in the car park somewhere."

Sanders blinked. "I'm shutting this fair down right now!" he snapped.

Logan turned to face him, blood dripping from his chin. Big Ed's bulk forced him to lean sideways to see the detective. Wiri had stopped fighting him and clung around his neck, his face pushed into Logan's shoulder. "You needn't do that," he replied, his voice filled with authority. "The incident happened here. It's a staff car park."

"I'll shut the gate so nobody can get in." Lincoln turned his tall body and his blond hair glinted in the sunshine. "Come with me." He waved to the guards. Gravel scrunched beneath his boots as he stalked away.

Big Ed edged himself along the gap between the cars and his hip spun Whaea's wing mirror back the other way. It gave a sickening creak. "I'm in charge!" he called after Linc's retreating back.

"Hey, Linc!" Logan called and Lincoln turned. His eyebrows drew into a line.

"Yeah?"

"Thanks," Logan replied.

Lincoln's handsome face creased into a smile and his eyes held amusement. "Yeah, I know." He turned and walked away, waving backwards over his shoulder. "I won't tell anyone I decked Logan Du Rose."

"I'm shutting it down." Sanders fixed his hands on his hips and his jaw worked as though eating the air. Hana groaned and leaned over to place her hands on her knees.

"No, you're not." Logan's voice contained latent fury and Hana closed her eyes as exhaustion coursed through her. She heard him shift Wiri onto his hip so he could rub Hana's back with his other hand. Caroline shifted in the gravel next to them and pushed herself to a sitting position.

"Odering's here." Red spots littered the ground as Hana spoke. The pain in her neck radiated up to her head and caused a thumping ache. "Get him."

"This is my case!" Sanders postured and Hana heard Logan release a sigh of irritation. His hand disappeared from her back and she opened her eyes to see him digging in his jeans pocket for his phone.

Odering picked up straight away and Logan delivered the facts without preamble. "He's on his way," he announced, ending the call and shoving his phone back into his pocket. He jabbed his finger at Caroline and Hana forced her spine to uncurl. She rose with difficulty and the world spun less. "He wants her arrested and the gun sealed in an evidence bag." Hana glanced sideways at the hard look on her husband's face. "He said now," Logan growled.

Sanders flapped around in a panic at the knowledge of Odering's imminent arrival. He dropped to his knees and retrieved the revolver from beneath Hana's truck, using a pen to hook the trigger guard. When he rose, he spent more time worrying about holding the pen so the revolver didn't slide towards his fingers than considering arresting Caroline. Hana glanced away from the detective's entertaining antics to see

Caroline using the side of the truck to stand. Blood dribbled down her face in rivulets from her nose and one eye looked partially closed. She rubbed the back of her head where Hana's chin contacted it with force.

"Don't!" Hana snapped. "Don't even think of trying to run." Her voice wavered. "I should never have trusted you. Kane's still walking around but you couldn't resist trying to take my husband, could you?" Hana's voice rose and Sanders jumped. The revolver slid to the end of the pen nearest his fingers and he released a groan as he contaminated the evidence. Hana turned her body to face Caroline and for the first time in their relationship, she captured the upper hand and kept it. "And when he refused to choose you over me, you shot at him. Move and I swear I'll do more than break your nose for this." Hana's hands balled into fists.

"She killed my dad." Wiri's chest hitched and Hana took her gaze from Caroline for a moment. Red splotches covered the child's face and snot mingled with tears on his cheeks and chin. He levelled an index finger at Caroline. "Why did you do it?" he begged. "Why? I didn't tell him I loved him."

Hana took a step back and crashed into Logan. Her eyes widened in alarm as puzzle pieces fitted together in her mind. "You've been here the whole time!" she gasped. "You changed units on the camp ground after you got the call about Kane's death. The receptionist called you by your maiden name. You registered as Miss Marsh when you arrived days before, didn't you?"

Caroline's jaw tensed and she closed her eyes. The left one looked swollen and she raised a shaking hand to touch her eyelid. "I needed the money from the bond," she said, her voice a hiss. "Kane's sick."

Sanders' footsteps scraped against the gravel. He tipped the revolver onto the hood of the truck with a clunk before striding over. "Kane Du Rose is dead," he said, moderating his tone to sound more sympathetic than irritated. "Remember?"

Caroline let her backside sink to the gravel and used her sleeve to mop blood from beneath her nose. "Nev is dead. I followed him into Alfred's apartment. I knew he'd take the money for himself and needed to stop him. Kane won't listen, but he needs to get help. That's why I wanted the cash. I've found a private doctor, but he's expensive. Please can you find Kane?" She directed her question at Logan. "I didn't mean to shoot Nev. He told me something I didn't want to hear. It shocked me and I pulled the trigger. Then I panicked and pushed him. Logan, I'm sorry. Find Kane if he's still alive. He won't see a state doctor. Reuben never trusted them, so his boys won't either." She swallowed but her eyes maintained their silent plea. "When you find him, please tell him I don't hate him?"

"You need to stop talking until we get to the station." Sanders waggled his fingers at Caroline. She grasped his hand and hauled herself upright.

Fury lit Hana's breast, like a child denied the last page in a storybook. "No!" she gasped. "We have a right to hear this! She just shot at my husband!"

Logan heaved out a breath and to Hana's dismay, he turned away with Wiri still in his arms. "I don't wanna hear it," he said, his tone heavy. His footsteps crunched in the gravel as he walked away.

60

Unexpected Gift

Hana abandoned her quest for information and followed Logan across the car park. The local police officer arrived with Odering in tow. She didn't look at the detective, refusing help for her injuries as she followed her husband's rigid back through the crowds. "Logan, wait!" Her breath heaved in her chest and she paused and rested her hands on her knees. Her phone vibrated in her pocket and she ignored it. Logan stopped and he blinked back at her as guilt took hold of him.

"Sorry, sorry." He caught her beneath the elbow and helped her upright. "I need to get him away from here," he said, jerking his head towards Wiri.

Then Hana noticed the low mewling sound issuing from the child's lips. His eyes appeared glassy, mirroring the trauma trapped within his soul. He'd locked his fingers around Logan's neck and his body looked rigid like a plank. "Okay," she whispered, forcing her spine to straighten and following Logan to the private entrance behind the stables.

They used the spiral staircase to get to the third floor and Hana looked back to see spots of blood in her wake. She lifted her fingers and held them beneath her chin to catch the drips.

The door to Alfred's apartment stood ajar and Logan rolled his eyes at their lax security. The clatter of their footsteps on the wooden stairs brought Leslie to the top and she glared at them. "There you are!" she shouted. "You gived yer poppa heart failure!" She jabbed a shaking finger at Wiri before noticing the state of Hana's face. She turned and hollered into the apartment. "Wiri's here! They've found him. And Hana's hurt again."

Phoenix appeared at the top of the stairs before Alfred managed to lumber his old bones across the lounge. He held Leslie's battered mobile phone in his fingers. "I've rung you heaps of times." His tone sounded accusatory and his brow furrowed at the sight of the blood on Hana's face. "Wiri bolted and Leslie couldn't find him anywhere." He jabbed a finger at Wiri. "That's the second time today. You need to stop worrying us like this." He switched to Māori as Logan reached the top of the stairs with his burden. Logan shook his head, thwarting Alfred's demand for details.

"Mama?" Phoenix's brows furrowed and she reached out to clasp the leg of Hana's torn jeans in probing fingers. A rip in the knee exposed grazed skin. "What happened, Mama? Are you okay darling?"

"I'm fine." Hana's voice sounded muffled. "I fell and cut my lip. Mouths just bleed heaps. Nothing to worry about." She dropped her hand into the soft fingers which reached for her.

"But Mama, your pants is ripped and you cut your leg."

Hana looked down at the tear. Blood oozed through the gap. "It's nothing," she promised. "I can't even feel it."

Logan tried to set Wiri down, but the child clung to him and the volume of his mewling rose. Defeated, Logan slumped into an armchair and gave Hana a look of apology. She shook her head to tell him she'd be fine. Wiri flattened himself against Logan's broad chest and hid his face.

"Sit at the table." Leslie tugged her arm and led Hana through the partition to the dining room. She shoved her into a seat before leaning close and lowering her voice. "He ran away," she whispered and hurt infused her brown irises. "From me. He just took off again. Can you believe it?"

Hana sighed and reached for a tissue. She mopped at the blood on her chin and stared at the livid red stain against the fragile, white fabric. "It wasn't personal," she whispered. Phoenix wrapped her fingers around Hana's wrist, but her gaze strayed towards Wiri's distressed mewling.

Leslie shook her head. "He hates that woman, doesn't he?"

"What woman?" A sense of alert returned to Hana's brain and she removed the tissue from in front of her mouth. She snaked her spare arm around Phoenix and dragged her daughter close.

"Caroline." Leslie widened her eyes and mouthed the name.

"You okay darling?" Wide grey eyes stared up at Hana and she nodded, hearing her own platitudes from her baby's lips. "Who's Caroline?"

"Nobody for you to worry about. And Nonie will fix me," Hana promised, wincing as speaking hurt. Her tongue found a loose flap of skin inside her cheek and she hissed in pain. Phoenix's eyes widened and her brow puckered into a landscape of soft creases.

"Will Nonie fix Papa too?" she whispered. "And Wiri?"

Hana nodded, the lie unable to proceed from her lips. She cuddled Phoenix into her side and focussed on Leslie's rambling. "Bloody Caroline." The old woman whispered the name louder as she dug in her depleted first aid tin. "You're going through my medical stuff like a dose of salts, girly. You gotta stop getting hurt. I've run out of gauze."

"When did you see Caroline?"

"On the way up the spiral staircase. I found her lurking at the bottom with that little girl she's dragging around."

"She was inside the house?" Hana rose and pushed the chair away. She kept hold of her daughter and hoisted her onto her hip as she stood. "What happened?"

"Calm down." Leslie flapped a hand at her and dumped antiseptic wash and cotton wool on the table. "Is yer mouth cut inside or out?"

"What happened with Caroline?" Hana demanded, frustrated as Leslie dipped forward to peer at her lip.

Leslie's eyelashes fluttered and guilt spread a pink flush across her neck. "I was gonna tell yer," she breathed. "She didn't give me a chance to say no."

"To what?" Hana's voice rose and she heard the steady rumble of Alfred and Logan's conversation cease. "What did you want to say no to?"

"Hush! Hush!" Leslie flapped her hands and with gargantuan force, shoved Hana back into the dining chair. Phoenix let Hana drag her onto her knee. "She dumped her girl on me. I've put her down for a nap with Mac for now. She promised she'd come back, so don't get cross. It's only for half an hour."

Hana groaned and rested her painful chin on the top of her daughter's soft head. "It'll be for much longer than that," she whispered.

61

The Sound of Silence and Rejection

Phoenix held Wiri's hand under the dining table and Hana rolled her eyes. The little girl had refused all requests to release him and though he seemed unwilling to converse with anyone else, Wiri still spoke to her. Hana turned her back on the sight of her daughter attempting to eat scrambled eggs one handed and plunged her rubber gloves back into the washing up water. Logan leaned against the counter next to her, a mug of coffee in one hand and toast in the other.

"Don't worry." His tone held reassurance and he offered her a shallow smile. "We've been here before. He'll come around, Hana. I've asked Michael for the name of a good child psychologist."

"You're speaking to Michael?" Hana's voice held surprise and she raised an eyebrow. The saucepan in her hand dropped back into the water with a splash.

"Yeah." Logan wrinkled his nose. "It's about time, don't you think?"

Hana shrugged. "Maybe run it by Tama before you get too chummy."

"Not chummy, Hana." Logan's tone held rebuke. "And it's my business, nobody else's."

"Fine. Then make sure it doesn't become mine."

Hana jumped at the scrape of chairs behind her. Phoenix dragged Wiri towards the door. "Hey!" Soap bubbles tracked down the front of the cupboard and onto the tiles as she turned. "You need to ask before leaving the table."

"Sorry, Mama. Please may we get down?"

"You're already down!" Hana felt her nerve endings jangle and looked to Logan for assistance.

He blinked and leaned sideways as he straightened his body. "Get back up at the table and then ask before getting down. The rules haven't changed."

Phoenix blinked sideways at Wiri and then widened her eyes. "Can I say it for both of us?"

Hana darted a frantic look towards her husband. His jaw clenched. "Say it for yourself. Wiri and I need to have a chat."

The children clambered back onto their chairs, not an easy feat while holding hands. Phoenix gave an exaggerated sigh and complied with Logan's request, although her tone held attitude. "Thank you for my breakfast. Please may I get down?"

"Yes, you may." Hana gave the requisite reply and let her hands rest in the warm water. Heat seeped through the rubber gloves and warmed her from the outside in. She let her gaze focus on the bush beyond the garden fence and allowed the hues of colour to blend into a bottle green mist. Logan's sleeve brushed against hers as he set his mug and toast on the counter and moved his hands.

"You too, Mac. Good boy," he replied to his son's signed request. Hana heard the scrape of the child's chair against the tiles and the patter of his bare feet walking across the room. A plate littered with crumbs appeared on the counter next to her. Glancing down, Hana saw the concentration on his face as he pushed it up and over the lip and then added his cutlery. He'd put his tee shirt on backwards and the tag flipped over the collar and dangled beneath his chin.

Hana leaned sideways, leaving her hands in the soapy water. She pursed her lips for a kiss. He mouthed something as he delivered the wet offering, the words only a breath of warm air across her skin. He tripped over his own feet in the last second and Hana felt the cut inside her mouth give as his lips slammed against hers. The taste of metal infused the residue of the scrambled egg she'd forced down.

"Ouch," she whispered as her son left the room. Mac closed the door behind him and the handle remained down, the door clunking against the frame a few times before the handle pinged upright again. Hana's muscles tightened as Logan's arms snaked either side of her waist.

"You're tired," he said. "Why did you stay up so late?"

Hana wrinkled her nose. "I couldn't sleep. And I have this book on my phone I wanted to finish."

"Have I told you today that you're beautiful?" he whispered. He waited long enough for her to discard the rubber gloves before wrapping her into an embrace which hid her from the world. Hana buried her face in his armpit and shook her head. Her denial sounded muffled. "Well, you're beautiful," he breathed. "Do you want to talk about yesterday?" Hana shook her head again, doubting they could find anything left to say. Logan kissed the top of her head and released a sigh. "Can you stay home if I take the children to Leslie? I assumed you wouldn't want to go to church today."

Hana tilted her head back on her neck and blinked up at him. The cuts and grazes on his right cheek and chin still oozed. Black and grey whiskers grew through the painful skin and he'd avoided shaving. "Why?" Her voice sounded small and feeble.

"David Allen's coming up to change the locks. I asked him to do it after breakfast." At her frown, Logan lifted his right hand and brushed a lock of red hair from in front of Hana's eyes. "I know you don't want to talk about it, Hana, but some of it will continue to affect us. Caroline has been remanded in custody for shooting Nev and pushing him backwards over the balcony rail. She's also admitted stealing Leslie's bunch of keys from behind the apartment door."

"Oh." Hana swallowed. "The spare key to our house is on there." She clicked her fingers. "That's why Leslie acted so odd the night they got back. She didn't want to tell me."

Logan raised his eyebrows and tilted his head in irritation. "Yep."

Hana's fingers looped through Logan's belt behind his back and she drew closer. "Caroline's been in our house?"

Logan nodded and his arms tightened around her ribs. "The cops are keeping the keys as evidence, but it's easier just to change everything, don't you think?"

"Yeah." Hana pushed her cheek against Logan's broad chest and felt his collarbone press against her ear. She closed her eyes. "She still wanted you. If Annalise hadn't intervened, you'd be married to Caroline now. It makes my brain hurt to imagine it."

Logan inhaled a breath and released it in a whoosh. "All life hangs in the balance, Hana. There's an old saying in Kawhia, 'He manu ka motu i te mahanga e kore e taea te whai.'"

Hana lifted her head and her brow furrowed. "Manu means a flying creature. A bird, isn't it?"

Logan nodded and pressed a kiss to the end of her nose. "A bird which has once escaped from the snare will not be caught again." Creases created laugh lines at the corners of his eyes and his grey irises flickered. "I love you, Hana. I'm yours. Nothing else matters."

Hana reached up and smoothed the space behind Logan's right ear. His hair tickled the backs of her fingers. "Take the children to Leslie and then come back to me," she whispered. "Put David off and come to bed."

Logan's head jerked backwards and he studied her eyes as though searching for something. He swallowed and a dark shadow crossed over his expression. An act of will chased it away. "Bed?" he repeated.

"Yeah. There's this thing I want to try. It might take our minds off everything that's happened." Her eyes sparkled with the knowledge of her midnight reading and her lips quirked upwards. The cut inside her mouth split again and she groaned.

"Probably not a great idea." Logan released her and turned away. "I'll take Phoe and Macky to see the olds and I'll tell Wiri I need his help with the clean-up from the fair. He might speak to me if it's just the two of us."

"Okay." Hana sounded doubtful and watched his rigid back as he stalked away. The kitchen door clicked shut behind him. "Right then," Hana said to herself, reaching for her rubber gloves. "I think that was a definite no."

Her phone rang and she lifted it from the bench, slipping one hand in the glove and holding the phone with the other. The school principal's voice spoke into her ear, silky smooth and nauseating. "Ah, Mrs Du Rose, I'm glad I've caught you. Is your husband there?"

"On my mobile number?" Hana dragged the phone away from her ear and stared at it. Definitely hers. "No. He's nipped out."

"Please can you let him know our mutual difficulty sorted itself out?" He gave a small cough. "I took a walk around the fair yesterday. It looked well put together. I'm hoping we raised a lot of money for the school."

"Probably." Hana closed her eyes and waited for the odious man to get to the point. He didn't want Logan. He knew he'd called her number and she held her breath, imagining all the reasons he might want to check Logan's proximity before stating his case. Hana allowed a sigh to escape. Logan hadn't exactly promised not to intervene in Phoenix's dilemma.

"Do you think we might repeat the format next year?" the principal asked. "It ran so much better than usual and the hotel is a fantastic venue."

"No." Hana kept her reply short.

"Oh, sorry, I thought you said no." The principal gave a fake laugh. "Please ask your husband for me. We met yesterday and erm..." His voice trailed off and Hana imagined the meeting as something he'd not wish to repeat.

"I did say no, but you're welcome to ask Logan yourself." Hana flicked the glove off her hand and wrinkled her nose as it sank in the washing up water. "I'm busy. Is there something you wanted?"

"Erm, just to say we won't be moving your daughter into the older class. The family have given notice. I just got an email." He sighed. "We're losing a couple of families, actually."

"What a shame." Hana's patience snapped. "Just as you were so desperate to sort things out too. You must feel so disappointed."

"I was sorting it out," he blustered. "We don't tolerate bullying at our school. I tried to tell your husband the same thing yesterday."

"Unless the offenders make big donations," Hana bit. "Then it's okay. Did you get the money for your gym equipment?"

She heard a definite gulp. "No. The apparatus arrived on Friday and our budget appears a little short right now. I'm sure we raised enough yesterday. How long do you think it will take for your husband to tally up the profits and pass them across? A bank transfer would be quickest."

Hana pressed her finger over the red button to disconnect the call. A flame of injustice heated in her stomach and became a fireball in her chest.

62

A Taonga - A Family Heirloom

Hana cursed as the knock on the front door shook the house. She forced her anger into a compartment in her mind and opened the door to David Allen and his impressive assortment of hammers and chisels. English politeness dictated she offer him a mug of coffee and she held it for him while he wrestled the first lock mechanism free.

"Thanks." His blond eyebrows rose and he jerked his head towards the hall cupboard. "Stick it there please. I just need to finish this." He dropped the lock onto a blanket protecting the tiles and reached for a contraption like the numbered panels at the hotel.

"Code entry?" Hana winced. "I have enough trouble remembering my phone number."

"It's what the boss wants." David rose and fitted the device into the hole. He gave a satisfied nod and laid it on the blanket. Black grease covered his fingers as he reached for the mug of coffee. He took a long sip and then smacked his lips. "You gonna stand over me all day?" he asked, a twinkle in his eyes.

"Maybe." Hana switched a photo of Jas with one of Elizabeth and sighed. Then she switched them back again. "Are people talking about what happened yesterday?" She didn't look at him as she asked the question.

David scoffed. His fingers reached for the plate of chocolate cookies Hana set next to the mug. "Is the Pope Catholic?"

"What are they saying?"

David Allen settled with his spine against the door frame, his outline backed by the high kauri trees. He waited until Hana lifted her eyes before speaking. "You know I don't gossip," he said. "So why ask me?"

Hana shrugged and switched the photographs again. One disgorged a ball of lint and she picked it up and rolled it between her fingers. "You're here," she replied. "And I know you'll tell me the truth."

"Fair enough." David relaxed and slurped another gulp of his coffee. "They're saying she was always a few biscuits short of a packet. Nobody sounds surprised."

"Who said that?" Curiosity burned in Hana's chest.

David raised one blond eyebrow and gave her a quizzical look. "Now you want names too?"

Hana smiled and stretched their truce to its limits. "Yep," she whispered.

"The local cop. He saw me installing a camera over the corridor which leads to the family side of the house. He's a talkative chap. Probably shouldn't be."

"What did he say?" Hana pushed an index finger in front of her lip and let the pain ground her.

David gulped the last of his drink and held the mug out for her. Hana stepped forward and took it, moving it the short distance to the cupboard without comment. She dropped into their familiar game of one-upmanship with a flicker of relief. Not everything had changed. David wiped his fingers on his jeans and bent forward to pick up the hacksaw. "He said she confessed to killing Neville Du Rose. Nev wanted all the money for himself and she needed it for her husband's medical treatment. He also told her in a throwaway statement that she'd married her half-brother and Caroline lost it. She shot him twice and pushed him backwards over the balcony." David heaved out a sigh tinged with sadness. "I thought I'd seen all the cruelty I could take in Afghanistan. Seems there's still more no matter where you hide."

Hana swallowed and avoided eye contact. "It shows a degree of arrogance to stand on a balcony of an apartment you broke into looking like you belong there. You think it was cruel for Caroline to push him?"

"Yes!" the former soldier exclaimed. "And he was cruel for telling her something so damaging. Ignorance is bliss sometimes, Hana. He destroyed her world because he could." He shook the hacksaw at her. "And I checked those balcony fixings, despite what everyone thinks. They were fine."

Hana nodded, snatched up the mug and strode back to the kitchen. If David thought her exit hurried, he made no comment as always. She flung the mug in the dishwasher and closed it with a clang. A strange, pent up emotion weighed heavy in her soul and the ball of rage ignited again. She'd known about Caroline and Kane's fraternal relationship and said nothing on Logan's insistence. At the thought of Edin camped out at Leslie's and continually asking for her mummy and daddy, her heart clenched.

"Sorry, I need to go out," Hana said as David looked up. She stepped over his tools and strode onto the driveway. Logan's truck sat in its usual place, but he'd taken hers containing the car seats.

"Everything okay?" David watched her as she floundered and Hana turned to him and nodded. She sifted through the keys on her bunch until she found the fob for Logan's truck and pressed the button. The indicator lights flicked on and the wing mirrors turned outward in response.

Hana clambered into the driver's side without looking at David. Her fingers searched down the side of the seat to find the button which moved everything into her position. When she could finally reach the pedals, she pressed the ignition at the same time as the brake and the engine fired. David had left the gate open at the top of the hill and Hana sped past the old kauri tree standing sentry over the mountain. She longed for space just to think.

A pukeko ran from the bushes ahead as she navigated the tricky lane along the ridge. Hana saw its awkward legs and the blue-black of its feathers as it dashed in front of the truck. She slammed on the brakes and two late chicks ran behind it in a messy line. She missed them with just centimetres to spare and they pushed through the wire fence to the left and fluttered down the cliff in search of the stream below. Something hit the back of her seat with a muffled clang.

Sadness and dread coursed through Hana's bloodstream and her legs shook on the pedals. Tightness began in her chest and she fumbled to secure the handbrake. She lay her head back against the seat and closed her eyes as the diesel engine idled beneath the massive hood. Unexpected tears filled her eyes as she contemplated the near miss. Logan's words returned to her as a sense of wisdom washing through her soul. "All life hangs in the balance." She knew that better than most. The fingers of her right hand fluttered up to touch the pacemaker beneath her collar bone. Then the livid pink scar on her left wrist. She remembered Kane walking away from her nursing his grievous, unnamed illness and her mind drifted to Edin's sweet little face looking up at Mac. "Is this mountain cursed?" she asked out loud. "Does everyone who comes here find themselves abandoned?" Her chest hitched and sticky wet tears warmed her cheeks. The bush canopy rustled beside her and it felt as though the spirit of Logan's elders crowded around the truck.

"*No,*" their ancient voices whispered. *"But those who find themselves abandoned come here."*

It brought perspective. Everything changed relating to perspective. A vendetta became a cry for help. A spiteful act seeped desperation. Hana dried her tears on her sleeve and turned in her seat. Logan's guitar had fallen into the foot well behind her. She wrestled it free and stroked the polished wood beneath her fingers. "Sorry," she told it. "I'll be more careful." She tried to lay it on the passenger seat, but the body slid onto the floor. It looked unsafe and Hana hauled it back up by the headstock. One of the bridge pins looked loose and guilt prickled in the back of her neck. The guitar represented the only link Logan had with his father. Something ugly lurked beneath the surface of her marriage and she'd never felt so offside with her husband. Bashing up his guitar wouldn't help.

Hana ran a hand across her face and caught her painful lip in the action. "Damn! Damn! Damn!" Hitting the steering wheel offered no release and she wound the window down to help cool her rising temper. Then she tried again, pulling the guitar up by its neck and leaning it back against the seat. "Fine," she bargained, "I'll take you to the music shop in Auckland myself and pay to have you properly restored. Deal?" The guitar remained silent. Clambering over the handbrake gave Hana enough leverage to drag the passenger seat belt around the instrument to hold it in place.

The breeze through the open window rustled a fragile piece of paper hidden inside the body of the guitar. Taped there decades ago by a man who loved his son, it hung by a single thread of sticky tape. It created the odd resonance which Logan had always loved. And it embodied love, hope and great sacrifice.

Oblivious, Hana sat back in her seat, collected herself and released the handbrake. She drove to the hotel with more care and parked near the dusty red car in the quiet bus lane of the car park. Voices sounded from the hotel grounds as staff and school volunteers cleared up after the summer fair. Hana used the rose garden to skirt the activity, heading for the paddock and the comfort of her unpredictable white horse.

63

A Gift Reclaimed

A retired mare stood with her head over the fence and her eyes jerked open at Hana's approach. She blinked and opened her mouth in a wide yawn to display a long tongue and worn, yellow teeth. "Sorry, did I wake you?" Hana reached out a hand and stroked the white blaze which defined the high forehead. The bay head nodded and the eyes closed again. "Sacha!" Hana called and gave a low whistle, searching for the white mare's rounded rump in the group which grazed near the stable's back wall. Stamping hooves disturbed settling flies and the equine bodies milled around a pile of hay like garments sloshing in a washing machine. Hana climbed onto the bottom rung of the fence and searched for her horse, dread filling her heart when she didn't see her.

The snoozing mare jerked her head back as Hana turned away. A half-closed eye watched her run across the paddock and through the gate to the stable yard. "Rawhiti!" Hana shouted.

"What?" The faint reply came from a window above and Hana ran towards the open barn door and the stairs. She clambered up two at a time and stuck her head into the tack room.

"Rawhiti!"

"What?" He emerged from his apartment, his dark features shrouded in irritation. He wore a shirt for once over his defined muscles and the fresh creases seemed incongruous with his usual ruffled appearance. The hair which always stuck up like a cockerel's plume looked tamed beneath a layer of slick gel. "What do you want?" he demanded, his tone brusque to the point of rudeness.

Hana swallowed and pressed her fingers over the balcony rail. "Sacha's gone," she said. Her gaze took in the smart trousers and shiny shoes and panic tightened her chest. "You shot her, didn't you?"

Rawhiti's shoulders slumped. "No. Logan took her out about half an hour ago." He turned and walked back into his bedsit. Curious, Hana followed, finding the bedroom and tiny kitchen in disarray. A battered suitcase sat on the unmade bed, looking like a hand grenade detonated off inside. Clothing spewed out as though trying to escape. Rawhiti clattered around in his tiny bathroom, packing his few wash items into a supermarket bag.

"Where are you going?" Hana's brow furrowed. "Did Logan fire you?"

"No." Rawhiti glanced back at her and a look of torment danced in his glittering brown eyes. He wiped his nose on his shirt sleeve and then looked at it in dismay. "He doesn't know I'm going. I saw him earlier when he bunged me a hundred dollars for helping with the pony rides at the fair." Rawhiti swallowed. "I need to leave before he finds out."

"Finds out what?" Hana's voice hardened and she took a step back towards the door. Talking made her painful lip ooze and reminded her she'd had enough of other people's unpredictability to last her a lifetime. She swallowed the metallic taste of blood and waited for him to answer.

"That I've made a mess of the accounts." Sadness shrouded him like a black swarm and his voice caught. "I thought I could do it, but I hate it. I told him I'd got the books ready so he could pay the GST due at the end of this month, but I haven't. It's best I just leave."

Hana released a sigh of exasperation and her hands slapped against her thighs. "Bloody hell, Rawhiti!" she groaned. "Why didn't you say something? Logan's under the impression you'd done accounts before. He's not an idiot. Risking his business isn't something he'd do."

"I know! I know!" Rawhiti's face creased into a mask of pain. "Ryan said he'd help me but then Logan let him go on that six-month chef's course and now I'm stuck."

"Ryan? As in Ryan, son of Michael?" Hana rolled her eyes. "You knew he wouldn't get back until the end of the semester." She could calculate the length of Ryan's absence based on Logan's complaints about the downhill slide of food quality in the restaurant. Venturing back into the room, Hana leaned against the door frame. "I thought you loved it here," she said, her tone soft. "Apart from my horse. I know what you think of Sacha."

"I do love it here." Rawhiti turned away to swipe his sleeve across his face without her seeing. "Except for Sacha. I have an interview with a racehorse trainer in Hamilton this afternoon, but it's not what I want."

Hana released a held breath and shook her head. She pointed at the mess on the bed. "Then unpack," she ordered with authority in her voice. "And get on with your work. I'm officially busting you back down to a stable hand and that goes for your wage too."

"Really?" Rawhiti spun around and she saw the glint of tears on his cheeks. He wiped his nose on his sleeve again. Hana kept a straight face; not sure she'd ever seen anyone so pleased with a demotion.

"Yes," she replied. "I have some grovelling to do and then we'll get those accounts fixed up before the deadline."

"Thanks Mrs Du Rose. Hana." Rawhiti corrected himself and Hana smiled.

"Hurry up, Ra. Bee's waiting for you by the paddock gate. She's given up fighting the others for the hay. I'm guessing you sneak her an apple around now."

Rawhiti's cheeks flushed and he nodded. "I do," he admitted. His fingers wrenched at the shirt collar constricting his neck and buttons popped open as he tugged. His familiar uniform of bare chest and stubby shorts peeked from beneath the interview clothes and Hana waved over her shoulder and walked down the stairs. She heard him yanking things out of his suitcase and eager footsteps pad back and forth across the floorboards.

Hana dragged her feet. Jack's office door mocked her from the other side of the stable yard and she braced herself and strode towards it. Logan had updated the paintwork and spruced up the outside of the low cabin, but it remained Jack's office. Hana sorted through the bunch of keys in her pocket and found the right one, pressing it into the lock and turning. She clasped the door handle and held her breath as it moved beneath her fingers.

The office looked tidier than she remembered. Rawhiti had moved the desk to face the window and removed the pictures of Jack's history with the Du Roses. Lincoln took them down first, but they'd remained stacked against the aged closet door like sentries. The walls looked bare despite the crisp white paint covering the brickwork on three sides. Memories flooded back to Hana of happier times. She'd sat in the office and signed to Jack more times than she remembered, the only other person in his life he could communicate with using his hands. Hana saw him holding Phoenix in his lap and the way her daughter giggled when she touched his bristled chin. The child had loved the grizzled old man as though recognising the blood tie despite the secrecy.

Staring at the wall of book shelves, Hana stiffened her resolve. Will had requisitioned the old records stretching back beyond Phoenix Du Rose's time at the helm of the mountain property. They sat in a box in the museum in archive quality wrappers, waiting for her to pluck up the courage to scan them. She had avoided anything bearing Jack's crawling script for fear of the nightmares beginning again. Will had stopped asking her to do it, tired of her list of never-ending excuses which didn't include the embarrassing truth.

Hana sighed. Her fears had affected everyone without her realising. She needed to make herself scan the breeding records and load them into the expensive software Logan had purchased the previous year. Then the fragile books could rest easy in the museum while remaining useful to the men in charge of the bloodlines. "Okay! I'll do it." Hana made herself the promise and moved towards the shelves. She fingered the few dusty items but didn't find what she needed.

She found it in the bottom drawer of Jack's old desk. His neat handwriting covered every page of the address book and the scent of mildew drifted up from the age spotted leaves. Hana searched for the section she needed, holding her finger in the page as she pulled her phone from her pocket and dialled the number.

"Hi." His voice sounded calm and even. Hana drew in a breath and held it.

"Linc." She swallowed and her request emerged on the crest of her breath in a rush of words. "Please come back and work for us? We need you."

64

The Cost of Compassion

Hana rode as far as the town boundary in search of her husband. The gelding beneath her jogged with impatience at the sight of the knot of creamy cattle grazing in a far corner. The Charolais moved as a mob, never taking their eyes from the grass beneath them. It looked shorter than days ago and she guessed Logan planned to move them on soon. The gate clasp clanked as she leaned down to release the chain and Logan turned his head in her direction. She moved her horse so she could fasten it and half expected her husband not to be there when she spun back around. To her surprise, Logan tapped the rope against Sacha's neck and the stunning white mare moved towards home.

Logan sat like a statue in the saddle, right hand wielding the rope with a featherlight touch and the other resting on his thigh. His body moved with a fluidity which mirrored Sacha's walking hoof beats. Hana pushed her gelding into a lazy canter and they met in the middle.

"Hey." Logan's eyelashes fluttered, hiding a pit of buried emotions. "Sorry."

"For what?" The horses touched muzzles between them and Sacha gave a high-pitched whinny. The young gelding jerked backwards but his ears pricked forward as Sacha tossed her mane.

"Stop it." Logan tapped her neck with his index finger and she shook her mane again. Hana smiled as the blue wall eye communicated mischief. The gelding blew out a breath and fidgeted. Logan's face relaxed and the stress lines lessened. "He couldn't do anything to you even if he wanted, you horny mare." A tap of the rope against her neck and Sacha moved forward, Hana falling into step beside her. She said nothing, waiting for Logan to speak first.

He lasted until before the first gate. "Sorry for taking Sacha. I just needed to get away for a while." Hana leaned down and struggled with the gate clasp. "How did you find me?"

She inhaled and drew the gate towards her. The gelding back stepped until it swung clear. "Sacha gave you away." She passed through and left Logan to close it behind them. He grasped the chain and towed the gate, Sacha rolling her wall eye and keeping her legs out of the way. Logan sat up after fastening it shut.

"How?"

Hana released a laugh and pushed the gelding into a trot. At the sound of Sacha taking off behind him, his ears flattened against his head and he surged into three strides of a canter before stretching into a gallop. The rushing air snatched Hana's laughter and threw it aside as she stood in her stirrups and crouched over the gelding's neck. Sacha's hooves pounded behind her and as Hana pulled up at the next gate, a blur of white flew over the fence and into the next paddock. Logan pulled Sacha up and they doubled back in a lazy, rocking-horse canter. He leaned down to open the gate. "That's how." Hana's breath came in heaves and she felt exhilarated. "She wanted to jump the fences and pitched a fit whenever I dismounted. She played up worse on the next one and I cut my finger on the catch." Hana pushed the gelding through the gap and waited for Logan to close the gate. When he sat up in the saddle, she faced him. "You come here often, don't you? This mob of cattle is tiny. You just move them from one of JD's paddocks to the next and back again. They're your excuse to come here."

Logan swallowed and examined the scarred hand holding the rope. His jaw worked in his face and he appeared lost for words. When he looked up, his eyes shone with unshed tears and the grey irises sparkled like a stormy sea. "I miss him. So bloody much." He inhaled and stared at the ridge of mountain sheltering the hotel. "He tried to kill you and I miss him. What does that say about me?" Logan ran a hand across his eyes and Hana saw the yawning chasm in his soul. "You can't stand any mention of his name, but for a long time he was all I had. Teacher, adviser, advocate and friend. I was just a teenager when Jack told me he was my grandfather. It's impossible to reconcile the man I knew with the crazy guy who held a gun to your head and wanted my newborn son dead. I know whenever you watch Mac struggle you blame him. We tell everyone your mother was deaf, but so was Jack. He never spoke a word his whole life and yet he made me who I am. Something happens and I wanna stop by the stables and tell him, share a tot of whisky and watch him use his hands to show me I've done good. He's not there anymore Hana. But was he ever? Who was he really?"

Hana pushed the gelding closer, using her heels to enforce the command. He sidled alongside Sacha, uncomfortable near the unpredictable hooves and teeth, yet he obeyed. Hana reached across and laid her hand over Logan's writhing fingers. The rope felt smooth against her skin. "He was JD, Jacob D'Arcy Du Rose," she breathed. "Jack. A man who lived too long and ended up ruining the good things he'd achieved. I've let anger stop you grieving and I'm sorry. It's no better than my brother banning me from my mother's funeral all those years ago. Forgive me?" Hana ducked her head to look under the brim of Logan's cowboy hat. He kept his head bowed and his shoulders seemed to fold in on his chest. He accepted her apology with the tiniest bob of his head. The yawning chasm threatened to eat him whole and Hana held his hand and kept him afloat. The horses shifted beneath them and the gelding's tack clanked. As though Logan's seat plugged him into Sacha's soul, the mare held onto her impatience and allowed the gelding to bump against her as he champed on his metal bit and sighed.

Logan inhaled and his head rose by degrees. Determination sparked behind his irises. "I loved him, Hana." His voice wavered. "How can I take his memory back to the man who just loved me for myself?"

"I don't know." Her fingers strayed to Sacha's regal neck. The mare's dinner plate hooves carried the stain of Jack's blood. "Time helps to heal though. I know that from personal experience."

Logan shrugged. "Time heals the pain, but it also blurs the memories. I'm not sure which is worse."

Hana frowned. He spoke the truth and she had no good answers for him.

Logan closed his eyes and breathed in a fortifying breath. "There's something else."

"What?" Hana baulked at the tone of his voice, serious with a hint of danger. "What else is there?"

He swallowed. "Hana, I'll ask you this once and I want the truth. It's eaten away at me for a while and I can't stand it anymore." His grey eyes flicked to her face and pinioned her beneath an interrogative stare. She forced a blank expression into place, feeling guilty before he'd even asked her. "Don't lie because I'll know. Are you having an affair?"

Breath whooshed from Hana's lips and she almost laughed. She raised a hand to cover her painful mouth and relief slouched her shoulders. "Really?" She cocked her head to one side. "That's your big question?"

Temper flared behind Logan's irises and his teeth ground his mouth shut so he snarled through his lips. "Yes!"

Hana shook her head as though clearing her thoughts and sighed. "Then no, Logan. Absolutely not." He swallowed and stared at her, his hips rocking with Sacha's motion as she rested a back leg. He said nothing and frustration burgeoned in Hana's chest. "Why even ask me that? What have I done?"

Logan swallowed and looked towards the mountain. He ran a shaking hand over his chin. "Wiri said you were secretive about your phone. You wouldn't let him play games on it." His voice wavered and he lowered it to a whisper. "You seemed okay with what Libby's doing. I looked at your phone and couldn't find anything suspicious, so I got Toby to watch you for a while. Then I wondered if you were seeing him." Logan inspected a healing cut on his index finger. "I took the SIM card from the truck's dash cam and downloaded the footage. You kept leaving it on and I wondered if it captured whoever pushed Nev. I saw you bump into Toby in the car park and how he looked at you." He licked his lips. "Then you keep trying this new stuff in the bedroom."

"Ohhhh." Hana tasted salt as the sea breeze lifted the surf and dispersed its distinctive tang far and wide. "That's why the camera wouldn't work. You picked a fight with Toby, didn't you? Wiri told me about the first one, but the next one was worse. That's how you got bashed up." Logan pursed his lips and neither confirmed nor denied her conclusion. The gelding sighed and blew out a warm breath. "Logan, Logan, Logan," Hana breathed. She shook her head. "You're an idiot."

The fire revived behind his eyes and he bridled at her insult. Darkness flashed across his face. "Then what's going on, Hana?" he demanded. "Just tell me."

She cringed and a groan escaped her lips. An embarrassed flush crept up her neck and she turned away from his critical gaze. "Did you like it?"

"What?"

"The bedroom stuff." Hana swallowed and felt her throat dry. "Did you like it?"

"What do you think?" He sounded exasperated. "I loved it, but not if some other guy's teaching you stuff."

"I bought a book, but needed to read it on my phone. You should have looked in my digital library." Hana closed her eyes as the hot flush crept into her cheeks and her ears turned to fireballs. "Women always look at you, Logan. It makes me feel vulnerable. I wanted to make sure you always ended up in my bed and the book promised to teach me how to keep you there." She covered her eyes with her left hand, the reins dangling from her fingers. The scent of leather comforted her. "This is so embarrassing."

She heard Logan gulp. "You bought a book?"

"Yes. It's a study of the Kama Sutra."

"With pictures?"

"No." Hana sighed. "It's a sanitised version, but I should have got the one with pictures. I didn't want you or the kids to find it, so that's why I'm reading it on my phone." She stole a sideways glance at Logan, expecting him to laugh at her foolishness. She saw no mirth in his expression, just a veiled emotion she couldn't decipher. "I want to make you happy and find another way to reach you." The notion seemed ridiculous in the cold light of day. "You think I'm stupid."

Logan closed his eyes and inhaled. "No, Hana. I think you're beautiful. I love you more than you could ever understand." He leaned sideways and reached for her hand, his fingers rough from hard work and the acidic mountain soil. "I don't know why you stick with me."

"Because I want no one else, you wally." Hana saw embarrassment in his eyes and released his fingers. He'd shown more weakness in that few moments than she'd seen in all their tumultuous years together. "Can this horse jump?" she asked, making the question sound casual.

Logan wiped an olive forearm across his face and Hana saw his tattoo appear from beneath his tee shirt sleeve before disappearing as the fabric moved back into place. The cuts on his forearms leaked clear fluid through the waterproof plasters which kept out infection. "Yeah. Methuselah sired him. Course he can jump. Why?"

The gelding took off with a leap which almost unseated Hana and she squealed in shock. She released her heels from his sides and he flattened his body and ran. Her fingers gripped the horn of the saddle and she dipped forward as the fence loomed ahead. The gelding bunched his shoulders and took a flying leap. His back hooves clipped the top rail, but he landed square, picking up his pace and clearing the next paddock with ease. Sacha's easy gallop drummed behind them, a pause breaking the stride as she jumped the fence and followed. Logan caught up just before the next fence, circling in front of them and halting the chaotic journey. "Not this one," he shouted. "He won't clear the ditch the other side. Sacha's used to it."

Hana nodded and let the horse drop back to a canter. They arrived at the gate at a jog. Logan opened it and let Hana through, closing it behind them. They rode in companionable silence and Logan jumped no more fences despite Sacha's irritation with the sedate pace. The mountain range rose before them with its familiar ridges and tree covered surface. It resembled rough green fabric and Hana realised she thought of it as home. She released a sigh which sounded like relief. Logan gave her a sideways smile. "Did the dam accept the orphaned calf?" she asked. Her brow knitted. "I've been scared to ask."

"Yeah." Logan nodded and pushed his hat further back on his head. "I guess there's a lesson there."

"What do you mean?" Hana shielded her eyes from the sun with a forearm across the bridge of her nose.

"Edin."

"You're saying I'm a cow?" Hana tightened her lips and feigned offence. "That's nice."

Logan snuffed out a laugh and shook his head. "Yeah, Hana. You're a real cow." His expression didn't match his words. "I think we should take her. Wiri knows the truth, I think he always has. Does it matter who parents them as long as someone does a half decent job?"

"I guess not. Did you talk to Wiri about the not-speaking-to-us thing?"

Logan nodded. "Yeah. The kid's scared. Just as he gets settled, another threat comes. It's like he's always scrambling. That's why he makes it his business to know what's going on. The kid's sharp, Hana. He's always mitigating the next unseen disaster."

"You know Anahera will come back for him one day, don't you?" Hana sighed. "Nothing we can do about that."

"Yeah and Phoenix will never forgive us if we let her take him." Logan shook his head. "You left your phone in the truck after your bang on the head. The hospital rang you and left a message, so I've made an appointment to see Anahera next week. I'm asking her to let us adopt Wiri."

Hana sighed and watched a hawk ride the up-draughts searching for dinner. "Wow. That's a huge step."

"Sorry." Logan winced. "I should have asked you first. I'll agree to unconditional access, but we need to stop her taking him in the future. It's what terrifies him."

Hana nodded. "Want some company when you see her?"

"Yes please."

"This is the cost of loving, isn't it?" She frowned. "I doubt Caroline will serve sixteen years in prison which means she'll take Edin one day. There's no way she'll let go of her daughter. Edin's all she has left." Hana's gelding skipped beneath her as a rabbit shot from the long grass. She sat heavy in the saddle and waited for him to settle. "What do you think made Caroline push Nev after she shot him? The shove came from a place of real anger. The local cops think it was because of what he told her."

"Yeah, I think she lost control when he told her she was Kane's half-sister. Maybe he meant to blackmail her into forgetting about the money. It doesn't sound like Nev, but who knows who Nev really was. He let Lincoln serve a prison sentence in his place and then went on the run." Logan squeezed the bridge of his nose between finger and thumb. The cuts on his face oozed less in the sunshine as his faulty clotting worked overtime. "This ticket thing is worth fifty grand. Did you know that? And they didn't need the bond, just my signature and identification. If they'd explained, I would have given them the cash up front."

"Even Nev?" Hana frowned. "Knowing he wanted it to escape justice."

"I don't know about him. But Kane and Caroline, yeah. Although they wanted it for different reasons. She needed to get him medical help. I don't know why he wanted it." Logan exhaled.

"I do." Hana let the reins run through her fingers. "He needed to leave Caroline and Edin enough to get by for a while after he'd gone." Hana clenched her jaw to stop the pity turning into tears. "Is it strange that I feel sorry for her?"

"No. You have a big heart," Logan replied.

"I should have said something when the receptionist from the campground called her Miss Marsh. It seemed odd at the time but not enough to make me investigate. She must have come straight here looking for Kane just after he turned up at our place. Registering as Caroline Du Rose would have raised too many red flags." Hana sighed. "All those years of trying to get the Du Rose name added to hers so she could feel part of the family and she had to arrive using her old one. It must have killed her inside. I should have realised."

Logan shook his head. "You couldn't have known, Hana." He rolled his neck to shake off the ghosts and smiled at Hana. "So, Mrs Du Rose. What's next?" He lifted his feet from his stirrups and stretched his long legs. He slotted them back in without looking, saddle and horse an extension of his body.

Hana fixed her gaze on a kauri tree on top of the nearest mountain. It stretched its uppermost branches towards the sky, head and shoulders above the canopy. She sighed. "I guess we use the opportunity to teach Phoe and Mac some mercy and compassion. Adopt Wiri so he feels secure and just love little Edin. Whānau is about more than blood, or so you always say." She smiled and reached out a hand towards her husband. "Maybe we're not too old to learn some lessons with them."

"You think?" The crow's feet returned to the corners of Logan's eyes as he accepted her hand, lifting it to kiss her fingers.

"What should we do about Kane?" Hana released a sigh. "He'd gone downhill so fast since he turned up at our place, Logan. We watched him push that breakfast around in the video footage at the golf lodge, but he ate none of it. I'm not a doctor, but he looked in the final stages of something terminal. He had that smell about him too, like when people are close to death. I'm sorry." She squeezed his fingers. "How do we find him? Maybe get him some help."

Logan shook his head. "I paid the guy at the airstrip to search the bush from first light this morning. He rang me after I dropped Wiri back at the apartment. He saw smoke curling up from the bush. Looked like a campfire."

"So, you can go to him?" Hana's expression brightened but her brows knitted into a line at the shake of Logan's head.

"No. He's made sure no one can get him out. He's trapped himself at the bottom of that sheer ridge on the Port Waikato side of the mountain. It's impassable. He's used ropes to climb down there." Logan released a sigh. "We'd need a rescue helicopter and a team of paramedics to get to him. He's gone there for a reason and he won't come out. I get the message, Hana. He's come home to die and he wants me to leave him alone. I've passed the coordinates to Sanders. It's up to him now."

Hana blinked away the sadness and clung to Logan's fingers for comfort. Kane's last words echoed through her memory. "Take care of Edin for me," he'd asked. But she remembered something else and swallowed, trying to formulate the words on her tongue. Then she spoke them and let them drift onto the warm breeze. "It isn't his last message to you though," she whispered. "Kane asked me to tell you he was sorry. For what it's worth, I believe him."

Logan nodded and pursed his lips. He turned his face away to prevent her seeing him break. Hana kept hold of his hand and led the last of Reuben Du Rose's sons home, Sacha's hooves plodding against the hard baked earth.

Glossary of Maori Words and Phrases

Each tribe had its own complete language in the old days, not dialects as the English settlers made everyone believe. The tribes were independent people groups, much as England, Ireland, Scotland and Wales didn't use dialects of each other's language. Te Reo is now the nationally accepted native language of New Zealand, embodying much of the heart and sentence structure of the old. That's what I've used in my novels because it's what I've learned. Where I've used Te Reo, I've made sure there's a translation in place right there in the text, either through another character repeating it in English, or just clarifying in the next sentence so you become familiar.

I love this language. I attend a class at our local arts centre every Thursday afternoon and have done for some time. The teacher is a volunteer retired headmaster and his classes typically begin running for 10 weeks and keep going for 6 years. We've become a family as we've greeted each other in a lost tongue each week. Our oldest student is in her eighties and is learning to speak the words she heard at her grandmother's knee but buried through oppression. It's an amazing experience and I feel truly grateful to be part of the Te Reo revival.

Things to remember

wh is pronounced as *f*

ng is pronounced with the *g* as very faint behind the *n*

I've given the definitions as I've used the words.

Some words have different meanings for verb and noun use.

ara line of weaving, way, path, passage.

aroha - noun means love, verb means to love.

hapu - sub tribe, extended family group linked by ancestry.

haraheke - New Zealand flax.

inoi - prayer to God.

iwi - people group, tribe, race. The noun also means 'strength, bone' which is relevant. It's the thing which holds everything together. Logan's **iwi** is the Waikato tribe, but his **hapu** is Ngāpuhi in Northland through family relationships. A famous Ngāpuhi ancestor is Hōne Heke, who kept chopping the English flag down in Russell, Northland when the English refused to honour the Treaty of Waitangi.

kai - noun means food. Verb means 'to eat'. Mac is always hungry.

kia ora - be well, used as a greeting.

karakia - blessing.

kōtiro - girl. Term of affection.

Kuia - elderly woman, grandmother, female elder.

karanga - formal ceremonial call, welcome.

kaumātua - respected elder.

koha - gift, present, offering, nowadays often financial.

marae - gathering place for different tribes.

Matua kēkē -uncle, aunt.

maunga - mountain.

mihi whakatau or mihimihi - This is a greeting during which the male will give his credentials or lineage. Logan's **mihi** involves declaring the landmarks and people which make him Logan Du Rose.

mokopuna/moko - grandchildren, the next generation.

rākau - this is a length of wood or a stick. The noun refers to a challenge stick laid down before distinguished visitors on a marae. It was used as a weapon of war.

raranga weaving.

Tainui - one of the boats which navigated to New Zealand from Polynesia. Most Māori can trace their lineage back to the boat which their ancestors arrived on. They navigated using the stars and came back and forth often over thousands of years. There was no great invasion as the English settlers would have everyone believe. It was small groups of adventurers who arrived over the centuries and stayed. The ancestors of the Waikato tribes arrived at Kawhia on the west coast of New Zealand on the **Tainui.**

tāne - husband, man.

tangata whenua - I've used this as 'people of the land', often Logan's ancestors.

taonga - heirloom, treasure, something of value.

tēna koe - there you are (used as a greeting).

urupā - cemetery, burial ground.

waka - canoe. Latterly it also means 'car, vehicle.'

Whaea noun for mother, aunt, aunty.

whakapapa - noun means genealogy. Verb means to recite a genealogy. There are many ways to do that, either through senior males, including spouses, or single lines of descent. Logan's used to include Alfred, but you saw how that went for him. Because the mitochondria is the energy particle in an ovum before conception, the energy comes through the female line. Female lineage is very important for Māori for this reason. Logan has chosen to rely on his female genealogy in this novel because his male descent has become unreliable.

whānau - noun means family group.

wharenui - big house, often the sleeping house on a marae.
whenua - land, for Logan that means the mountain where his placenta was buried.

Dear Reader,

I would love it if you could leave a review at your usual retailer.

I find the opinions of readers helpful and constructive. Reviews are the Holy Grail to an author as they cause our work to sink or swim. It is the bench mark for other readers and can determine whether our work will be successful and reach many or none. It doesn't have to be an essay or a literary criticism. A few words about what you liked would be most appreciated. The shortest review I ever received for my work was, 'Great,' accompanied by five stars and the longest was a whole video from a gorgeous woman in the USA. My favourite to date has to be the lady who said, *'I read until my eyes fell out.'* I keep looking at that one because it makes me laugh.

You can review on my website, ktbowes.com

And hey, let me know when you've done it. I'd love to hear from you.

Say Hello

You can find the author hanging out on social media in the following places.

Check in and say hello. Maybe suggest she gets back to writing and stops watching cat videos.
FACEBOOK
https://www.facebook.com/NZauthorKTBowes/
INSTAGRAM
https://www.instagram.com/k_t_bowes

About the Author

K T Bowes is a bestselling teen and women's author. Her novel, *A Trail of Lies*, was the winner of the genre award for Author's Cave in 2014.

Phoenix Du Rose was considered for the prestigious Ngaio Marsh awards for 2021 and *Her Quiet Legacy* in 2022.

K T Bowes is an Englishwoman in exile in New Zealand, swapping rugged cosmopolitan for mountain ranges and terrifying rivers. She loves Māori culture and has learned to weave flax using traditional methods. Her other passion is Rongoa Māori, which involves creating medicines from native plants. She is a student of Te Reo Māori.

Also by this Author

The Hana Du Rose Mysteries Series:
Logan Du Rose
About Hana
Hana Du Rose
Du Rose Legacy
The New Du Rose Matriarch
One Heartbeat
The Du Rose Prophecy
Du Rose Sons
Du Rose Family Ties
Du Rose Vendetta
Phoenix Du Rose
Wiremu Du Rose

The Calculated Risk Series:
The Actuary
The Actuary's Wife
The Actuary in Trouble
The Heart of The Actuary

Troubled series for teens:
Free from the Tracks
Sophia's Dilemma
A Trail of Lies
Gone Phishing

Escaping the Back Country NZ Series:
Pirongia's Secret
Deleilah

Standalone novels:
Artifact
Demons on Her Shoulder
All Saints
Her Quiet Legacy

Humorous Cozy Mystery Series from New Zealand
Dead Straight
Bad Hair Day
Side Parting